A PRINCE *of the*

JOHN BUCHAN (1875-1940) was born in Perth on 26th August 1875, the eldest son of a minister in the Free Church of Scotland. He spent part of his childhood in Fife, before the family moved to Glasgow in the 1880s. In 1894 he went to Oxford University and began to write, publishing several books and many articles while still a student. After Oxford he had a successful career as a barrister and Member of Parliament, while continuing to write highly-acclaimed novels such as *The Thirty-Nine Steps*, *Greenmantle* and *The Three Hostages*. He also wrote widely on other subjects, including biographies of Cromwell and Montrose, and an autobiography *Memory Hold-the-Door*.

John Buchan was created Baron Tweedsmuir in 1935 and became Governor-General of Canada the same year. He died in Canada in 1940, soon after completing his last great novel, *Sick Heart River*.

DAVID DANIELL is Emeritus Professor of English in the University of London. For twenty-five years he was director of Shakespeare studies at University College London, and has published a great deal on Shakespeare. A long-standing interest in the English Bible has produced articles and books, particularly editions of William Tyndale's New and Old Testaments, and a biography of that translator. He has published,

Other B&W titles by John Buchan

JOHN BURNET OF BARNS
THE FREE FISHERS
A LOST LADY OF OLD YEARS
THE BLANKET OF THE DARK
SICK HEART RIVER
HUNTINGTOWER
MIDWINTER
THE POWER-HOUSE
THE COURTS OF THE MORNING
THE GAP IN THE CURTAIN

A PRINCE
of the
CAPTIVITY

JOHN BUCHAN

"As when a Prince
Of dispers'd Israel, chosen in the shade,
Rules by no canon save his inward light,
And knows no pageant save the pipes and shawms
Of his proud spirit."

First published 1933
This edition © 1996
B&W Publishing Ltd
Edinburgh
Introduction © David Daniell 1996
ISBN 1 873631 68 5

British Library Cataloguing in Publication Data:
A catalogue record for this book is available
from the British Library

Cover illustration:
French Troops Resting, 1916
by C. R. W. Nevinson
reproduced by kind permission
of The Imperial War Museum

Cover Design by *W. Creevey & Co.*

Printed by Werner Söderström

INTRODUCTION

PROFESSOR DAVID DANIELL

John Buchan wrote *A Prince of the Captivity* in the summer of 1932. He had by then been living at Elsfield Manor, outside Oxford, for over a dozen years. He was a Member of Parliament (for the Scottish Universities, a seat since abolished) and Deputy Chairman of Reuters: he had not long before left the Edinburgh publishers, Thomas Nelson and Sons, where, from the London office but travelling north frequently, he had been an energetic partner for over twenty years. His enterprise there made a powerful mark on English and Scottish letters.

In the course of that year, 1932, as usual he wrote reviews and articles, often weekly, many of them requiring a good deal of reading. He spoke frequently in debates in the Commons. Also that year he published his novel *The Gap in the Curtain*, the children's story *The Magic Walking-Stick*, his big biography of Sir Walter Scott, and a shorter life of Julius Caesar. *A Prince of the Captivity* was his ninety-ninth book, and twenty-third novel. It was published on 6 July 1933 by Hodder and Stoughton, his regular publishers: the American edition from Houghton Mifflin followed in August.

The new novel received mixed reviews. Buchan's friend T. E. Lawrence wrote about it to Edward Garnett on 1 August.

> Did you read his latest? He takes figures of today and projects their shadows on to clouds, till they grow surhuman and gro-
> tesque: then describes them! Now I ask you—it sounds a filthy technique, but the books are like athletes racing: so clean-lined, speedy, breathless. For our age they mean nothing: they are sport, only: but will a century hence disinter them and proclaim him the great romancer of our blind and undeserving generation?

Lawrence of Arabia's puzzlement was shared: but his insight is shrewd. Only now, not so far off a century later, are we beginning to understand what might be going on in *A Prince of the Captivity*. This is not unusual: one work of a good writer can simply fall into the ground. To stretch the scale of significance rather far, we recall that Shakespeare's *Troilus and Cressida*, so much a play of our later twentieth century, had no performance at all from when it was written until a single night in 1907, and then *The Times* said it was best forgotten: and Melville's *Moby Dick*, no less, written in 1851, lost him his reputation and was not discovered until after the Second World War.

Lawrence was right about the 'athletes racing': Buchan is always properly much admired for his skill with pace of narrative, and *A Prince of the Captivity* is, surprisingly, no exception. People have been puzzled by it—but it has still sold over 100,000 copies up to 1990: it is a thunderingly good read.

Buchan's life at Elsfield Manor, with his wife and growing family of daughter and three sons, was very much as he wanted it. His study, his treasured garden, nearby Oxford, the surrounding Cotswolds known and loved from frequent thirty-mile walks, the quiet days of trout-fishing, all made a highly creative life for him (in the sixteen years he had there he wrote some sixty books, and much else). To some extent, Elsfield was a place of retreat from London. But, as is again apparent here in *A Prince of the Captivity*, he was still in love with Tweeddale and all the Scottish Border country of his childhood and youth: he went to Scotland as many times in the year as he could. And many people from the world over came to Elsfield to see him: from the study windows of Elsfield Manor, the view was global.

One of John Buchan's achievements, still not properly recognised, was the twenty-four volume publication of *Nelson's History of the War*, well over a million words written by him as the war happened, from 1915 onwards. There one notices at once the lack of overheated propaganda, and the world view of a world calamity. The lasting damage from that appalling war is the ground on which *A Prince of the Captivity* is built. Post-war Britain, and with her Europe, Buchan tells us, are in a bad condition. Lack of good leadership opens the way to barbarism:

'the wilderness is still only across the road' (the end of Book Three). We are coming now to see the prescience of Buchan in being alarmed about the rise of Fascism: even as early as 1924, in *The Three Hostages*, that concern is visible. Here, in *A Prince of the Captivity*, it is central.

The first thing to notice about the novel is that the war itself, though felt intensely, is seen obliquely, from the side. At the end of Section II of Book Two, Chapter II, the hero, Adam Melfort, says 'I didn't say I wasn't in the war. I said I wasn't fighting'. His tasks behind the enemy lines had been more dangerous even than life in the trenches. The second is the range both geographic and social. Scenes are set with Buchan's usual atmospheric economy in London clubs, on a Hebridean shore, by Worcestershire streams, in rural Belgium, in the slums of 'Birkpool' (Birmingham or Wolverhampton), in arctic Greenland, in German-controlled Turkey, in English country houses, in Scandinavia, in a medieval German town, on a cross-channel ferry, in the Black Forest, in Paris, in the Italian Alps, and so on, with strong references to life in South Africa or on a Scots moor. Cabinet ministers (the Prime Minister is shadowy) and lords and ladies are vigorously mixed with trades union officials and a popular preacher; with an American millionaire philanthropist and a Belgian half-witted farm worker; with vicious international villains and Knightsbridge hostesses, and so on again, all in the powerful world of political belief. It makes for an especially dense, rich texture—it is like a tin of condensed Disraeli, as from *Coningsby* or *Sybil*, and now with pace and international philosophical alarm. Yet here again the view is oblique: there is no one group which resonates with the narrator's particular passion.

That this is deliberate can be easily shown. Buchan has been accused of poor characterisation, particularly here, and in this book of trying to make a novel of ideas out of his usual kit for making a thriller—the secret anarchist organisation, the assassination-attempts, the fallen Lucifer, the amazing disguises, the hunt on the bare hillside. Certainly all are present, and more, and they do a lot to help the pace. As certainly, the book is a

vii

novel of ideas; it is a more active *A Lodge in the Wilderness* (1906), or *The Island of Sheep* (1919)—the first inspired by, the second written with, his wife Susan. But *A Prince of the Captivity* is something quite different.

Consider the title. Those who know the Jewish Scriptures, to Christians the Old Testament, know at once what it means. The Jews were taken to exile in Babylon, as a nation, from 598 BC, some not returning to Jerusalem some eighty years later but remaining there for centuries. Such exiles chose 'Princes of the Captivity'. A Jewish 'Prince' in Babylon, exiled from the proper holy ground, would have power and authority, even be treated with some pomp and ceremony, but his rule would be necessarily oblique, as it was not from Jerusalem.

The two epigraphs give clues. The first, on the title page, is four lines of Miltonic verse, not by Milton (though that poet is significantly read by the hero, as we learn at the end of the fourth Section of Chapter I of Book One). They may be taken to be by Buchan himself. The content divides into two notions, the Prince 'of dispers'd Israel' (the adjective is in Isaiah 11), and the inward light. Though (and the same is true of the title) no phrase there is an exact biblical quotation, the words are biblical: the musical instruments, 'shawms' (oboes), are in the *Book of Common Prayer's* Psalm 98 (a suggestive psalm for this book, about rejoicing in right rule, the sea making a noise, and the round world, and more as we shall see). It is no surprise to find Buchan deep in the Prayer Book; it was part of his culture; four years earlier he had used a phrase from Psalm 68, 'he letteth the runagates continue in scarceness' for the title of a collection of stories with some relation to *A Prince of the Captivity* in range of experiences. There, in *The Runagates Club* (1928), is also Buchan's excitement about double lives:

> the lawyer and financier were also soldiers; the Greek scholar had captained a Bedawin tribe; the traveller had dabbled in secret service; the journalist had commanded a battalion; the historian had been a mate on a novel kind of tramp . . .

We know we are to read *A Prince of the Captivity*, from that first epigraph, as being about oblique rule from an 'inward light'. It is the essential clue to the irregular development of the hero, Adam Melfort. That movement is not easy to grasp, as often Adam is not centre-stage: Buchan is using a fictional device of some sophistication, the off-centre hero.

The second epigraph, described as '*The Emperor Akbar's inscription at Fatehpur-Sikri*', continues the clue of obliquity. The great Mogul emperor Akbar, a descendant of Tamberlaine and Genghis Khan, in the late sixteenth-century AD united the entire sub-continent of India. He began to build his capital, Fatehpur Sikri, near Delhi, in 1570, but abandoned it in 1586. With a global view, he relished the stimulation of cultural encounter, where Hindu, Muslim and European Christian met. He is said to have been an enlightened, even admirable, governor: but though under him the élite amassed great wealth, the peasants starved. So Buchan's epigraph apparently expresses some oriental gem of wisdom: but Jesus never said any such thing, and the powerful inscriber himself is flawed.

There is thus more cunning in the epigraphs than may be first apparent. As there is in the structure of the novel. The four Books are of unequal length; the last two are half as long as the first two. Books One and Two each have four chapters, the first three subdivided into sections, the last standing complete. Patterns become visible. Thus the third section of each chapter tends to be about, or to include, a process of healing in a context of unusual suffering (Adam's prison dream of Eilean Bàn; Adam, still behind enemy lines, convalescent after pneumonia; Adam in the Arctic night bringing Falconet from death; Adam curing Marrish of his murderous jealousy). The last section of each of the first three chapters takes Adam into new territory virtually alone—Northumberland, Turkey, the return to the Greenland base. The last section of each of the three chapters in the second Book has group scenes showing ideals defeated. The fourth, undivided, chapter at the end of Books One and Two puts together two strongly-related characters whose relation might change everything, Adam and Creevey, and then Adam and Jacqueline.

The important word is 'might'. In a different novel, Adam

and Creevey would have increasingly complex personal encounters, subtle exchanges, in a struggle for something felt in them to be of intense importance. One thinks of what Henry James would have made of the matter. Likewise, Adam and Jacqueline's love, obvious to the reader, could have intensified through pages of feeling to burn fiercely in some extended consummation. One thinks of what D. H. Lawrence would have made of it.

Books Three and Four have different shapes again, allowing the pace of action to increase, until the solitary climax. In this is enacted a structural image from the book, the pyramid. In Book Two, Chapter I, in the second Section, Utlaw despairs of overcapitalised business 'trembling like a pyramid stuck on its point . . . the whole thing will topple over'. Book Four opens with Creevey musing on an old General's image of the war-effort as 'a great pyramid with its point directed at the enemy': but 'Mr Creevey . . . inverted the pyramid' seeing himself as 'the single point' from which 'all great human activities expanded'. Adam's final superhuman act (which saves Creevey) is the point to which the whole elaborate book is directed.

More could be said: but we might begin to be aware that there is in *A Prince of the Captivity* evidence of certain kinds of serious novelistic craft, 'of scope and structure' as the *TLS* review briefly noted. So why is the novel dismissed by critics as unsatisfactory? The metaphor is said not to work, by contrast, for example, with Thomas Mann's *The Magic Mountain.* Why is Buchan accused of not stopping to think?

There are many ways by which a novelist might deal with conditions at a particular national moment: by painful quest for the eternal city, like Bunyan in *The Pilgrim's Progress*; by satire, like Swift in *Gulliver's Travels*; by high romance and drama, like Fielding in *Tom Jones* (and all three books influenced Buchan, the first greatly). Buchan's method was always to marry popular fiction, with its simple characterisation and driving action, with acute alertness about the nation at that moment. Thus *The Thirty-Nine Steps*, driven as it is, sees, like that spotter-plane, with the eye of God—that the fate of civilised Europe hangs on the ability to read the code, to penetrate the impossible disguise, to get there in time. Human appearances of normality deceive, always. Barbarism is, always, only a step away. All Buchan's Richard Hannay novels, and Edward Leithen novels, tell the same story—as do the historical novels like *The Blanket of the Dark*. For an ambitious 'Condition of England' novel (the tag given to Disraeli's stories and their immediate Victorian successors) Buchan does just the same. The anonymous *TLS* reviewer described it as 'a Buchanorama of the upheaval, physical, mental and spiritual, of the last twenty years'.

The locking-in to 1932 is partly done through *A Prince of the Captivity* being a *roman à clef*. Adam's opening self-sacrifice, as his first readers would have known, was based on a true event, even to the jailed officer later running spy networks in Belgium. Falconet is recognisable as Edward Harkness, to whom the novel is dedicated, a co-founder with Buchan of The Pilgrim Trust (Falconet, incidentally, is the title of Disraeli's last, unfinished, novel). Loeffler has elements of the Weimar Chancellor Brüning, whose economic adviser was Buchan's friend Moritz Bonn. Creevey (with his fine Dickensian name) is said to be based on Maynard Keynes.

The book ends with the future apparently lying with a somewhat roughened Creevey: but nothing is spelled out. Everyone else left alive is disappointed. The condition of England is grave indeed. There are no saviours: Adam's near-invisible quest for a leader has, apparently, failed. William Plomer, in his hostile review, was exactly wrong in seeing in the book 'a wildly romantic view of human nature'. There is no embrace in the sunset. Adam finds his brief consummation in death; the end is his moment of private peace. His sacrifice does nothing for Europe, except perhaps to make one force in economics have a slightly more human face for a while.

What, however, is even more shadowy than Adam as 'Prince . . . in the shade', but novelistically just as present, is the awareness that Europe's failure leads to one particular disaster even worse than the Great War—Fascism. Alarm at the power of a few evil men, perhaps one man, over the minds of a country like Germany, runs like a stain through the book. Buchan knew what he was talking about. To write a book in 1932 in which the fate of modern Germany is central to Britain's survival is sound. To have the book in the shops six months after Hitler seized power is far-seeing.

To do all this without 'pageant . . . pipes and shawms' is good. Buchan was not Henry James, D. H. Lawrence or Thomas Mann: he had his own ways. He took the familiar scenes and types from popular fiction—the men in the club in the opening chapter, including their stilted talk; the empty-hearted, pretty, silly woman that the strong, silent hero ruinously marries; the journey of impossible hardship, and so on: and then he negates both his main plot and his hero. The plot, as plot, gets nowhere: after a succession of disappointments, a troubled man dies in the Alps. Contrary to popular form, that hero, who has an interestingly untypical repeated mystical experience, is often barely present. Characterisation, too, is odd, done here by slightly turning the normal view: the sermon we are given of the popular preacher (Book Two, Chapter I, Section II) is no sermon at all, when examined. Andrew Amos, so vivid in *Mr Standfast* in 1918, is here not quite Andrew Amos. Utlaw's apparently fiercely loyal and politically enraptured fiancée in the slums is called Miss Covert—and then pronounced 'court'. Nothing is quite as it 'should' be. The standard elements of a popular, or even of a mainstream, novel are here oblique. It is not a fault; it is exhilarating.

John Buchan was brought up a Calvinist, and became at university a Platonist as well. Both go into the making of this novel. Under God, the real matters at stake are cosmic in importance—'the Lord' as that Psalm 98 says 'is come to judge the earth'. Buchan was right to be afraid for Europe. And as in Plato, the power is in what is unseen. Take this novel of ideas so imperfectly stitched, we are told, on to a thriller: now turn it a few degrees, and see what begins to appear. The ideas are not made to cohere; the thriller ends abruptly, and with disappointment. Instead a serious alarm appears about the Condition of Europe and its almost inevitable Fascist future, a fear obliquely stated inside a gripping, and still neglected, story.

Thus said Jesus, upon whom be peace.
The World is a bridge; pass over
it, but build no house upon it.

*The Emperor Akbar's inscription
at Fatehpur-Sikri*

BOOK I

CHAPTER I

I

ON a warm June evening three men were sitting in the smoking-room of a London club. One was an old man, with a face which had once been weather-beaten and was now intricately seamed with veins and wrinkles. His bearing, his shoulders trimly squared even at seventy, spoke of the old style of British regimental officer. The second was in his early thirties, a heavy young man, with nothing of the Guardsman about him except his tie. The third might have been any age between forty and sixty, and had writ plain upon him the profession of the law.

The newsboys were shouting in Pall Mall.

"They can't have got the verdict yet," said the last. "Jenks was only beginning to sum up when I left. We shall hear nothing for another hour."

The old man shivered. "Good God! It is awful to be waiting here to know whether Tom Melfort's boy is to go to prison for six years or ten. I suppose there's no chance of an acquittal."

"None," said the lawyer. "You see, he pled guilty. Leithen was his counsel, and I believe did his best to get him to change his mind. But the fellow was adamant."

The young soldier, whose name was Lyson, shook his head.

"That was like Adam. There never was a more obstinate chap in his quiet way. Very easy and good-natured till you presumed just a little too much on his placidity, and then you found yourself hard up against a granite wall."

"How well did you know him?" the lawyer asked.

"I was at school with him and we passed out of Sandhurst together. He was a friend, but not what you would call an intimate. Too clever, and a little too much of the wise youth. . . .

Oh yes, he was popular, for he was a first-class sportsman and a good fellow, but he had a bit too much professional keenness for lazy dogs like me. After that he went straight ahead, as you know, and left us all behind. Somebody told me that old Mullins said he was the most brilliant man they had had at the Staff College for a generation. He had got a European war on the brain, and spent most of his leave tramping about the Ardennes or bicycling in Lorraine."

"If this thing hadn't happened, what would you have said about his character?"

"Sound as the Bank of England," was the answer. "A trifle puritanical, maybe. I used to feel that if I ever did anything mean I should be more ashamed to face Adam Melfort than any other man alive. You remember how he looked, sir," and he turned to the old man. "Always in training—walked with a light step as if he were on the hill after deer—terribly quick off the mark in an argument—all fine and hard and tightly screwed together. The grip of his small firm hand had a sort of electric energy. Not the kind of man you would think likely to take the wrong turning."

"I am not very clear. . . . What exactly happened?" asked the old man.

"Common vulgar forgery," the lawyer replied. "He altered a cheque which was made out to his wife—part of her allowance from a rich great-uncle. The facts were not in doubt, and he made no attempt to dispute them. He confessed what he had done, and explained it by a sudden madness. The funny thing was that he did not seem to be ashamed of it. He stood there quite cool and collected, with a ghost of a smile on his face, making admissions which he must have known were going to wreck him for good. You say he was wrapt up in his career, but I never saw anyone face a crash more coolly. . . . The absence of motive puzzles me. Were the Melforts hard up? They never behaved as if they were."

"Adam was supposed to be fairly well off. He was an only son, and his father died years ago. But I fancy his lady wife made the money fly."

"I saw her in the witness-box," said the lawyer. "Pretty as a

4

picture and nicely dressed for the part. She gave her evidence in a voice like music and wept most becomingly. Even old Jenks was touched. . . . Poor little soul! It isn't much fun for her. . . . Who was she, by the way? Somebody told me she was Irish."

"She was Camilla Considine," said Lyson. "Sort of far-away cousin of my own. Adam first met her hunting with the Meath. I haven't seen a great deal of them lately, but I shouldn't have said that the marriage was made in Heaven. Oh yes! She was— she is—angelically pretty, with spun-gold hair and melting blue eyes—the real fairy-tale princess type. But I never considered that she had the mind of a canary. She can't be still, but hops from twig to twig, and her twigs were not the kind of perch that Adam fancied. They each went pretty much their own way. There was a child that died, you know, and after that there was nothing to hold them together. . . . Adam had his regimental duties, and, when he got leave, as I have said, he was off to some strategic corner of Europe. Camilla hunted most of the winter— she rode superbly, and there were plenty of people ready to mount her—and in London she was always dancing about. You couldn't open a picture-paper without seeing her photograph.

"No," he continued in reply to a question, "I never heard any suggestion of scandal. Camilla lived with rather a raffish set, but she was not the kind of woman to have lovers. Not human enough. There was something curiously sexless about her. She lived for admiration and excitement, but she gave passion a miss. . . . She and Adam had one thing in common—they were both fine-drawn and rarefied—not much clogged with fleshly appetites. But while Adam had a great brain and the devil of a purpose, Camilla was rather bird-witted—a lovely inconsequent bird. God knows how he ever came to be attracted by her! I thought the marriage absurd at the time, and, now that it has crashed, I see that it was lunacy from the start. I reckoned on disaster, but not from Adam's side."

"It's the motive I can't get at," said the lawyer. "If, as you say, Melfort and his wife were more or less estranged, why should he risk his career, not to speak of his soul, to provide her with more money? The cheque was made out to her, remember, so she must have been privy to the business. I can imagine a doting husband playing the fool in that way, but I understand that they scarcely saw each other. He didn't want money for himself, did he? Had he been speculating, do you suppose?"

"Not a chance of it. He had no interests outside soldiering—except that he used to read a lot. . . . I daresay Camilla may have outrun the constable. Her clothes alone must have cost a pretty penny. . . . No, I can't explain it except by sudden madness, and that gets us nowhere, for it's not the kind of madness that I ever connected with Adam Melfort. I can see him killing a man for a principle—he had always a touch of the fanatic—but cheating, never!"

The newsboys' shouting was loud in Pall Mall. "Let's send for the last evening paper," said the lawyer. "It ought to have the verdict. . . . Hallo, here's Stannix. He may know."

A fourth man joined the group in the corner. He was tall, with a fine head, which looked the more massive because he wore his hair longer than was the fashion. The newcomer flung himself wearily into a chair. He summoned a waiter and ordered a whisky-and-soda. His face was white and strained, as if he had been undergoing either heavy toil or heavy anxiety.

"What's the news, Kit?" the younger soldier asked.

"I've just come from the court. Two years' imprisonment in the second division."

The lawyer whistled. "That's a light sentence for forgery," he said. . . . But the old man, in his high dry voice, quavered, "My God! Tom Melfort's boy!"

"Leithen handled it very well," said the newcomer. "Made the most of his spotless record and all that sort of thing, and had a fine peroration about the sudden perversities that might overcome the best of men. You could see that Jenks was impressed. The old chap rather relishes pronouncing sentence, but in this case every word seemed to be squeezed out of him unwillingly, and he did not indulge in a single moral platitude."

"I suppose we may say that Melfort has got off easily," said the lawyer.

"On the contrary," said the man called Stannix, "he has been crushed between the upper and the nether millstone."

6

"But on the facts the verdict was just."

"It was hideously unjust—but then Adam courted the injustice. He asked for it—begged for it."

Lyson spoke. "You're his closest friend, Kit. What, in God's name, do you make of it all?"

Stannix thirstily gulped down his drink. "I wish you had seen him when he heard the sentence. You remember the quiet dreamy way he had sometimes—listening as if his thoughts were elsewhere—half-smiling—his eyes a little vacant. Well, that was how he took it. Perfectly composed—apparently quite unconscious that he was set up there for all the world to throw stones at. Think what a proud fellow he was, and then ask yourself how he managed to put his pride behind him. . . . Mrs. Melfort was sitting below, and when Jenks had finished Adam bowed to him, and looked down at his wife. He smiled at her and waved his hand, and then marched out of the dock with his head high. . . . I caught a glimpse of her face, and—well, I don't want to see it again. There was a kind of crazed furtive relief in it which made my spine cold."

"You think . . ." the lawyer began.

"I think nothing. Adam Melfort is the best friend I have in the world—the best man I have ever known—and I am bound to back him up whatever line he takes. He has chosen to admit forgery and go to gaol. He drops out of His Majesty's service and his life is ruined. Very well. That is his choice, and I accept it. . . . But I am going to say something to you fellows which I must say, but which I will never repeat again. I sat through the trial and heard all the evidence. I watched Adam's face— you see, I know his ways. And I came to one clear conclusion, and I'm pretty certain that Ned Leithen reached it too. He was lying—lying—every word he spoke was a lie."

"I see!" said the lawyer. *"Splendide mendax!"*

The old man, who had not listened very closely, took up his tale. "Lying!" he moaned. "Great God! Tom Melfort's boy!"

II

Adam Melfort began his new life in a kind of daze. The stone walls which made his prison did not circumscribe him, for he was living in a far narrower enclosure of the mind. The dismal fare, the monotonous routine were scarcely noticed: he was allowed books, but he never opened them, visitors were permitted on certain days, but he did not welcome them, and the few who came—a cousin, a brother officer or two, Christopher Stannix—found a man who seemed to have lost interest in the outer world and had no need of consolation. His wife was not among these visitors.

The truth was, that ever since the tragedy Adam's mind had been busied with a problem of conduct. He believed that he had acted rightly, but doubt intervened with maddening iteration, and a thousand times he had to set the facts in order and review his decision.

It was a long story which he had to recount to himself and it involved a stern inquisition into his past. Much he could pass lightly over—fortunately, for the recollection was like opening graves. . . . His boyhood, for example, the intricate, exciting world of school, the shining months of holiday on Eilean Bàn— the pictures which crowded on him were almost too hard a trial for his fortitude. . . . Sandhurst was easier, for there he had entered manhood and begun the life which had now shipwrecked. There the vague dreams of boyhood had hardened into a very clear purpose which absorbed all his interests, and for which he believed that he had a special talent. Military problems fascinated him, and he had the kind of brain, half-mathematical, half-imaginative, which they demand. There is no higher pleasure in life than to discover in youth a clear aptitude and to look forward to a lifetime to be spent in its development. He had been very serious about the business, and had prided himself on keeping mind and body in perfect discipline, for at the back of his head he had a vision of a time coming when every atom of his power would be requisitioned. He felt himself dedicated to a cause far higher than personal success. But this success had come to him—at Sandhurst, in his regiment, at the Staff College.

Adam had little vanity, but he could not be insensitive to the opinion of his colleagues, and that opinion had, beyond doubt, marked him out for high achievement.

Then into his absorbed Spartan life Camilla had come like a disquieting west wind. She was the kind of woman with whom men like Adam have fallen in love since the beginning of time— that Rosalind-youth, which to the mystery of sex adds the mystery of spring, the germinal magic of a recreated earth. He had marvellously idealised her, and had never sought to penetrate the secret of her glancing, bewildering charm. His carefully planned scheme of life went to pieces, and for three tempestuous months he was the devout, unconsidering lover.

Disillusion came in the first year of marriage. The woman he lived with could no longer be set on a pedestal for worship; he had perforce to explore the qualities of head and heart behind the airy graces. His exploration yielded nothing. Camilla was almost illiterate, having been brought up in a ramshackle country house among dogs and horses and hard-riding squireens. That he had known, but he had not realised the incurable lightness of her mind. During their courtship her eyes had often been abstracted when he talked to her, and he had fancied that this betokened a world of private thought. He learned now that it meant only vacuity. Her brain was featherweight, though she had many small ingenuities in achieving her own purposes. Into his interests and pursuits she stubbornly refused to enter. At first she would turn the edge of graver topics with a laugh and a kiss, but presently she yawned in his face.

He discovered, too, that her tenderness was only skin-deep. Her soft melting eyes were not an index to a sensitive heart. Her nature had a hard glossy enamel of selfishness, and her capacity for emotion seemed to be limited to occasional outbursts of self-pity. Her light laughter could be cruel indeed, and often cut him deep, but he hid his wounds when he saw that she could never understand in what she had offended. She lived for admiration and gaiety, blind to anything but the surface of things. She was curiously obtuse to human values, and made intimates of all who flattered her; but she was safe enough, for she had no passion, and her bird-like flutterings carried her through dangerous places. . . . A child was born after a year of marriage, in whom she took little interest, except now and then to pose with him, as the young mother, to a fashionable photographer. The boy died when he was five years old, and after an hour's sobbing Camilla tripped again into the limelight. The broken-hearted Adam sat down to face the finality of his blunder. He realised that he had been a romantic fool, who had sought a goddess and found a dancing-girl. His wife was untamable, since there was nothing to tame.

He did not blame her; his reproaches were all for himself. He understood that if she gave him no affection, his affection for her was also long ago dead. He had been in love with a dream, and had awakened to detest the reality. Not detest perhaps; his feelings were rather disillusion, pity, and self-reproach. Especially self-reproach. He blamed himself bitterly for his folly and blindness. He had married this woman on false pretences, loving something which she was not; so from the first the marriage had been stained with infidelity. Adam was one of those people who keep so much space around their souls that they are always lonely, and this leads often to quixotic codes of conduct. The hard good sense which he showed in his profession was absent in his inner world. He tortured himself with remorse; he had domesticated a being without mind or heart, but the blame was wholly his.

So he schooled himself to make reparation. He let Camilla go her own way, and stinted himself that she might have money to spend. His Continental wandering was done in third-class carriages and on a bicycle, while she had the car on the Riviera. Occasionally they dined out together, but for the most part they went their own roads. Some of her doings and many of her companions gravely hurt his pride, but he made no complaint. His manner towards her was always courteous and friendly, and if now and then his face showed involuntary disapproval she did not observe it. She set him down as a part of the conventional background of her life, like the butler or the chauffeur—a pleasant piece of background which was never out of temper.

After seven years of marriage the crash came. Camilla had always been extravagant, and for the past year she had been rapidly amassing debts. Twice she had appealed to Adam, who had paid off all the liabilities she confessed to, liabilities which were far short of the true figure. Then had come a final reck-lessness, so wild that she was afraid to approach her husband again. For a certain fancy-dress ball she bought a jewel for which she had no means of paying, and when a little later she was in need of immediate money for a trip to Nice, she sold it at a heavy loss. The jewellers became pressing, her bank refused to allow her a further overdraft and clamoured for a reduction, and in a panic she had recourse to the money-lenders. That settled the jewellers, but it left her a prey to periodical demands which she had no means of meeting. Somewhere at the back of her mind she had a real dread of the fraternity; a tradesman's per-tinacity could be overcome, but the soft-spoken people with Scots names and curved noses would take no denial. For all her light-headedness, she had a certain sense of social decorum, and she shrank from a public scandal like a child from the dark.

For a week or two she was a harassed woman, and then her great-uncle's quarterly cheque seemed to offer a way of escape. He was a rich man and would never notice a few hundreds less to his credit. If she asked him for the money he would be certain to give it to her; but she was afraid to plague an old man in bad health with her affairs. She presumed on his generosity, for he had always been indulgent to her. She was behaving well, she told herself, since she was saving him trouble. . . . She was neat-handed and took pains with the forgery, and when it was done she breathed freely. She paid in the cheque and had once again an easy mind.

But suddenly dreadful things began to happen. It was like a volcanic eruption in ground where no volcano had ever been dreamed of. There were inquiries from the bank, urgent inquir-ies. Then came a visit of solemn, smooth-faced men who, she realised with terror, were detectives. After that there was a wild fluttering panic, a breakdown in tears, an incoherent confession like that of a bewildered child. . . .

Adam, she thought, behaved well, for he invented a very clever story. She had changed the figure—that could not be denied and she had admitted it—but Adam with a very white

11

face had declared that she had done it by his command, that he had forced her to it. . . . After that no-one seemed to trouble about her, only to look at her sympathetically, but they troubled a great deal about Adam. It appeared that he had done something very wrong—or said he had—Camilla was rather confused about the whole affair. Of course he had not touched the cheque, but perhaps he was right, and she had altered it under his influence—she had heard of such things happening—anyhow, Adam always spoke the truth. She was sorry for him, but immensely relieved that she was out of the scrape, and soon she was far more sorry for herself. For Adam had to leave the house and be tried in a court and perhaps go to prison, and that would be a terrible business for her. . . .

For a moment Camilla had felt a glow of gratitude towards him, but that was soon swamped in self-pity. If only she had not meddled with the wretched cheque! But Adam said he was responsible for that and she would not let herself think further about it. . . . After all, she did not care much for him, though he seemed to care for her. Their marriage had been comfortable but nothing more. And now the comfort was gone, and she foresaw endless worries. Camilla took refuge in tears.

Adam's action had surprised himself, but he realised that it was the consequence of a long process of thought. For years he had been convincing himself that he had wronged Camilla, and that it was his duty to make restitution, and his sudden resolve on that tragic morning in Eaton Place was the result of this premeditation. . . . For a little the necessity of playing a part and brazening it out kept him from thinking, but during the trial he had been beset with doubts.

He had smashed his career. Well, that was inevitable, for in making reparation something must be broken. . . . He had cut himself off from serving his country. That was more serious, but private honour must come first with a man. . . . But this private honour! That was what most concerned him. He had lied deliberately, and never in his life had he lied before. Adam felt himself smirched and grubby, fallen suddenly out of a clean world into the mire. He was no casuist and this tormenting doubt pursued him to the dock, and from the dock to his prison cell. A man was entitled to sacrifice much in the way of duty, but was he entitled to sacrifice his soul?

Peace came to him at last because of one reflection. The alternative was that Camilla should be sitting in this place of bare walls and rude furniture. Such a wheel would have broken the butterfly. God would forgive, thought Adam, a man's sin if it was designed to shield the weak.

III

The peace did not last long. He had settled a scruple, but he had still to face the litter of a broken life. He had been desperately in love with his work, and had developed a loyalty to his service and to his regiment the stronger because it had no rival in his home. The task of a modern soldier is a curious compound of those of the mathematician and the imaginative creator, for he has to work meticulously at intricate combinations of detail, and at the same time allow for the human factor's innumerable permutations. Adam's mind had wrought happily among the undergrowth, but he had also an eye for the trees, and in his moments of insight for the shape of the wood. It was these last flashes of vision which had been the high moments in his career, and had impressed his colleagues. He had always been an assiduous student of military history, and that had led him into other history, and he had learned the major part played by economics and civil statesmanship in the art of war. As he studied Europe he seemed to see forces everywhere straining towards the point of clash, and he had set himself to work out the problems which that clashing involved. Along with one or two other young men he had established a new school of military thought, to which one distinguished statesman had been converted. There was a cognate school in the French Army, and the two exchanged memoranda. Academic for the moment, but soon, he believed, to be an urgent reality. . . . And now this happy activity, this happier companionship, was gone for ever.

For days Adam lived in blank, unrelieved misery. This was

not a problem to be solved, but a judgment to be endured, and he could only meet it with a leaden stoicism. . . . He had settled a large part of his income on Camilla, but he had enough left to support existence. Existence it would be, not life. He was a disgraced man to whom all honourable careers were closed. His interest had been so concentrated on his profession that outside it the world was blank. He struggled to attain fortitude by reminding himself of others who had built up broken lives—disgraced men who had fought their way back, blind men who had won new energy from their handicap. . . . But what could he do? He had but the one calling, and he could not force the gate that had clanged behind him. There was the Foreign Legion, of course. But could he face the blind monotony of the rabble at the foot of the tower when he had once been the watchman on the battlements?

He slept badly, and would lie and torture himself with a retrospect like a chessboard. He saw everything in cold black and white, so that what he looked at seemed scarcely human life, but a kind of cosmic puzzle for which there was no solution.

One morning he woke with an odd feeling that something pleasant had happened. He had been dreaming of Eilean Bàn.

It was different from the island which he remembered. There were the white sands that he knew, and the white quartz boulders tumbled amid the heather. There were the low hills, shaped into gracious folds, with the little sea-trout river running through green pastures to the sea. There was the forest of wild-wood on Sgurr Bàn, where the first woodcock came in October, and Sgurr Bàn, with its queer stony fingers that used to flush blood-red in the sunset. There was the whitewashed lodge among the dwarfish oaks and birches, the mossy lawn, and the pond where the wildfowl thronged in winter.

But the place seemed to have grown larger. Beyond Sgurr Bàn should have been the cliffs where the choughs bred, and the long slopes of thyme and bent stretching to that western sea which in the stillest summer weather did not cease its murmur. But now the sea had fled from Sgurr Bàn. In his dream he had been walking westward, for he wanted to visit again the sandy cove where he used to bathe and look out to the skerries where the great grey seals lived. But it seemed to him that the thymy downs now extended for ever. He had stridden over them for hours and had found delectable things—a new lochan with trout rising among yellow waterlilies, a glen full of alders and singing waters, a hollow with old gnarled firs in it and the ruins of a cottage pink with foxgloves. But he had never come within sight of the sea, though it seemed to him that the rumour of its tides was always in his ear.

That dream opened a new stage in Adam's life. His mind ceased to move in a terrible wheel of abstractions, and he saw concrete pictures again. Two especially, on which he would dwell with an emotion that had in it more of comfort than pain.

The first was a small child in a London house slowly ascending the steep stairs that led from the day-nursery to the night-nursery. Nigel, named after Adam's grandfather, was a solemn, square boy with a Roman head set finely upon stalwart little shoulders. Adam led a busy life in those days, but he usually contrived to return home just as the child, his hair still damp from his bath, was moving bedwards. Nigel would never permit himself to be carried by the nurse up those stairs. Very slowly he made his progress, delaying on each step, impeded by bedroom slippers slightly too large for him. He carried in both hands his supper—a glass of milk, and a plate containing two biscuits, an orange or a banana. It was part of the ritual that he should be his own food-bearer, and it was his pride that he never spilled a drop of milk, except on one disastrous day when over-lengthy new pyjamas had tripped him up, and he and his supper had cascaded back to the landing. Adam generally found him on the second lowest step, and used to applaud his grave ascent. Then he would tuck him up in bed, when the supper was eaten, and listen to his prayers repeated slowly and dogmatically to his Scots nurse. Sometimes, when there was no dinner engagement, Adam would tell Nigel a story, most often a recollection from his own childhood, and always about Eilean Bàn.

Camilla rarely appeared on these occasions, except to hurry

Adam's dressing when they were dining out. She had not much to say to Nigel, or he to her. But the father and the son had an immense deal to confide to each other. The child was fanciful, and had invented a batch of familiar spirits out of his sponge, his toothbrush, his dressing-gown, and an old three-pronged poker which stood by the nursery fireplace. He would recount the sayings of these familiars, who held strong and damnatory views on unpleasant duties like nail-cutting and hair-washing and visits to the dentist. But especially he would question his father about Eilean Bàn. Adam drew many maps of the island in a realistic Elizabethan manner, and Nigel would make up stories about sundry appetising creeks and provocative skerries. He never visited Eilean Bàn, for Camilla was bored by it when she was taken there at the end of her honeymoon, so it had been let for a term of years to a Glasgow manufacturer. But any seaside place to which Nigel journeyed was contrasted by him unfavourably with that isle of dreams. There were too many houses at Bournemouth, and too many people at Broadstairs, and a horrible band in green jackets at Eastbourne, and a man who made ugly faces at Littlehampton, but at Eilean Bàn there would be only his father and the sea and the grey seals and the curlews and a kindly genie called "Peteross".

When Nigel died of meningitis after two days' delirium the bottom dropped out of Adam's world. Fortunately at the time he was desperately busy, and his duties took him on a two months' mission to a foreign capital. He drugged himself with work, and when the strain slackened and his mind could again make timid excursions, he found that he could patch up his world with stoicism. Stoicism had always been Nigel's strong suit, for the little boy had been wonderfully brave, and had taken pride in never whimpering. Adam told himself that he must do likewise to be worthy of the child who had so brightened his house of life. One regret tormented him—that he had never taken Nigel to Eilean Bàn.

He put the thought of the place from him in distaste, for it awoke an unavailing bitterness.

But now he found that by some happy magic the two memories

16

had intertwined themselves. Nigel had taken possession of Eilean Bàn. He was to be met with not only on the nursery stairs in Eaton Place, but on the white island sands and on the slopes of the hills, a tiny figure in shorts and a light blue jersey, with hair the palest gold against a sunburnt skin.

Adam had found a companion for his dream revisitings. He would let himself fall into a waking trance, and spend happy hours recaptured from childhood. . . . Nigel was a delight to behold. It had been a hot summer when he died, and the child had been ailing a little before his last illness. Adam remembered meeting him one sultry evening as he returned with his nurse from the Park, and a pang had gone through his heart at the sight of the small pale face and clammy forehead. He had then and there resolved to send him to the country; indeed, the very day when the child sickened he had been negotiating for rooms in a Cotswold farm. . . . But now Nigel was as firm and sweet as a nut, and nearly as brown. It was a joy to see his hard little legs twinkle as he ran shouting in the ripples of the tide.

In Nigel's company Adam seemed to live over again his very early childhood, when the place was as big as a continent, and as little explored as central Arabia. Peter Ross, the keeper, was the tutelary deity of those days. Peter was a very old man who did not belong to the islands, but had come ages before from the mainland in the time of Adam's grandfather. The Melforts had been a mainland family, until Kinloch Melfort was sold by the grandfather in the time when Highland deer-forests fetched fancy prices. That grandfather had been a famous diplomat, whose life had been mostly spent out of England, and he had longed for an island in which to spend his old age. Consequently the lodge at Eilean Bàn was filled with strange foreign things—rugs on which were pictured funny little men and horses, great jars of china and many-coloured metals, and heads of grim wild beasts among which the island deer-horns looked shy and feeble. To the boy's eye the house had been full of enchantments, but Peter Ross made the out-of-doors more magical still.

Peter was full of stories, in all of which he had himself played a part. He had been down among the whales like Jonah, and he had heard the silkies singing at dawn on farther islets than

17

St. Kilda, and he had seen in the gloaming the white hind, which means to the spectator death or fortune according as he behaves in face of the portent. Peter could tell tales far more exciting than those in the big *Grimm* in the nursery, since most of them were laid in Eilean Bàn. There was a mermaid who once lived on Craiglussa, and her songs used to wile ships on to cruel reefs; at low tide you could see some of the timbers of the lost merchantmen. Up in a cave on Sgurr Bàn a holy man had dwelt, so holy that his prayers could bring the fish into Ardmore bay, and immoblise pirates so that they remained stuck fast a mile from shore, where they danced in fury on their decks. The tumbled grey stones in the heather as you went south to Silver Strand had once been the house of a witch who flew daily to France to dine in the French king's kitchen. The old folk knew the sound of her flight, which was like the whistle of gigantic wild geese before a frost. And Peter had other stories into which the great ones out of history entered. The good King Robert had sat on the topmost rock of Sgurr Bàn watching for the spire of smoke from the far mainland which would tell him that he might safely go back to Scotland and take up his quest for the crown; and only the other day, so Peter reckoned it, a young prince with yellow hair had hidden for a week in the caves beyond the Strand, while English ships, his enemies, quartered the seas. Peter had sung many songs about this prince, and he called him the Prionnsa Bàn, which made Adam fancy that Eilean Bàn must have been his peculiar kingdom.

So the whole island had been a haunted place, and every day an adventure. Adam went over in minutest detail each step of the ritual. There was the waking to the sound of clucking hens, and corncrakes in the meadow, and very far off the tinkle of anvil and hammer in John Roy's smithy. Through the open window drifted the scent of climbing white roses and new-cut hay. That was part of the morning smell of the house, and the rest was a far-away odour of cooking, a faint flavour of paraffin lamps, and the delicious mustiness of an old dwelling. When he went to school there was a corner in one of the passages where you could get the same kind of smell, and Adam used to hang about and sniff it hungrily till his eyes filled. . . . Then came breakfast—porridge and milk, with the stern eye of a lady called Missmass watching to see that the bowl was tidily emptied. Miss Mathieson was part housekeeper and part governess, a kindly dragon who could be cajoled into providing a snack of scones and jelly, and permitting a meal to be eaten on the hills or by the sea instead of in the nursery. But she was iron on one point—that all expeditions beyond the garden and the home meadow should be accompanied by Peter Ross. . . .

Then with beating heart Adam would set out with Peter—Peter with his old gun in the crook of his arm, and at his heels a wall-eyed retriever called Toss. Sometimes they fished, with worm when the Lussa was red and swollen, but more often with black hackles of Peter's dressing. Sometimes Adam was permitted to fire a shot, the gun resting on a dyke, at a ruffian hoodie crow. Usually Adam would go into camp, on his honour not to stray beyond certain limits, while Peter departed on his own errands. These were the happiest times, for the boy could make a castle for himself and defend it against the world; or play the explorer in deep dells of the burn where the water-crows flashed and sometimes an otter would slide into a pool; or climb the little rocks at the tide's edge and discover green darting crabs and curious starfish. When they returned home Adam felt that he had been roaming the wide earth and had been in touch with immense mysteries. There were certain specific smells which belonged to those wonderful days—thyme hot in the sun, bog-myrtle crushed in grubby hands, rotting seaweed, and the salty wind which blew up the Sound from the open seas of the south. Freshness above all, freshness which stung the senses like icy water.

For a time Adam in his memories stuck to his childhood, for he wanted Nigel's company. But gradually he seemed to be growing up in the dream world, while the little boy remained the same. Almost before he knew he had become a youth, and was no longer at Eilean Bàn in June, that month which is the high tide of the northern spring. He was at school now, in his last year there, and his holiday was at Easter, when the shadow of winter had scarcely lifted. . . . Nigel was still at his ageless play in the glen below the house and on the nearest beach

19

under Peter Ross's eye, but Adam himself went farther afield. He remembered the first time he climbed Sgurr Bàn and saw the mysterious waters on the far side, and the first sea-trout caught by himself in the Lussa's sea-pool, which filled and emptied with the tides. Once in a long day he had walked the whole twenty-three miles of the island's circumference. The place, before so limitless, had now shrunk to a domain which could be mastered. Soon he knew every cranny as well as Peter Ross himself.

But if the terrestrial horizon had narrowed, the spiritual was enlarged. Adam was back in the delirious mood when youth is first conscious of its temporal heritage. In those April days he would stride about Eilean Bàn with his thoughts half in the recesses of his own soul and half in the undiscovered world which lay beyond the restless seas. The landscape suited his mood, for it was still blanched with the winter storms, and the hills would look almost transparent under the pale April skies, the more since a delicate haze of moorburn brooded over them. The hawthorns, which in June were heavy with blossom, were scarcely budding, and this bareness discovered the primrose clumps at their roots. The burns were blue and cold, and there was a perpetual calling of migrant birds. To Adam it seemed the appropriate landscape and weather for his now-conscious youth, for it was tonic and austere, a spur to enterprise, a call to adventure. . . . He had discovered poetry, too, and his head was a delectable confusion of rhymes. As he sat in his narrow cell he had only to shut his eyes, and croon to himself the airs which he had then sung, to recover the exquisite delirium of those April days. Shakespeare especially, it was Shakespeare's songs that had haunted him then. "Blow, blow, thou winter wind"— that had been his accompaniment on tempestuous mornings, when from the south-west came the scurries of chill rain. "Sigh no more, ladies," had been for him the last word in philosophy. "O mistress mine! where are you roaming?"—was there not in that all the magic of youth and spring? He hummed it to himself now without a thought of Camilla, for the mistress he had sung of was not of flesh and blood. And then there was "Fear no more the heat o' the sun", which made a noble conclusion to the whole matter. The race must have a goal, or it would be no race; some day man must take his wages and go bravely home.

A scent is the best reviver of memories, but there were no scents in his cell except those of scrubbed wood, yellow soap, and new linoleum. But a tune is the next best, and, as Adam *soothed* to himself the airs which had entranced the boy, he seemed to slip happily into his old world.

Gradually the feeling grew upon him that everything was not lost. He had still Eilean Bàn, and only now he understood that it was the dearest thing to him in life. It was still his—the lease to the Glasgow manufacturer would be up in a year's time. It was there waiting for Nigel and himself. The thought of it obliterated all the misery of the last years. To return there would be like the sick Naaman bathing in the waters of Jordan.

For a little while Adam was happy in this resolution. He would go back to the home of his fathers, and live as they had lived in simpler days. The world had broken him, so he would flee from the world. People had gone into monasteries after disasters to remake their souls, and why not he? The very thought of the green island gave him a sense of coolness and space and peace. Youth was waiting there to be recaptured, youth and happiness. And Nigel too—Nigel would be lonely without him. He had dreamed himself into a mood in which the little figure in shorts and blue jersey was as much a part of his home as Sgurr Bàn itself.

And then one morning he had a dismal awakening. All the rosy veils of fancy seemed to be ripped from the picture as if by a sharp east wind, and he saw the baselessness of his dreams.

For what had been the magic of Eilean Bàn to the heart of youth? A call to enterprise, nothing less. A summons to go out and do great things in the world. Once, long ago, when he had realised his passion for the place, he had toyed with the notion of making his life in it, and had instantly rejected the thought. Eilean Bàn would scorn such a weakling. Its ancient peace was not for the shirker. It was a paradise from which a man might set out, and to which he might return when he had fought his battles, but in which he dared not pitch his camp till he had won a right to rest.

Miserably he understood that the peace for which he had longed had to be fought for. . . . But now he was tragically out of the fighting-line for ever.

IV

There followed a week of more bitter emptiness than he had ever known before. He had let his dreams run away with him, and had suddenly awoke to their baselessness. Eilean Bàn seemed to slip out of the world into some eternal ocean where Nigel, for ever out of his reach, played on its sands. He felt himself naked, stripped to the buff, without a rag to call his own.

Those were days of dull misery and nights of dreamless sleep and unrefreshed awakening.

And then one morning he arose with a verse in his head. He had always been a voracious reader of poetry, and had remembered the things which caught his fancy. This verse was about the soul and body being ploughed under by God. He had forgotten the author, but bit by bit he managed to build up one quatrain, and it seemed to run something like this:

> "Come ill, come well, the cross, the crown,
>   The rainbow or the thunder—
> I fling my soul and body down
>   For God to plough them under."

There was a strange fascination in the idea. Adam had the underlying fatalism which is the bequest of ancestral Calvinism, even though its specific tenets may have been long ago forgotten. He had always drawn comfort from the thought that, while it was a man's duty to strive to the uttermost, the result was determined by mightier things than man's will. He had believed most devoutly in God, though he would have been puzzled to define his creed. Suddenly there came over him a sense of the microscopic littleness and the gossamer fragility of human life.

Everything lay in the hands of God, though men fussed and struggled and made a parade of freedom. Might not there be a more potent strength in utter surrender?

His mind became acid-clear. He had nothing—nothing. His chances in life, so zealously cherished, had departed like smoke. His reputation was shattered for ever. He had sunk into the underworld of those who are eternally discounted. . . . But if he was stripped to the bone, that meant also that he had nothing to lose—nothing but Eilean Bàn, which was not really of this world. . . . But had he nothing left? He had health and an exercised body—brains—much knowledge. Was there no use to be made of these even in the underworld of the disconsidered? Might there not be a tremendous power in complete submission? If soul and body were offered to God to plough under, might not there be a harvest from the sacrifice?

The thought came upon him with the force of a revelation. His feebleness had suddenly become strength. He asked nothing of life, neither length of days, nor wealth, nor fame, nor comfort. He was out of the daylight and honour of the firing-line, but there must be work to do in dark places for one who was prepared to keep nothing back. Desperate men he had been told were always formidable, but desperation was commonly a wild neurotic thing, incalculable and undirected, based on ignoble passions like jealousy and fear. What of a desperation which had in it no taint of self, which was passionless and reasoned, not a wayward lightning but a steady flame? He might win the right to Eilean Bàn by other means than the glittering career he had once mapped out for himself.

A new kind of peace fell upon him. It was not the peace of the fakir who has renounced everything for the high road and the begging-bowl, but something more absolute still, for Adam did not ask for a hope of Heaven. Even Eilean Bàn dropped out of his picture. He was content to lay himself under the eternal plough. . . . He took to prayer, which was a kind of communing with his own soul. . . . And finally there came a night when he dedicated himself humbly yet exultingly to whatever uttermost service might be asked, and rose from his knees with the certainty that his vow had been accepted.

Christopher Stannix, who was his most regular visitor, noticed a change in Adam. The muddy prison colour in his face had given place to the hue of health, which was inevitable, for he was now striving consciously to keep his body fit. His old alertness had returned, and, instead of the dull apathy of the first days, he showed a lively curiosity about events in the outer world. He asked for books, and an odd collection they made. Milton was the only poet—naturally, Stannix thought, for Adam seemed to have pulled himself together and to be making a stand against fortune, and Milton in his blindness had done the same. There were various books of philosophy, including a newly published volume of Bergson, and various works on the higher mathematics. Also there was a mass of travel literature, and many grammars. There was no request for any military books.

Adam had resolved to equip himself for his task in this enforced leisure which had been granted him. The first thing was to keep his mind bright and clear, so he toiled at the stiffest mental gymnastics which he could find. The second was to enlarge his knowledge, for one who worked in the shadows must know more than those in the daylight. He had decided that soldiering, the scientific side of it at any rate, was no more for him, so he put his old interests aside. Since he did not know where his future service might lie, he set about informing himself on those parts of the globe which were strange to him. He had always had a passion for geography, and now, by much reading and poring over maps, he acquired an extensive book-knowledge of many countries. Languages, too, for which he had a turn. He already spoke French and German well—German almost like a native, and he had a fair knowledge of Italian and Spanish. To these he now added Russian and Turkish, and, having in his youth learned enough Icelandic to read the Sagas, he made himself a master of the Scandinavian tongues. He found his days pass pleasantly, for he had an ordered programme to get through, and he had the consciousness that he was steadily advancing in competence. Every scrap of knowledge which he acquired might some day, under God's hand, be of vital import.

But there were two tasks which he could not yet touch—the most urgent tasks of all. He must school his body to endure the last extremes of fatigue and pain, and prison gave him no chance for such a training. Also he must acquire a courage like tempered steel. It was not enough to hold one's life cheap: that was merely a reasoned purpose; what was needed was to make fortitude a settled habit, so that no tremor of nerves should ever mar his purpose. On that point alone he had qualms. He had still to lift his body, with all its frailties, to the close-knit resolution of his mind.

V

Adam came out of prison in March 1914. His lawyer had seen to the preliminaries, and Camilla intended to divorce him for desertion under Scots law. He had settled upon her most of his income, leaving himself one thousand pounds a year, apart from Eilean Bàn. She ultimately married a hunting baronet in Yorkshire, and passed out of his life. The island he let for a further term of seven years to its former tenant. If he was ever to return there, he had a heavy road to travel first.

Most of the summer was spent in getting back his body to its former vigour, for the effects of a long spell of confinement do not disappear in a day. He took rooms at a farmhouse in Northumberland and set himself to recruit his muscles and nerves as steadily as if he had been preparing for an Olympic race. He spent hours daily on the moors in all weathers, and the shepherds were puzzled by the man with the lean face and friendly eyes who quartered the countryside like a sheepdog. At one of the upland fairs he entered for a hill race, and beat the longest-legged keeper by half a mile. His mind needed no recruitment, for it had been long in training. He spent the evenings with his books, and once a week walked to the nearest town to get the London newspapers. He was waiting for a sign.

That sign came in the first days of August with the outbreak of war.

CHAPTER II

I

IN Whitehall on an August morning Adam met Stannix.
The latter had just left the War Office, which had changed
suddenly from a mausoleum to a hive. He was in uniform, with
scarlet gorget-patches, and was respectfully saluted by whatever
wore khaki. At sight of Adam he cried out.

"The man in all the world I most want to see! Where have
you come from?"

"From Northumberland, where I have been getting fit. It
looks as if I had finished the job just in time."

"And where are you bound for?"

"To join up."

"As a private?"

"Of course. I'm no longer a soldier."

"Nonsense, man. That can't be allowed. We're running this
business like a pack of crazy amateurs, but there's a limit to the
things we can waste. Brains is one."

"I must fight," said Adam. "You're doing the same."

"Not I. I'm stuck at home in this damned department store.
I want to go out tomorrow, for I've been in the Yeomanry for
years and know something about the job, but they won't let
me—yet. They told me I must do the thing I'm best fitted for.
I pass that on to you."

Adam shook his head.

"I'm fit for nothing but cannon-fodder. You know that well
enough, Kit. And I'm quite content. I'll find some way of
making myself useful, never fear."

"I daresay you will, but not the best way. This wants perpending.
Promise me on your honour that you'll do nothing today, and
lunch with me tomorrow. By that time I may have a plan."

Adam protested, but the other was so urgent that at last he agreed.

Next day they lunched together and Stannix wore an anxious face.

"I've seen Ritson and Marlake," he said, "and they think as I do. If you join up as a private, you'll presently get your stripes, and pretty soon you'll be offered a commission. But in a battalion you'll be no better than a hundred thousand others. I want you to have a show. Well, it can't be in the open, so it must be in the half-light or the dark. That means risks, far bigger risks than the ordinary fellow is now facing in Flanders, but it also means an opportunity for big service. How do you feel about it?"

Adam's face brightened.

"I haven't much capital left, and I want to spend it. I don't mind risks—I covet them. And I don't mind working in the dark, for that is where I must live now."

Stannix wrinkled his brows.

"I was certain you'd take that view, and I told Ritson so. But Adam, old man, I feel pretty miserable about it. For a chance of work for you means a certainty of danger—the most colossal danger."

"I know, I know," said Adam cheerfully. "That's what I'm looking for. Hang it, Kit, I must squeeze some advantage out of my troubles, and one is that my chiefs should not concern themselves about what happens to me. I'm a volunteer for any lost hope."

"I may be helping to send my best friend to his death," said Stannix gloomily.

"Everybody is doing that for everybody. You'll be doing the kindest thing in the world if you give me a run for my money. I've counted the cost."

The result of this talk was that during the following week Adam had various interviews. The first was with Ritson at the War Office, a man who had been one of his instructors at the Staff College. Ritson, grey with overwork, looked shyly at his former pupil. "This is a queer business, Melfort," he said. "I think you are right. You're the man I would have picked above

27

all others—only of course I couldn't have got you if certain things hadn't happened. . . . You know what's expected of you and what you're up against. Goodbye and God bless you! I'll be like a man looking down into deep water and now and then getting a glimpse of you moving at the bottom."

Thereafter Adam entered upon a varied life. First he made a journey into the City, to a little street in the neighbourhood of Leadenhall Market. On the door of every narrow, flat-chested house were a score of names, mostly attorneys and notaries public. At the foot of one such list he found J. N. Macandrew, who professed to follow the calling of an average-adjuster. Mr. Macandrew was hard to come at. Adam was received in a dingy slip of an office by a pallid boy, who took his card and disappeared. He returned and led the way up a maze of wooden stairs and murky passages, till he left him in a room where sunlight was pouring through a dirty window. There for half an hour Adam kicked his heels. The place had all the cheerful features of an attorney's waiting-room. On the walls, where the paper was dark with grime, hung an ancient almanac, a bad print of Lord Chancellor Cairns, and a faded photograph of the court of some livery company in the year 1889. On a rickety table stood three venerable Law Lists, an antediluvian Burke, a London directory, and a pile of shipping journals. There was a leather armchair which looked as if it had seen service, and a pile of cigarette ends in the empty grate, which suggested that the room was much in use.

Adam examined the scanty properties, and then stared out of the window at the jumble of roofs and house-backs. The place was oddly depressing. Here in this rabbit-warren life seemed to shrink to an infinite pettiness. What part could it have in the storm which was scourging the world? . . . He turned, to find that Mr. Macandrew had entered the room, though he had heard no door open.

Mr. Macandrew's name was misleading, for he was clearly a Jew, a small man with a nervous mouth and eyes that preferred to look downward. He seemed to have been expecting Adam, for he cut short his explanation. "Yes, yes, yes," he said. "Please take a seat. Yes, I know all about you. We can have a little talk, can't we? Will you smoke?"

Adam sat in the rubbed armchair, while the other perched himself on the table. It was a curious interview, of which the purpose only gradually became clear. Macandrew asked a few questions about a corner of Belgium which Adam had often visited. Ritson knew about those visits, and might have told him. Then he suddenly broke into the guttural French which is talked in the Meuse valley. "You understand that?" he snapped. "Every word?" Adam replied in the same patois, and was corrected on a point or two. "Pretty good," said Macandrew. "Good enough, perhaps. You have the right gurgle, but not all the idioms."

Then he spoke Flemish, which Adam translated after him. "That is good—very good. You do not need to speak it, but it is well to understand it." He drawled a few sentences in some tongue which sounded mere gibberish. "You do not follow? No matter. That is the speech of the hill people in the high Ardennes—peasant people only, you understand. There are gipsy words in it."

There followed a series of interrogatories. Adam was asked to describe the daily life on a farm in south-east Belgium. "You have stayed in such a place. Now, give me the duties of the farmer's son, beginning with the first daylight." Adam ransacked his memory and did his best, but the catalogue was sketchy. He pleased his interlocutor better with his account of a wayside estaminet, a cattle-fair, and a Sunday pilgrimage. "You can observe," said Macandrew. "Not yet with sufficient nicety. Yet you have eyes in your head."

He was suddenly dismissed. The pallid boy appeared, and Macandrew held out his hand. "Goodbye, Mr. More. Perhaps we shall meet again soon."

As Adam re-threaded the labyrinth of stair and passage, he wondered why he had been addressed as More. That must have been Ritson's arrangement, and he had not been told of it because his chiefs assumed that he knew enough to be passive in their hands.

A few days later he found himself a guest in a country house which lay under the Hampshire Downs. The invitation had been sent to him by Ritson, and in it he figured as Mr. John More. His host was called Warriner, a fine, old, high-coloured sportsman, who looked as if his winters had been spent in the hunting-field, and his summers in tramping his paternal acres. There was a son, in his early twenties, who had come over from a neighbouring training-camp. It appeared that young Warriner was a noted mountaineer, and Adam remembered his name in connection with ascents in the Caucasus. At dinner the talk was very little of the war, and there was no hint of any knowledge of Adam's past. The father and son, with all the courtesy in the world, seemed to be bent on discovering his tastes in sport and his prowess in games, so that he set them down as the type of Englishman who never outgrows the standards of his public school.

"You look uncommonly fit," said the son, as they left the smoking-room.

"I try to be," said Adam. "I haven't got many things to my credit, but one of them is a hard body."

"Good," was the answer. "We'll have a long day tomorrow. You'll be called at five. Put on something old and light—flannel bags will do—and strong shoes. We have a bit of striding before us."

It was a clear cool morning when they started, and Adam thought that he had never seen such a light-foot walker as Frank Warriner. He led him out of the vale up on to the Downs at a steady pace of nearly five miles an hour. Presently the sun grew hot, but there was no slackening of their speed. Adam's spirits rose, for he understood that his endurance was being tested, and he had little fear of the result. To his surprise their first halt was at a country rectory, where a parson in slippers gave them a tankard of home-brewed beer. He was a fantastic old gentleman, for he directed all his conversation to Adam, and engaged him in a discussion on Norse remains in Britain, which appeared to be his hobby. Adam thought it strange that he should have hit on a subject which had always been one of his private interests, and for the half-hour of their visit he did his best to live up to the parson's enthusiasm. "Good," said

30

Frank Warriner, as they left the house. "You managed that quite well."

In the early afternoon they came to a stone wall bounding a great estate. Frank led the way over the wall. "Follow me," he said. "Colonel Ambridge is a devil about his pheasants. We'll have some fun getting through this place." They found themselves in a park studded with coppices, and bordered by a large wood full of thick undergrowth. Frank took an odd way of crossing prohibited ground, for he began by making himself conspicuous, walking boldly across the open in full view of a keeper's cottage. Presently a man's voice was heard uplifted, and the two became fugitives. They doubled back behind a group of trees, and Frank made for the big wood. They were followed, for as Adam looked behind him he saw two excited men running to cut them off.

In the wood Frank led him through gaps in the undergrowth, stopping now and then to listen like a stag at pause. There was no doubt about the pursuit, for the noise of heavy feet and crackling twigs was loud behind them. Frank seemed to know the place well, and he had an uncanny gift of locating sound, for he twisted backward and forward like a rabbit. Adam found running bent double and eel-like crawling through bracken a far harder trial than the speed of the morning, but he managed to keep close to his companion. At last Frank straightened himself and laughed. "Now for a sprint," he said, and he led the way at a good pace down a woodland path, which ended in an alley of rhododendrons.

To Adam's surprise, instead of avoiding the house they made for it. Frank slowed down at the edge of a carriage drive and walked boldly across the lawn to a stone terrace, and through French windows into a library where a man was sitting. "Hallo, Colonel Ambridge," he said. "We're out for a walk and looked in to pass the time of day. May I introduce my friend Mr. More?"

The Colonel, a lean dark man of about sixty, behaved like the parson. He gave them drinks, and plunged into military talk, most of it directed to Adam. This was no somnolent retired soldier, but a man remarkably up-to-date in his calling. He spoke of the French generals whose names were becoming familiar in

Britain—of Joffre's colonial service and of Foch's *Principes de la Guerre*, and he was critical of the French concentration in Lorraine. France, he maintained, had departed from the true interpretation of the "war of manoeuvre," and he was contemptuous of false parallels drawn from Napoleon's *bataillon carrée* at Jena. He seemed to have an exact knowledge of the terrain of the war, maps were produced, and Adam, the sweat on his brow and the marks of brier scratches on his cheek, found himself debating closely on points of strategy. There was something sharp and appraising in their host's eye as they took their leave. "Good," said Frank again. "You handled old Ambridge well. Now for home, for we mustn't be late."

The last part of the ground was covered mainly in a loping trot, which took them back along the ridge of the Downs till they looked down upon the Warriners' house. Adam calculated that they had done nearly thirty miles, but he realised that the day had not been meant as a mere test of bodily endurance. Those queer visits had had a purpose, and he guessed what it was. To his delight it seemed to him that his companion was flagging a little—at any rate the edge was off his keenness—while he himself had got his second wind.

He found a large tea-party at the Warriners'. "I'm going to cut it," Frank said, "but you must show yourself. You look all right. You've kept amazingly tidy." Adam obeyed, for he thought he understood the reason.

He could have drunk pints, but he was only given one small cup of weak tea. But he had a full dose of conversation. It appeared to be the special purpose of everyone to talk to him. He had to listen to schemes of hospital work from local ladies, and to amateur military speculations from an old Yeomanry colonel. A Bishop discussed with him the ethics of the war, and a parliamentary candidate had much to say about the party truce. He felt hot, very thirsty, and rather drowsy, but he collected his wits, for he saw that his host's eye was continually fixed on him. The elder Warriner managed to add himself to any group where Adam talked, and it appeared that he was adroitly trying to draw him out.

"You have been drinking in the peace of England," the

Bishop told him. "Today will be a cool oasis to remember in the feverish months before you."

When the guests had gone and he was left with his host, the rosy country squire seemed to have changed to somebody shrewd and authoritative.

"We shall be alone tonight," he said, "for Frank has gone back to camp. You acquitted yourself well, Mr. More. Frank is pretty nearly all out, and he is harder than most people. I daresay you realise the purpose of today's performance. In the game you are entering physical fitness is not enough. A man must have full control of his wits, and be able to use them when his bodily vitality is low. The mind must have the upper hand of the carcass, and not be drugged by exertion into apathy. You appear to fill the bill. . . . Now you'll want a bath before dinner.

"By the way," he added, "there's one thing you may like to know. We won't talk about the past, but long ago at school I fagged for your father."

Adam's next visit was of a different kind. Slowly there had been growing in his mind the comforting reflection that he might be of use to the world, since other people seemed to take pains to assess his capacities. He recognised that the tests were only superficial—what could anyone learn of a man's powers from a few experiments?—but that they should have been considered worth while increased his confidence. So when he was sent down to spend a day with a certain Theophilus Scrope in a little market-town in Northamptonshire he speculated on what might next be put to the proof. Certain branches of his knowledge had been probed, and his bodily strength, but no-one had attempted to assay his mental powers or the quality of his nerves. The latter, he believed, would now be the subject, and he thought of Mr. Scrope as a mixture of psychologist and physician.

Mr. Scrope was neither. He was a small elderly man with a Chinese cast of face, who wore a skull cap, and sat with a tartan plaid round his shoulders, though the weather was warm. He had a dreamy eye, and a voice hoarse with age and endless cigarettes. At first his talk meandered about several continents.

33

It appeared that he had spent much of his life in the East, and he entertained Adam with fantastic tales of the Tibetan frontier. His experiences seemed to have impressed themselves on his face, for he had the air of a wise and ancient Lama. He was fond of quoting proverbs from native languages, and now and then he would deliver oracles of his own, looking sideways under his heavy eyelids to see how they were received.

Adam spent a confused morning, sitting in a little garden heavy with the scents of autumn flowers. Mr. Scrope seemed to have a genius for the discursive. But gradually it appeared that his reminiscences were directed to one point especially, the everlasting temperamental differences of East and West. His chief instance was the virtue of courage. The East, he said, which did not fear the hereafter, was apathetic towards the mere fact of death, but it had not the same fortitude about life. It was capable of infinite sacrifice but not of infinite effort—it was apt to fling in its hand too soon, and relapse upon passivity. The West, when it had conquered the fear of death, demanded a full price for any sacrifice. Rightly, said the old man, since man's first duty was towards life.

Then they went indoors to luncheon, which was a modest meal of eggs, cheese, and vegetables. After that his host must sleep for an hour, and Adam was left alone to his reflections in a chair on the veranda. . . . He was beginning to see some purpose in the talk of this ancient, who looked like a Buddhist holy man. Mr. Scrope must have been informed about his case, and realised that he was dealing with one who had nothing to lose. The moral of his talk was that desperation was valueless by itself and must be subordinated to a purpose. A man's life was an asset which must be shrewdly bargained for. Adam wondered why he had been sent down into Northamptonshire to hear this platitude.

But when the old man appeared he changed his view. For Mr. Scrope, refreshed by sleep, became a shrewd inquisitor, and probed with a lancet Adam's innermost heart. Never had he dreamed that he could so expose his secret thoughts to any man. More, he had his own beliefs made clear to himself, for what had been only vague inclinations crystallised under this treatment into convictions. His companion was no longer a whimsical old gentleman with the garrulity of age, but a sage with an uncanny insight into his own private perplexities. Duty was expounded as a thing both terrible and sweet, transcending life and death, a bridge over the abyss to immortality. But it required the service of all of a man's being, and no half-gods must cumber its altar. Adam felt himself strangely stirred; stoicism was not his mood now, but exaltation. "He that findeth his life shall lose it, but he that loseth his life shall find it," the other quoted. "That is not enough," he added. "He that findeth his soul shall lose it— that is the greater commandment. You must be prepared to sacrifice much that you think honourable and of good report if you would fulfil the whole Law."

There was a kindly gleam in his dim old eyes as he bade his guest goodbye. "You have the root of the matter, I think," were his last words. "You will make your soul, as the priests say, and if you do that you have won, whatever happens—yes, whatever happens." It seemed almost a benediction.

After that Adam was sent back to the City of London. There he was no longer received in the dingy waiting-room, but in Macandrew's own sanctum, a place to which the road was even more intricate. He realised, though he had had no word from Ritson, that his services had been accepted.

For weeks he worked hard under the tuition of a very different Macandrew. His instruction was of the most detailed and practical kind. From plans and books he studied a certain area of Flanders, and was compelled to draw map after map and endure endless cross-examinations till his tutor was satisfied. He was made to learn minutely the routine of the country life. "You will work on a farm," he was told, "but as you will have come from the town you must have urban knowledge, too, and that I will provide." It was provided at immense length, for his master was not easily satisfied. "There is nothing too small to be unimportant," Macandrew said. "It is the very little things that make the difference." He had to commit to memory curious pieces of slang and patois and learn how to interweave them naturally with his talk. Disguises, too; there were afternoons when Adam had to masquerade in impossible clothes and be taught how to live up to them, and to acquire the art of giving himself by small changes a different face. His special part was kept always before his mind. "You must think yourself into it," he was told, "and imagine that you have never been otherwise. That is the only real disguise."

Then there was the whole complicated business of cyphers and codes. These must be subtle and yet simple, for Adam must carry them in his head. He had to practise his powers of memory, and was surprised to find how they developed with exercise. And he was told of certain people who were key-people, the pivots of the intelligence system in which he would serve. This was the most difficult business of all, for these persons would take on many forms, and it was necessary to have certain marks of identification and passports to their confidence. Adam was almost in despair at the mass of knowledge, vital knowledge, which he must keep always in the background of his mind. "It is altogether necessary," said Macandrew. "You are a quick learner and will not fail. The clues are intricate because the facts are intricate. There is no simple key to complex things."

As the weeks passed Adam had moments of impatience. "There will be peace before I am ready," he complained, and was told, "Not so. The war will be very long."

A new Macandrew had revealed himself, a man confident and eager and untiring, but one who still kept his eyes lowered when he spoke. Adam often wondered what was in those eyes. It appeared that his real name was Meyer, and that he was a Belgian Jew, who had long foreseen the war and had made many preparations. Adam discovered one day the motive for his devotion to the British cause. The man was an ardent Zionist, and the mainspring of his life was his dream of a reconstituted Israel. He believed that this could not come about except as a consequence of a great war, which should break down the traditional frontiers of Europe, and that Britain was the agent destined by God to lead his people out of the wilderness. He would not speak much on the subject, but it was the only one which made him raise his eyes and look Adam in the face, and then Adam read in them the purpose which makes saints and martyrs.

When they parted at last he gave Adam a tiny amulet of silver and ebony, shaped like a blunt cross. "You will wear that, please—people will think it a peasant charm—it may be useful when we meet, for I am not quick at faces. . . . Assuredly we shall meet. Are we not both working for the peace and felicity of Jerusalem?"

II

In the second week of January, in the year 1915, those who passed the untidy farm of the Widow Raus might have seen a new figure busy about the steading. When the neighbours inquired his name they were told that he was the Widow's nephew Jules—Jules Broecker, the only child of Marie, her dead sister. The Widow was volubly communicative. The poor Jules had no near kinsfolk but her, and she could not leave him alone in Brussels, for he was simpler than other folk—and she meaningly tapped her forehead. He would be useful about the farm, for he was a strong lad, and would have his bite and sup and a bed to lie on in these bad times as long as she was above ground. Madame Raus was a short plump woman with grey hair neatly parted in the middle and plastered down with grease. Out of doors—and she was mostly out of doors—she wore a man's cap to keep her head tidy. She had a name for closeness, and she was the soul of discretion, for she did not grumble like most people at the high-handed ways of the local German Commandant. She has no proper feelings, that one, her neighbours said, and they looked on her with cold eyes as being apathetic about her country's wrongs. But the Widow had had an only son who never returned from the Yser, and she did not forget.

Jules Broecker appeared suddenly one morning at the farm, having come on foot from Brussels, his little trunk of bullock-hide following him in a farm-cart. When summoned before the Commandant he had his papers in good order, his certificate of residence in the city, his permission to leave, and the *visé* on it stamped by the officer at Nivelles. The neighbours knew all about him, for they remembered Marie Broecker and had heard of her simpleton son. But no-one had met him on the Brussels road—which was natural, for he came not from Brussels but from the south, having been landed from an aeroplane in a field twenty miles off during the darkness of a January night.

His appearance supported his aunt's commendation. He seemed wiry and strong, though he slouched heavily. He had a wispish blond beard which looked as if it had never been shaved, and sandy hair which was cut at long intervals by the blacksmith in Villers l'Evêque. His clothes were odd, for he wore corduroy trousers, much too small for him, which had once belonged to the deceased Raus, and though the first months of the year were chilly he was generally coatless. His face was always dirty, which, said the neighbours, was a disgrace to the Widow; but on Sundays he was smartened up, and appeared at Mass in a celluloid collar and a queer old jacket with metal buttons. From long before the first light he was busy about the farm, and could be heard after dark had fallen whistling lugubriously as he fed the cattle.

The steading was an ill-tended place—a vast midden surrounded by wooden pens and byres, with at one end a great brick barn, and at the other the single-storeyed dwelling-house. There was not much grown in the way of crops, only a few roots and a patch of barley, but the grasslands along the brook were rich, and the Widow pastured no less than six cows. She had a special permit for this, which was ill-regarded in the neighbourhood, for she was a famous cheesemaker, and sold her cheese (at a starvation price) to the nearest German base-camp. Jules had a hard life of it, for he was cowherd, milker, and man of all work; but he bore it with a simpleton's apathy, clumping about the dirty yard in his wooden clogs, his shoulders bowed and his head on his chest. Now and then he was observed to straighten his back and listen, when the wind brought from the west the low grumble of distant guns. Then he would smile idiotically to himself, as if it was some play got up for his entertainment.

Clearly a natural, all agreed. Marie's husband was remembered as having been a little weak in his wits, and the son plainly took after him. Jules had large vacant blue eyes, and when he was

38

spoken to his face took on a vacant simper. His habits were odd, for he would work hard for a week and then go off wandering, leaving his aunt to make the rafters ring with maledictions. On such occasions she would reveal shamelessly the family skeleton. "He is Jean Broecker's own son," she would declare, "feckless, witless, shiftless! But what would you have? An old woman cannot control an able-bodied idiot. Would that Raus were alive to lay a dog-whip on the scamp's shoulders!" But the Widow's wrath was short-lived, and when Jules returned he was not given a dog-whip but a special supper, and she would even bathe his inflamed feet. For it appeared that he was a mighty walker, and in his wanderings travelled far up and down the Meuse valley to places which no-one in Villers l'Evêque had ever visited. He would tell foolish empty tales of his travels, and giggle over them. Beyond doubt, a natural!

But a harmless one. Jules was not unpopular. For one thing he was socially inclined, and when he was idle would gossip with anyone in his queer high voice and clipped town accent. Sometimes he would talk about his life in Brussels, but his stories never reached any point—he would break off with a guffaw before the end. But he seemed to have picked up some good ideas about farming, and in the Three Parrots estaminet, which was the farmers' house of call, he was sometimes listened to. He liked of an evening, if his work was finished in time, to go down to the village, and he patronised all three of the alehouses. He never stood treat, for he was not entrusted with money, and he never drank himself—did not like the smell of beer and brandy, he said, and made faces of disgust. His one vice was smoking, but unlike the other countryfolk he did not use a pipe—only cigarettes, which he was clever at rolling when anyone gave him tobacco. Now and then he was presented with a packet of cheap caporals which lasted him a long time, and he had generally a cigarette stuck behind his left ear as a sort of iron ration. People tolerated him because he was quiet and simple, and many even came to like him, for so far as his scattered wits allowed he was neighbourly. Also he provided the village with perpetual surprises. He seemed to be oblivious of the severe regime of the military occupation, and many prophesied early disaster.

But no disaster came to this chartered libertine. Villers l'Evêque was a key-point, for it stood at the crossing of two great high roads and not three miles from the junction of two main railways. Therefore the discipline for its dwellers was strict. There were always second-line troops stationed near, and the beershops were usually full of Landsturm. At first Jules was made a butt of by the German soldiers, raw young peasants like himself for the most part, with a sprinkling of more elderly tradesmen. They played tricks on him, pulled a chair from beneath him, slipped lighted matches down his neck, and once gave him an explosive cigarette which badly burned his lips. But he was so good-humoured under this persecution that it presently ceased, and he was treated more like a pet dog or a mascot. They taught him their songs, which he sang in an absurd falsetto that became a recognised evening's entertainment. Also they talked freely to him, for they could not regard anything so feckless as an enemy. Homesick boys who had picked up a little French would tell him of their recent doings—he was a good listener and quick at helping them out when they were at a loss for a word and relapsed into German. His pale eyes had sympathy in them, if little intelligence.

Word of this village natural came to headquarters, and every now and then he had to appear before the local Commandant. These officers were frequently changed, but for the most part they were of the same type—elderly dug-outs who asked only for a quiet life. At such interviews Jules produced his papers, and told in a wailing recitative the simple story of his life. The worst that happened was usually a warning to stay at home and not tramp the country, lest he should find himself one fine day against a wall looking at a firing squad—at which he would grin sheepishly and nod his head. But one day he had a terrifying experience. There was a new Commandant, a Bavarian captain who had been temporarily invalided from the front line, a young man with an eye like an angry bird's, and no bowels of compassion for simple folk. For two hours he kept Jules under the fire of his questions, which he delivered with a lowering brow and a menacing voice. "That animal may be dangerous," he told his lieutenant. "He is witless, and so can be used as a tool by

40

clever men. A telephone wire, you understand—a senseless thing over which news passes. He must be sent farther east." But this Commandant was moved elsewhere in a week, and nothing more was heard of his threat. A more dangerous man, if Jules had had the sense to realise it, was a friendly, fatherly personage, who tried to draw him into confidences, and would suddenly ask questions in German and English. But Jules only stared dully at such experiments, until his inquisitor shrugged his shoulders and gave them up.

Had anyone from Villers l'Evêque met Jules on the road on one of his tramps he would have seen only a shaggy young peasant—rather better shod than most peasants, since he had got the cobbler to make him a stout pair of marching boots—who seemed in high spirits, for he cried a greeting to every passer-by and would sing silly child's songs in his high falsetto. But much of Jules's travelling was done off the roads, where no-one saw him, and in the dark of moonless nights. Then he was a different being. His clumsy gait and slouching carriage disappeared, and he would cover country at a pace which no peasant could have matched. Into queer places his road often took him. He would lie for long in a marshy meadow till a snipe's bleat made him raise his head, and then another man would crawl through the reeds, and the two would talk. Once he spent two days in the undergrowth of a wood close to a road where German columns passed without end. He seemed to have many friends. There was an old woodcutter in the hills between the Meuse and the Ourthe who several times gave him shelter, and foresters in the Ardennes, and a blind woman who kept an inn outside Namur on the Seilles road. Indeed, there was a host of people who had something to say to him in whispers, and when he listened to them his face would lose its vacancy. They seemed to respect him too, and when they spoke to him their tone had not the condescension of the Villers folk. . . .

Sometimes he did strange things. In a lonely place at night he would hide himself for many hours, his head raised like that of a horse at covert-side who waits for the first music of the hounds. Often he waited till dawn and nothing came, but sometimes there would be a beat of wings far up in the air which was not the beat of a Fokker, and the noise would follow of a heavy body crushing the herbage. He would grope his way in the direction of the sound, and a man would appear from the machine with whom he spoke—and that speech was not French or Flemish. By and by the aeroplane would vanish again into the night sky, and Jules would look after it, wistfully for a little, before by devious paths he took his road home.

A close observer, had there been one at hand, would have been puzzled by his treatment of cigarettes. On his travels he was always giving and receiving them, and some he never smoked. A barmaid would toss him carelessly a dilapidated caporal, and it would go behind his ear, and no match would come near it. More than once in the Three Parrots a pedlar from Liège, or a drover who had brought to the valley some of the small cattle of the hills, would offer him a box from which he would take two, one to smoke and one to keep. In turn he would give away cigarettes which he had rolled himself, and some went to very special people, who did not smoke them, but carried them with them in their travels, and in the end handed them secretly to somebody else. If such cigarettes had been unrolled, it would have been found that the paper was stiffer than the ordinary and more opaque, and that on the inner side next the tobacco there was something written in a small fine hand. Jules himself could write this hand, and practised it late at night in his cubbyhole of a bedroom next to Widow Raus's cowshed.

These cigarettes wandered far, most of them beyond the frontier. A girl who had been a mannequin in a Paris shop took some of them to Holland; some went into the heavens with the airmen whom Jules met in the dark of the night; and some journeyed to Brussels and Antwerp and then by devious ways to the coast and overseas. There was that in them which would have interested profoundly the Commandant at Villers l'Evêque— notes of German troops and concentrations, and now and then things which no-one knew outside the High Command, such as the outline for the Ypres attack in the spring of '15, and the projected Flanders offensive which was to follow the grand assault on Verdun. . . . Only once was Jules in danger of detection, and that was when a Würtemberg captain, who was a little fuddled, plucked the cigarette from his ear and lit it. He swore that the thing drew badly and flung it on the floor, whereupon the provident Jules picked up the stump and himself smoked it to a finish.

Twice he went to Brussels to see his relatives, journeys arranged for by much weary intercession with the Commandant, and duly furnished with passes. On these visits he did not see much of his kin, but he interviewed a motley of queer persons in back streets. Under the strictest military rule there are always a few people who can move about freely—women who are favoured by high officials, bagmen of the right sympathies who keep the wheels of commerce moving, all the class, too, who pander to human vices. With some of these Jules mixed, and Villers would have rubbed its eyes to see how he bore himself. Instead of a disconsidered servant he became a master, and in back rooms, which could only be reached by difficult alleys and through a multitude of sentries, he would give instructions which were docilely received by men and women who were not peasants.

Once it was necessary that he should cross the Dutch border by what was called in the slang of his underworld the "Allée Couverte". He started his journey as an old mechanic with a permit to take up a plumber's job at Turnhout. But long before he got to Turnhout he changed his appearance, and he had a week in the straw of barns and many anxious consultations with furtive people till early one dark autumn morning he swam a canal, crawled through a gap in the electrified wire (where oddly enough the sentry was for a moment absent) and two hours later breakfasted with a maker of chemical manures who seemed to be expecting him. His host spoke to him in English and lent him clothes which made him look like a young merchants' clerk after he had shaved his beard. . . . Jules spent four days in Holland, and at an hotel in Amsterdam had a meeting, which lasted late into the night, with an English businessman who was interested in oil—a businessman whose back was very straight for one who spent his days in a counting-house. Jules called him "Sir" and stood at attention till he was bidden to sit

43

down. This Englishman had much to tell him and much to hear, and what he heard he wrote down in a little black notebook. He addressed Jules as "More", but once he slipped and called him "Melfort". Then he seemed to recollect himself. "I think you knew Melfort," he said. "Adam Melfort. You may be interested to hear that his D.S.O. has just been gazetted—he is a second-lieutenant on the Special List."

Jules was absent that time for more than a month from the Raus farm. He returned at last from Brussels with a doctor's certificate duly countersigned by the military, which testified that he had been ill with typhoid in the house of a second cousin. His beard had been shaved during his fever, and his lean cheeks and the sprouting growth on his chin were visible proof of his sickness. He returned to his old routine, except that the Widow for a little did not work him so hard on the farm. "That Jules!" she complained to the neighbours. "The good God is too hard on him. He has bereft him of sense, and now He has made him as feeble as a pullet." Also his wanderings ceased for the space of more than a month.

Time passed and the Widow's half-witted nephew grew into the life of the place, so that he was as familiar an object as the windmill on the rise above the Bois de Villers. Commandant succeeded Commandant, and the *dossier* of Jules was duly handed on. The tides of war ebbed and flowed. Sometimes the neighbourhood of Villers was black with troops moving westward, and then would come a drain to the south and only a few Landsturm companies were left in the cantonments. There was such a drain during the summer of '16 when the guns were loud on the Somme. But early in '17 the movement from the east began again, and Jules took to wandering more widely than ever. Great things seemed to be preparing on the Flanders front.

In two years he had acquired a routine and a technique. He had taken the advice of Macandrew and thought himself so comprehensively into his part that his instincts and half his thoughts had become those of a Flanders peasant. In a difficulty he could trust himself to behave naturally according to his type. Yet there remained one side of him which was not drugged. He

44

had to keep his mind very bright and clear, quick to catch at gossamer threads of evidence, swift to weave them into the proper deductions, always alert and resourceful and wholly at his command.

It was this continual intellectual stimulus which made bearable a life as brutish as a farm animal's. Now and then, to be sure, he had his moments of revolt which were resolutely suppressed. He had long ago conquered any repugnance to his physical environment, the smells, the coarse food, the bestial monotony, the long toil in mud and filth. But there would come times when he listened to the far-off grumbling guns in the west with a drawn face. His friends were there, fighting cleanly in the daylight, while he was ingloriously labouring in the shadows. He had moods when he longed desperately for companionship. British prisoners would pass on their way to Germany, heavy-eyed men, often wounded and always weary, who tried to keep their heads high. He would have given his soul for a word with them. And once he saw in such a batch some men of his own regiment, including an officer who had joined along with him. The mere sound of English speech was torture. In those moods he had no source of comfort save in the bare conviction that he must stick to his duty. At night on his bed he could recapture no healing memories of Eilean Bàn. He was so deep in a hideous rut that he could not see beyond it to his old world.

He had two experiences which shook his foundations. Once at a midnight rendezvous with an English aeroplane there was a hitch in taking-off, an alarm was given, and soldiers from a German post appeared at the edge of the meadow. Jules knew that with his help the machine could get away, but that it would mean a grave risk of discovery. As it was, he obeyed the airman's hoarse injunction, "For God's sake clear out—never mind me," and, crawling down a little brook, found safe hiding in the forest. He saw the airman badly wounded and carried off into captivity, but not before he had reduced the 'plane to ashes; and he realised that he could have saved him. That was a bitter draught of which the taste long remained. It was no good reminding himself that he had done his duty, when that duty seemed a defiance of every honest human inclination.

The other experience was worse. There was a girl who had been a prostitute in Lille, and who served in an estaminet on the Brussels road. She was one of his helpers—M 23 on the register of his underworld. Now a certain Bavarian sergeant, who desired to be her lover, but whom she had repulsed, discovered her in some small act of treachery to the authorities which was no part of Jules's own affair. He exacted his revenge to the full, and Jules happened to enter the estaminet when the sergeant and another soldier were in the act of arresting her. They made a brutal business of it, the sergeant had her arms twisted behind her back, and her face was grey with fear and pain. For an instant Jules forgot his part, the simper left his mouth, his jaw set, and he ran to her aid. But the girl was wiser than he. She flung at him a string of foul names, and the black eyes under the tinted lids blazed a warning. He had to submit to be soundly cuffed by the soldiers, and to see the woman dragged screaming into a covered wagon. After that it took him a long time to recover his peace of mind. The words of the old man in the Northamptonshire village were his chief comfort: "You must be prepared to sacrifice much that you think honourable and of good report if you would fulfil the whole Law."

On a certain day in March '17 an urchin from the village brought Jules a message which had been left for him by a farmer from the Sambre side—that he had better bestir himself about the summering of the young beasts. It was an agreed password, and it made Jules knit his brows, for it meant that the long chain of intelligence which he supervised was in danger. That night he went on his travels and presently his fears were confirmed. The enemy had discovered one link and might discover the whole, for the interconnection was close, unless his suspicions could be switched on to a different track.

Three nights later Jules found a British aeroplane at a place agreed on for emergency meetings, meetings appointed by a very delicate and bold method which was only to be used in an hour of crisis. There was a passenger beside the pilot, an officer in a great blanket coat, who sat hunched on the ground and listened with a grim face to Jules's story.

"What devil's own luck!" he said. "At this time of all others!

The Arras affair, as you know, is due in three weeks—and there are others to follow. We simply cannot do without your crowd. Have you anything to suggest?"

"Yes," was the answer. "I have thought it all out, and there is one way. The enemy is on the alert and must be soothed down. That can be done only by giving him good ground for his suspicions—but it must not be the right ground. We want a decoy. You follow me, sir?"

The other nodded. "But what—or rather who?" he asked.

"Myself. You see, sir, I think I have done my work here. The machine is working well, and I can safely hand over the direction of it to S. S. I have taught him all I know, and he's a sound fellow. It's the machine that matters, not me, so my proposal is that to save the machine I draw suspicion on myself. I know the Germans pretty well, and they like to hunt one hare at a time. I can so arrange it that every doubt and suspicion they entertain can be made to fasten on me. I will give them a run for their money, and after that S. S. and his lads will be allowed to function in peace."

"Gad, that's a sporting notion," said the officer. "But what about yourself? Can you keep out of their hands long enough?"

"I think so. I know the countryside better than most people, and I have a good many possible lairs. I shall want a clear week to make arrangements, for they are bound to be rather complicated. For one thing I must get Mother Raus to a hole where she cannot be found. Then I press the button and become a fugitive. I think I can count on keeping the hounds in full cry for a week."

"Won't it be hard to pick you up if the pace is hot?"

"I don't want to be picked up. I must draw the hunt as far east as possible—away from the front. That will make S. S. and his machine more secure."

The other did not reply for a little.

"You realise that if you're caught it's all up with you?" he said at length.

"Of course. But that has been true every moment during the past two years. I'm only slightly speeding up the risks. Besides, I don't think I shall be caught."

"You'll try for Holland?"

"Holland or Germany. It will probably take some time."

The officer stood up and glanced at his luminous wristwatch. "We should be safe here for the next hour. I want all the details of the new layout—S. S. I mean."

When this conference was finished he turned to Jules and offered his hand.

"You are right. It's the only way, and a big part of the fate of the war hangs on it. I won't wish you good luck, for that's too feeble for such an occasion. But I'd like to say this to you, More. I've seen many gallant things done in my time, and I've met many brave men, but by God! for sheer cold-blooded pluck I never knew the like of you. If you win out, I shall have a good deal to say about that."

Two days later the Widow Raus set off for Brussels to visit her relations. She took with her a great basket of eggs and butter, and she got a lift in a German transport wagon to save the railway fare. Thereafter she disappeared, and though her whereabouts were sought by many they were never discovered. She did not emerge into the light again till a certain day in December 1918, when she was one of many women thanked by her King, and was given a red ribbon to wear on her ample bosom.

Left alone at the farm, Jules went on his travels for two days, during which he had interviews with many people in retired places. Then he returned and showed himself in the Three Parrots. But that night he left the farm, which was occupied next morning by soldiers who were in a hurry. They ransacked every room, slit the mattresses, pulled up the floors, probed in straw heaps in the outhouses. There were wild rumours in the village. Jules the simpleton had, it appeared, been a spy—some said an Englishman—and a confederate had betrayed him. A damning message from him had been found, for it seemed he could write, and he had been drawn into rash talk by a woman in the German pay. Much of the leakage to the Allies of vital secrets had been traced to him. He would be taken soon, of course, and set up against a wall—there was no hope of escape from the fine-meshed net which enveloped the land. But the bravery of it! Many a villager wished he had been kinder to the angel they had entertained unawares, and dolefully awaited the news of his end.

It did not come, for Jules seemed to have slipped out of the world. "He has been taken," said one rumour. "He will be taken," said all. But the best-informed knew nothing for certain. Only the discipline was uncomfortably tightened in the countryside, and the German officers looked darkly on every peasant they met. "Curse that Jules!" some began to say. "He has only made our bondage more burdensome."

Meantime Jules was far away. He had made his plans with care, and began by drawing the hunt northward as if he were making for Brussels. The first day he took pains to show himself at places from which the news could be carried. Then he doubled back to the Meuse valley, and in the dark, in a miller's cellar, shaved his beard, and was transformed into a young woodcutter who spoke the patois of the hills and was tramping to Liège, with papers all complete, to a job in a timber yard. His plan was to change his appearance again in Liège, and, having muddied the trail, to get to Antwerp, where certain preparations had been made in advance.

But on one point he had miscalculated. The chase became far closer than he had foreseen, for Belgium was suddenly stirred to a fury of spy-hunting. The real Jules had been lost sight of somewhere in the beet-fields of Gembloux, but every stranger was a possible Jules, and a man had to be well-accredited indeed before he could move a step without suspicion. He realised that he simply could not afford to be arrested, or even detained, so he was compelled to run desperate risks.

The story of his month's wanderings was never fully told, but these are the main points in it.

In Liège the woodcutter only escaped arrest on suspicion by slipping into a little civilian hospital where he knew the matron, and being in bed with the blankets up to his chin and bandages round his forehead when the military police arrived in quest of him. . . . He travelled by rail to Malines as a young doctor who had taken a Berlin degree, and was ready to discourse in excellent German on the superior medical science of the exalted country

49

where he had had his training. At Malines there was danger, for his permit was not strictly in order, and he realised that five minutes' cross-examination by a genuine doctor would expose the nakedness of the land. So he had to sink again into the gutter, and had a wretched week in a downpour of rain doing odd jobs among the market gardens, where there was a demand for labour. He was now a Dutch subject, speaking abominable French, and had been provided with papers by a little man who wore a skull-cap, was rarely sober, kept a disreputable pawnshop, and was known to certain people by a letter and a numeral. . . .

He tramped his way to Antwerp, and there suffered so severe an interrogation that he did not return for his *permission de sèjour*. Instead he found lodging in a street near the docks, where his appearance was considerably improved by the attentions of a lady of doubtful fame who had many friends. He was still a Dutchman, but of a higher class, for he had now a good black coat and a white collar, and his papers showed that he was a clerk in a Rotterdam office, who had come to Antwerp on his firm's business. He had permission to return to Holland, a permission which expired two days ahead.

Then, as bad luck would have it, he fell ill—the first time in two years. The drenchings in the rain and the scanty food had reduced his vitality, and he caught some infection is his squalid lodgings. For twenty-four hours he was in a high fever, and when he rose he could scarcely stagger. He dared not delay. If he stayed he must go to hospital, and there he would suffer a stern inquisition. As it was, before he had the strength to move, he had outstayed by one day the limits of his permit. . . . There was nothing for it but to take the risk. With a blinding headache, and legs that gave at the knees, and a deadly oppression on his chest, he took the tramway which jolted him to the frontier. There he was examined by the German post.

"Back you go," said the sergeant. "You have outstayed your permitted time. This permit must be corrected at the office of the Military Governor."

"Let him pass," said another, who seemed to have more authority. "The Dutchman is sick—mortally sick. We have no use for another bloody consumptive."

The Dutch sentries did no more than glance at his papers. That afternoon he took the train for Rotterdam, drove to a good hotel, and sent a message to a man he knew. Then for the next month he descended into the pit of pneumonia and very slowly climbed up the farther side.

III

Adam took a long time to recover his strength. There were friends who came to sit with him when he was permitted to receive visitors, one especially who was of a family long settled in Java, and whose dark colouring and yellow-tinged eyeballs suggested a dash of native blood. He called himself Lassom, and seemed to be a man of influence, for he managed to procure little comforts which were hard to come by in that difficult time. On his watch-chain he wore a little amulet of ebony and silver. From him the convalescent got the first news of the progress of the war on all fronts, for hitherto he had been shut up in a narrow enclave. Lassom, whose name had been Macandrew in the office near Leadenhall Street, required an exact report of all that had happened during the past two years in the neighbourhood of Villers l'Evêque.

Once an Englishman came to see Adam as he sat in a corner of the hotel balcony in the sunshine of early summer. "In the Army List," he told him, "you still figure as a second-lieutenant on the Special List. That, however, may not be for long. By the way, they have given you a bar to your D.S.O. for your last performance. I take it that for some time you have been shooting at your limit, as the gunners say. Well, you won't have anything so arduous for a bit—anyhow, till you're fit again. Lassom will give you your instructions when you are ready, and will make all arrangements."

The Englishman was a friendly person, and showed himself ready to gossip, but the man whom he called John More seemed curiously uninterested. The news about the bar to his D.S.O. left him cold. The truth was that he was suffering from a heavy drop in mental vitality. He had been like a squirrel going steadily

51

round a cage, and he found it hard to realise the world outside
the bars, or to think of any other form of motion but the
treadmill. The fact that so far he had succeeded gave him no
satisfaction. Lassom divined his mood and took the best way of
doctoring it. Having got the information he wanted, he strove
to draw the convalescent out of the abyss of the immediate past
and to wash from his memory the Raus farm and all it stood
for. There were bigger duties before him, he said, and he tried
to divert his thoughts, so to speak, from minor tactics to major
strategy, thereby giving his mind new subjects to play with. But
above all he looked after his body, and in the beginning of June
carried him off to a village on the Texel coast.

There, in a little painted wooden inn above the salty dunes,
the invalid became whole again in mind and body. But it was
not the wholesome food and the tonic sea winds that worked
the cure, but the fact that he had recovered Eilean Bàn. Something in the tang of the air, the scents, and the crying of curlews
along the shore did the trick, and Adam, who had long been
excluded from the happy isle, found that once more his dreams
and his waking visions carried him swiftly to its greenery. . . .
Nigel was there unchanged; it was two years since he had been
able to see the child clearly, but now he heard his voice, felt
the firm cool clutch of his hand, saw the grey eyes light up with
recognition. . . . The boy accompanied him in his rambles, a
docile little figure trotting at his heels. It was to the west side
of Sgurr Bàn that they went most often, where the magical
western ocean always sounded in their ears. But they never came
within actual sight of its waters, so he could not show Nigel the
far skerries, the black ribs of wave-scourged basalt where the
grey seals lived. There was always a ridge of hill or a thicket
which shut off the view. But Adam felt no impatience. Some
day he would cross the last rise and descend upon those sands
which were whiter than Barra or Iona.

One day he began to bestir himself and asked about his next
job.

"Ha!" cried the delighted Lassom. "For this I have been
waiting. You are cured now, and we talk business. In your next
job you enter Germany with the approbation of her Imperial

52

Government. You will be a Danish *commis-voyageur*, who is confided in by the authorities. You will give these authorities information, and most of it will be true—but not all. You will likewise gather information, which must all be true. You will not be alone as in Flanders, for I accompany you. But for the purpose it is necessary that we approach the Fatherland by what you call a voluptuous curve. Next week we cross the Skager Rack.

"You have been happy these last days," Lassom said that night after supper. "Your eyes bear witness. You have been seeing pretty pictures. Tell me."

Then for the first time Adam told another of Eilean Bàn—not much, only a sentence or two about his childhood's home, and its lonely peace. But Lassom understood.

"Ah," he said, "it is as I guessed. We have each our Jerusalem."

The two men had a difficult journey, mostly in coasting smacks, whose skippers demanded a great price before they would tempt the infested seas. In the end they reached Gothenburg, where a noted merchant of the place, who had a Scots name, but whose family had been Swedish for three centuries, assisted them to a change in their mode of life. Adam became a high-coloured businessman in early middle age, who wore horn spectacles like an American—he professed to have been much in America—dressed carefully, and had a neat blond moustache. He spoke Swedish like a Dane, said his host. He travelled in wood-pulp propositions, and was minutely instructed in the business by the merchant with the Scots name. Presently he knew enough to talk technicalities, and he met at dinner various local citizens in the same line of business, to whom he paraded his experiences in Britain, Canada, and the States. Lassom also was different. He had let his beard grow, and had trimmed it to a point, and he too wore glasses. He was an American citizen of German descent, and of an extreme German patriotism—by profession a lecturer in chemistry at a Middle Western university. His country's entry into the war on the Allied side had left him without a home, and driven him for comfort to

53

pure science. He had much to say of new processes in the making of chemical wood-pulp, which he hoped to perfect. Altogether a gentle academic figure, who woke up now and then to deliver an impassioned harangue on the wickedness of the world.

The two went to Stockholm at different times and by different routes. In that city of the isles Adam found himself in a society which was strongly sympathetic to Germany, and he met many unobtrusive folk in whom it was easy to recognise German agents. Presently with some of them he began to have highly confidential conversations, especially when Lassom arrived, for Lassom seemed to have a vast acquaintanceship. One day in an office on the top floor of a fine new apartment-house he had an interview with a thin, grey-bearded man, who spoke openly of his visiting Germany. "It can be arranged," he was told, "for one who is discreet and well-accredited, such as you, Herr Randers." He bent his brows on Adam, and his small bright eyes seemed to hold a world of menace and warning. "You are neutral, yes," he continued, "but neutrality is no protection for the bungler—or the traitor." He gave him certain provisional instructions with the same heavily charged voice and the same lowering brows.

Lassom, when he was told of the interview, laughed. "That is according to plan," he said. "That is he whom we call the Cossack. Formidable, is he not? He has also another name and a number, for he is one of us. He is a Czech, and the Czechs, having no fatherland at present, are the greatest secret agents in this war."

Then they went to Copenhagen, a precarious journey, and in Copenhagen Adam spent two weeks of crowded busyness. His Danish was fluent, but, said his friends, the speech of a man who had been much about the world and had picked up uncouth idioms. But oftenest he found himself talking German, for that tongue was favoured by the men—and women—whom he met by appointment at odd hours in back rooms in hotels and suburban tea-houses and private flats. Lassom did not appear at these conferences, but he was always at hand to advise. "It is necessary that you have open communications behind you," he

54

said, "for you are a channel between an enclosed Germany and the world—one of a thousand channels. You must have a conduit both for your exports and your imports."

Adam met, too, many people in Copenhagen who made no secret of their sympathy with the Allies, and with such he had to be on his best behaviour. The florid bagman had no bias one way or another; the war was not his war, and would to Heaven it was over, that honest men might get to work again! "These folk do not like you," Lassom told him, "but it is necessary that the others should know that you have access to their company. . . . Now, my friend, to work. There is much to talk over between us, for the day after tomorrow you cross the frontier."

Adam left Copenhagen alone. But, when five days later he sat in the lounge of a Cologne hotel, he saw Lassom at the other side of the room behind a newspaper.

Flanders had been lonely enough, but this new life was a howling desert for Adam, because he could not even keep company with himself. For every waking hour he was on the stretch, since he lived in the midst of a crowd and had to maintain a tight clutch on his wits. No more days and nights of wandering when he could forget for a little the anxieties of his task. His existence was passed in a glare like that of an arc-lamp.

Lassom he saw regularly, but only for hurried moments, for Lassom was constantly on the road. He recrossed the Dutch and Danish frontiers frequently; sometimes the Swiss too, for he was busy in mysterious negotiations with neutrals on the supply of vital chemicals. Adam himself had a double role. He was supposed to be engaged in various branches of neutral trade, and carried samples which, with Lassom's assistance, were periodically renewed, But his main task in the eyes of the authorities was to be the means of bringing them news through neighbouring countries of the Allied plans. This meant that he, too, occasionally passed the borders, and was fed with titbits of confidential information by several people in Zurich and Copenhagen. These titbits were mostly of small importance, but they were invariably true, and their accuracy was his prime credential. But now and then came pieces of weightier news, which he made a point of offering diffidently, as if not perfectly sure of their source. Yet, on the credit of the many accurate details he had furnished, these other things were as a rule believed—and acted upon—and their falsity did not shake his credit. For example, there was the report of a British attack due at Lens in February '18, which led to a wasteful and futile German concentration.

That was one side. The other was not known to the stiff soldiers who received him for regular conferences and treated him so condescendingly. All the time he was busy collecting knowledge for export—knowledge of the condition of the people and the state of the popular mind, and word of military operations, which great folk sometimes discussed in highly technical language in his presence, believing them beyond his comprehension. It was Adam's news that largely filled those desperately secret reports on Germany's internal condition which circulated among the inner Cabinets of the Allies. Now and then he sent them fateful stuff—the story, for instance, of the exact sector and day of the great German assault of March '18, which the British staff alone believed. Lassom was the principal agency for getting this information out of Germany, but sometimes impersonal means had to be found—sealed Kodak films, the inner packets of chewing-gum, whatever, in the hands of innocent-looking returning nationals, might be trusted to escape the eye of the frontier guards.

Adam had still another task. There was much ingenious Allied propaganda already circulating in the country, based for the most part on Switzerland. It was not anti-German but anti-war, and its distributors were largely members of the Socialist Left Wing. He had to keep an eye on this, and now and then to direct it. It was a delicate business, for it would have been ruin to one of his antecedents to be seen speaking to the intellectuals of the pavement. Yet this was the only duty from which he extracted any comfort, for each encounter involved a direct personal risk which steadied his nerves.

For the rest he hated his work bitterly—far more bitterly than at any moment of his years in Flanders. There was no groove to get into where one could move automatically, since every day, almost every hour, demanded a new concentration of his powers. It was work which he loathed, dirty work, all the dirtier for being done under conditions of comparative bodily comfort. He had nothing to complain of; he lived as well and slept as soft as other people; he had even a certain amount of consideration paid to him; the risk, so long as he kept his head, was not great, and he had a task which kept his mind working at high tension. There were immense ultimate dangers, no doubt, but they did not come within his immediate vision. What irked him was the necessity of thinking another's thoughts and living another's life every minute of his waking hours. He felt the man who had been Adam Melfort slipping away from him, and his place being taken by a hard, glossy, fraudulent being whom he detested.

Now and then he had narrow escapes which helped his self-respect. Once he was all but caught in the kitchen of a man who had a cobbler's shop in Freiburg, and who had for some time been closely sought in Westphalia. Adam got out of a back window, and had two days of circuitous tramping in snowy forests before he was certain that he had shaken off pursuit. Twice, when his secret information had proved false, he looked into the barrel of a pistol in the hand of a furious *Erster Generalstabsoffizier*. More than once he was rigorously examined and every detail of his *dossier* tested. But he had grown an adept at this business, and each syllable of his bourgeois bewilderment rang true.

Once, when his soul was sick within him, he laid it bare to Lassom.

"I have learned nothing," he told him, "except to be an actor of character parts, and to keep the shutter down on my thoughts."

"Not so," said the other. "You have sharpened your mind to a razor edge, and made steel hawsers of your nerves. You have acquired the patience of God. You have taught yourself to look at life uncoloured by the personal equation. What more would you have?"

"Tell me, am I honestly and truly serving my country?"

"You served her nobly in Flanders—that you know as well as I."

"But here?"

57

Lassom looked grave. "Here you are worth to her—how shall I put it?—more than a division of good troops. More, I think, than an army corps."

There came an hour in May '18 when Lassom arrived by night and sat on his bed.

"There are commands for you to leave Germany," he said. "You have finished your task. This people is breaking, for the last gambler's throw has failed, and your work now lies elsewhere."

"Am I suspected?"

"Not yet. But suspicion is coming to birth, and in a week, my friend, it might be hard for you to cross the frontier."

"And you?"

"I stay. I have still work to do."

"You will be in danger?"

"Maybe. That is no new thing."

"Then I will not leave you."

"You must. You add to my danger, if danger there is. I am a man of many shifts, remember. Also it is your duty to obey orders." He passed to Adam a slip of paper with a few words on it, which Adam read carefully and then burned.

"*Au revoir*," said Lassom gaily. "We will meet some day outside Jerusalem."

On the fourth morning after that visit Adam was speaking English to two men in a small hotel in a side street of Geneva. A few hours earlier, in the courtyard of a military prison in a certain Rhineland city, a small man with a pointed beard and a nervous mouth had confronted a firing squad. On that occasion he did not look down, as had been his habit, but faced the rifles with steady, smiling eyes.

IV

On the quay at Marseilles, as Adam was embarking in a converted liner, he met Lyson, the brother officer whom we have seen waiting in the Pall Mall club for the verdict. They said much to each other before they had to separate.

58

Lyson, who was on his way to Palestine, was now an acting lieutenant-colonel on the staff. He looked curiously at Adam's Special List badge, second-lieutenant's star, and undecorated breast.

"I suppose your rig is part of the game," he said, "but it is a little behind the times. What has become of your order ribbons?"

Adam smiled. "They're not much use in this show. I have been on enemy soil till a week ago, and I fancy I am going back to it."

"Still, you're among friends for the present, I should have thought too that you'd take your proper rank on your travels." When Adam looked puzzled, he exclaimed. "Didn't you know? It was in the *Gazette* months ago. You have been reinstated in the regiment without any loss of seniority. Also they gave you a brevet."

Adam was surprised that the news excited him so little. The regiment and all it stood for seemed a thing very small and far-away. The name on his passport was John More, and he did not trouble to have it altered. But he held his head a little higher among the crowd of officers, mostly very young, who for the next fortnight voyaged in his company over dangerous seas.

At Salonika after various interviews he was handed over to a Greek doctor, whose profession seemed to embrace many queer duties. In his house he stayed for three days, and during that time he exchanged his khaki uniform for reach-me-down flannels. Also various things were done to his appearance. His face had become very lean, but his skin was puffy and white from a sedentary life, so now it was stained to an even brown. During those days he talked nothing but Turkish, and his host had something to say about his pronunciation. Then one evening, with a brand-new kit-bag, he embarked in a seaplane and headed eastward. Two days later he was in occupation of a back room in the house of a man called Kuriotes, a Greek fruit-merchant in the town of Kassaba, where the railway line from Smyrna climbs to the Anatolian plateau.

Here he suffered a complete metamorphosis and acquired a new set of papers. It appeared that he was a Hanoverian by

59

birth, who had for ten years been in business in Stambul—there were all kinds of details about his past life set down very fully in close German typescript. His identity card was signed by the German Ambassador, and stamped by the Turkish Ministry of the Interior. It seemed that he had been commissioned, and had served on the Balkan front as an interpreter, and was now to act in the same capacity with a Turkish division.

To the back room came a certain Circassian colonel, Aziz by name, who commanded a battalion in the same division, and from him Adam learned many things. One was that the best German troops had been withdrawn from the Palestine front to stop the gaps in Europe, and that many of the guns were following. The latter were being replaced by an odd assortment, including Skoda mountain howitzers which had once been destined for the Hedjaz. The word of Germany was now all in all, and Enver was sulking. But the great Liman was not loved, and the Turks were very weary of the business. "They will send us south," said the colonel, "but if Allah wills, the war may be over before we reach Aleppo." He winked, for he had been much in Egypt and had picked up foreign manners.

Adam joined his division at Afium Karahissar on the great Bagdad railway, and found his task as interpreter a delicate one. The Austrian officers of the Skoda batteries were sullen and puzzled, and perpetually quarrelling with the divisional staff. . . . But bit by bit he discovered other duties. His business now was not that of a spy but of a fomenter of mischief, a begetter of delays—for great things were preparing in the south, where Liman was holding a long line in face of an enemy who showed an ominous quiescence. Adam had been instructed in his role, and he found many helpers. Aziz, for one, who during the endless delays of the journey was very busy and often absent from camp. Everywhere in the army there seemed to be disaffection, and the countryside was plagued with brigandage and full of deserters and broken men. Purposeless brigandage it seemed to be, for there was a perpetual destruction of bridges and culverts and telegraphs, which can have offered no booty to the destroyers. Adam, as the only German officer in the division, was the recipient of the complaints and curses of many furious Teutonic colleagues. More than once he was placed under arrest, and was only released by the intercession of his corps commander. He was set down by his German superiors as lazy and incompetent, one whose natural loutishness had been swollen by the idleness of his years in Stambul. Yet he was quietly busy, and in his own purposes he was rather efficient.

Orders from headquarters, frequently countermanded and habitually misinterpreted, kept the division north of the Bulgar Dagh till early August, and it did not reach Aleppo till the beginning of September. During the summer heats Adam had been a good deal away from headquarters by permission of Colonel Aziz, and had been in many strange places and among many queer folk in his task of tangling up the connections which linked the embarrassed Liman to his base. . . . These were laborious and difficult days, but he found them curiously exhilarating. He felt himself within the electric zone of war, an actor in a drama which was moving to some stupendous climax. The toil of it rejuvenated a body which had been too long cramped and under-exercised. Moreover, he was among novel scenes, and his interest in the unfamiliar revived in him. Almost he became young again.

By way of motor-car, motor-bicycle or weedy horse, and sometimes on his own feet, he prowled about a land which had been for many thousands of years the cockpit of war. It was all pared and gnawed to the bone. He found everywhere irrigated fields where the water-furrows were dry, and orchards which had been felled for firewood. He entered towns where the lattices hung broken, and the mud walls crumbled, and only a lean child or a beggar showed in the narrow streets. He had days of blistering heat, when the sky was copper above and the earth iron below, and when hot winds stirred the baked mud into dust-devils. He had days, too, when bitter blasts blew from the north-east, or when the rainstorms swept in battalions till he could almost cheat himself into the belief that he was on a Scots moor and that the tamarisk scrub was heather. The open air and the weather's moods put new vigour into his body, and never for one moment was he sick or sorry. There was disease every-where among the troops, but, while his colleagues went down like ninepins with fever and dysentery and heatstroke, Adam in his shabby field-grey went steadily about his business. "You are a mountaineer like my own folk," said the admiring Aziz. "You are as hard as the hillside quartz."

As they moved south he began to mix with new types—shaggy Druses, sleek Damascenes, Arabs from the Syrian desert as thin and fine as sword-blades. His imagination caught fire, and he had visions of the vast hidden life astir behind the front where Liman played his mechanical game of war. That life was breaking loose from the game, and it was his task to expedite the breaking. For a blow was in preparation, and its force must be aided by defection in the rear, so that when it fell it would strike not a solid but a hollow shell.

The blow came, as all the world knows, at dawn on the 19th of September, by which time Adam's division had not reached the Asian corps in Djevad's Eighth Army to which it had been attached as reserve. It was still a mile or two short of Nablus. Presently it was caught up in the backwash of the great defeat, and turned its face northward. Down upon it came the fog of war, nay the deeper fog of a pell-mell retreat. . . . These were busy days for Adam—and for Aziz and for many obscurer folk. There was a German staff-officer who used to appear mysteriously at crossroads and give authoritative orders to fleeing columns. He must have been raw to his job, for most of his orders contrived to shepherd those who obeyed them into the arms of Allenby's terrible horsemen.

Adam had one moment of indecision. Liman was routed, so his task must be over. Was not the next step for him to be picked up by the pursuit and restored to his own people? But a thought deterred him. He did not know what might be happening in the north. There might be a stand beyond the Lebanon at Homs or Aleppo, or in Anatolia itself, and work for him to do. So he clung to his fleeing division, and struggled with it past Rayat to the broad-gauge line, and across the Orontes till the minarets of Aleppo rose above its orchards—on past the junction with the Bagdad railway, and up the long slopes of the hills which circle Alexandretta. The division was now only a rabble of scared and starving men, and soon he was convinced that Turkey's last shot was fired, and that for her broken army not even the shores of the Marmora would be a sanctuary. His work was done.

He realised something more—that it was high time for him to go. Aziz had left him, and there were ugly faces turned on him among the troops. He was a reminder of the race that had led the children of Islam into the mire. One night he had to run for it to escape a rifle bullet at the hands of a crazed sergeant. He had for some days dropped his uniform, retaining only his field-boots, and wore a ragged Turkish tunic and great-coat. He had made ready, too, a slender packet of food, and he had a map, a compass, and twenty rounds for his revolver. Thus equipped, he hid for one night in the scrub of a nullah, and next morning started, like Xenophon's Ten Thousand, on his march to the sea.

For three weeks he was a hunted man, and had his fill of the hardships which those British soldiers suffered who escaped from a Turkish prison-camp. To be sure, there was no pursuit, but there was a more menacing thing, a land where all order and discipline had gone, and a stranger was like a sheep among wolf-packs. The countryside was starving, with the people fighting like wild beasts for food. Also it was strewn with broken men on the same desperate errand as himself, striking out frantically for safety like a weak swimmer in a heavy sea. He moved only by night, and in these weeks he learned the shifts of primeval man whose mind is narrowed to a single purpose—the purpose of the meanest sentient thing. He had schooled his body to need the minimum of food, but even that little was in constant jeopardy. He had twice to fight for his life with famished dogs, and used up four of his pistol cartridges. Once he stumbled on a group of Kurdish soldiers who had set up as bandits, and only the fortunate approach of a moonless night enabled him to escape. Every day he felt his strength growing less, so he husbanded it like a miser. Light-headedness was what he feared: too often the scrub and the hills would dance about him, and he would lie face down, his fingers pressed on his throbbing eyeballs, till he won touch with earth again.

63

It was a nightmare time, but he was not unhappy, for a veil seemed to be lifting from his horizon. He had recaptured his own country. The most alien sights and scents were translated into the idiom of home. As he lay in the hot tamarisk at midday he smelled thyme and bracken, and under a sky of glittering stars he could make believe that he was belated on some familiar moorland. Especially in rain could he retrieve these links, for the odour of wet earth seemed to recreate for him a whole world of ancient comfortable things. His body might be stretched to its ultimate endurance, but his mind was at peace. . . .

One afternoon he came over a scarp of hill and looked down at last on the sea. There was a little bay below him and a few fishers' huts; off shore lay a British destroyer, from which a watering-party had just landed. He looked at this assurance of safety with no quickening of the pulse, for he was too weary for such emotion. Besides, he had somehow expected it.

He was taken on board and met by a brisk young lieutenant. There had been a conversation between the lieutenant and a petty officer. "Escaped prisoner, I suppose. Good God, what a scarecrow! I suppose we must take charge of the poor devil. Bring him along at once."

A few words from Adam sent the lieutenant's hand to his cap.

"Adam Melfort! Of course I know all about you, sir! What almighty luck that we put in to this God-forgotten hole! You want a long drink, and then a bath, and a square meal, and then you ought to sleep for a week. I can lend you some kit. . . . Hold on, sir. Perhaps you haven't heard the news. It came through to us last night. The jolly old war is over. Yesterday morning Germany got down from her perch."

But Adam scarcely listened, for he was in a happy dream. The lapping of green water and the tang of salt had carried him over great tracts of space and time. He had found Eilean Bàn.

CHAPTER III

I

IN the smoking-room of the club where this story opened Christopher Stannix sat on a warm June evening. It was the day of the Peace celebrations in London, when the returning generals had passed through the streets, and from Pall Mall came the shuffling sound of homing spectators. The war had grizzled Stannix's thick dark hair above the temples, and had slightly rounded his shoulders, for he had spent four years at office work. Also it had hollowed his cheeks, and made faint pencillings at the corners of his eyes. His face was that of a man a decade older than his age. The lawyers' primness of mouth had gone, for he had given up the Bar, and, having been in the House of Commons since 1913, had now turned definitely to politics. He was one of the younger men who were beginning to make their mark in the dull and docile Coalition Parliament.

Lyson, his companion, was in uniform, for he had been engaged in the day's procession. He was skimming an evening paper while the other ordered tea, and dispensing fragments of news.

"Hallo!" he said, "I see Falconet is lost. No word of him for four months, and he is more than a month overdue at his base. You remember him, Kit? The long American who had a hospital at Arville? Began the war as a French airman, till he smashed himself up. He was a bit of a nuisance to us at G.H.Q."

"He was a bit of a nuisance to us at the War Office," said Stannix. "I never saw a man with his temper so handy. I daresay that was due to his left arm giving him neuritis. Also he was some kind of multi-millionaire and used to getting his own way. Well I remember his lean twitching face and his eye like a moulting eagle's. Where do you say he has got to now?"

"That's the puzzle. He has gone over the edge somewhere in Northern Greenland. He always made a hobby of exploring unholy corners of the earth and financed several expeditions, and he had some theory about Greenland, so, as soon as he was certain that the Allies were winning, he bolted off to have a look at it. Funny business, if you come to think of it, changing the racket of the front for the peace of an Arctic desert! And now he has gone and lost himself, and this paper says they're talking of a relief party."

"We're in for a lot of that sort of thing," said Stannix. "There's going to be all kinds of queer by-products of the war. You know how after a heavy day you are sometimes too tired to sleep. Well, that is the position of a good many today—too tired to rest—must have some other kind of excitement—running round like sick dogs till the real crash comes. The big problem for the world is not economic but psychological—how to get men's minds on an even keel again."

"I daresay that is true," said the other. "But the odd thing is that it is not the people who had the roughest time that are the most unsettled. There was a little chap at home who was the local postman. He enlisted at the start in a Fusilier battalion and had four of the most hellish years that ever fell to the lot of man—Gallipoli and France—blown-up, buried, dysentery, trench-fever, and most varieties of wounds. Today he is back at his old job, toddling round the villages, and you would never guess from his looks or his talk that he had been out of Dorset. . . . Then take Adam Melfort. I suppose he had about as nerve-racking a show as anybody, but you couldn't tell it on him. I ran across him the other day, and, except that he was fined down to whalebone and catgut, he was just the same quiet, placid, considering old bird."

Stannix smiled. "Funny that you should mention Adam, for he was the case I had chiefly in mind. With him it's not so simple an affair as your postman. You see, he was in the war, but not *of* it. He stood a little way apart and got a bird's-eye view. For him it was only a spell of training for something much bigger, and now he is looking at the world like a philosopher and wondering what his real job is to be."

Lyson's face kindled into interest. "Tell me about Adam. You see a lot of him, I know, and I don't often manage to run him to ground. I'd give a good deal to get back to the old terms with him."

Stannix shook his head. "You never will. I can't myself. Adam has made his choice. When he crashed, he decided that God meant him to drop out of the firing-line, and had work for him somewhere in the rear. He has gone deliberately underground, and means to stay there. That was why he was by miles the best secret-service man we had—he took to the job like a crusade, something to which he was specially called by the Almighty. He is the complete philosophic fatalist, waiting for destiny to show him his next move. He's a lonely man, if you like, but he doesn't mind that, for he knows that it is his strength. Every journalist is talking about the 'brotherhood of the trenches'—a silly, rhetorical phrase, but there's something in it—people who went through the same beastliness together did acquire a sort of common feeling. Well, Adam had no chance of that; he was as much outside it as if he had been a conchie. He has missed all the comfort one gets from a sense of companionship, but he has missed, too, the confusion of the mass-mind. He has no delusions and no sentimentalities. He is looking at our new world with clear dispassionate eyes, like a visitor from another planet. But, all the same, when he finds his predestined job it will be like the releasing of a steel spring."

"By Jove, that sounds like trouble for somebody. What is it to be? Russia?"

"It might be. He talks the language, and might put a spoke in the Bolshie wheels. But he hasn't made up his mind—at least he hadn't last week. He has been spending recent months having a general look round."

"Go on. Tell me," said Lyson. "I'm deeply interested."

Stannix laughed. "It was a funny business, and I saw something of it, for I had to chaperon him in most of his investigations. You see, he had lost touch a little with his kind, and he realised that he must find it again if he was to be of any use. . . . The first thing was to meet the people who had been fighting, of whom he knew nothing at all. He saw a fairly representative lot,

67

from the hearty fellows who had found it rather a lark and were half sorry it was over, to the damaged sensitives who had a grievance against humanity. I fancy he did not get much out of any of them, and decided that it would be many a day before we could be certain what effect the war had had on our people. . . . Then he made a tour of the serious folk—the internationalists and the social reformers. He hung about the universities to have a look at the young entry, and went into W.E.A. circles, and put in some time with a Glasgow riveter. Adam was never very communicative, so I don't know what conclusion he came to, but he did not seem to be depressed by his experiences. . . . Oh, and he sat out a good many debates in the House of Commons. He found them a dusty business, and used to come down from the gallery with puzzled eyes. I wanted to get some of the politicians to meet him, but he wouldn't have it—didn't want to hear other people's conclusions—wanted to make his own."

"Can't we get him back into the Service?" Lyson asked. "I know he has sent in his papers, but that could be arranged. There are twenty jobs on hand for which he would be the spot man."

"Not a chance of it. I put that to him, for it seemed to me common sense. I told him that he was a brilliant soldier and should stick to the profession for which he had been trained. No earthly use. You know that look of intelligent obstinacy which is more unshakable than the Pyramids. 'You forget,' he said, 'that in the past four years I've had a training for other things.' "

"A pretty desperate training," Lyson commented.

"Yes," said Stannix, "that is the right word. Remember that Adam is a desperate man. There is nothing in Heaven or earth left for him to fear."

One night later in the summer Stannix dined with Adam Melfort at a restaurant. Thereafter they made a curious progress. First they went to a meeting of a group of serious people who were perturbed about the state of the world, and listened to a paper on the "Economics of Victory". It was held in the drawing-room of a private house and the paper was read by a brilliant young Oxford don who had made a high reputation for his work abroad on behalf of the British Treasury. . . . They did not wait for the discussion, but moved on to a newly formed club, patronised mainly by ex-cavalry officers, which boasted a super-excellent American bar. There, as they drank cocktails, they listened to the gossip of youth. Stannix knew many of the members, but he did not introduce Adam. The talk was chiefly of money, for most of the young men seemed to have gone into business and precociously acquired the City jargon. They were determined to have a good time, and had somehow or other to find the cash for it.

Then they went to a ball, given by a celebrated hostess who was making a resolute effort to restore the pre-war gaiety. It was gay enough; dementedly gay, it seemed to Adam, as he recalled the balls where he had once danced with Camilla. The female clothes were odd, the dances were extravagant things, the music was barbarous, and the men and women seemed to be there not for amusement but for an anodyne. Adam and Stannix stood in a corner and looked on.

"Isn't that Meeson?" the former asked, mentioning the name of a Cabinet Minister.

"Yes," said Stannix. "He comes to this sort of thing, for he thinks it smart, and smartness was beyond him in his old days in the suburbs. There's Wendell—that man dancing with the Jewess. He comes because he wants to be thought young—age, you know, is the chief crime today. Most of the boys want to make up for the war, and the girls have four dull years to forget. It's all perfectly natural, I suppose, but rather foolish. Half the world is destroyed, so we caper among the ruins. You don't seem as shocked as I expected."

"I'm not in the least shocked," was the answer. "I'm only wondering how long it will last. We must pull up our socks pretty soon, or the rest of the world will go."

Late that night the two sat in Stannix's rooms.

"Well, you've had your look-round," the host said. "I take it that tonight was the last lap. I hope I took you to the right places. What do you make of it all?"

69

"Nothing very clear." Adam had acquired a trick of speaking very slowly and softly, as if words were precious and had to be respectfully treated—a common thing with men who for a long season have had to forgo their own language. "There must be a time of confusion—another year at least, I should say. Everybody is self-conscious and egotistical. Creevey tonight was not trying to solve an economic problem, but to show how clever he was. The lads at the Pegasus have had too much in the way of duty and want to make pets of themselves. The dancing people were not natural—they were all trying to make-believe and play a part. That is going on for a little while till the ground begins to quake under them. I'm not wanted yet, I think.

"And I'm not ready myself," he went on. "I've been coming to realise that for some time, and now I'm sure. First of all, I'm not fit enough. . . . Oh yes, I'm fitter than you, far fitter than most people, but I'm not in the hard training I should be in. Today I couldn't make my body do what it ought to do. I want some good, tough, physical toil."

"Anything else?" Stannix asked. He smiled as he looked at Adam's lean face, his frame without an ounce of needless flesh, and the alert poise of his head.

"Yes, I want a spell of quiet. You see, I have been living for four years in a circus. It hasn't damaged my nerves in the ordinary sense—they're under pretty good control—but it has made my mind airless and stuffy. I want to get some sort of poise again, and that means being alone. What I need is space and silence—frozen silence."

"How are you going to find it?"

"I'm on the road to it. I've been busy for weeks making arrangements with the Danish Government and with his American relatives. The day after tomorrow I sail for Iceland. I'm going to find Falconet."

II

On the last day of September Adam sat on a hummock of snow looking east to where, far below Danmarks Fjord, lay a blue gash

70

in the white ice-cap. The cirrus clouds of the afternoon before had been a true augury, and all night a gale had howled round the little tent. But the wind had blown itself out before morning, and now the air was clear and quiet. It was the first peaceful hour he had had for days when he could review his position.

At Shannon Island he had found the schooner which Falconet had instructed to meet him in June. A base had been erected there like a lumber-camp, huts and store-rooms and dog-houses, for money had not been spared, but there was no sign of its master. Falconet had made elaborate plans. A sealing sloop had crawled up the coast as soon as spring opened the shore waters, and its crew had pushed on when navigation became impossible, and had laid down depots and caches of food at points up the coast as far north as Independence Fjord. Such spots had been carefully marked on the latest map, which was Rasmussen's. Falconet himself had set off with two sledges and dog teams in March to cross the inland ice. His objective was a bay on the extreme north shore of Greenland, of which Rasmussen had heard rumours through the Arctic Highlanders of Thule. They called it Gundbjorns Fjord—a curious name, thought Adam, who remembered that to the old Norsemen Gundbjorns Reef had been the legendary edge of the world. Falconet had his own theories about Greenland travel. He had taken but the one companion, his stores were of a scientific compactness, his dogs were the best that money could buy, and he held that by travelling light he could reach his goal in early summer, replenish his supplies from bear and musk-ox (he was a famous shot), and return by the coast depots in time to rejoin his ship at the end of July.

But something had miscarried. Ship's parties had gone up the coast almost as far as Kronprinz Christians Land, and had found no sign of him. He could not be returning by the inland ice, for his food supplies would not permit of that. His American friends had been anxious, and Washington and Copenhagen had laid their heads together, so Adam had found his proposal welcomed. Falconet might be ill, or he might have had an accident; if he did not come south before the winter he would perish; clearly someone must go and look for him. Time was of

71

the essence of the business, so the route must be the inland ice, the road Falconet had himself travelled, for the coast road would mean a detour round two sides of a triangle.

So Adam started from Shannon Island with three sledges and two companions—one a Danish naval officer called Nelles who had been with Koch, and the other a young American, Myburg, who had explored the Beaufort Sea before the war. Their plan was to find Falconet somewhere in the north of Peary Land and bring him down the coast by the chain of depots, before the sun disappeared. If they were delayed they would winter on Shannon Island and go home in the spring. Nine years before Ejnar Mikkelsen had covered most of the ground in a couple of months, and Nelles, who was the local expert, believed that, if Falconet was alive, he could be found and brought back before the close of September. It was arranged that in that month relays of dog-teams should be waiting at points on the coast as far north as Danmarks Fjord.

At first fortune had been with Adam and his party. They climbed on to the ice-cap a little south of Cape Bismarck, and, keeping the nunataks of Dronning Louises Land on their left, travelled for five days on tolerable ice in good weather, with few bergs to surmount and no crevasses to delay them. Then suddenly their luck turned. A wind of 120 miles an hour blew from the east, and the plateau became the playground of gales. They came on ice-fields like mammoth ploughlands, where they scarcely made three miles in the day, and mountainous seracs which would have puzzled an Alpine climber. They found valleys with lakes and rivers of blue ice out of which they had to climb painfully. There was trouble, too, with the dogs. Five of them one night broke into the stores and ate one-half of the total dog-feed. Several died of gashes from the sharp ice, and two more from eating the livers of their dead companions. For nearly a week the party was stormbound, lying in their tents in the lee of an ice-scarp, while blizzard after blizzard threatened to blow the whole outfit to Baffin's Bay.

The culminating disaster came in the fourth week out, when one of the sledges, driven by the young American Myburg, broke through the crust and disappeared in a bottomless abyss.

Adam and Nelles made vain efforts at rescue, and Adam had himself lowered on a cable made up of haul-ropes into the cruel blue depths. There was no sign of life; hundreds of feet down in the bowels of the ice-cap, man and dogs had met their death. The tragedy was followed by a storm which delayed the survivors for three days, and gave Nelles too good a chance to brood. He was a dreamy, morose man, and an indifferent companion, and from that day onward Adam found his moods hard to deal with. Death and the madness which is worse than death had cast their shadow over him.

Adam himself had found the weeks pass quickly. He had a straightforward task—to shape a course which he more or less understood, and to complete that course in the shortest possible time. It was only a question of common sense, resolution, and physical fitness; the difficulties were known, and had been surmounted by many others since the days of Henry Hudson; if each of them put out his powers to the fullest stretch they would reach Gundbjorns Fjord, barring accidents, and whether or not they found Falconet was in the lap of the gods. Such was his mood at the start, and even the tragic fate of Myburg did not greatly change it. Death was an irrelevant factor in any enterprise, and since one could not ensure against it one must leave it out of reckoning. His fatalism was more than a creed now, and had become an instinct of which he was conscious in every waking hour. Always, above and around him, was the sense of guidance.

He had got the solitude he desired, and the long white distances streaked with blue shadows, the unfeatured universe in which nothing moved but winds and clouds, soothed and comforted him. . . . But it was a kind of comfort which he had not expected. He had wanted to get away from men and their littleness, but he found that the littleness was in nature. All his life he had dreamed of exploring the last undiscovered geographical secrets, and had thought of the world as a field of mystery of which only the edge had been lit up. Now he realised that the globe had suddenly gone small, and that man had put his impress upon the extremist wilds. The forgotten khanates of central Asia were full of communist squabbles. The holy cities of Arabia had been bases and objectives in the war. Epidemics, germinated in the squalor of Europe, had destroyed whole tribes of savages in Africa. He remembered conversations he had heard that summer in England, when untrodden equatorial forests had been thought of only as reservoirs of wood alcohol, and plans were preparing for making a road by air to every corner of the inaccessible. The world had shrunk, but humanity was extended—that was the moral that he drew from his reflections. Many things had gone, but the spirit of man had enlarged its borders. The problem of the future was the proper ordering of that spirit.

As they moved north from the head of Danmarks Fjord over the snow-cap of Erichsens Land, there was one human spirit that troubled him. Every day Nelles became more difficult. He was a big fellow, and with his heavy clothes and matted hair and beard and red-rimmed eyes he looked like a bear wakened out of its winter sleep. He had always been silent and uncompanionable, though a magnificent worker, but since Myburg's death he had taken to talking—wild incoherent talk in a voice that rose often into a scream.

He wanted to turn back. They had lost time and would for certain be caught by winter. Falconet was dead—must be dead long ago—and what advantage was there in finding a corpse? His passion made him eloquent, and he would draw terrible pictures of an ice-cave at Gundbjorns Fjord, and two dead men with staring eyes awaiting them. "I will not go!" he cried. "I will not meet the dead. For the love of God let us turn now, or we shall be wrapped in the same winding-sheet."

Adam reasoned with him patiently, but the madness grew with every hour. He became slovenly, and one night left the dogs unfed, with the consequence that next day two were sick. He would eat little himself, and his blackening lips showed signs of scurvy. Adam decided that this state of affairs could not go on, and that it would be better to send him home with one sledge. He had no doubt where his own duty lay. Even if Falconet was dead he must reach him and make certain of his fate. He might be alive and crippled or ill; in that case the only hope was to winter with him and nurse him. If provisions ran short he would get him down to the nearest depot on Independence Fjord, the farthest north of those which the schooner parties had established. Adam, with his blistered flaking skin and bleared eyes, would not have seemed to an unskilled observer a man in the best physical condition, but he knew that his body had never been harder, and he believed that he had strength enough and to spare for his purpose.

He gave Nelles one final trial. Down perilous icy shelves they descended to the shore of Independence Fjord, and, travelling half a day to the east, found without trouble the beacon which marked the ultimate food depot. The cache was a large one and in good order, and they strengthened with boulders its defences against inquisitive bears. A fresh snowfall had covered all but the top of the dwarf Arctic willows and the heather, but there was at least a hint of vegetation, the first they had seen for many weeks. They went into camp, and since the place had a reputation for game they went hunting. A seal was killed which gave the dogs fresh food, and, though each of the men had a touch of snow-blindness which made stalking difficult, they managed to get a young musk-ox and a brace and a half of ptarmigan. That night they had a feast of fat things.

But the meal did not change Nelles's purpose, though it seemed to give him a better balance. The sight of something other than snow and ice and the taste of fresh meat had increased his determination to go back. He began by arguing reasonably. This, he said, was the last chance, and there was just time, if God willed, to reach the ship before the winter gales. They would go down the coast and get supplies from the chain of depots. He understood sledging on shore ice better than on the ice-cap, and he had no fear for the journey. Otherwise only death awaited them—death beside a dead man, if indeed they ever found Falconet's corpse. When his arguments did not prevail his voice grew wild and shrill, he gesticulated, implored, and wept. Adam came to a decision.

"I am going on," he said, "for I have a charge laid on me. You are different. If I find Falconet you will only be another mouth to feed, and if I fail you will be another victim. I order

75

you to go back. You have a map with the depots marked, and you already know something of the coast route. I put you on your honour to take no more food than you need from the caches, for Falconet and I must depend on them on our way south. If the ship has gone when you reach Shannon Island you can winter comfortably in the huts. If she is still there, you will tell Captain Tonning to come back as soon as the seas are open and to send his sloop to scout up the coast. Tell him I will have Falconet home by next summer."

That night Adam heard Nelles babbling in his sleep. Next morning he set off with four dogs and one of the sledges for Cap Rigsdagen, and did not once look back. He was whistling as far as his cracked lips allowed him.

Beyond Independence Fjord Adam entered a fantastic world. The shadow of the coming night was beginning to droop over it, but it had a queer sunset opalescence, so that often it was hard to believe that there was substance behind the dissolving shapes of cloud and rock and snow. For the first days there was little wind, the four dogs travelled well, and Adam had peace to consider his plans. He had enough food and petroleum to last him till the spring, but not enough for more than one. Falconet and his companion had taken ample stores with them for the time they expected to be absent, but not enough for a winter. There was no chance now of getting back to the ship before it was forced to escape from the grip of the ice, so, if he found Falconet and supplies were short, there would be nothing for it but to make for the nearest depot—Independence Fjord—and work their way from cache to cache down the coast. Even in winter such short journeys would be feasible. He must find Falconet, alive or dead, for he could not have missed him on the road. He had never met him, but he had heard much of his furious energy and resolution. That was not the sort of man to be easily beaten by difficulties. Adam was fairly certain of his course, and had taken observations as regularly as a deep-sea skipper. In four days—a week at the most—he should be across the low ice-cap of Peary Land and looking down on the ultimate Polar Sea.

But suddenly the weather worsened. A gale blew from the north while he was among a chain of nunataks glazed into black ice, where the going was hard. One evening he saw a great white wall moving towards him, which was the snow blown into a solid screen by the wind. He and his dogs were almost smothered; in the teeth of it movement was impossible, and it was late before the tent could be pitched and the stove got going. For the first time he really felt the Arctic cold, since that night the heat of his body seemed powerless to conquer the chill of his soaked clothes. As he peered through the blizzard he began to share Nelles's forebodings of what might lie beyond it.

The storm died down, and there fell a strange calm; the air was still and not too cold, but even at midday there was a sense of twilight. At last one afternoon he found himself looking down on a long sword-cut which cleft the ice-cap, and beyond it to a wilderness of opal and pearl, and he knew that he had reached his goal. But the gale had blown the sun out of the sky. The whole heavens were a pale gold, and pinnacles of the land ice were tipped and flushed with fire. Even as he gazed a grey shadow seemed to creep slowly from the horizon and one by one put out the fairy lights. Adam realised that he was watching the Polar night emerge from the Polar Sea, and that for a third of the year the world would be sunless.

He guided the dogs without difficulty down a cleft of the ice-cap to the edge of the fjord. There he saw what he expected. On a mound of snow a discoloured American flag hung limply from a post. There was something beside it which startled him— a little cross of wood, with an inscription burned on it—*M. P., July 27th, 1919*. He remembered that Falconet's companion had been called Magnus Paulsen.

His first thought was that he had arrived too late. Falconet was gone, after burying his dead comrade under his country's flag. . . . Then a little to the left, under the lee of a cliff, he saw something which was not a hummock of snow. A boulder, riven from the precipice by some winter storm, made a small cave over which a kind of roof had been stretched. Inside there was darkness, and Adam stumbled over something which he recognised as a food box. He struck a light, and saw a rough bed on which lay the figure of a man. He thought he was dead, till his breathing told him that he was asleep.

III

Adam found a lantern and lit up the interior of the cleft. It made a lopsided hut, but, except at the mouth, where blocks of snow had been piled to lessen the aperture, the floor was dry. The light woke the sleeper, who started up as if to reach for a weapon, and then dropped feebly back. Adam saw a face as thin and beady as a crow's, with pallid skin showing between a black, tangled mane of hair.

"Who the devil are you?" The words came out in slow gasps.

"I was sent to find you. Melfort's my name—an Englishman. You're Falconet, aren't you?"

"What is left of him," was the answer. "You can't move me. . . . I think my back is broken. . . . Paulsen is dead—his head was smashed to pulp by an accursed ice-fall. The dogs too—I had to shoot the last to put him out of pain. I'm for it all right. . . . But I'm glad to see you, whoever you are. . . . I'd like company when I peg out."

"You're not going to peg out. Let me have a look at you before I put things straight."

Slowly and painfully layers of filthy clothing were stripped off, till Falconet's body was revealed. His back and shoulders were a mass of bruises and unhealed scars, and his left arm was broken and unset. He was in the last stage of emaciation. Adam had enough medical knowledge to decide that there was no damage to the spine, but that lacerated muscles had induced a partial paralysis of one side. The man was worn to a shadow by pain, malnutrition, and poisoned blood.

Bit by bit Falconet's story came out. He and Paulsen had reached Gundbjorns Fjord a month later than they had planned, owing to storms on the ice-cap. They had made camp in the cleft, and, believing that they had still ample time to rejoin the ship by the coast route, had set out to explore the coast to the west. Their dogs had been reduced to six, but, since the coast depots would enable them to travel light, this loss did not trouble them. They had pushed forty miles or so along the shore and had discovered and surveyed a new fjord, living largely off the ptarmigan and duck which they shot. On their return, when they were within a mile of their camp, they passed under a great nose of ice, which had been loosened by a spell of warm weather. It fell on them, killing Paulsen, killing or maiming all the dogs, and leaving Falconet himself unconscious under a corner of the avalanche. He had come to his senses, extricated Paulsen's body, and somehow dragged it and himself back to camp.

All this had happened nine weeks earlier. Since then he had been in constant pain, and had had much ado to get himself the means of life, for every movement had become agony. He was almost too weak to cook meals, and had subsisted largely on chocolate and meat lozenges. But indeed food mattered little to him, for the torture of his body forced him to have recourse to opiates from the medicine box, and thirst vexed him more than hunger. He had made up his mind for death, and had been growing so light-headed that he was scarcely conscious of his surroundings. Adam's arrival had startled him into sanity, but presently he fancied that it was Paulsen he saw, and his mind wavered miserably between the living and the dead.

Adam boiled water on the stove and washed the foul body. He set the broken arm in splints, and dressed such of the wounds as had become sores. He forced him to drink a bowl of hot soup, found him a change of shirt, and did his best to make him a softer bed. Falconet was asleep before he had finished these ministrations. It was rough nursing, but the best he could give. As he watched the figure in its restless sleep, looking for all the world like some peasant victim of a Russian famine, he could not refrain from smiling, for he remembered that this was Jim Falconet, who had once captained a famous polo team on their visit to England, and was believed to be the third or fourth richest man in the world.

Then he set about making an inventory. There was enough dog-feed to last the winter, and Falconet's stores and his own ought to carry the two of them through. The risk lay in running

79

short of petroleum, which would have to be strictly rationed. Clearly the man could not be moved for weeks. Adam believed that he had suffered no serious mischief, and that with care his strong physique would right itself. . . . He tidied up the hut, which was in a hideous mess, and found quarters for his dogs in an alcove near the entrance. Then out of some broken packing-cases he made a fire, more for the comfort of his mind than of his body, and as he watched its tiny glow struggling with the velvet dark he had a moment of satisfaction. He had carried out the first part of his task.

Very soon Adam found that what had been his fancies on the ice-cap had become grim truth. For the wide Arctic world was narrowed for him to a few stuffy cubic feet in a cranny of rock, and his problem to a strife not with wild nature but with a human soul.

Falconet's body was the least part of the task. The problem was to avoid blood-poisoning, and Adam put all his wits to the job. His own case of medicines was well stocked, but Falconet's was in dire disorder; but out of the two he got enough drugs on which to base a simple regime. Diet was the trouble, for to a sick man the coarse satisfying Arctic food was ill-suited. Adam managed, before the last daylight disappeared, to shoot some ptarmigan on the fringes of the ice-cap, and to give the patient a few days of fresh chicken-broth. With careful dressing the sores began to mend, and the swollen and displaced muscles after much bandaging came slowly into order. The arm, too, set well, and presently Falconet was able to move more comfortably. But acute attacks of neuritis followed, and the flow of returning strength into the man's veins seemed to be as painful as the running back of the blood to a frozen limb.

Meantime the daylight ebbed, till at noon there was only a misty grey twilight. There was a spell of fine weather in November, when the stars blazed so bright that they seemed to be set not in two dimensions on a flat plane, but hung solidly in receding avenues of utter blackness. The brightest time was night, when there was a moon, and the cliffs and the fjord swam in frosty silver. With December came storms, which howled among the crags and blocked up the entrance to the hut with forty-foot drifts. The place became as cold as a hyperborean hell, cold and yet airless. There was no means of making fire, and there was little light, for the petroleum, if it was to last the winter, had to be jealously conserved. Already with the constant melting of snow and boiling of water for Falconet's dressings, it had run lower than Adam's plans allowed. He would have made an effort to get a further supply from the cache at Independence Fjord if he had dared to leave the sick man alone for a week.

By Christmas Falconet's body had mended, and he was able to walk to the door in a lull of the weather and breathe fresh air. But this return of his physical powers seemed to be accompanied by a disorientation of mind. In his lonely vigil, before Adam's arrival, he had brought himself to face death with calmness, but, having been plucked from the grave, it appeared that he could not recover his bearings. He was morose and peevish, and liable to uncontrollable rages. The spirit of a grown man had been exchanged for the temper of a suspicious child. He had lost the power of self-restraint, and there was no companionship to be got out of him. He babbled to himself, his voice acquired a high, querulous pitch, and he became the prey of childish nightmares. For no apparent cause he would lie shivering and moaning, and when Adam tried to soothe him he screamed like an animal. . . . On Christmas night a little extra feast was prepared, a fire was made of empty boxes, and two cigars were added to the rations. But the festival was a tragic failure, for the cigar made Falconet sick, and, when Adam tried to cheer him with talk about the world they had left, he cursed and wept and went sulking to his sleeping-bag. For the better part of a week his wits seemed to leave him altogether, and Adam had to watch his every movement lest he should cut his throat.

The two men in the hut came to loathe each other. Adam confessed it to himself with shame. His tending of the other's body in all its noisomeness had given him a horror of it. As the cold increased it was necessary for warmth that they should creep close together, and he shrank with a kind of nausea from such contacts. Falconet's growing witlessness added to the

81

repulsion, for the gaunt hairy creature seemed to have shed all that made humanity tolerable. Days and nights were alike dark, for they could afford little light. They rarely spoke to each other, and never conversed. They sat or lay in their sleeping-bags in a dreadful frozen monotony of dislike. Adam's one relaxation was to tend the dogs. He would bury his head in their fur, for the smell of it brought back to him a happier world. To feed them and exercise them seemed his one link with sanity. The dark world out of doors was a less savage place than the squalid hut.

He realised that he was facing the severest test of his life, for he had himself to conquer. Here at the back end of creation he was bound to a lunatic, and all the terrors and perils of the Polar night were narrowed to the relation between two human souls. In his loneliness during the war he had had at any rate the free use of his mind, but now, under the strain, he felt his mind warping. He had to fight down crude and petty things which he thought he had long since put behind him—above all, he had to conquer the sane man's horror of the insane, the clean man's repulsion from the foul. This was a fiercer trial than he had envisaged when he set out from England. He had desired space and solitude, and he had found them; he had wanted to inure his body to extreme fatigue, and he had done it; but he had not reckoned upon this spiritual conflict in a kennel darker than a city slum. . . . But he must go through with the job he had undertaken. Falconet had been a great man, and was worth saving, and the task could not be left half-finished.

Adam nerved himself for a supreme effort. Through all his outbreaks and spasms he nursed Falconet with patient tenderness. He soothed him and coaxed him, and in the end he quieted him. By the beginning of February Falconet's increased bodily well-being reacted on his mind. Now and then he talked rationally. He began to fuss about Paulsen's grave, which, he feared, might be exposed when summer thinned the snow. Once or twice he stammered a few words of gratitude.

One February day, while Adam was feeding the dogs, he saw in the south a strange glow. For a moment he was puzzled, and thought of some new kind of aurora borealis; then an explanation flashed on him, and he called excitedly to Falconet to come out. The two men watched the glow deepen, till their eyes, so long accustomed to darkness, ached at the sight. Then suddenly one of the ice peaks above the fjord flushed into deep rose, and the glow from the south seemed to run across the frozen ocean to meet them. A ray, an authentic ray of sunlight, made a path in it, and over the edge of the world appeared a semicircle of blood-red. The dogs in the hut felt its advent, for they set up a wild barking. The sun had come back to the world.

Adam and Falconet moved down towards the shore, bathed in the cold primeval radiance. For the first time for months they saw their shadows—ghostly indeterminate things running far behind them into the north. Then they heard a croak overhead, and looked up to see a raven. He had been flying west to the ice-cap, but the sight of the sun made him change his course, and with a steady beat of wings he flew south to welcome it.

Falconet grinned, and his face was that of a sane man.

"We've got to follow that old bird," he said. "It knows what's good for it."

IV

They started for home on the first day of March, when the allowance of daylight was still scanty. The easier road to Independence Fjord was by the shore ice, but it would have been three times as long, so, since the petroleum supply was very low, Adam decided to return as he had come, by the ice-cap.

The advent of spring had worked a miracle with Falconet. His great bodily strength came back in waves, the hollows in his cheeks filled out, his voice lost its ugly pitch, and he became at moments almost jolly. Adam shut away the memory of the dark days of hatred, and set himself to rediscover his companion. One thing he realised with alarm. The winter's strain had told on his own health. He looked at food with distaste, and he began to suffer from blinding headaches.

The ice-cap greeted them with violent gales, and once again

among the nunataks they had to lie up for days, desperately cold, for they had only a minimum of petroleum to carry them to Independence Fjord. The dogs' pads had become soft during the winter, and every one went lame and left blood in its tracks. After the gales came a clammy fog, through which the sun's rays never penetrated. It was hard travelling for both men, for their reindeer-skin kamiks had been worn into holes, and there was no fresh sedge-grass with which to stuff them. The novel light induced snow-blindness in both, and they had to fumble along with their eyes partially bandaged. Adam felt his strength steadily ebbing. Tasks, which on the outward journey he would have made light of, were now beyond his power. His gums were swelling, and the skin all over his body was mysteriously peeling off in strips. Worst of all, he suffered from distressing fits of light-headedness, during which every ice-fall became an Alpine peak and the nunataks danced like dervishes around him.

When they reached the depot at Independence Fjord and could get warmth and light again, Falconet insisted that they should keep camp for two days to give Adam a chance to recover. The rest cured his snow-blindness, and, since Falconet managed to shoot a bear, he had a diet of beef-tea which put a little vigour into his bones. Also the signs of the returning spring seemed to unlock his past again. There were gulls about— Sabine's gull and the ivory gull—and skuas and king-eiders, and the sight brought back Eilean Bàn. In baking days in Anatolia he had thought most pleasantly of that island as wreathed in mist or scourged by spring hail, but now he pictured it as green and flowery, sleeping in the blue of summer afternoons. In this world of ice and rock he drew warmth from the vision of its graciousness.

The winter roles were reversed, and Falconet took charge. There was a fierce kindliness in the man and, as they lay at night in the little tent, he talked—talked well, with an obvious purpose of cheering his companion. He asked many questions about Adam's past, and, since two men in such a position have no need of reticence, he heard the full truth.

"I was a soldier," Adam told him. "Then I had to leave the army, for I went to prison."

"So!" Falconet whistled. "I wonder whom you were shielding. Skip that bit, sonny, and get on to the war. What front were you on—the Western, Palestine, Mespot?"

"None. I wasn't a combatant—except for a few months when I wore German uniform with the Turks. For nearly four years I was behind the enemy lines."

Falconet's eager questions bit by bit drew out the story. Adam told it candidly, for he had no self-consciousness about it—he saw small credit in the course which had been the only one open to a man in his position. But Falconet was loud in his exclamations.

"Say," he asked. "What did your Government give you for your four years in hell?"

"I was restored to my regimental rank."

"Yes. That's the sort of thing you would want. . . . Great God, man, I never heard a yarn like yours. You must have a nerve like a six-inch cable. What's to be done with you? You're not going to throw all that training away?"

"Not if I can help it. I came out here to round it off."

Falconet pondered. "I see the sense in that. You wanted to get away from mankind for a bit . . . and you struck the most ill-conditioned specimen on the American continent. You saved that specimen's life, too. But for you I should have been a corpse in that bloody hut. . . . Now you're going to drink some soup and get off to sleep again."

They moved on in a flash of fine weather, and crossed the mouth of Danmarks Fjord on snow which was beginning to break up into channels and rivulets. The sun shone, and they journeyed in a world of gleaming crystal, out of which would rise towards evening wonderful mirages of hills and cities. Close to the land the ice was smooth and bare, and it was possible to hoist a sail and travel fast. But the first day out Adam realised that the days of rest had not cured his malady. So far he had had no fever, but now his temperature rose, and he became so weak and giddy that he could not keep up with the sledge, even when holding on to the uprights. There was nothing for it but that he should become a passenger, which was possible, since they travelled light, having the depots to count on for supplies.

85

He wandered off into a mad world, and one day he was so delirious that he had to be tied on to keep him from rolling off in his wild starts. To make things worse, they struck a bad patch of shore ice, seamed with water lanes and acres of deep, slushy snow.

Of these days Adam had no clear remembrance. He seemed to be perpetually sinking into gulfs and screaming warnings . . . and then he would know nothing till he saw Falconet's anxious face and felt hot soup being fed to him in spoonfuls. Nelles had carried out his orders, and had taken little from each depot, so there was no lack of petroleum and man's food and dogs' food. Once they made camp on a shore where the spring had begun to melt the snow, and mosses were showing, and willow scrub and greening grass. Here Falconet was lucky enough to shoot a bear, and, following some wild lore of his boyhood, he stripped Adam and wrapped him in the reeking pelt.

The fever may have run its natural course, or the bearskin may have had some therapeutic power, for from that night Adam began to mend. His temperature fell, the giddy world became stable, his limbs moved again according to his will. Soon he could leave the sledge and stagger beside it, and he could help to set up the tent in the evening. Falconet would have none of his aid till he was satisfied that he was a whole man once more.

"There's one thing you've got to learn," he said fiercely, "and that's to *take*. So far you've only known how to *give*. But if a fellow isn't ready to take from a friend when he's in need, then his giving is only a darned insult and an infernal bit of patronage. Put that in your pipe and smoke it, Mr. Melfort."

Suddenly something went wrong with the depots. They came to one which looked as if it had been pulled about by wild beasts. The boxes were stove in and their contents scattered and spoiled, and there was not a drop of petroleum in the cans. They put the mischief down to a bear, and, since the stage from the last depot had been over difficult ice, it did not seem worth while to go back and collect the supplies which still remained there. They decided to push on to the next cache.

But the next cache, reached after a desperate toil over shore ice from which the snow was fast melting, proved no better. Nelles seemed to have made a fire and burned up everything, for among the ashes they found only a crumpled petroleum tin and some twisted iron fragments which had once been the hoops of a barrel.

They held a council, for the position was grave. Nelles had broken faith—or he had lost his wits—or someone or something coming after him had rifled the depots. They had with them food at the utmost for seven days, and petroleum for a little longer. They could not go back, for though they had left a fair quantity of stores at the first caches, there was not enough to enable them to reach Shannon Island. On they must go in the hope that in the next depot, or the next, there would be supplies, or that they might meet a search-party from the ship, which by this time must have reached the Greenland coast. They slept ill that night, and next morning reduced their rations to a pound a day. There were no biscuits left—only pemmican, some tinned vegetables, and a little tea.

At the next depot they found the same devastation, and they found also the clue to it. Two of Nelles's dogs lay dead with split skulls, their bones picked clean by the ravens. The man had gone mad—berserk mad—and had raged down the coast rioting in destruction. Adam remembered his lowering brows and sullen, brooding eyes.

Every day the going became harder. From the ice-cap above the shore cliffs waterfalls were thundering, and the beaches were chains of little torrents. The snow was melting fast from the sea ice, and soon that ice would begin to break up, and they would be forced to keep to the terrible moraines of the land. They were now on half a pound of food a day and the dogs had become miserable bags of skin and bone. Presently one died, and his companion lost his senses and ran round in circles till they were forced to shoot him. The sledge was light enough, but with only two dogs they made slow going among the slush and the waterlogged ice. Once the sledge toppled into a voe, and Falconet's diaries were only rescued by a miracle. Each depot told the same tragic tale of blackened desolation, except that in one they found an undamaged tin of cocoa.

87

Presently they were forced to kill the remaining two dogs, and relinquish the sledge. This meant that each had to carry a load, and stumble painfully along the boulder-strewn shore. Their one hope now was a search-party from the ship, and that was only a shadow. Dog-flesh is not good for human beings, but it was sufficient to keep life in them, and that and a little tea were all they had. They had petroleum to last for two days more. In grim silence they struggled on, savage with hunger, their feet so heavy that to lift them at all was an effort. They made short days with long rests, and the nights in the open were bitter. They would rise from the tortures of cold and emptiness and take the road without looking at each other, as if each feared what he might see in his companion's eyes.

Once Falconet said: "If we come out of this, we two are going to keep together for the rest of our lives. How do you reckon the chances? A million to one against?"

"Evens," said Adam. "They're never worse than evens if you keep up your heart."

That day Falconet shot a goose, and, finding a patch of scrub and heather on the edge of a small fjord, they made a fire and roasted it. The meat carried them on for two days, while they traversed a much-encumbered beach under huge dripping cliffs where there was no hope of game. After that they had half a pound of pemmican and a rib of dog to carry them to the next depot—their tea and petroleum were finished.

Next morning Adam's bleared eyes studied the map.

"We shall make the depot before evening," he said.

"And leave our bones there," said Falconet.

That day their exhaustion reached the outside limit of what man can endure. The sharpness of the hunger-pangs had gone, but both men were half-delirious. They constantly fell, and Falconet twisted his ankle so badly that they could only move at a snail's pace. Neither spoke a word, and Adam had to concentrate all his vanishing faculties to keep in touch with solid earth. Sometimes he thought that he was walking on clouds, till he found himself lying among the stones with blood oozing from his forehead. He took Falconet's pack on his own shoulders, and had to give Falconet a hand over the icy streams. "I will not go mad," he told himself, and he bent his mind to the road, fixing a point ahead, and wagering with himself about the number of steps he would take to reach it. According to the map a depot lay beyond a rocky cape which bounded the long beach over which they were floundering.

They turned the cape in the late afternoon and looked on a little bay with a beacon on a knoll. A wild hope rose in Adam's heart. Surely this place was still intact—the demented Nelles must have broken down before he reached it. Hope put strength into his legs, the more as he found his feet suddenly on soft herbage.

But Nelles had reached it. There was something dark and crumpled lying half-buried by a patch of old snow. He had reached it and died beside it, for the stones had not been moved from the cache's mouth. Adam's feeble hands uncovered the food box, which was intact. "We have won on the post," he whispered to Falconet, for his tongue had swollen with starvation. "Lie flat on your back till I get a fire going. We touch nothing but soup tonight, but tomorrow we shall breakfast in style."

They made a mighty bonfire and slept beside it for twelve hours. Next day Falconet nursed his ankle, and dozed in the sun, and in the evening two men, plucked from the jaws of death, feasted nobly, since the rest of the depots were safe and there was no need to hoard. Falconet had come out of his stupor, and sat staring into the green dusk, which was all the night at that season.

"We're two mighty small atoms," he said, "to have beaten old man Odin and his bunch. And the dice weren't kind to us. My God, I've taken some risks in my day, but nothing like this. . . . Do you know, I asked you a week back what the chances were, and you said 'Evens'. I expect you were a bit loony at the time—we both were."

"No, I meant it," said Adam. "It's the strength of the human spirit that matters. Man can face up to anything the universe can pit against him if his nerve doesn't crack. Our trouble was not snow and cold and famine but the human part. Something gave in Nelles's brain, and he played the deuce with a perfectly sound

89

scheme. The hell of that winter hut of ours was not the cold and the dark but the boredom—the way you and I got across each other. . . . We're going back to a badly broken world, and the problem is to find the men big enough to mend it. Our business is to discover genius and put quality into humanity."

"That's the job you've been training for?"

"I think so."

"Well, you can count me in to my last dime," said Falconet.

A week later the two men met the party from the ship which had been sent out to find them.

CHAPTER IV

AT Reykjavik in Iceland Adam and Falconet were met by the latter's yacht. Falconet was, among other things, a newspaper proprietor on a large scale, and he was able to control the curiosity of the press. The message which he sent off from Reykjavik merely announced his safe return, accompanied by his companion Mr. Melfort, after wintering in North Greenland, adding that the scientific results of the expedition would in due course be given to the world. This was published copiously in the American press, and, to a lesser degree, in the English papers, many of which left out the name of Falconet's companion. Not more than half a dozen people realised that Adam was back from the wilds.

The yacht touched at Liverpool, where Falconet turned a flinty face to inquiring journalists. There Adam left it, and, dressed in a suit of Falconet's which did not fit him, returned to the rooms in the Temple which he had taken when he came out of prison, and had retained ever since. His first business was to provide himself with clothes and other necessaries. Then he engaged a servant, a man called Crabb, who had once been his footman and had lost his left arm in the war; he had found on his arrival a letter from Crabb asking for employment, and had some difficulty in disinterring him from a Rotherhithe slum. After that he set himself down for two long days to read the weekly papers for the past year. Then, having got his bearings, he rang up Christopher Stannix, who, he gathered from his reading, had become lately a prominent figure in the national life and was now a member of the Government.

Stannix came to the Temple that evening during a slack interval in the House. To Adam's eyes he seemed to have put on flesh, and his face had acquired that slightly frozen composure which is a necessary protection for those who are much in the limelight. What he thought of Adam may be judged by his behaviour. He dragged him to the window and looked at him from all sides, and then dropped into a chair and laughed.

"Man, you have come back ten years younger—more—twenty years. You don't look twenty-five. I've seen Falconet, who told me something. Not much, for he said you didn't want it talked about—but I gather that the two of you went through a rather special hell. It has shaken Falconet, but you seem to have thriven on it. . . . But for God's sake, get a new tailor. . . . What's your next step? Whom do you want to meet? I'm rather tied up just now, but I'm entirely at your service. . . . Oh, Adam, old fellow, I'm glad to see you. You're like somebody recovered from the dead."

"I want to meet Scrope, if he's alive. I told you about him—the old fellow in Northamptonshire that Ritson sent me to see in September '14."

"That's a queer thing, for he wants to meet *you*. I had a letter from him this morning. He knows that you're home, as he knows most things. I'll get in touch with him at once."

Stannix telephoned next morning that Scrope was coming to town, and desired Adam to dine with him three days thence. That afternoon there arrived an emissary from Scrope in the shape of a tall young man with perfect clothes and a pleasant, vacant face. He introduced himself as Captain Frederick Shaston, late of the 9th Lancers, and now an idle sojourner in the metropolis.

"Mr. Scrope sent me to be kind to you, sir," he said with a very boyish grin. "I gather you've been having a tough time, and he thought you ought to frisk a bit, so I've come to show you round. . . . It's a jolly morning, and I've got my car here. What about a run down to the country? You'd like to see England again at her best."

So Adam spent a day of clear sunshine on the roads of the southern midlands. They climbed the Chilterns, where the beeches were in their young green livery, and ran across the Aylesbury vale among blossoming hawthorns and through woods which were a mist of blue. High up on Cotswold they had the kingdoms of the earth beneath them, and from the Severn scarp looked over to the dim hills of Wales. Shaston would stop at some viewpoint, and make some enthusiastic comment, but Adam noted that the banality of his speech was at variance with the cool, appraising eyes which he turned on him. In the bright afternoon they slipped slowly down the scented valley-roads of Thames. Adam said little, but after a year of barrens and icy seas the ancient habitable land was an intoxication.

That evening Shaston took him to dine at a restaurant with a party of young men, who treated him at first with nervous respect. But, though he was not disposed to talk of himself and had still the slow, formal speech of one who had not spoken English much for years, his friendliness presently dispelled their shyness, and the evening ended merrily with a visit to a boxing match and a supper of broiled bones and beer. Next day Shaston took him to Roehampton to watch polo, where he, who had not spoken to a woman for years, was compelled to mingle with a group of laughing girls. They went to a play that night with a party, and Adam did not fall asleep.

"Please don't thank me," said Shaston when they parted. "I've had the time of my life. I can't tell you what a privilege it is to show you round. I hope you'll tell Mr. Scrope that I didn't bore you too much."

"How do you come to know Mr. Scrope so well?" Adam asked.

"I don't know him well," was the surprising answer. "No-one does. But he knows all about me, and about everybody else and everything. He's about the largest size of man we've got, don't you think?"

Adam rubbed his eyes at the sight of Scrope in the little restaurant in Jermyn Street. He had been a few minutes late, and found his host already seated at a table in a quiet corner. When he had last seen him six years before he had thought him very frail and old, a valetudinarian nearer eighty than seventy, shivering under his plaid on a mild autumn day. The man now before him looked a hale fellow not beyond the sixties, and his Mongolian countenance was ruddy instead of ivory-white. Two things only remained unchanged, his voice, husky from cigarette smoking, and his dreamy heavy-lidded eyes.

Scrope seemed to be no longer a vegetarian, for instead of the mess of eggs and vegetables with which he had once regaled Adam, he had now ordered a well-considered normal meal. He seemed to divine his guest's surprise.

"I have come out into the world again. I thought I had found sanctuary, but it was ordained otherwise; and if I am to be of use in the world I must conform—ever so little. So must you, my friend. You liked Shaston?"

"Yes. You sent him to find out if I had become a fossil. What did he report?"

Scrope laughed.

"Shaston is what you call a flat-catcher. He looks innocent, and sometimes foolish, but he is very, very acute. He reported that you had not lost touch with common life. He described you as 'bonhomous', which is old-fashioned slang, for he is sometimes old-fashioned. That has laid my fears, but I confess that it has also surprised me: I have acquainted myself with your doings for the past six years, and they have been the kind to drive a man back inside himself, and make him an alien from the ordinary tastes of mankind. By all the rules you should have become a prig, Mr. Melfort, and somewhat inhuman. Shaston reports otherwise. He says that you can still feel the elation of a May morning, that you can laugh with simple people at obvious things, and even condescend a little to play the fool. That means that there is something about you that I do not yet know. What is it? You have falsified rules which cannot be falsified. I expected to find you stiff and angular and insensitive, and I thought that it would be my first business to crack your shell. But lo and behold! there is no shell to crack. What has kept you mellow?"

"I will tell you," said Adam. With this man, as with Meyer, the Belgian Jew who had called himself Macandrew, he could have no secrets. He told him the story of Eilean Bàn.

Scrope listened with his eyes downcast, and his fingers playing tunes on the tablecloth. When Adam stopped his face was marvellously wrinkled by a smile, so that he looked like the good mandarin from a willow-pattern plate.

"That is right. You have had a fountain in the desert. That means that you are hard-trained, but not, as I had feared, over-trained. Eilean Bàn! I think I too could be happy with dreams of such a place. Our race must turn its eyes west when it looks for Mecca."

Till the meal was over Scrope talked of what had been going on in the world since Adam went behind the northern ice. He talked brilliantly, with hoarse chuckles and much gesticulation of delicate hands, and again the many-wrinkled smile. But when coffee had been served and he had presented Adam with a cigar from a case like a sarcophagus, he fell suddenly silent. There was a party dining a little way off, with a man in it who seemed to claim his attention.

"You know him?" he asked.

Adam saw a short, squarely built young man with a big head of dark hair, a sallow face with a lofty brow and high cheekbones, and a strong, slightly protuberant chin. He was talking volubly, and kept his chin thrust forward so that there was something almost simian in his air. He looked like an immensely intelligent ape, poised and ready to bound upon an enemy. But his face was pleasant, for he had a quick smile, and everything about him from the crouched shoulders to the glowing eyes spoke of an intense vitality.

"No. . . . Wait a moment. I think. . . . Yes, I have seen him before. A year ago I heard him read a paper at a club—I've forgotten its name. Creevey, isn't he? Some kind of university swell?"

"Creevey—Warren Creevey," said Scrope. "A very remarkable man. Take a good look at him, for you will see him again. I've a notion that you will have a deal to do with him before you die."

Adam obeyed.

"I don't like him," he said.

Scrope laughed.

"You have had to learn in the last five years to judge men rapidly and to go mainly by their faces. I don't quarrel with your verdict. You have learned also to judge ability by the same test. How do you place Mr. Warren Creevey?"

"I should try to avoid antagonising him. If he were my enemy I should cross to the other side of the road."

"So! Well, you will not meet him just yet, for he swims in a different pool. He is very clever and is making a great deal of money, and he also lives the life of pleasure. But some day . . ."

Scrope kept his eyes fixed on the party for a second longer, and then swung round and looked Adam in the face.

"I have seen Falconet. Have you found your work yet?"

"I know what the world needs."

"Come, that is something. That's more than the world itself knows. What is it?"

"Quality."

"By which you mean leaders?"

Adam nodded.

"Are you going to take on the job yourself?"

"No. I can never be in the firing-line. I belong to the underworld. But I can help to find the men we want, and perhaps give them confidence."

"I see. A midwife to genius."

There was a big mirror opposite where the two men sat, and, as it chanced, both were gazing at it and saw their faces reflected. Adam had not much interest in his own looks, but as he gazed and saw Scrope's ruddy Mongolian countenance beside him, and, a little way off, half the profile of Creevey, he could not but be aware that he looked different from other people in England. Scrope saw the distinction in sharper contrast. He saw a face, irregular and not specially handsome, in which supreme concentration had brought all the parts into unity, and to which cool nerves and peace of spirit had given the bloom of a boy. He laid his hand on Adam's shoulder.

"You accept that? And yet you are also disappointed? Confess that you are disappointed."

"I have no cause to be disappointed."

"Which means that you are. You must be. You have fined down your body till it is like that of a blood-horse—you have every muscle and nerve in proper control—you have taught yourself to endure in silence like a fakir—you have a brain which is a noble machine and which is wholly at your command—and you have forgotten the meaning of fear. Such a man as you was meant to ride beside Raymond into Jerusalem. As it is, you propose to be bottle-holder to something called genius, which you will probably have to dig out of the mud."

"I might have wished for something different," was Adam's reply, "but I must take what is sent me."

The old hand patted his shoulder.

"You are wiser than Naaman the Syrian," said Scrope. "I was afraid that I should have to say to you like Naaman's servant 'My lord, had the prophet commanded thee some great thing'— but I find that you have renounced the great thing."

"Not the great thing. But we cannot expect the spectacular thing, we who work in the shadows."

"I stand corrected." Scrope withdrew his hand from his companion's shoulder, and sat farther back in his chair from where he could see Adam's face clearly in the glow of a neighbouring lamp.

"Yes," he said. "You are a formidable fellow, Melfort. You are the rational fanatic—the practical mystic—the unselfish careerist—any blend of contradictories you please. . . . You should have been a preacher. You might have been a second John Wesley, riding on his old white horse throughout England preparing the day of the Lord."

"I have no gospel to preach. My business is to find the man who has."

"Oh yes, I know. I agree. . . . All the same, you are a leader, though you may pretend only to follow. For before you follow you will have to create your leader."

Scrope flung himself back in his chair and looked at Adam from under wrinkled brows.

"You say you have no gospel? Man, you have the gospel which the world needs today, and that is, how to get comfort. What said old Solomon?—'Behold the tears of such as were oppressed and they had no comforter; and on the side of their oppressors there was power, but they had no comforter.' . . . Do not be afraid, my son. I may not live to see it, but every atom of your training will be called into play before you die.

You are right to stick to the shadows, but I think that before the end you will be forced out into the sunlight. You may yet enter Jerusalem by the side of Raymond."

The party at the next table were leaving. Mr. Warren Creevey was putting a cloak about a pretty woman's shoulders, and his rich voice, thick as if it came through layers of chalk, was elevated in some species of banter.

Without raising his chin from his breast Scrope nodded in his direction.

"But I think that first you will have left that paynim skewered on your lance."

Falconet was raging about London. A year's seclusion from the world seemed to have released a thousand steel springs in his body and mind. He lectured to the Royal Geographical Society on his discoveries in North Greenland, which were of some importance, but he kept to his bargain, and so minimised the hardships of his journey that he had no need to bring in Adam's name. But what filled his days and encroached on his nights was a series of consultations with every type of man—financier, merchant, journalist, politician—on the organisation which he meant to set up in his own country. It was characteristic of Falconet that in an enterprise he began by seeking advice from all and sundry, and ended by following strictly his own notions.

Adam's words at the end of the Greenland journey had sunk deep into his mind. The hope of a broken world was to find men big enough to mend it. Quality, human quality, was the crying need, and just as the war had revealed surprising virtues in unlikely places, so this quality must not be sought for only in the old grooves. He gave a dinner at a flat which he had taken in St. James's Street, and to it he summoned Stannix and Adam.

"I've seen your wise man," he told Stannix. "Had two hours with him on Monday and an hour yesterday. He impressed me considerably, but I couldn't quite place him. Say, what's his record? He looks as if he had been a lot about the globe."

"It would be hard to say exactly," Stannix replied, "for Scrope has always been something of a mystery man. He began, I believe, as a famous Oriental scholar and a professor at Cambridge. Then he had a call, and went out to India on his own account as some kind of missionary. He led a queer life, if all tales be true, on the Sikkim frontier, and became our chief authority on Tibet—he accompanied Younghusband's 1903 expedition. After that he disappeared for years, during which he is believed to have been wandering about the world. . . . No, I don't think he has written anything since his Cambridge days. He amasses knowledge, but he gives it out sparingly. . . . When he returned to England he somehow or other got in touch with the Government, and the War Office especially thought the world of him. He was by way of being a sick man, and never left his country retreat. Then during the war he picked up amazingly, and now he looks a generation younger. I fancy he can't be more than sixty-eight. He is the most knowledgeable creature alive, for if he doesn't know a thing himself he knows how to find out about it. You press a button and get immediate results. But his wisdom is greater than his knowledge. I don't know anyone whose judgment I'd sooner trust about men or things."

Falconet listened intently.

"I admit all that. Anyone with half an eye could see it. Where he falls down is that he isn't interested in organisation. He is like an oracle in a cave that gives sound advice but doesn't trouble about seeing it carried out. He agrees with our view, Adam's and mine, but he isn't worrying about what to do next. Now that man Creevey—"

Falconet broke off to expound his own plans. "Organisation is nine-tenths of the fight," he proclaimed. "I'm going to start a great machine for the inquisition of genius." He produced from a pocket of his dinner-jacket a formidable sheaf of papers. "See here," he said as he spread them on the table. "First we have the geographical layout. I'm going to have informal committees up and down the land to consider likely cases. No advertising, you understand—all the work must be private and underground— but I shall have on these committees just the people who will make good sleuths. Then here is my system of checking-up on their reports. We can't afford to make mistakes, so I've got this elaborate arrangement for getting cross-bearings—the schools, the universities, the bankers, the business folk, and a lot of shrewd private citizens. . . . So, when we get a likely case, it will be sifted and winnowed, and before we bank on it we'll be certain that it's the best-grade wheat."

Falconet's dark hawk-like face was flushed with enthusiasm.

"Here's the kind of thing I figure on. There's a lad on a farm in Nebraska who has mathematical genius. Well, he won't be allowed to drift into a third-class bank or a second-class job in a school—we'll give him a chance to beat Einstein. Another is a natural-born leader of men. That kind of fellow is apt to become an agitator and end in gaol, but we'll see that he gets a field where his talent won't be cramped and perverted. . . . We'll cast our net wide over all sorts of talent—art and literature, and philosophy and science, and every kind of practical gift, but it's the last I'm specially thinking about. I want to spot the men who might be leaders—in business, politics, I don't care what—for it's leaders we're sick for the lack of. We've got to see that our Miltons don't remain mute and inglorious, but above all that our Hampdens are not left to rot on a village green."

"Is the real Hampden ever left to rot?" Stannix asked.

"You bet your life he is. It's only one in a hundred that gets his feet out of the clay. And in these days it's only going to be one in a thousand, unless we lend a hand.

"It's a question of organisation," Falconet continued. "We have all the parts of a fine excavating and sifting machine if we can assemble them. That's going to be my business till I cross Jordan—to see that the best man gets his chance."

"It will cost a lot of money."

"I have money to burn. I've been spending nothing for two years, and God knows how my pile has been mounting up. This is a darned lot better way of getting quit of it than founding dud libraries or paying hordes of dingy fellows to cut up frogs. . . . Say, Adam, you'll need some cash. I'm sticking to my own country, but you'll need the same kind of machine here. Remember what I told you. I expect you to draw on me for all you want."

"I don't think I shall want much," said Adam. "I have a little of my own, and it may be enough."

"But that's idiocy," said Falconet fiercely. "You can't do anything without a machine. Take it from me, that's sound, though old man Scrope doesn't understand it. And a good machine costs a hell of a lot."

"But I'm different from you. You're a big man in the public eye, and you can do things on the grand scale. I must keep in the background."

"Well, if that isn't the darnedest nonsense! I'm speaking seriously, Adam. I count myself your best friend—at any rate you are mine—and Stannix here is another. You've got to forget all that's by and gone. The prison business, as all the world knows, was an infernal blunder, and it's been washed out by what happened since. Weren't you restored to your regiment with full honours? You did a hundred men's jobs in the war, and if people had been allowed to know about it you'd have been as famous as Lawrence—the Arabian fellow, I mean. In Greenland you were the largest scale hero, but your infernal modesty wouldn't let me breathe a word about it. What's the sense of it all? You could do the job you're out for a million times better if every man and woman in England had your picture in their album."

Adam shook his head.

"I'm afraid that is impossible. You see, I know best where my usefulness comes in."

"That you don't, and you won't get any sane man to agree with you. Creevey . . ." Falconet stopped.

"Creevey?" Stannix asked. "Do you mean Warren Creevey?" There was a sharp note in his voice.

"That's the man. About the brightest citizen I've struck on these shores. Mailsetter put me on to him, and he has helped me some. I never met a fellow with such a lightning brain. *He* understands organisation, if you like. If you throw out a notion he has a scheme ready for carrying it out before you have finished your sentence. He'd be worth half a million dollars salary to any big concern. They tell me he's a pretty successful businessman anyway. Well, Creevey takes my view about Adam."

101

"But Creevey knows nothing about him—never heard of him—never met him," said Stannix. His face wore an air of mystified apprehension.

"Oh yes, he does. I can't remember how Adam's name came up, and of course I gave nothing away—about Greenland and the other thing. But he seemed to know a lot about him and to be very interested. . . ."

The door bell rang, and Falconet looked a little shy.

"Speak of the Devil! I expect that's our friend. I asked him to come round this evening. You know him, Stannix, don't you? I want to introduce him to Adam."

The man who followed Falconet's servant looked different from the crouching, sparkling figure, set among appreciative women, whom Adam had seen at the restaurant. Creevey wore a dark morning suit, and explained that he had been sitting on a currency committee at the Treasury till eight-thirty. He had snatched a mouthful of dinner at his club, but he accepted a glass of Falconet's old brandy and a cigar.

It was strange how he seemed to take up space in the room. He in no way asserted himself. The thick chalky voice was low-pitched, the forward thrust of the jaw was rather inquiring than aggressive, and the dark glowing eyes were friendly enough. He talked brilliantly about common things—the last news of the Europe-Australia flight, the obstructiveness of M. Poincaré, Mr. Shaw's latest mammoth drama, and—with a compliment to Stannix—the level of debate in the new Parliament. He seemed to take the measure of his company, and effortlessly to dominate it.

Yet he did not put it at its ease. Stannix was coldly polite, and his haggard face was set hard. Falconet, anxious to be showman to his phoenix and at the same time detecting Stannix's dislike, was patently unhappy. Only Adam seemed oblivious of the strain. He looked at Creevey's blunt, mobile features, agreeable because of the extreme intelligence that lit them up from behind, and his fathomless eyes, and they seemed to cast him into a trance. His face had the air of one in mazes of curious dreams.

That night Stannix wrote in his diary:

102

"I have seen in the body two anti-types—Warren Creevey and Adam Melfort. I believe they were conscious of it too, for Creevey has been making inquiries about Adam, and Adam tonight sat fascinated, as if a snake's eyes were fixed on him. A queer contrast—the one all grossness and genius, the other with his 'flesh refined to flame'. I thought of other anti-types in history—Marius and Sulla, Pompey and Caesar, Lorenzo and Savonarola, Napoleon and Wellington—but none seemed quite to make a parallel: Ormuzd and Ahriman were the nearest. . . .

"Of one thing I am certain. That meeting in Falconet's flat had fate behind it. Tonight two remarkable men for the first time saw each his eternal enemy."

BOOK II

CHAPTER I

I

ADAM'S first sight of Utlaw was on a dry-fly stream on the Warwick and Gloucester borders.

He had been down for a weekend to stay with Kenneth Armine, who had been at school with him, and on the Saturday morning he went out to remove a few grayling from Armine's little river. It was a quiet November day, windless and very mild. Early frosts and the gales of late October had stripped the leafage from the coverts and yellowed the waterside meadows, but the woods had not yet taken on their winter umbers and steel-greys and the only colour was in the patches of fresh-turned plough. It was a moment in the year which Adam loved, when the world seemed to rest for a little before beginning its slow germinal movement towards spring.

To take the soft-mouthed grayling on a dry-fly needs a good eye and a deft hand. Fishing the shallow stickles with a long line, Adam had failed to satisfy himself, and he was in the fisherman's mood of complete absorption when, turning a corner, he was aware of another angler on the water. He waded ashore, intending to begin again at a point some distance upstream. As he passed the other he stopped for a moment to watch him. He was a young man with a shock of untidy fair hair, who had an old-fashioned wicker creel slung on his back. He was fishing earnestly but clumsily the tail of a deep pool—a good place for trout in June, but not for a grayling in November. He turned and cried out a greeting. "Done anything?" he asked. "A few," said Adam. "Good for you. I can't stir a fin." The voice was attractive, and the half-turned face was merry.

An hour later the sun came out, and Adam sat himself on a ridge of dry moss to eat his sandwiches. Presently he was joined by the other fisherman, who came whistling up the bank. He was a young man who might be thirty, but no more. He was of the middle size, square-shouldered and thickly made, and his shock head was massive and well shaped. He wore a tattered trench waterproof and what looked like ancient trench boots, and his walk revealed a slight limp. He had wide-set friendly grey eyes, which scanned Adam sharply and seemed to approve of him.

"May I lunch beside you?" he asked, and again Adam noted the charm of his voice. The accent was the soft slur of the west midlands.

He peered inside the fishing-bag which lay on the moss.

"Great Scot! You've a dozen beauties, and I've nothing to show for my morning. I raised several, but they wouldn't take hold. Not nippy enough at the striking, I expect. But what does it matter on a day like this? It's enough to be alive."

He inhaled a long breath of the soft air, and then fell to work vigorously on a packet of bread and cheese. Clearly he was lame, for when he sat down he stretched out his left leg stiffly. His fishing paraphernalia was not elaborate, for, besides the old wicker basket, he had a cheap rod with an antiquated type of reel.

He had nothing to drink with him, so Adam handed him over the bottle of beer with which Armine's butler had provided him. The young man required some pressing, and only accepted it on the donor's assurance that he never drank at meals, and did not want to carry the beastly thing home.

"I say, this is fine," he exclaimed after a long draught. "Bass tastes its best out of doors. This reminds me of my first drink after Bourlon Wood—about the same time of the year as this, and much the same weather. It's funny to think that that was only three years ago. Were you on the Western Front?"

"I didn't fight in the war."

The grey eyes, regarding Adam's lean fitness, had a shadow of surprise in them.

"Lucky for you! I got a bit too much of it, but mercifully the worst was a crooked leg. I can still enjoy life, not like the poor devils who have gas in their lungs or damaged guts. It must be

108

rotten to come out to a place like this and get no good of it because of your vile body. Thank God, that isn't my way of it. I don't often get a day in the country, but when I do it makes me daft. If I hadn't a game leg I could dance a jig. . . . No, I'm not much of a fisherman, though I love it. I get few chances on a stream like this—mostly bait-fishing in the Canal, or an odd day after perch on one of the Club reservoirs. You must be a dab at the game. Do you live hereabouts?"

Adam told him that he lived in London, but that his job took him a good deal about the country. He could see that his companion set him down as a commercial traveller.

"I do a bit of moving about too," he said. "But not in places where you can catch fish. I come from Birkpool, and my beat is a score or two grimy villages round about it. I'm not complaining, for I'm after bigger things than fish, but I thank Heaven that there are still places like this in the world. When things get too beastly, I think about a bend of a river with a wooded hill above and a meadow between."

Adam felt oddly attracted to this expansive young man. There was such frank gusto in his enjoyment, and his eyes looked out on the world with so much candour and purpose.

"I'm going to help you to catch a few grayling," he said. "You mustn't go home with an empty creel."

So till the dusk fell the other was given his first lesson in the mysteries of the dry-fly. Adam made him take his own rod and instructed him how to cast the tiny midge on a long line, how to recognise the gentle sucking rises, and how to strike with a firm but delicate hand. The young man proved an apt pupil, for he had excellent eyesight and a quick wrist. By the end of the afternoon he had half a dozen fragrant fish of his own catching.

"I must be off to catch my train back," he said, as he reeled in regretfully. "You're staying the night at the pub? Lucky dog! What does a rod like that cost? I must save up my pennies for one, for this old weaver's beam of mine is no earthly . . . I wish you'd tell me your name. Milford? Mine's Utlaw—Joe Utlaw. I'm district organiser for the Associated Metalworkers—not a sinecure these days I can tell you. Look me up the next time your round takes you to Birkpool. Here's my office address, and also my private digs." He tore a leaf from a notebook and scribbled something on it.

"I'm very much obliged to you, Mr. Milford. You've given me the afternoon of my life. If I can do anything for you in return . . ." The carefree boy had gone, and the young man became suddenly formal and rather impressive. But as he disappeared up the farm road to the station Adam could hear his whistling begin again. The tune was "The Lincolnshire Poacher".

The way back for Adam lay through a wood of tall beeches which lined the northern slopes of the valley. The air was clear and sharpening with a premonition of frost, while behind the trees the sun was setting in a sky of dusky gold. Beyond the wood the ground fell to the hollow in the hills where the Court lay among trim lawns. Adam stopped to admire the old brick which glowed like a jewel in the sunset. From the chimneys spires of amethyst smoke rose into the still evening.

A cocker spaniel fawned at his feet, a wire-haired terrier butted its head against his knees, and the owner of the dogs swung himself over a fence.

"Had one of your idyllic days?" he asked. He looked into the fishing-bag. "Not bad. We'd better leave the fish at old Perley's, for Jackie can't abide grayling."

Kenneth Armine was three years Adam's junior. At school he had been his fag, and their friendship had been sincere ever since, though till lately their converse had been intermittent. He had gone to Oxford and then to an honorary attachéship at an Embassy, after which followed half a dozen years of travel in outlandish places, varied by two unsuccessful contests for Parliament. In the war he had fought his way up from second-lieutenant to the command of a famous line battalion, and he had acquired a considerable reputation as a fire-eater. He was adored by his men, who let their imaginations expand on his doings. But the repute was unjustified, for he was the least pugnacious of mortals, and had a horror of suffering which he jealously concealed. The truth was that he had one of those short-range imaginations which are a safeguard against common fear, so that under shellfire he was composed, and in an attack

110

a model of businesslike calm. One young officer who accompanied him in a morning's walk in an unpleasant part of the Ypres Salient reported that at a particularly unwholesome sunken road his commanding officer seemed to be deep in thought. But his mind was not on some high matter of strategy, for when he beckoned the nervous youth to him it was only to observe that this was a place where the partridges would come over well.

Like many others of his type Armine went through the war without a scratch or an ailment. For some months he had a job with the Army on the Rhine, and then he came home and married. His father, the old Marquis of Warmestre, lived secluded with his collection of coins and gems at the main family place in Devonshire, and gave over Armine Court to his son. Armine was a friend of Christopher Stannix, in whose company Adam met him again and picked up the threads of their friendship. He had the slight, trim figure of one who has once been a good lightweight boxer. Like all his family he was sallow and dark, with a hint of the Celt in his long nose and quick black eyes. Yet his stock was solid English, descending without admixture from the ancientry of Saxondom, and his Scottish Christian name was due to a mother's whim.

His muddy boots fell into step with Adam's brogues, as they descended the slope to a ha-ha which bounded the lawns.

"I've had a heavy agricultural afternoon," Armine said. "Been round the near farms, and must have walked ten miles in mud. I can't get these fellows to see reason. Old Stockley wants to buy his farm—made a bit of money, and would like to feel himself a landowner. I don't mind, for very soon land is going to be a millstone round a man's neck, and I'd be glad to lessen the size of mine. But what on earth is old Stockley to do when he has spent his nest-egg on becoming a squire and is pinched for working capital? He is a fine Randolph Caldecott type with a red face and a bird's-eye neckcloth, but his notion of farming is to hunt two days a week and to potter round his fields on a fat cob. How is he going to live when prices drop and there's a glut of production throughout the globe? Labour costs are bound to go up—the labourer has higher wages but is a dashed lot worse off than his father for all that. And when trouble comes Stockley and his kind won't have me to lean on, if they set up for themselves. A good thing for me, you say? Maybe, but we've been too long here for me to take a bagman's view of property. I know it's absurd, and Jenkinson keeps pressing me to take the chance of a good bargain, but I simply can't do it. Too infernally unconscientious. There's another chap called Ward—started ten years ago with a hundred pounds, and now has a pedigree flock of Oxford Downs, and a big milk run in Birkpool, and his wife and three sons and two daughters all work on the farm like blacks. I'd sell him his land tomorrow, but he is far too wise to buy—he likes a squire as a buffer. The trouble is that everybody wants to pinch some little advantage for themselves out of things as they are today, and nobody bothers to look ahead."

Armine expanded on the topic. He had large dreams for English agriculture. He wanted more people on the land—smaller farms, more arable, less pasture—but the drift seemed to be towards letting plough slip back to prairie. Stock, he held, was the English staple, for the quality of English stock would always beat the world, so he held that arable should be subsidiary to stock, and that the full richness of English pasturing was untapped. Adam, who knew nothing of midland farming, listened with half an ear.

"I wish to Heaven," his host concluded, "we could get the right kind of leader for our country labourers, somebody who would act as a gadfly and make our jolly old bucolics sit up and think. It's the only chance of salvation for master and man. But the common breed of Labour leader has a head like a doorpost."

"There was one on the river today," said Adam, "a man called Utlaw from Birkpool."

Armine awoke to a lively interest.

"Utlaw! the chap was in my battalion. Got a commission after Cambrai. Now I come to think of it, he wrote to me about fishing, and I told Jenkinson to give him a day whenever he asked for it. Why the devil doesn't he look me up when he comes here? I've heard about his doings in Birkpool. He's a big swell in his Union, and I'm told as red as they make 'em. They

112

want me to be Mayor of the delectable city, and if I am I daresay I'll run up hard against Mr. Utlaw. . . . But I don't know. He was a dashed good battalion officer, and a very decent sort of fellow."

Armine continued to soliloquise.

"I'm glad you mentioned him, for I must keep my eye on him. Horrid the way one forgets about all the good fellows one fought beside. I tell you what—Utlaw is some sort of shape as a leader. He had no luck in the war or he would have had his company. Bit of a sea-lawyer he was, but reasonable too. Now I remember, he put up a good show at Calais in December '18. You remember there was a nasty business with the troops there, for the demobbing was mismanaged and some of the older men were getting a dirty deal from the War Office. So far as my lot was concerned there was no trouble, for Utlaw got hold of them at the start, found out their grievances, made himself their spokesman, and gave me the case I wanted to put up to head-quarters. It needed some doing to hold a lot of tired, disgruntled men and talk them into reason. . . . What's he like now? The same tow-headed, cheery, talkative blighter? The next time he comes here I must get hold of him. I want a yarn with him, and he'd amuse Jackie."

Adam descended the broad shining staircase very slowly, for he felt that he was recovering a lost world. He had had a bath and had dressed leisurely before a bright fire, and his senses seemed to have a new keenness and to be quick conveyers of memories. The scents of the Court—half-sweet, half-acrid—wood-smoke, old beeswaxed floors, masses of cut flowers—blended into a delicate comfort, the essence of all that was habitable and secure. He had dwelt so long in tents that he had forgotten it. Now it laid a caressing touch on him, and seemed to clamour to have its spell acknowledged. He found himself shaking his head; he did not want it, and very gently he relaxed the clinging hands. But it was something to preserve—for others, for the world. As he descended, he looked at the pictures on the staircase, furni-ture pictures most of them, with their crudities mellowed by time. There were two tall ivory pagodas at the foot of the stairs,

113

loot from the Summer Palace; in the hall there were skins and horns of beasts, and curio cabinets, and settees whose velvet had withstood the wear of generations, and above the fireplace a family group of seventeenth-century Armines, with the dead infants painted beneath as a row of tiny kneeling cherubs. The common uses of four centuries were assembled here—crude English copies of Flemish tapestry, a Restoration cupboard, Georgian stools, a Coromandel screen, the drums of a Peninsular regiment, a case of Victorian samplers—the oddments left by a dozen generations. This was a house which fitted its possessors as closely as a bearskin fits the bear. To shake loose from such a dwelling would be like the pulling up of mandrakes. . . . Need there be any such shaking loose? Surely a thing so indigenous must be left to England? But at the back of his head he heard the shriek of the uprooted mandrakes.

A young woman was standing on the kerb of the fireplace with her head resting on the ledge of the stone chimney. When she saw him she came forward and gave him both her hands.

"Such a damned disinheriting countenance!" she quoted. "I never saw such a solemn face, Adam dear. Do you disapprove of my new arrangements? You can't pull the Court about much, you know—something comes in the way and the furniture simply refuses to be moved. . . . I only got back an hour ago, and I'm stiffer than a poker. Thirty miles in a car driven by myself, after a day in those rotten Mivern pastures! Ken will be down in a moment. He has been farming, and I left him getting the mud out of his hair."

Jacqueline Armine had a voice so musical and soothing that whatever she said sounded delicious. She was tall, and the new fashion in clothes intensified her slimness. One could picture her long, graceful limbs moving about the great house, followed by a retinue of dogs and children. Dogs there were in plenty—two terriers, the cocker that Adam had met that afternoon, and a most ingratiating lurcher, but the children were represented only by a red-haired urchin of one year now asleep upstairs in bed. He drew his colouring from his mother, for Jacqueline's hair was a brilliant thing, a fiery aureole in sunlight, but a golden russet in the shadows. It was arranged so as to show much of the forehead, and the height of the brow and her clear, pale colouring gave her the air of a Tudor portrait. She came of solid East Anglian stock, for the Albans had been settled on the brink of the fen-country since the days of Hereward, but a Highland mother had given her a sparkle like light on a river shallow, as well as a voice which should have been attuned to soft Gaelic. Her manner seemed to welcome everyone into a warm intimacy, but it was illusory, for the real Jacqueline lived in her own chamber, well retired from the public rooms of life. The usual thing said about her was that she oxygenated the air around her, and made everything seem worth doing; consequently she was immensely popular, as those must be who give to the world more than they take from it. Having been brought up largely in the company of grooms and gillies, she had a disconcerting frankness about matters commonly kept out of polite conversation. Someone once said that to know her was to understand what Elizabethan girls were like, virgins without prurience or prudery.

At dinner Armine, who had gone without luncheon and tea, was very hungry, and it was his habit when hungry to be talkative. He discoursed on his farming investigations of the afternoon.

"They keep on telling me that the one part of England that isn't shellshocked is the deep country. Like the country line regiments, they say—honest fellows that did their job and won the war, and never asked questions. It's all bunkum. The old shire-horse of a farmer is just as unsettled as the rest of us, and wants to snaffle a bit for himself out of the pool. There is a lunatic idea about that we won something by the war, and that there's a big pile of loot to be shared out. Whereas of course we won nothing. All we did was to lose a little less than the other chap, and that's what we call a victory. The fellow that said that no war could ever be profitable to anybody was dead right. Yet everybody's after his share in an imaginary loot. Old Stockley wants to become a squire, and Ward's reaching out for another farm over Ambleton way. And Utlaw and his lot want higher wages and shorter hours. You must meet Utlaw, Jackie. He was in my battalion, and Adam forgathered with him today on the river. You've often said you wanted to make a domestic pet of a Labour leader. And the politicians are promising a new earth, and the parsons a new Heaven, and there's a general scramble each for the booty he fancies. But there's no booty, only an overdraft at the bank."

"That's nonsense," said his wife. "You shouldn't go too much into agricultural circles, Ken. It goes to your head, my dear, and you grouse like an old moss-back. You shall come to London with me at once and get your mind clear. You shall meet my Mr. Creevey."

"Now who on earth is your Mr. Creevey?"

"He's a friend of Aunt Georgie, and the cleverest thing alive. When I was up shopping last week, Aunt Georgie gave a party, and I sat next to Mr. Creevey—rather a hideous young man till you notice his eyes. Somebody was talking just like you, how we had won the war only to lose the peace—that kind of melancholia. Up spake Mr. Creevey and made us all cheerful again. I can't repeat his arguments, for he talked like a very good book, but the gist of them was that we had gained what mattered most. He called it a quickened sense of acquisitiveness, and he said that the power to acquire would follow, if we had a little intelligence."

Armine shook his head.

"That's begging the whole question. It's the lack of intelligence I complain of. What's the good of wanting to acquire if you haven't the sense to know how to do it. There's a get-rich-quick mania about—that's my complaint. Everybody wants to take short cuts—those rotten painters who splash about colours before they have learned how to draw, and those rotten writers whose tricks disguise their emptiness, and those rotten politicians who—who—well, I'm hanged if I know what they want to do. I don't say we haven't a chance, for the war has burned up a lot of rubbish, and you can't go through four years of hell without getting something out of it—being keyed up to something pretty big. There's a great game to be played, I don't deny, but nobody is trying to understand the rules. We're all muddled or feverish—all except Adam, who stands aside and smiles."

"I wish I knew what you were doing!" Lady Armine turned to Adam.

"I've cross-examined him, Jackie," said her husband. "He

116

never tells me anything, and I've known him ever since he used to lick me for burning his toast."

Adam had slowly felt his way back into the social atmosphere. He was no longer tongue-tied, and his words were not drawn slowly and painfully as out of a deep well. But he was still the observer, and even the friendliest of company could not make him expand.

"It wouldn't interest you to hear what I've been doing. I've been exploring queer places."

"Among what Utlaw calls the 'workers'?"

"Yes. I've had a look at most of the big industries. From close at hand, too. I've lived among the people."

"And the intellectuals? They're an uneasy lot. Every batch of them has got a different diagnosis and a different cure, and they're all as certain about things as the Almighty."

Adam smiled. "I've sampled most varieties of them—the half-baked, the over-baked, and the cracked in the firing."

"Have you tried the uplift circles?" Jacqueline interposed.

"You mean?"

"Oh, all the fancy creeds. The gentry who minister to minds diseased. The mystics who lift you to a higher plane. The psychotherapists who dig out horrors from your past. The Christian Scientists with large soft hands and a good bedside manner. The spooky people. Aunt Georgie has them all. The last I saw there was a drooping Hindu who was some kind of god."

"No," said Adam, "I left the toy-shops alone!"

"Well, and what do you make of it?" Armine was fiercely interrogative. "You've had a look round politics. Is there any fellow in that show who can pull things straight? They're playing the old game in which they are experts, but it isn't the game the country requires. I had hopes of Kit Stannix, but I'm afraid the machine is too strong for him. He has become just a cog in it like the rest. And the Church—the Churches? Have you discovered a prophet who can put the fear of God into the tribes of Israel?"

"Do you know my brother?" Jacqueline asked.

Armine raised his head.

"Yes," said Armine. "What about Frank Alban? You haven't

117

run across him? Well, you ought to. Brother Frank is just a little different from anybody else. He takes my view of things, but, being a saint, he is hopeful."

"He's at St. Chad's now," said Jacqueline. "There are tremendous crowds at his Wednesday afternoon sermons. They are the strangest things you ever heard—mostly the kind of slangy familiar stuff he used to give the troops, and then suddenly comes a sort of self-communing that you can't forget, and an impassioned appeal that makes you want to howl. Ken, this must be seen to at once. Adam and Frank must meet. They'd do each other good."

"That's the best we can do for you," said Armine. "Frank Alban with only one lung, and plenty of people who think him loony. . . . Another glass of port? Well, let's get round the library fire, for it's going to freeze. 'Pon my soul, things are so dicky that I may have to take a hand myself."

II

Mrs. Gallop, at No. 3 Charity Row, in the dingy suburb of Birkpool which went by the incongruous name of Rosedale, had found a tenant for the back room on her upper floor. The houses in the Row were a relic of happier days when Rosedale had been almost country, for they were small two-storeyed things, built originally to accommodate the first overspill of Birkpool residents. Today their undue lowliness contrasted oddly with the tall tenements which hemmed them round.

Her tenant was a pleasant gentleman who, she understood, was by profession an insurance agent or a commercial traveller. The room was not easy to let, for it was small, and its outlook was on the blank wall of the new block behind Charity Row. She had two good rooms on the ground floor, which Mr. Utlaw occupied; he needed space, for he had many visitors, and what had once been the best parlour, before Mr. Gallop's decease compelled his widow to take lodgers, was often full of folk who stayed till all hours—Mrs. Gallop was apt to be kept awake by their talk. But Mr. Milford, for that was her upstairs tenant's name, was easily satisfied and never complained. He was not often there, so there was little profit from his board, but he kept the room on during his absences. He was a quiet gentleman, very easy and soft-spoken, and he was a friend of Mr. Utlaw, so the household at No. 3 was a happy family.

Adam's base was his chambers in the Temple. There for perhaps half the year he lived an ordinary London life. He saw his old friends—few in number now, for the war had cut deep swathes in that group—and he made new ones. He forced himself to move in as many circles as possible, and in the lax post-war society this was easy enough. To his satisfaction he found that he was taken as a newcomer, cumbered with no past. No-one associated him with the ancient scandal, and his doings in the war were known to only a dozen or two people who held their tongues. He was good to look upon, still young, apparently comfortably off, and something remote and mysterious about him, his modesty and reticence in an expansive world, gave him the charm of strangeness. He might have been a social success if he had allowed himself to be exploited. As it was, he was a Cinderella who departed before the stroke of midnight; no-one saw enough of him to place him, but he had the gift of whetting people's appetites for a fuller knowledge. Only with Stannix, Shaston, and a few others did he put off his defensive armour and live in any intimacy.

With the help of his servant Crabb he made his Temple rooms a starting-point for a descent into a variety of new worlds. He was very clear that to understand these worlds he must live in them as a veritable inhabitant, and the power of adapting his personality, which he had acquired during four difficult years, stood him in good stead. An odd figure often left the Temple whom only Crabb could have recognised as his master, and after a long interval an odder figure would return, sometimes with its fingers flattened and stained by unfamiliar tasks, once or twice very ragged and the worse for wear. It had been easy for him to slip into the bagman of Mrs. Gallop's lodgings—a few Cockney vowels, clothes slightly astray from the conventions of Mayfair, one or two mannerisms unknown to his class; his homeliness and friendliness did the rest.

Utlaw took him for what he professed to be, one of the cogs in the commercial machine, who had a better mind than was usual with his type, and aspired to higher things. Two nights after his first arrival, Adam had been invited to a coffee-drinking in Utlaw's rooms. There was nearly a score of people there, who made the air solid with cigarette smoke, strained the resources of the establishment in the matter of black coffee, and argued till three in the morning. Most of the guests were young, and about half of them were returned soldiers, while the others had been exempted for bodily weakness or munition work, or had had a stormy conscientious career in and out of gaol. By tacit consent the war was never mentioned, and all were very busy in pegging out claims in the new world. It was an atmosphere with which Adam was familiar, the crude, violent, innocent disputation of bewildered youth. One man he found who was busy educating himself in tutorial classes, reading Plato no less, with a dream of a university far ahead. Another preached the pure Marxian gospel, and there was a heated argument between a group who found their spiritual home in Russia and a League of Nations enthusiast who upheld the virtues of law. All were poor, each had a precarious present, but all believed in a better future which with their hands and brains they would wring out of the reluctant lords of society. Adam had heard it all a hundred times, but he was impressed with Utlaw's handling of the talkers. He seemed to treat the whole thing as a relaxation from the business of life, an adventure not to be taken too seriously. He would prick a speculative bubble with a hard fact and reduce the temperature of debate with his homely humour. Once he interposed with a cold douche.

"How on earth can you get Lenin's workers' paradise in Britain?" he cried. "For that you want a self-supporting country. We're parasites and must live by our exports, and that means capitalism until the day comes when we have halved our population and can be independent of our neighbours. We're as complicated as hell, and for Bolshevism you want simplicity. . . ." "Savagery," someone suggested. "Aye, savagery," he said. "You can't have it both ways. Our job is to make the best of what we've got."

120

Adam found it hard to see much of Utlaw. The man was furiously busy. There were the weekly lodge meetings and a host of less formal gatherings to be attended. There was the day-to-day work of health insurance, and pensions, and workmen's compensation cases—work equivalent to that of a solicitor in a large practice. There were endless little disputes to be arranged before they became acrimonious, difficulties with arrogant foremen and with slack workmen, and now and then full-dress diplomatic conferences with employers singly and in combination. There was a daily letter-bag like that of the editor of a popular newspaper. But if he heard little of Utlaw's work from Utlaw himself, he heard much of it from other people. At the coffee-party a man called Bill Wrong had been present, an official of another Union, and with him Adam struck up an acquaintance, which presently ramified into many acquaintances in Bill's class. Everywhere he found Utlaw spoken of with a curious respect.

"He's got guts, has Joe," said Wrong. "The best kind, for he'll not only stand up to the enemy, but he'll knock his own folk about if he thinks they're playing the goat."

He had a dozen stories to tell of how Utlaw had fought with the masters and won, and the fights had left no unpleasantness behind them. "He's got a wonderful gift that way. Learned it in the army, maybe. . . . My varicose veins kept me out of that kind of thing and I often wish to God they hadn't. Joe can hand you out the rough stuff and you only like him the better for it. If I call a man a bloody fool I'm apt to get a bloody nose, but if Joe does it he gets stood a drink."

One Saturday afternoon Adam was bidden to tea in the rooms downstairs. There was another guest, a girl in a biscuit-coloured coat trimmed with some cheap fur, who moved away from Utlaw's side when Adam entered. She was small and slight and pale, with dark hair rather badly shingled. The moulding of her face was fine, and the deep eyes under the curiously arched eyebrows made her nearly beautiful. The impression which Adam received was of ardour and purpose and speed—almost of hurry, for she seemed to have spared little time to attend to her

121

appearance. She was untidy, but she suggested haste rather than slovenliness.

"I want to introduce you to my fiancée," Utlaw said. "Florrie, this is Mr. Milford—Miss Florence Covert. Since we're all going to be friends, you'd better get her name right at the start. It's spelt Covert and pronounced Court in the best Norman style. But that's the only oligarchic touch about Florrie. Otherwise she's a good democrat."

Miss Covert, as Adam learned afterwards, was the daughter of a country clergyman of ancient stock. Finding the tedium of vicarage life unbearable, she had broken away to make her own career. The family were very poor, but she had managed to get a scholarship at a women's college where she had taken a good degree, and she was now a welfare-worker in Eaton's, the big biscuit factory. Adam was at first a little nervous, for this girl had sharp eyes and might penetrate his disguise, so he was at some pains to accentuate the idioms of his new role. He must have succeeded, for her manner, which was at first suspicious and defensive, presently became easy and natural. She accepted him for what he professed to be—one of Joe's friends of the lesser bourgeoisie, who were to be tolerated but not encouraged, since they could never be of much use to him.

It was easy to place her. She was devouringly ambitious, first for her man and then for herself. There could be no question but that she was deeply in love. Her protective, possessing eyes followed Utlaw with an ardent affection. He had spruced himself up for the tea-party, and wore a neat blue suit, coloured linen, and the tie of his old grammar-school, but his smartness only accentuated his class. He was the child of the people, and the girl, for all her dowdiness, was clearly not.

"I saw our new Mayor yesterday," Utlaw observed, "Viscount Armine—ain't Birkpool going up in the world? I've told you about, him, Florrie. He commanded my battalion, and he's given me some fine days fishing on his water at the Court. A good chap, old Sniffy—that was the men's name for him, for when he gave you a telling-off he would look down his nose and sniff as if he had a cold in his head. Bet he wakens up some of the frozen feet on the Town Council, for he's a pretty good imitation of a Bolshie. Half these young lords are, for the war has stirred 'em up, and being aristocrats, and never having had to bother about ways and means, they're of the spending type, and quite ready for a new deal."

"It won't last," said the girl scornfully.

"I don't say it will—with most. With some, maybe. When they get down to rock facts, most will be scared and run away. But I daresay one or two will finish the course. You see, that class of fellow is accustomed to take risks—loves 'em—the sporting instinct, you'd call it, while the middle-classes play for safety. So if you're going to have a big experiment you'll always get one or two of the old gentry to back you. Their fathers were shy of the working man apart from their own folk, for they knew nothing about him; but this generation has lived four years with him in the trenches, and is inclined to make a pal of him. No, it isn't patronage. It's a natural affinity, just as a pedigree hound will make friends with a tyke, and both combine to maul a respectable collie. If you set Armine down among our boys, in half an hour they'll be calling each other by their Christian names, whereas a man like Tombs will be 'sirred' till the end of time."

"I don't think these public-house affinities count for much," said Miss Covert. "Charles Tombs is a stick, but he has a wonderful mind. What has your Lord Armine to give to the world?"

"Oh, I don't say that Sniffy is much of a thinker, but he's a human being, which is something. The world could do with more like him today. He's very friendly to yours truly. He wanted to know all about my work. You haven't to tell him a thing twice, for he's very quick in the uptake. He asked if I was married, so I told him about you, and he said he must meet you—said his wife would like to know you. I've never seen Lady Armine."

"I have. She was pointed out to me the other day in Bertram Street. A lovely lady with Titian hair, who walks as if she knew she was somebody and expected people to make way for her. Don't let's have any nonsense, Joe dear. I'm not going to be taken up by Lady Armine, and I won't let these grandees make a fool of you. There's no more contemptible figure than a Labour leader who allows himself to be made a lapdog by the enemy. We're a class army, and we must stick together till the battle is won."

Utlaw laughed. "Good for you, Florrie. You would have made a fine *tricotreuse* in the French Revolution."

The girl neither assented nor demurred to any of Utlaw's generalities; what attracted her was the technique of the game. Adam drank his tea and listened in silence to a discussion on Utlaw's prospects, for it appeared that Miss Covert accepted him as a loyal friend of her lover's, though not a friend who could be of much use. At any rate his advice was never asked. There was the question of a seat in Parliament. Not just yet, perhaps, There was no chance of a vacancy in Birkpool, and a constituency in the North, where his Union was powerful, was too rich a prize to be had at the first time of asking. Besides, the present Parliament was hopeless, and to be a member of it would only compromise him. . . . But he must keep himself before the public. He must speak at Mr. Twining's big meeting next month, and he must be ready for a great effort at the next Conference. Who were his real friends? Deverick was no use, but Judson, and Gray, and Trant himself were friendly. Trant had said to someone who had told a friend of hers . . .

Adam had the impression that Miss Covert was suffering from inverted snobbery. She was contemptuous about the Armines, and would have Utlaw stick to his class, but she was determined that he should be high in that class's hierarchy. She pronounced the names of Labour notables with an almost sacramental reverence. She retailed what she believed to be the gossip of the inner circle as an aspiring hostess exults over the doings of Royalty. Trant, the party leader, Gray, with his wizard locks and wild eloquence, Judson with his smashing repartees were all to her creatures of romance, as fascinating as a duke to a novel-reading shopgirl. . . . Well, that was no bad thing. If the woman who adored Utlaw had this minor worldly wisdom, she would keep his feet on the ground. The danger was that he would think too much of ultimate things and forget the gross and immediate facts.

Yet Adam felt that he had not succeeded with Miss Covert. She had held him at arm's length, not because she was suspicious of him, but because she considered him negligible. An incident a few days later did not help matters. In the street he met Jacqueline Armine.

"Carry this puppy for me, Adam," she cried. "My car's parked at the Town Hall and I've mislaid my chauffeur. I had to bring the little brute to the vet, for he has damaged his off hind paw. I won't ask what you're doing here, for Ken says that is what I must never ask. You're very shabby, my dear. Have you come down in the world?"

"The Court!" she exclaimed in answer to his question. "Ken is there, and half a dozen young couples who have planted themselves on us uninvited. What is to be made of the youth of today? They're all penniless, and they all want to get married at once. When their parents frown they fly for refuge to me, because I'm believed to have a large heart. I can tell you it's no fun having your house made a rendezvous for amorous paupers. The chaperone business is beyond me, so I don't try. They're scarcely out of the nursery, you know. What is to be done about this craze for child marriage? It's worse than India. Why couldn't we adopt a good Indian custom when we were at it? Suttee, for example. The world is cluttered up with superfluous widows."

Just before they reached the car Miss Covert passed them. Adam lifted his hat with difficulty owing to the puppy, and to Jacqueline's hand, which at the moment was affectionately laid on his arm. He received a curt bow and a surprised glance from the deep eyes.

"Who's that Charlotte Corday?" Jacqueline asked.

"The girl Utlaw is engaged to. You've heard Kenneth speak of him."

"Rather. I want to meet him. Her too. We're going to take our Mayoral duties very seriously. Hallo, there's Simpson. Give him the puppy, and thank you so much, Adam dear. Can't you come on to us and see our Abode of Love? Oh, by the way, brother Frank is coming here soon to preach. If you're in Birkpool, go and hear him. It's an experience."

If Miss Covert remained aloof, Adam found that he was moving towards a closer friendship with Utlaw. His silent ways made him a good listener, and presently he became the recipient of the other's confidences. Utlaw was one of those people who discover their own minds to themselves by talking, and often he would ascend to Adam's little room before going to bed and unburden himself of some of his cogitations of the day. The man had an explosive vitality which carried him through the roughest places. His maxim was that you must always be, as he phrased it, "atop of your job". Once let it crush you, or tangle you, and you were done. But it was not always easy to keep this pre-eminence, and he had often, in Adam's presence, to argue himself out of moods which inclined to lethargy or depression. His humour was his salvation, for he had a pleasant gift of laughing at himself. "Life's a perpetual affair of going over the top," he said; "and it doesn't provide a rum ration. You've got to find that for yourself. Mine is a jack-in-the-box elasticity. If I'm suppressed, I can't help bobbing up. Also my feeling about the comedy of it all. Once I can see the idiocy of a fellow and laugh at him, I know I've got him in my hand.

"Florrie tells me she saw you with Lady Armine," he said one evening. "I didn't know you knew her."

"I don't know her very well. She asked me to carry her lame pup. She's a sister of a parson called Frank Alban, who's coming to preach next month in St. Mark's."

"Alban! You don't say! I met him in France. I don't trouble Church much, but I shall go to hear him. He used to have fire in his belly."

One morning a strange figure presented itself in Adam's room. It was that of a short elderly man, who was nearly as broad as he was long. He must have been over sixty, for his mop of hair was white, and his square face was deeply lined. His eyes under bushy eyebrows were a steely grey; his chin and portentous upper lip were clean shaven, but hair like a fur muffler enveloped his cheeks and throat. His name was Andrew Amos, and in the war he had been a pillar of a service so secret that the name of no one of its members and no one of its reports ever

126

appeared on paper. Adam had been sent to him by Scrope, and had lodged with him during some illuminating months on the Clyde. Amos was as inflexible in his politics as he had been in his patriotism; he was a Radical of the old rock and no Socialist, but his class loyalty was as vigorous as Miss Covert's. He had a conception of the rights of the wage-earner which he held as stoutly as he held his own creed of militant atheism, and he would never deviate one jot from it as long as he had breath in his body. Eighty years earlier he would have been a Chartist leader.

He accepted a second breakfast—tea and two of Mrs. Gallop's indifferent eggs.

"Maister Scrope sent me here," he explained. "He wanted me to get a line on Joe Utlaw, and as I ken a' the Union folk and they ken me, he thocht I would be better at the job than you. I've been here three weeks, and I think I've made a fair diagnosis. He'll dae. Utlaw will dae. Yon yin has the root o' the matter in him."

When his clay pipe was lit Mr. Amos expanded.

"There's twae types o' Labour prophets on the road the day. There's them that canna see an inch beyond bigger wages and shorter hours, and there's them that takes the long view. I ca' them the arithmetical and the pheelosophical schools. Utlaw belongs to the second. The warst o't is that most o' his school are inclined to a windy Socialism. He is not, at least not in the ordinary sense, and that's a proof o' an independent mind. The feck o' the workers o' my acquaintance wad spew if they properly understood what the Socialism was that a man like Tombs preaches. They've mair in common wi' an oppressive Tweedside laird than wi' the wersh callants that ca' themselves Marxians. But unless there's folk to guide them richt they'll be stampeded like sheep intil a fauld whaur they dinna belong. Utlaw kens this, and that's why I say he's a man wi' a superior and independent mind.

"He's a queer yin too." Amos removed his pipe and grinned broadly, thereby revealing a dazzling set of new, ill-fitting teeth. "He doesna care muckle what he says. He can be dooms funny when he likes—whiles not altogether decent—like Robert Burns he can give ye a waft o' the kitchen-midden. But his great gift is for rough-tonguing without offence. I've heard straight langwidge in my time, but no often as straight as his. He can misca' an audience till ye'd think they'd want his blood, and yet they only like him the better for't. I've been considerin' the why and wherefore o't, and my conclusion is this. He's the common denominator of a' that's English. Not Scotch—he wadna gang down wi' our lads, and he'd get his heid broke afore he was a week on the Clyde. But he's English to the marrow o' his banes, and the folk that listen to him ken that they're listenin' to their ainsels if they had just the power o' expression.

"His danger?" he said in reply to a question of Adam's. " 'Deed, I think that he'll maybe be ower successful. He has an uncommon gift o' the gab, and he's young, and he has imagination, and guid kens this warld's a kittle place for them that has ten talents. I whiles think that there's mair to be gotten out o' the folk that has just the yin talent—or maybe twae. Brains and character are no often in equal proportions, and if they're no, the balance, as Robert Burns says, is wrang adjusted."

Adam attended St. Mark's when Frank Alban preached. The church was in the centre of a large slum parish, and had been famous in the past for certain audacities of ritual which had led to episcopal interference. Its vicar had recently died, and at the moment the living was vacant. There was a movement abroad which called itself the Faith and Brotherhood League, and under its auspices special sermons were being preached in the industrial cities. St. Mark's had been selected in Birkpool because of its size and its situation.

The place was crowded, for Alban's recent utterances had given him some celebrity in the popular press. The congregation was made up largely of women, most of them well-dressed, but there was a fair proportion of young men. Adam went there expecting little, but eager to see Jacqueline Armine's brother. He had not been greatly impressed by what he had read in the newspapers. The Wednesday services at St. Chad's, from the published extracts, had seemed to him clever nonsense, the provocative utterance of paradoxical youth. He expected this,

128

combined with some breezy, man-to-man padre talk, for Alban had made a considerable reputation among the troops in the war.

The first sight of the man confirmed this expectation. Frank Alban had none of his sister's colouring. He had a finely cut pale face like a tragic actor's, dark hair thinning into a natural tonsure, and nondescript deep-sunk eyes. He looked a fragile, almost a sick man. . . . Then came a series of surprises. To begin with, there was the voice. It was sweet, not powerful, husky and a little breathless, the voice of a man with weak lungs. But it had a curiously attractive, even compelling, power. One could not choose but listen. The face of the man, too, was transfigured when he spoke, as if a light had been lit behind it. The impression he gave was one of intense, quivering earnestness. He read the New Testament lesson, a chapter of St. John's Gospel, and Adam thought that he had never heard the Scriptures more nobly interpreted. It was not that the voice and elocution were pre-eminent, but that the reader seemed to be communicating to his audience exultingly a revelation which had just been granted him.

The next surprise was the sermon. Here was none of the jolly man-and-a-brother business which Adam had anticipated. Alban stood in the pulpit like some mediaeval preaching friar, and held his hearers in a sort of apocalyptic trance. He had no topical allusions, no contemporary morals; his theme was the eternal one of the choice which confronts every mortal, the broad path or the narrow path, the mountain-gate which is too narrow for body and soul and sin. It reminded Adam of sermons he had heard from old Calvinistic divines in his youth. The tenor was the same, though it was notably free from the language of conventional piety. In a world, said the preacher, where everyone was clamouring for material benefits, there was a risk of soul-starvation. He pictured the Utopia of the *arrivistes* and the Utopia of the social reformers, the whole gamut of dreams from the vulgar to the idealistic. But did even the noblest express the full needs of humanity? He repeated in his wistful voice the text which Scrope had once quoted to Adam: "Behold the tears of such as were oppressed and they had no comforter; and on the side of their oppressors there was power, but they had no comforter."

In the church porch, as the solemnised and rather mystified congregation dispersed, Adam ran across Andrew Amos.

"What did ye think o' him?" asked the old man, who had not forgotten the sermon-tasting habits of his youth in spite of his latter-day scepticism. "Yon's an orator and no mistake. Man, it's queer to reflect that if he strippit his discourse of Biblical jargon, it would be a very fair statement of faact. There's a sound biological basis for the doctrine o' the twa roads. In a' evolution there's a point where a movement must swither between progress and degeneration, and that's just the amount o' free will I'll admit in the universe."

That night Utlaw came up to Adam's room before going to bed. He, too, had been to St. Mark's.

"That's dangerous stuff," was his comment. "I've heard a lot about Frank Alban, but I never thought he was that class. Oh, wonderful, I allow! If anybody in my job could talk like that he'd be leading the country inside four years. But all the same it's dangerous stuff. That's the 'otherworldliness' that our Marxians are terrified of. If you take his view, then all we're trying to achieve is futile, and the only thing that matters is for a man to save his soul though he lives his life in hoggish misery. That sort of thing is the anodyne that blankets reform. . . . All the same there's some truth in it, but I can't quite fix it. No soft soap about Frank Alban. He is out to make the world uncomfortable, and, by God, he succeeds. My mind felt all rubbed up the wrong way. . . . By the way, he's staying some days in Birkpool. He's coming to tea with some of us at the Institute on Wednesday. You'd better come along. You know his sister and might like to meet him."

Frank Alban out of church was a most unclerical figure, for he turned up on the Wednesday night in a tweed suit and an Eton Ramblers' tie. He had none of the hearty ways of the traditional army padre, and none of the earnestness of his preaching manner. He looked a retiring delicate man, perhaps a few years over thirty. His voice was low and hoarse, and he was liable to fits of coughing.

But he had the gift of putting people at their ease. There was something about his shy friendliness which bound together in

130

one fraternity the motley group in the upper room of the Institute. The guests were all Utlaw's friends and associates—minor
Union officials, the organisers of W.E.A. classes, a Socialist
parson who had won a seat on the town council, one or two
women, including Florrie Covert. Alban greeted Adam as a
stranger, at which Florrie opened her eyes. She had gathered
from Utlaw that Adam knew Lady Armine through her brother.

It appeared that Alban had been spending his time looking
at housing conditions in Birkpool and going over some of the
chief works. He deplored the flimsiness of his London life.

"St. Chad's is too fashionable. How can I speak to men's
hearts if there is a microphone two feet off broadcasting my
sermon as if it were a music-hall turn, and half a dozen reporters
looking out for spicy titbits? I know it is all well meant, but it
kills freedom. The result is that I dare not be unprepared, and
must write everything beforehand, and that you know, Mr. Utlaw,
is the end of sincere speaking. You can't hope to persuade
unless you can look into people's eyes. . . . Also there are too
many women."

"What ails you at the women?" Florrie asked tartly.

"There are too many of them, and they are there for the
wrong purpose. They are either good souls who lead a sheltered
life, or girls looking for a new sensation."

"You mean they're in love with you?" said Florrie.

He flushed. "God forbid! I mean that I've nothing to say to
them. If I'm any use it's not in confirming believers in their faith
or giving the idle a new thrill. My job is to trouble people's
minds as my own is troubled. I want to be a gadfly to sting
honest lethargy into thought. We're done, you know, if we go
on being self-satisfied."

"That's my complaint about you," said a shaggy youth in a
red tie. "You want to keep us in a state of blind torpor about
the dirty deal we're getting in this world, and satisfy us with
celestial husks."

Frank did not answer. Instead he asked questions—questions
about the way in which the Birkpool workers lived. He had seen
enough for himself to make his interrogations intelligent, and
Utlaw, who did most of the answering, took him seriously.

131

"They've a better life than their fathers had who were in the same job. You can say that if you can say nothing else. Big wages were earned in the war, and there were a good many nest-eggs laid by. At present there's not much poverty and only the average amount of unemployment. That will come, for the whole system is rotten. The firms have been afraid to declare too big dividends, so they've been 'cutting the cake', as we call it, and distributing bonus shares to their shareholders. What's the result? Every business is over-capitalised and trembling like a pyramid stuck on its point. Once let the draught come—and it's coming all right—and the whole thing will topple over. It's a mug's game, and do you think our fellows don't know it? It's maddening for an intelligent man to see a business on which his livelihood depends at the mercy of stock-jobbing finance and him and his friends powerless to interfere. The human touch has gone today. There's a board of bigwigs in London, and a general manager who spends his life in the train and doesn't know a single man by head-mark, and, as like as not, a works manager who knows the men all right but whose job is only to be a slave-driver. Oh, there's plenty of decent fellows among the masters, but the system is bad. Capital gets too much out of the pool, and labour and brains too little. That's the first thing we've got to change."

The parson town-councillor replied to one of Frank's questions about housing. Birkpool, he said, was as bad as any place in the land, except some of the mining villages in the North. There was little comfort and not much decency. The parson was a dreamer, but he was also full of facts.

"The life is hard," he said, "but that by itself wouldn't matter. It's not so hard as a miner's or a deep-sea fisherman's. The trenches were foul enough, but our men learned there the blessings of cleanliness, and they haven't forgotten it. The younger lot don't take well with six days of filth year in and year out and a perfunctory clean-up at the weekends. The marvel is that they manage somehow to keep their self-respect."

The talk ranged at large, Frank interrupting many times with questions. He never looked at Adam, but he kept his eyes steadily on Utlaw.

"You say we're at the crossroads?" he asked. "You mean, that the men want more of everything—money, leisure, chances? Their horizon has been enlarged? That's partly the spread of education, I suppose, and partly the war."

"Yes, but we're at the crossroads in another sense. Unless I'm wildly wrong we're on the brink of devilish bad times. Britain has lost her monopoly in most things, and she has to compete against rivals who can undersell her every day. How are we going to meet that situation? By scaling down our standard of life?"

"By God, no," said the young man with the red tie. "We can't scrap what we have so painfully won. There'll be a revolution first."

"I don't know about that," said Utlaw. "It's no good kicking against the pricks. Our people will stand up to an economic crisis as they stood up to the war, if it's put fairly before them. But they must be prepared for it. You must take them into your confidence. Above all, they must be certain that they are getting a fair deal."

"I want you to tell me something," said Frank. He had been sitting on the table dangling his legs, and he now stood up before the gas fire. "I see generally what you're after—a fairer share of the reward of industry for labour and more say in its management. You want first of all security, and, after that, better chances, better conditions and more leisure. You want to give the ordinary fellow a better life. But merely tinkering at his material environment won't do that."

"Agreed," said Utlaw. "We've got to go farther and think of what you call his soul. Leisure's no use to him unless he is fitted to make something out of it. He must be given access to all the treasures of thought and knowledge which till the other day were the perquisites of the few." Utlaw delivered this oracularly, for it had been the peroration of a speech.

"I know, I know," said Frank. "There's fine work being done in that direction—I've seen something of it in Birkpool this week. But does it go far enough? After all, everyone hasn't a capacity for culture. But everyone has a soul to be saved and perfected."

There was an odd silence in the room, for Frank's voice had lost its easy friendliness and suddenly become hoarse and strained. He was not looking at Utlaw now, but through him to something very distant.

"This is my point," he said, and the words seemed to come with difficulty. "Succeed as much as you please, recast industry on a better pattern, and manual labour will still be the ancient curse of Adam. It has lost the interest of the craftsman, and is for the most part a dismal monotonous grind. . . . Again, you may tidy up your shops and factories, but most of the work will have to be done among dirt—and not honest country muck but the hideous grime of man's devising. Too much of that kind of dirt is bad for the human spirit. . . . Then you say that even the material side is insecure. At any moment, in spite of all you have done, the worker may have to face an economic blizzard, and he has no shelter against it such as his master possesses. But you admit that he must stand up and face it, for there is no other way. . . . What does all that mean? Surely that the one thing which matters is to strengthen the man's soul. Open his eyes, enlarge his interests as much as you please, but make certain above all that he has an inner peace and fortitude of spirit."

"How are you going to do it?"

Frank smiled.

"I apologise for talking shop. My answer is by what theologians call the grace of God. The way to it was laid down nineteen hundred years ago, and it is still open. . . ."

"Christ was a red-hot Socialist," said the young man.

"Not the ordinary kind," said Frank. "He did not call the rich men knaves—he called them fools."

Adam found his arm seized as he made his way home, and to his surprise saw Frank at his side.

"I didn't introduce myself properly," he said, "for I gather that you don't want to have attention called to you. I noticed you never opened your mouth tonight. But I know a good deal about you from Jackie. Lyson, too—you served with him, didn't you? He's an old friend of mine, and once he told me a little—

a very little—about your doings. I want to talk to you—not now, but somewhere soon—a long talk. You can help me a lot."

The street was well lit, so he may have seen surprise in Adam's face, for he laughed.

"Oh, I know I'm supposed to be officially helpful, but I'm a broken reed. I'm as much adrift from my moorings as anybody. I'm sick to death of my work in London, and unless I chuck it I shall become a public scandal. I believe in God, but I'm not very clear about anything else. I call myself a Seeker. You remember Cromwell's words—'The best sect next to a Finder, and such an one shall every faithful humble Seeker be at the end.' That's my comfort, and I'm on the lookout for others to keep me company. . . . You're one. Kenneth Armine's voice becomes reverential when he mentions you, and he has no great bump of veneration. . . . And I think Utlaw is another. You agree? One man with faith can move mountains, but three might be an Army of the Lord."

III

A month later Adam noticed that Utlaw's face had begun to wear a curious look of strain and worry. He dated it from Twining's great meeting in the Town Hall, a Labour rally at which Utlaw had proposed the vote of thanks in a speech which completely outclassed the banal rhetoric of the principal orator. Twining was a man who had grown grey in the service of the party, and was very generally respected, but constant speaking out-of-doors had stripped his voice of all tone, and his ideas were those of the last little official handbook. After him Utlaw's living appeal was like champagne after skim milk. It had been a fine performance, but it had been interrupted. He got no such respectful hearing as Twining got. Clearly there were elements in Birkpool hostile to him, and one man in particular had made himself conspicuous by savage interjections.

Ever since then Utlaw's manner had been constrained, as if he were cumbered with difficult private thoughts. He never appeared now in Adam's room before going to bed. He seemed to

135

avoid him, and, though very friendly when they met, showed no wish to meet often. Florrie, too, looked haggard and miserable. Twice Adam saw her leaving Utlaw's room, and he met her occasionally in the street, and each time he was struck by the anxiety in her face. Was it a lovers' quarrel? Or was Utlaw face to face with some serious difficulty in his work?

One evening came Andrew Amos, who enlightened him.

"I've been verifyin' my faacts," said Amos, "and now I've come to put them before you. Utlaw's in bad trouble—ye might say in danger. It's no blame to him, but it's not just that easy to see the way out o' it."

Then Andrew told his tale. There was a man called Marrish, who had once been an official of Utlaw's Union, and had indeed been the runner-up for the post of local organiser. After his rejection he had left his Union job and become a freelance journalist. He was a small dark man with a touch of the Jew in him, and had been born in the Transvaal and begun life in the Rand mines. For Utlaw he cherished an extreme jealousy, which was not improved by certain public encounters in which he got the worst of it. He was a fanatic of the Left, and Utlaw's moderation seemed to him treason to the cause, so public differences were added to private grievances. The situation was embittered by his lack of success in his new profession. Marrish had a clever pen, but he had not much sense of atmosphere, and he attributed the coldness of the Labour press towards his work to Utlaw's influence. The man had a delicate wife, and was himself threatened by diabetes, and the misery of his existence he set down at Utlaw's door. Utlaw, young, healthy, popular, expansive, seemed to his morose soul to be the enemy to whose sinister power all his misfortunes were due. He was excluded from lodge meetings, but whenever Utlaw appeared on a public platform Marrish was there to make a row, and at Twining's rally he had been especially violent.

Now things had become worse. Marrish had grown half demented. He had not enough to eat and far too much to think about. He had begun to drink, too, which was bad, for he had once been a fanatical teetotaller. Not in his cups only, but in cold blood he was announcing his intention of doing Utlaw in.

He had relapsed into the atmosphere of his early days when a revolver was apt to be the final arbitrament.

"It's a nasty business," said Amos. "Ye see the man is no what you might ca' certifiably mad. It wadna be possible to get him locked up. And his threats are no enough to bring him inside the law—he's ower clever for that—just a hint here and a hint there—nothing ye could frame a charge on. Besides, if ye sent him to prison or got him bound over, what good would that do? He would be wilder than ever and the mair determined to wait his chance. I've made it my job to see something o' the body, and, I tell ye, there's murder in his een. . . . Now, sir, what's to be done? Any moment Marrish may put a bullet in Joe's brain. After that they may lock him up or hang him, but the mischief will be done. Till Marrish is settled wi', Utlaw gangs in constant danger o' his life. It's like that auld story about the sword o' Damicockles."

There was that in Amos's eye which made Adam ask if he had ever been himself in the same predicament.

"Yince," was the grinning answer, "and I took the offensive. I lay in wait for the man and gie'd him sic a hammerin' that he never wantit to see my face again. But my yin wasna mad—just bad, and that was simple. Daftness is the wanchancy thing that ye canna deal wi'. My mind's clear that something must be done and the thing brocht to a heid, or Joe will get a bullet where he doesna want it, or gang in fear that will make his life a misery."

"Have you anything to suggest?" Adam asked.

"Not preceesely. But he canna go on dodgin' the body and keepin' him at arm's length. He maun get some kind o' settlement."

"And precipitate a tragedy?"

"Maybe. But onything is better than to gang as the Bible says in an awful looking for of judgment."

Adam spent a day in making inquiries, after telephoning to London to one or two obscure acquaintances. He had Marrish pointed out to him in a back room of a public house, and he did not like the look of his dead-white face and hot eyes. Utlaw had an evening meeting, and Adam attended it, and contrived to keep close behind him on his walk home. He entered the house a minute later and walked into the big downstairs room.

Utlaw was shuttering the window. He turned his head and Adam noted the quick, hunted look.

"I can't talk to you tonight, Milford," he said. "I've a lot of work to do. Sorry, but you must be a good chap and leave me alone."

"I'm afraid I must talk to you. Sit down and have a pipe. I've come to know about Marrish. You and I must have it out. The thing is too serious to let slide."

Utlaw dropped the bar of the shutter, and flung himself into an armchair. "Did you lock the front door when you came in? . . . You're right. It's damnably serious. I've been living in hell for the last week or two. And poor Florrie also. But it's no good. You can't do anything for me. It's my own show which I must go through alone."

"That's true. You must go through it alone. But possibly I can help you."

Utlaw said nothing for a minute. He was staring into the ashes of a dying fire with his brows knitted.

"I could ask for police protection," he said at last. "But that would mean publicity, and it would be no use, for Marrish if he means business would get me in the end. Or I could have my own bodyguard—there are plenty of young fellows who would be ready for the job. But that would be no good either, for there would be bound to come a time when Marrish would have his chance. So I have simply ignored the whole thing and led my ordinary life. My hope, if I have any hope, is that Marrish when he sees how little I care for his threats will think better of them—that my sanity will cure his madness."

"Isn't the other result more likely—that your contempt may increase his madness? Besides, he has only to catch a glimpse of you to see that his threats are taking effect. You're a different man since Twining's meeting. You look ill—sometimes you look as if you were under sentence of death."

"You've realised that? Well, that's exactly how I feel. But what else is there to do? Any action I take will merely postpone the trouble. The only thing for me is to set my teeth and go through with it, trusting to luck. But, my God! it's a stiff test of fortitude. I don't think I'm more of a coward than other folk, but this waiting and waiting and waiting turns my nerve to water. There are moments when I could go down on my knees to Marrish and ask him to shoot and shoot quick."

"You are an uncommonly brave man. But you're trying your-self too high. It would break the nerve of an archangel to go on as you're doing. Now, I'm going to prescribe for you. I'm older than you, and I've seen more of the world. Things must be brought to a head right now. . . . Listen to me and don't interrupt. You and Marrish must meet. Here—in this room—with nobody near. He must be given every chance, so that if he means to murder you he can do it and get away. You mustn't be armed. You must offer him the key and tell him to lock the door and put it in his pocket. . . . He may shoot at once, but it isn't likely. He will feel himself on the top of the situation and be in no hurry. Then you must talk to him—you know how to talk. Tell me, has he any earthly shadow of a grievance against you?"

"Not an earthly. It's all a wretched misunderstanding. I rather liked him and wanted to help him, but he went off at a bend into raving dislike."

"Good. Well, you must dig up all his grievances, and spread them out and explain them. Madmen get things in a tangled clump, and it is half the battle if you can sort out the threads. The clump looks big, but each of the threads looks small and silly. . . . You run a risk, of course, but you have a good chance, and if you don't do something of the kind the risk becomes a black certainty. You've got to end the thing once and for all—that's common sense, for you can't go on the way you're going. Marrish must leave this room satisfied—a sane man again as far as you are concerned—and he must leave it your friend."

Utlaw got to his feet. "Come now, that sounds good sense. It's action anyway, and that's easier for me than waiting."

They talked for an hour till Adam said goodnight. Utlaw asked a final question.

"Were you ever in deadly danger of your life?"

139

"Often."

"But I mean, a cold-blooded affair like this?"

"Yes. Worse than this."

"For God's sake tell me about it."

"Not now. Some day, perhaps."

"You're an extraordinary fellow, Milford, and I can't make you out. I thought of going to Lord Armine, for he was my old commanding officer, and I felt that my trouble might be a soldier's affair. But I didn't, for I reflected that Sniffy was a bit too thick in the head to take it in. But you—you order me about like a brigadier and you seem to have the wisdom of the serpent and the dove all in one. If I survive this next week I'm going to know what you were doing before you settled into your bagman's job."

Early next morning Adam saw Amos and dispatched him on an errand. An hour later Amos telephoned and his voice was grave.

"I've seen him, Mr. Milford. Things is waur than I thought. The man's bleezin' mad. He's a sort of a fisherman, and I said it was a grand mornin' and proposed that him and me should take a day on the Nesh. I saw that his thoughts were far awa' from fishing, but he agreed. He said he wanted to get a look at the countryside, for, says he, this is likely my last day on earth. He has a pistol in his pooch, and I can see that he's ettlin' to kill Joe and syne do awa' wi' himsel'. He has gotten his resolution up to the stickin' point, and means the blackest kind o' business. Joe's been in no danger afore, for the body hadna made up his mind, but now he's for it. What about speeritin' Marrish away for a month or two in the hopes that he will cool down? I could maybe arrange it. . . ."

"No, no," said Adam, "that would only postpone the reckoning. I'll join you at one o'clock at the bend of the Nesh below Applecombe Mill. Then I'll judge for myself. If he's stark mad we'll have him certified, and if there's any rudiments of sense in him we may straighten things out. Keep him off the drink at all costs."

"That'll be easy enough. He hasna tastit for three days. There's ower muckle fire in his heid to want alcohol. . . . Weel,

140

I'll expect ye at yin o'clock. It's no likely I'll have a very cheery mornin'."

Adam reached the river in the high noon of a May day, when the hawthorns were bowed down with blossom, and the water-side meadows were "enamelled", as the poets say, with daisies and buttercups. He was wearing an old suit of rough tweeds, and a broad-brimmed felt hat that gave him something of a colonial air. Amos sat stolidly on the bank watching his float, a figure as square and restful as a tree-stump. Marrish had given up the pretence of fishing and was walking about bareheaded, sometimes throwing a word to Amos, sometimes talking to himself. He looked ill; his face had the yellow pallor of the diabetic, he had not shaved for days, his thick black hair was unkempt, and his eyes were not good to look on. He started as Adam appeared, and his hand went to his pocket.

Amos slowly raised himself to his feet.

"Hallo, Mr. Milford. Are you out like huz for a day's airin'? Man, it's graund weather. But the fish are no takin', for I've had just the yin bite. Maybe there's thunder in the air. D'ye ken my friend, Mr. Marrish? He's out o' South Africa like yoursel'." He consulted an enormous silver watch. "It's about time for our meat. Haud on, and I'll fetch the creel wi' our pieces."

Adam held out his hand.

"I'm glad to meet you, Mr. Marrish. I've heard a lot of you from a friend, Johnny Sprot."

Marrish stared at him for a moment, and then extended an unwilling hand. Adam noted how hot and dry it was. He seemed to be wrestling with a painful memory.

"Johnny Sprot! That's a thousand years ago. I've forgotten all about that."

"Johnny hasn't forgotten," said Adam cheerfully. "He was in London the other day. He constantly talks about you. Says you were his best friend and a comrade of his boyhood and all that, and longs to see you again. Sit down and let's have a crack while old Amos fetches the lunch."

Marrish sat himself slowly on the grass as if his legs were cramped. Adam was so situated that he looked him full in the face, and his kindly domineering manner had its effect. Marrish's

141

hot gaze met his, and Adam's steady grey eyes seemed to hold him fascinated. He stopped jerking his shoulders and his lips ceased to mutter.

"I don't want to hear about Johnny Sprot," he said. "That's all dead and buried."

"Nonsense, man. You can't bury your youth, and you can't bury Johnny. He's the alivest thing on earth—the kind of friend that sticks closer than a brother. I'd rather lose twenty thousand pounds than wreck a friendship."

"I'm done with friends. I have only enemies."

"Well, that's better than nothing, for an enemy may be a friend tomorrow."

"By God, no. My enemies are enemies to the other side of Tophet. I stand alone."

"Not you. You've a wife, haven't you?"

"What the hell has that to do with you?"

Adam looked at him steadily.

"Look here, Mr. Marrish, you've got to mend your manners. When I ask a civil question, I expect a civil answer. I don't stand for insolence."

"You don't," Marrish almost screamed, and half rose to his feet. "Then, by God, you've got to lump it or clear out of this."

His right hand went to his pocket, but Adam was too quick for him. In a single deft movement he had one arm round the other's shoulders, pinioning Marrish's left arm to his side, while his right had grasped the hand in the pocket. Marrish, under-nourished and sick, had no chance against this exercised strength. The pressure of Adam's fingers on the other's right wrist paralysed it. Adam drew out the pistol.

He ignored Marrish utterly and examined the little weapon.

"A pretty toy. Loaded too. Isn't that unnecessary for an English riverside on a summer day? You're a bit of a marksman, Mr. Marrish, aren't you? Johnny had a story of a scrap with some drunken natives at Geduld where you were pretty useful."

Adam turned round and faced him. Marrish was sitting humped up with eyes like a sick dog's.

"Geduld, wasn't it?" he repeated.

"No, it was at the Vlak Reef."

142

"Well, it was a good show, anyway. Take back your gun and keep it for its proper use."

Marrish did not replace the pistol in his pocket. It lay on the grass between them. There was no sign of Amos with the lunch, for that worthy was obeying orders.

"Johnny said you were the best-natured chap going," Adam went on. "You're a little off-colour this morning, aren't you? You look to me like a sick man. Give me your hands. I know something about doctoring."

Marrish, who seemed in a daze, surrendered both hands, and Adam's strong grasp enclosed his wrists, and his cool eyes held the other's fevered ones in a strict control. "Do you remember this?" he asked. "It's not the English way of diagnosis. It's the trick of the old witch-doctor on the Black Umvelos', that you and Johnny Sprot met when you took a wagon-load of stores to peddle in Zululand. But it's mighty sound medicine. . . . Shall I tell you what I learn from the blood in your veins and the pupils of your eyes? You are sick in body, but not deathly sick. There's a whole man behind waiting to be cleansed of its leprosy. You are sick in mind, but not deathly sick, for there's a good fellow behind that ought to be released. But I see in the back of your eyes a small crazy devil. I know that devil well, and out he must come, for he's the source of all the mischief. . . . What a godless fool you were ever to come to Birkpool! You were never meant for a rotten black city like that. It has poisoned your blood and choked your lungs. And you were never meant for the game you've been trying to play—too good in one way—too stiff in your joints also. England wants a darned lot of understanding, and you hadn't the patience to learn. I'll tell you where you should be."

Still holding Marrish's wrists and mastering his eyes Adam began to talk about the High Veld. He had never been there himself, but he had made it his business from his early days at the Staff College to study the atmospheres of many parts of the globe. Once in the Rhineland he had escaped from a dangerous place by talking to a Bavarian of the Wettersteingebirge with apparently intimate knowledge. He knew enough of Marrish's early career to select the highlights. He spoke of prospecting journeys in Lydenburg and the Zoutspansberg, where the uplands break down in forested cliffs to the bushveld, and a man may look across a hundred miles to the blue peaks in Portuguese territory. He spoke of trading journeys in the Low Country, the red, scarred tracks through the bush, the slow milky rivers, and the camp in the evening with the mules kicking at their peg-ropes, and the wood fires crackling, and the guinea-fowl clucking in the trees. He spoke of hot middays on the High Veld, when the pans of Ermelo become in the mirage a shoreless ocean. Above all he spoke of that delectable climate where a man could go to bed supperless and weary on the cold ground and wake whistling with sheer bodily well-being—and of a world where there was hope and horizon, since everything was still in the making. Into Marrish's glazed eyes there came gleams of reminiscence, and now and then a flicker of assent. Sometimes he corrected Adam. "Not the Olifants," he would say. "It was farther north—the Klein Letaba."

By-and-by Adam dropped his wrists. He lifted the pistol.

"Johnny said you used to be a fine shot. Let me see you hit the grey knot in that willow stump across the river, three yards below the big elm."

Marrish automatically took the weapon and fired. He was within six inches of the knot.

"Let me try," said Adam. His shot was an inch nearer.

Marrish fired again, almost repeating Adam's shot.

Adam's next attempt was wide, but he fired a second time and just grazed the knot. Marrish almost plucked the pistol from his hand and sent a bullet plumb into the knot's centre.

"By Jove, that's pretty shooting. Johnny was right. Hallo, the gun's empty. Have you any more cartridges?"

Marrish seemed to awake to a maddened recollection. "Curse you!" he cried. "You've done me in. I wanted those bullets . . . I wanted them today for . . ."

"For what?" Adam asked, and once again he took the other's hands—his hands, not his wrists.

"For my enemy—the man who has ruined me . . . and a last one for myself."

"So?" said Adam. "You're a sicker man than I thought. There's

144

that small crooked devil to be got out of you. Now take your time—very slowly. I want to know all about that little devil."

The hands in Adam's grasp were quivering like a bird that a boy has caged. Marrish was talking rapidly, incoherently, words tripping on each other's heels. His voice had lost its shrillness, and had become low and intense. . . . He told of his coming to Birkpool, his dreams and ambitions, his successes—and then the appearance of the other man who jostled him aside. He did not mention Utlaw by name—he was only "he", as if the figure so dominated the world that even a stranger must recognise the incubus. There followed a long catalogue of injuries evidently carefully tabulated in his mind—many of them childish, but clearly to him a great mountain of wrongs. Little sayings were misconstrued, casual acts perverted, till all his troubles—his journalistic failures, the slights of his party, his poverty, his own ill-health and his wife's—were made to spring from the one tap-root of personal malevolence. Adam let him talk till his confession ebbed away in a moan of misery.

He dropped his hands.

"Poor old chap," he said. "You've made an infernal mess of things."

"Not me . . ." Marrish began.

"Yes, you. For you've lost your pride. You've forgotten the man you once were. Do you mean to say that when you and Johnny were partners you would have ever admitted that any man could down you? When you took a knock you blamed it on the cussedness of things and not on the other fellow. But now, when you've taken a collection of knocks because you're in the wrong groove and a world you don't understand, you're weak enough to put it all on the other chap. You're a fool, Marrish. And a bit of a coward."

"That's a lie. I've faced up squarely. . . ."

"Not you. You've knuckled under, and consoled yourself by putting it all down to an imaginary enemy, and nursing your hate for him till you can't see daylight. That's the behaviour of a sulky child. If you had faced up to things you'd have seen you were in the wrong place, cut your losses, and shifted yourself to a better. . . . Who, by the way, is the man you blame?"

145

Marrish muttered a word, and it was spoken not defiantly but shamefacedly. Adam had planned out beforehand every move in the game, and the slight change of tone told him that he was winning.

"Utlaw!" he cried, and then laughed. "Utlaw! Man, you've been barking up the wrong tree. Utlaw never had a hard thought about you. If he had, he would have scored heavily, for he has made you hate him, and that's the worst affliction you can put on a man. Have you ever had a happy moment since you started this grouch? No. It has come between you and food and sleep, and it's made the whole earth black for you. Utlaw would have scored, if he had wanted to—only he's not that kind of fellow."

"What do you know about him?" Marrish asked fiercely, as if he claimed a proprietary right in his enemy.

"I knew him in the war, where one learned a good deal about other people. Utlaw never in all his days cherished a grudge against anybody. He hasn't time for it—his head is too full of his maggots. He's a good chap, but he's a fool—like you, Marrish—the same kind of fool."

The other lifted his weary eyes.

"I'm a fool all right—Utlaw's a scoundrel," he said.

"No, he's a fool. He's like you—he's in a game where he can't win, and he'll eat out his heart in trying. He wants to build things up, and has all kinds of fine notions just as you had once. But he is working with tools that will break in his hand. He is slaving for people who, in the end, will turn him down. That's the curse of this rotten political game. In two years or five years he will be sitting with a broken heart in the dust among the ruins of his dreams. That is why I call him a fool. But he won't be such an utter fool as you, for he won't have invented an imaginary enemy, and be torturing himself with hating. He has too much guts and sense for that. . . . You thought of putting a bullet into him? Well, if he deserved it he would still have scored off you. He would have made your life a hell with your hate, and you would be putting him out of the world before he had lost his illusions. Not a bad way of dying, you know—only, of course, he doesn't deserve it. If you killed him, it would be like murdering a child."

Marrish had his eyes on the ground. Adam's steady gaze exercised some mysterious compulsion, for slowly he lifted them and looked him in the face. The heat of purpose had gone out of him, and what remained was bewilderment, almost fear.

"You meant your last bullet for yourself? Well, you'd probably make a mess of it. Then you would spend some weeks in a prison hospital till they patched you up. After that would come the trial. If you were well defended, they might find you mad, and put you away during His Majesty's pleasure. A nice kind of life for you! For of course you are not mad. You're as sane as I am. If you were lucky, the judge would put on a black cap, and presently you'd swing. You're a man of imagination—you started life with hopes and ideals—do you realise what the bitterness of those last days would be when you knew that they were all to end with a six-foot drop?"

"I wouldn't mind," the other muttered.

"Don't be too sure. God never meant you for a murderer—you're not a cool hand—when you saw Utlaw's brains on the floor you'd be sick and scared, and as like as not would blow away a bit of your jaw. It often happens that way. But assume that your shot went true. You'd be done with your troubles, you say. Maybe, but you'd also be done with life. You're still a young man. You've been living in a bad dream, but you know that there are still jolly things in the world. This countryside, for instance. You came out today to have a last look at it? Am I right? That shows that you have not lost the capacity for pleasure. When I was talking about the Houtbosch, I saw a spark come into your eyes. You're not the shrivelled husk you think yourself. There's still blood in your veins. Are you going to end all that—for a babyish whim?

"And there's another thing," Adam went on. "You've always been a proud fellow. You've been proud of yourself, and your friends have been proud of you. How are those friends going to feel when they hear that David Marrish has died shamefully—either by his own hand or by the hangman's? . . . And what about your wife? You thank God that you have no children, though there was a time when you didn't feel like that. But you're going to leave a wife behind who trusts in you. You've

147

been a good husband to her, but now you're going to inflict on her the uttermost wrong. . . . A murderer's widow. . . . Without a hope or a penny in the world. . . . You've been kind to her, and nursed her tenderly, and stinted yourself that she might have food and medicine. And now you're going to be savagely, brutally, hellishly cruel to a poor woman who gave you all she had."

For a moment it looked as if Marrish would attack him. The man got to his feet and stood with a contorted face and uplifted arm. Then he seemed to collapse into a heap. He was weeping, bitterly, convulsively, and his meagre body was shaken with sobs.

Adam flung his arm round his shoulders.

"Poor old chap," he said gently. "That's right. Let the tears come. When you've wept enough, you'll be yourself again."

For some time the two men sat there as the afternoon lengthened. Adam's arm seemed to comfort Marrish, and he lay back into the curve of it. Presently the sobbing ceased, and there was a long silence.

"I'm going to take charge of you," Adam said. "Never mind who I am. Say that I'm a healer of sick souls, and that I intend to make a proper job of you. This country's no place for you, and you're going back to the place where your roots are. You've plenty of good work in you, and I'll see that you get it out. Johnny Sprot wants you to join him. He has a tidy handful of propositions up in Rhodesia, and he wants a partner. Among other things, there's a newspaper for you to run. You're a good organiser, and there's a field with Johnny for your talents. . . . Are you hungry? For I am, ravenously, and Amos seems to have gone over the skyline with the lunch. I've got a little two-seater car, and I'm going to take you back to Birkpool. Then I'll tell you what you must do. Get shaved and tidied up, and you and Mrs. Marrish will come and feed with me. I'm at the King's Head. There we'll talk about plans, and tomorrow I'll take you up to London to see some friends. I'm in charge of this outfit, remember, and you must obey orders."

Marrish turned on him a white, tear-stained face. His eyes were quiet now, and a little dim.

"I don't know . . ." he began.

148

"You don't, but never mind that now—you will in time. One thing you do know, that you're the old David Marrish again. . . . Oh, by the way, you've another job before you tonight. You were going to see Utlaw—you had fixed that up, hadn't you? Well, you must keep the appointment just the same. He knows that you've been talking loose about him. Tell him you have come to apologise and make up the quarrel. Say that you have been all kinds of a fool. That's the amends that an honest man makes for an occasional folly. . . . If you like, you can tell him that he's a fool also—that he has got into the wrong game, the same as you, and will find it out some day."

Adam took up the pistol from the grass.

"There! You'd better take that," he said.

Marrish looked at it with a shudder.

"Take it," Adam repeated. "You can't leave it lying here. It's your property."

Marrish took the thing gingerly, as if it had been a hot iron. But he did not replace it in his pocket. Holding it by the muzzle he hurled it from him high into the air. It fell in the middle of the stream, and he watched till the last ripple made by it had died away. He had the face of one performing an act of reparation.

That night Utlaw came up and sat on Adam's bed. He looked like a man dog-tired but very happy.

"It's all over," he said. "I've seen Marrish. He asked for an appointment tonight, and I gave it him. I did all you advised me—nobody about, the key lying on the table ready to hand him, nothing to defend myself with—but I felt like a criminal going to the gallows. I opened the door to him myself, and I can tell you my knees were knocking together. . . . Then a miracle happened. I didn't offer him the key—I saw at the first glance there was no need. He looked quiet and sober and— and—kindly. Yes, kindly. He said he had come to apologise for playing the goat. Apparently he is leaving Birkpool at once. . . . We sat down and smoked a pipe together, and had a long friendly talk. I blame myself for not having had it all out with him before—it's a lesson to me I shall never forget. It was all a hideous misunderstanding. The man's a thundering good fellow—

149

a better fellow than me by a long sight. He has brains, too. He knows the difficult job I've got, and talked acutely about it—told me I was a bit of a fool myself for trying to do the impossible. We parted like long-lost brothers, and he's going to keep me posted about his doings. . . . Then I went round to see Florrie, and took her out and gave her supper, for neither of us has been able to eat a bite today. We both felt as if we had got a reprieve. She's fallen for you completely, Milford, and by God, so have I. You're the kind of friend to go to in a fix. . . . As I say, I've learned my lesson. Never funk trouble. It's Mount Everest when you fight shy of it, but when you face up to it it's a molehill. . . . Whew! I'm weary. I'm going to bed to sleep a round of the clock."

Adam did not go to bed. He sat and smoked long into the night. He thought of Utlaw; now that he had faced death in cold blood Utlaw would be twice the man he had been. But chiefly he thought of himself.

This was the kind of thing that he could do, for which his long training fitted him. But the other job—the main job? He believed that he had found the quality that he sought in three men, but it was still only potential, it had still to be shaped to leadership. At any moment one or the other, or all three, might crack in his hands. In his hands! That was the trouble. Had he the power, the brain, the mastery, to shape the career of a fellow-mortal? For a black moment of disillusion he felt that such a purpose was sheer arrogance. It was a task which should be left to God, and who was he to thrust himself in as God's vicegerent?

CHAPTER II

I

AS Adam dressed for dinner in his little Temple bedroom, which looked out on the top of a dusty plane tree and a flat-chested building of old brick, he had one of his rare moments of introspection when he tried to orientate himself with the world.

He was living a normal life again, in close contact with his fellows. To that he had schooled himself—not without difficulty after his six years of solitude. He had a task before him which absorbed all his energies of mind and body, but he had early realised that he must fail if he regarded people as only figures in a mathematical problem. So he laboured to cultivate the common sympathies. But he knew that his success was limited. He understood them and could use them, but they did not deeply move him. Marrish was a case in point. He had saved the man from disaster, and Marrish's letters now were full of a doglike worshipping affection. But for Marrish himself he had no strong feeling; he had been only an incident in Utlaw's life. Utlaw was the vital matter. Yet how much did he care for Utlaw apart from Utlaw's political career? . . . Adam laid down his brushes and regarded his face in the mirror. All his emotions were now tenuous things with a utilitarian purpose. Might not this lack of an ultimate human warmth be fatal in some critical hour?

It was the same, he reflected, with other things. He nominally shared in the ordinary tastes and pursuits of his kind, but how much did they mean to him? He was a brilliant fisherman, but he fished only to get solitude for his thoughts. Books he read only to extend his knowledge, the conversation of his fellows he welcomed only for the light it cast upon the talkers. The beauty of nature and of art scarcely affected him. He had no weaknesses of the flesh, no foibles of the mind. Had he any friends for whom he felt the true unself-regarding passion of friendship? Stannix, perhaps. Lyson, maybe? Kenneth Armine? He was not certain. He realised suddenly that he was living in a world where all things, except the one, were dim and subfusc and shadowy.

But was this wholly true? What of that steady exhilaration of his which was like a recovered youth? He had no need for stoicism. In his dingy Birkpool room, in the monotonous life to which for months he would condemn himself, he had never a moment of ennui. There seemed to be an inner fount of cheerfulness always flowing. His cause was an anchor to keep him steady, but it could not give this perpetual afflatus of spirit like a May morning.

He had no need to ask himself the reason. There was a secret world waiting for him across whose border he could step at will. It was only in moments of reflection like this that he understood how large a part Eilean Bàn played in his life. Half his time was spent among its cool winds and shining spaces. For him it was all that art and literature could give. How could he be rapt by the sight of a lush English meadow or a flowery woodland when his heart was given to his own place—the spire of Sgurr Bàn, the thymy downlands, the singing tides of the western sea? . . . And Nigel who trotted by his side and talked the wise talk of childhood. He had retained humanity because Nigel and Eilean Bàn were the passion of his innermost heart. His secret world was no lotus-eating paradise where a man squandered his strength in dreams. It was rather a vantage-ground which gave him a Pisgah view of the things of common life, and a half-contemptuous empire over them.

He laughed as he finished dressing, for he thought how inviolable was his secret. He went a great deal about in London, and had been at some pains to keep up a pretence of the commonplace. A few people, his old friends, knew something of him, but they respected his desire to be inconspicuous. The others, the men and women he casually met, regarded him as an agreeable, well-mannered *rentier* who filled a place at a dinner-party, took a gun at a shoot, and joined in a rubber of bridge at the club. He was aware that he was popular, since he trod on no toes and stood in no-one's light. . . . Women rather liked him, but women interested him not at all. Jacqueline Armine perhaps was an exception. With her he had advanced to a certain intimacy, for there was something about her which reminded him of Nigel. One or two had shown a desire for friendship, or at least flirtation, but his reserve had warned them off. He could, when he chose, become as wooden as a fence-post.

As he filled his cigarette case he remembered that there were two people who had seemed to detect more in him than he wished to reveal. The first was Warren Creevey, who was becoming a very notable figure in the public eye. On one side he was a professional sophist, a master of brilliant dialectic, who delighted in maintaining paradoxes of his own, and still more in shattering the platitudes of other men. But he was also a great figure in the City, a bold speculator in the wavering exchanges of the globe, and at the same time an acute economist who was frequently taken into the conclaves which discussed international settlements. Creevey had shown some wish for his acquaintance. They rarely met without Creevey trying to probe him with his delicate scalpel.

The other was Mrs. Pomfrey. Of her he had no fear, for she made no advances, but he had a lively curiosity about her. He was aware of her as a quiet figure with intelligent eyes, content to wait in the background, but wielding enormous power in her apparent detachment. She had succeeded in imposing her personality on contemporary life without obviously exerting herself. She had of course the advantage of great wealth. Her husband had been a shipowner whose fortune had become colossal during the war, and at his death, just before the Armistice, all of it had been left to her. The Pomfreys had come to London from the North in 1912, and, though they professed to be plain folk without social ambition, their house in Charles Street had very soon become a meeting-place for important people of diverse types. The attraction was the wife, for Pomfrey was a silent man, concerned with the cares of many businesses. Lilah Pomfrey had no beauty to help her, and only a sketchy education. She had been her husband's secretary in far-off days, and came out of a middle-class Northumbrian home; her one affectation was that she was disposed to exaggerate the humility of her origin, and to speak of herself as a "daughter of the people". She was short and powerfully built—had she been a man her physical strength would have been remarkable. Her face was broad, with strong cheekbones and a wide, kindly mouth; her colouring was a little dusky, and with her coal-black hair and dark eyes it suggested some trace of gipsy blood.

Most people when they talked of her set down her attraction to her gift of sympathy and her staunch fidelity. She never betrayed a confidence and was the most loyal of friends; she had proved on more than one occasion that she could also be an unforgiving enemy. She had succeeded where her rivals had failed. Lady Bland ruthlessly pursued every notable, and by dint of much asking swept a motley crowd of celebrities into her drawing-room, but she remained a comic figure and the target for malicious gibes. Mrs. Macrimmon collected bored royalties, most of them foreign, but her fame was confined to the picture papers. Mrs. Diamond from Chicago made a speciality of youth, and was consequently a frequent character in the novels of youth, and now and then the subject of odes in *vers libres* by young poets. These all had an ambition to be queens of salons to which intellect would gather and which would be a power-house of many movements; but their much-paragraphed entertainments were like circuses which were forgotten utterly when the last performer had made his bow.

Mrs. Pomfrey was different. She did not seek, she was sought; her invitations were to most people like royal commands. She spoke little, but what she said in her deep voice with its pleasant north-country burr was remembered. She dispensed not enter-tainment but friendship. Men of every type, leaders in finance and politics, were believed to seek her advice, but, since she was not vain, she never talked about it. . . . Adam was nervous when he caught her deep, appraising eyes fixed on him. Twice she had asked him to dinner, and both times he had found an excuse for declining.

154

Tonight he was dining with Lady Flambard in Berkeley Square. Sally Flambard was Mrs. Pomfrey's exact opposite, like her only in the absence of vanity. She was slight, fair, and volatile as a bird, living, as a French admirer once said, perpetually *sur la branche*. All that was new intoxicated her, but the waves of novelty passed through her life and left no mark. The basis of her character was her eager interest in things, and her human warmth. She was prepared to do battle to the death for her friends, and never refused a challenge, but her affection was not yoked with prudence, and those who liked her best had to be most on their guard. She was popular because of her power of aerating the atmosphere, but she was a dynamo, not an anchor. Those who went to Mrs. Pomfrey for counsel sought Lady Flambard's company for stimulus.

There were five people in the long, low drawing-room, which was dim with summer twilight. Sir Evelyn Flambard had gone down to the country to look at his young horses, so there was no host. Creevey, wearing knee-breeches and decorations, for he was going on to a ceremonial ball, was talking to Jacqueline Armine. The latter rose at Adam's entrance and came forward.

"Bless you, Adam," she said, "where have you been hiding yourself? Ken is dying to see you. He's Mayor of Birkpool, you know, and he's down in that filthy city today talking sense to town councillors. No, we're at the Court—we've no town house this summer—economy, I say—self-indulgence, Ken says, for he hates London. Have you heard the news about Frank? He has taken St. Mark's—the living is in the gift of the Corporation, and they were lucky to get him. . . . Hallo, here he is. Not dressed, too, like a sordid Member of Parliament. That's an affectation, for he can't be as busy as all that. . . ."

Lady Flambard took Adam's arm.

"You take in Mrs. Pomfrey. You know her, don't you?"

He bowed to a lady in the dusk behind Jacqueline. Mrs. Pomfrey was going on to the same ball as Creevey and wore a wonderful gown of black and red. Her jewels were emeralds. Adam realised anew the air of substance she carried with her—not material only, but a certain tough solidity of spirit. She

155

seemed like one who could command all the apparatus of life, moving in a sphere in which she was securely at home. Beside her Jacqueline Armine and Sally Flambard looked like gossamer visitants from a more rarefied planet. Frank Alban, too, with his lean plain face and shabby clothes, suggested failure, disquiet, the uncomfortable struggles of a lower order of things. But Creevey paired well with her, and it seemed appropriate that they should both be in gala dress. They were both assured and successful children of their world.

At the little round dinner-table Adam sat between Mrs. Pomfrey and Jacqueline. Sally Flambard and Frank Alban at the start did most of the talking. His hostess had much to say of Frank's flight from London.

"Don't tell me it's the call of duty. You're afraid, Frank, black afraid of the worshipping ladies in trouble about their souls."

"Not their souls," said Jacqueline. "Their emotions, my dear. It's the idle young women in search of a new sensation who scare Frank. Well, he won't have any in Birkpool. We've not a feminised society down there. Ken has forbidden me to powder my nose in public."

"Frank's afraid of women," said Sally firmly. "That's the drawback of British youth. In my country we bring up boys and girls together so that they mix naturally, but here you still hanker after the convent and the monastery till they reach what you call years of discretion. But discretion has to be learned and you expect it to come in a single dose. In America we break in our young bit by bit."

"It works well with your adorable ladies," said Creevey. "But what about the men?"

"They're well enough. A little apt to be run by their womenkind, but that's a fault on the right side. If I have any doubt it's about the girls. They don't transplant well. Our bright, brittle young things should marry into their own kind. I know I'm giving away my case to Lilah, who hates Englishmen marrying Americans. But take me—I'm a warning. I love every inch of England, but I shall never belong here. If I hadn't Evelyn to anchor me, I should be the most *déraciné* thing alive."

"What has an angel to do with roots?" Creevey asked.

"You should have been an American, Mr. Creevey," Sally replied. "That's just the kind of heavy compliment our menfolk are always paying. I mean what I say. When I look at the way you Englishwomen have your feet in your native mud, I could howl with envy. I know my cottagers at Flambard and all their troubles, and I doctor their babies, and look after the district nurse, and run a Women's Institute, and get up every sort of show, and yet I no more belong there than my pekinese."

"No, no, my dear," said Jacqueline. "You're a model. I wish I did my duty by Armine Court as you do yours by Flambard. All of us today are hopping about on the twigs. Ken gave me a talking-to yesterday—said I was of a composition to which water would add stability! He got that out of some book, and was very pleased with it."

She turned to Creevey, who was her neighbour on the left.

"We're becoming a new type—physically, I mean. There's very little need for slimming now. I agree with Julius Caesar— I prefer people about me that are fat and comfortable, and I can't find them. Look at us here. Sally and I are wraiths, and Frank is a mere anatomy. I often feel as wispish as a leaf in the wind. I want to be substantial. Lilah and Mr. Creevey are better, but of course they're not plump, and Adam looks like a prize-fighter in hard training. What has become of the nice, easy-going, well-padded people with soft voices and wide smiles? We don't breed 'em nowadays."

"What about Jimmy Raven?" someone asked.

"Oh, Jimmy! He used to be a beautiful young man, and now he is fat and waddles—but that's because he has taken up with some slushy religion, and believes that there is no such thing as pain or wickedness, and that we're all in a Pullman express bound for the Golden Shore. Charles Lamancha says it's biol-ogy—that atrophy of mind is usually attended by hypertrophy of body. Have I got the words right?"

"We're lean," said Creevey, and his voice belied his words, for its chalky richness seemed to argue a eupeptic body—"because we're dissatisfied, and that is not a bad thing to be. We're all seekers."

Adam glanced across the table at Frank and saw a whimsical

look on his face. These were the very words he had used during that walk home through the Birkpool streets.

"Seekers after what?" Frank asked. "A City of God? Or only some new thing?"

Creevey raised his massive head, and his eyes had an ironic seriousness.

"You can give it any fine name you like. Geraldine says it is a land fit for heroes, and President Wilson says it is a world fit for democracy, and the little poets call it a new renaissance. But we are not so much the slave of words today, and these pretty things are only meant for perorations. The motive at the base of everything is money. Call it economic stability if it pleases you, but that only means money. Everyone wants more out of the pool—workman, master, professional man, *rentier*, statesman, people. What's behind the League of Nations? Not the horror of war, not humanity, except in the case of a few old ladies and imaginative youths. It's disgust at having to waste good money in blowing things to bits."

"But Ken says that there is no pool to grab things out of," put in Jacqueline.

"My dear lady, there will always be a pool, and clever people will always have their hands in it."

"But what is to happen," Frank asked, "even if the pool turns out to be large enough and a great multitude can have a share in it? What are they going to do with their share? Is the new millennium to be like a Brighton hotel, all upholstery and rich cooking and a jazz band?"

"Why should it? Comfort need not be gross, it may have all the refinements. You can't have civilisation without money behind it. The great day of Athens was when she was cock of the Aegean and levied tribute from her dependencies. I'm no materialist, but I thank my stars I live in an age when people have an eye for facts. A little sound biology is what is needed. You've got to have a quantitative basis, as the wiseacres say, for qualitative progress."

"But how if quality is choked by quantity?" Frank asked.

"It needn't be. That's one of the arbitrary antitheses that your profession is always inventing—God or Mammon, the Church

158

or the World, the Narrow Road or the Broad Road, and so forth. Quality may be choked by quantity, but it will most certainly be starved by scarcity."

Adam, who had been talking to Mrs. Pomfrey, addressed Creevey for the first time.

"Perhaps you're right that the money motive is predominant with everybody. But assume that the confusion of the globe is only beginning, and that in a year or two the whole economic fabric will be cracking. Assume too that the only hope of saving it will be by a great effort of discipline and sacrifice. Will you get that effort merely for the money motive? Mustn't you bring in an altogether different kind of appeal?"

Creevey shrugged his shoulders.

"I don't think there need be any cracking if people show common sense. If there is, you won't mend it by any of the old-fashioned appeals. The world is out of the mood for them. It doesn't understand the language."

He broke off to answer a question from his hostess. Mrs. Pomfrey was speaking in her low-pitched husky voice, and Adam had to incline his head to catch her words.

"I think Mr. Creevey is wrong," she said. "Our troubles are only beginning, and we need a change of heart if we are to meet them. I want to see a new Crusade, and I want Mr. Alban to be its Peter the Hermit."

Frank Alban opposite seemed to be trying to catch her words, and Adam repeated them. The young man laughed, but there was no mirth in his laugh.

"I wish I had Peter the Hermit's job. It was a simple affair to persuade men who believed in God to set out to reclaim God's holy city from the infidel—and to go with them. To go with them, to share all their hardships and dangers. I have to persuade people that there is a God at all, and to make them believe that evil is a more awful thing than pain, and that a starved soul is worse than a starved body. I can't tell them to pack up and follow me across the globe—that would be straightforward enough. I can only tell them to go on as they are and grub along in their deadly monotonous lives. And the infernal thing is that I can't join them. I can't make my life like theirs.

159

If I tried it would only be a pose and they would see through it. People like me need never fear an empty belly or the loss of a roof over our heads. A preacher should be a little bit above his hearers, and I feel most of the time below mine. When I see a woman with a thin face and hands worn to the bone with toil, or a middle-aged workman struggling to keep his job against the handicap of failing strength—then I feel that my job is an infernal imposture. I wish that I were a penniless Franciscan in the fifteenth century, because then we should all be on a level. Only you can't put back the hands of your accursed clock. I'm suffering from the nightmare of other people's poverty . . . and I sometimes think that the nightmare is worse than the fact."

Mrs. Pomfrey nodded. "I think I know what you mean. But may not your suffering give you power? It will sharpen your sympathy."

She turned to Adam. "Don't you agree with me?"

"Melfort doesn't know what we mean," Frank said. "He's the real Franciscan if you like. He has been through so many kinds of naked hell that a consumptive tramp on a winter day expects more from the world than he does. He is the man who should be at my job—only if my perch is too low his is too high, and he could never drag an ordinary fellow within sight of it."

Adam shook his head.

"Nonsense, Alban," he said, "I can't lead men. The best I can do is to help those who can."

Mrs. Pomfrey turned to him.

"I wish you could tell me something about yourself," she said. "I have only heard rumours. But I am afraid you won't. You seem to me the only modest person left in an advertising world." She looked on him with her friendly eyes, and then turned them on Frank, and Adam seemed to see in the way in which she regarded the other something more than friendliness, something possessive and affectionate.

Jacqueline had caught a word.

"Modest!" she exclaimed. "You're utterly wrong, Lilah. Adam is the most immodest creature alive. We are wistful waifs compared to him. He knows where he is, and knows it so clearly that he never troubles to explain. Mr. Creevey says that we are

160

all seekers today. I don't think Adam is one. He has found something—only he won't tell."

Creevey lifted his head, which as usual had sunk between his broad drooping shoulders. He looked at Adam with his inscrutable, challenging smile.

"That is my notion of success," he said, "to have found what you want and to be able to keep it to yourself. Only there is no standing still in life. What one man has found may conflict with what others are seeking, and he may have to fight to retain it."

He lifted his glass of port.

"I drink," he said, "to the success of the best man. That the best should win is all that matters."

Afterwards, in the drawing-room, Adam talked to Jacqueline Armine.

"I can't make Ken out," she said. "I seem to have entirely lost the hang of him. He came back from the war declaring that he meant to enjoy himself for the rest of his natural life. He was crazy about the Court, and started putting it to rights—got the coverts tidied up, and began to rear pheasants in the old way. He spent a lot of money on the farms, far more than he'll ever get back. He wouldn't take the hounds, but he hunted regularly twice a week. Then you know how keen he is about horses—he has every kind of theory about how to breed up to an ideal—and he talked about a racing stable. Well, he seems to have forgotten all that. He's had a call, and has gone dotty about the public service, and I find it very wearing to keep pace with him.

"No, it's not Birkpool only," she said in reply to a question of Adam's. "It was quite natural that he should be Mayor—that's a family tradition. It's everything else. He naturally wishes he was in the House—not the Lords, but the Commons—he has so much he wants to say. You've seen from the papers that he has taken to making speeches? He has heaps of queer friends up and down the country, and they arrange meetings for him. Pretty strong meat he gives them too. The seventh Marquis has been sending anxious wires, and small wonder, if Ken said half the things he's reputed to have said! He's a mixture of high Tory

161

and rampant Bolshie—says he doesn't care a hoot for democracy and all the old Victorian idols, but that we have got to preserve the stamina of England, and that it can only be done by facing facts and having a fresh deal. He has big meetings and plenty of opposition, for he slangs all sides impartially, but it looks as if he were getting a following, and where it's to end I'm blessed if I know. The idyllic existence I had hoped for is all in smithereens."

"What about Birkpool?" Adam asked.

"Birkpool!" she exclaimed. "That's going to be a tough proposition. Instead of being content with a few functions—Lady Armine's Charity Ball, the Mayor's dinners—that sort of thing, after the peaceful fashion of his forbears, he must needs stick his nose into all the unsavoury corners, and shout his criticisms from the rooftops. He has quarrelled with half the councillors because he told them they were silly old men who didn't understand their silly old jobs. He is on to housing at present—says it's a howling scandal, and that he'll show up the grafters if he has to spend the rest of his days fighting libel actions. He has managed to hang up the new Town Hall—says that Birkpool must wash its face first before it thinks about a bib and tucker.

"Popular?" she went on. "Ken will always be popular with his own kind. Most of the respectables hate him and blackguard him in private, but they are too great snobs to attack him openly. The press crabs him respectfully and regretfully. The man in the street is ready to cheer him on as he would back a dog in a fight. I do my best to keep the peace by making love to the womenkind of the magnates. I stuff the Court with weekend parties that need the tact of an archangel, and my face is perpetually contorted in an uneasy smile. . . . Adam, I verily believe you had something to do with all this. Ken is constantly quoting you. If you have, you have done an ill turn to a woman that always wished you well."

"I think you rather like it," said Adam.

"I don't dislike it—yet, for I love a row. But I'm worried about where it is going to lead. I'm a wife and a mother, and I want peace. Birkpool is rapidly becoming a powder magazine. There's Ken, and there's the Labour man Utlaw. Of course you know him. And you know his sweetheart, too. There's a clever girl if you want 'em clever. I've made great friends with Miss Florence Covert, pronounced Court. I like Utlaw, and Ken swears by him, but the association of the two bodes trouble. Ken, if you please, is President of the Conservative Association, and spends most of his time with the Labour leaders, so honest Tories feel as if they were standing on their heads. Utlaw's salvation will be his wife—they are to be married next month, you know. You thought her very rabid and class-conscious. So she is, but I'm not quite sure which class. It may not be her husband's. . . . And last of all there's Frank, and he's the worst. It's hard luck for Birkpool that all the high explosives should be concentrated there. God knows what will happen when Frank gets into his stride, and adds the thunder of Sinai to the very considerable noise which Ken and Utlaw are making. Lilah may get her Peter the Hermit after all accompanying the crusade to Westminster."

She looked across the room to where Creevey and Mrs. Pomfrey were talking in a corner. The two heads seen in the shadowed light had a certain resemblance in their suggestion of massiveness and restrained power.

"What, by the way, do you make of Lilah?" she asked. "No, I forgot, you never attempt hasty summaries of people. You've only just got to know her? Well, I'll give you the benefit of my larger knowledge. Lilah fascinates me—she is so good, so unscrupulously good. There is no trouble she won't take to help a friend, and there's none, I believe, she wouldn't take to down an enemy, if she had one. She is always quite convinced that she is on the side of the angels. How blessed that must be! I wish I had half her conviction."

"She has an odd face," said Adam. "What do you read in it? A woman is the best judge of a woman."

"I read heart—genuine goodness of heart. I read brains. There's no doubt about that. I haven't any myself, but I can recognise them and admire them from afar. Ask Kit Stannix, and he will tell you that she knows more and can reason better than most men. . . . I read also complete lack of imagination. She has sympathy, but it is of the obvious kind, without insight—and she has no wings. She is devoted to brother Frank, and very good for him. She may be his salvation, just as Florence Covert may be the salvation of Utlaw. Oh no, I don't mean that they're in love or will ever marry. Frank is not the marrying kind, and Lilah has had all the matrimony she wants. But she will keep his feet on the ground, and prevent him becoming an ineffectual angel. . . . You don't look as if you liked the prospect. I believe you have a morbid weakness for angels."

II

After his marriage Utlaw moved to a little raw house in the Portsdown Road, and Adam occupied his former rooms on the ground floor in Charity Row. This was convenient in many ways, for it enabled him to put up Amos in his old room, when that worthy descended upon Birkpool from the North. Also he could leave the house inconspicuously at odd hours without distracting Mrs. Gallop.

In these days he had gone back to his former habits. The bagman remained only for the benefit of his landlady and the Utlaws. Marrish, before he left England, had put him in touch with the disgruntled section of Birkpool Labour, and with Amos's help he had penetrated to circles which even the Utlaws scarcely touched. He was now a Scot, back from South Africa, who had been much about on the Continent, and had the name of an extremist. He talked little, but he looked the part of a maker of revolutions, and hints from Amos skilfully established that repute. So bit by bit he got the confidence of the wilder elements without scaring the moderates. One conclusion he soon reached. He felt under his hand the throbbing of a great unrest which must sooner or later be dangerous. There was no confidence in the masters, and less in the Government; so soon as the economic strain began—and that was daily drawing nearer—there would be a perilous stirring of overwrought nerves and puzzled brains.

But there was confidence in Utlaw—that was plain. Even the fiercest was not prepared to do more than respectfully criticise.

The man had some demonic power which gave him an unquestioned mastery. Perhaps the main reason was that which Amos had once given, that he was Englishness incarnate, and therefore a natural leader of Englishmen. His familiar kindliness endeared him even to those who suffered from the rough edge of his tongue. He was credited with illimitable "guts". His joyous ribaldries were affectionately quoted. They were proud of him, too—he had placed their Union on the national map in a way that old Deverick had never done—he was a "coming man", and when he arrived his followers would not be forgotten. Deverick was due for retirement soon, and Utlaw must be his successor. There was talk of Parliament, too. Birkpool chuckled to think how Joe would batter the hard faces there, and set the frozen feet jigging.

One afternoon Adam went to call on Mrs. Utlaw. Jacqueline Armine had warned him of a change in that young woman.

"We had the Utlaws at the Court for the weekend before last," she told him. "It was rather a wonderful menagerie even for me. We had three couples of Birkpool grandees: Sir Thomas and Lady, Sir Josiah and Lady—war knights, you know—and the Clutterbucks, who have just bought the Ribstones' place and are setting up as gentry. Rather nice couples they were, very genteel, very mindful of their manners, and the womenkind had the latest Paris models. Their fine feathers made me feel a crone. Then we had the Lamanchas by way of pleasing Birkpool, and I must say Mildred played up nobly. But the real yeast in the loaf was the Utlaws. Do you know, Adam, that's an extraordinary fellow? He can lay himself alongside any type of man or woman and get on with them. He had been having all kinds of rows with the grandees and been calling them outrageous names, and making game of them, which is what they like least, but he hadn't been an hour in their company before they would have fed out of his hand. I think it's his gift of liking people and showing that he likes them. He had them roaring at his jokes, and I believe they actually came to regard him as a sort of ally, for I heard old Clutterbuck confiding to him some of his grievances against Ken. Charles Lamancha, too. You know how he behaves—elaborately civil to anybody he regards as an inferior, but shockingly impolite to his equals. Well, Charles was very

165

polite to the grandees, but he wasn't polite to Utlaw, and that's the greatest compliment he could have paid him. It was 'Sir Thomas' and 'Sir Josiah' and 'Mr. Clutterbuck', but it was 'Utlaw' and 'Don't be a damned fool'—Charles's best barrack-room form. I believe he asked him to stay with him when he could take a holiday—I know he liked him—you could see it in Charles's crooked smile. How does Utlaw manage it? I suppose it was his regimental training which has made him at home with Charles's type. He would have made a great diplomat if he had been caught young."

"And the bride?" Adam asked.

"That was the greatest marvel of all. Florrie—oh, we're on Christian terms now—was the perfect little lady. She cast back to her great-grandmother, who I believe was a Risingham. You would have thought she had spent all her life in the soft, lazy days of an old country house. She had the air, you know, of helping Mildred and me to put the Birkpool people at their ease. No effort, no show, very quiet and modest, but perfectly secure. She's beginning to learn how to dress herself, too. All the men fell in love with her, and Mildred took her to her bosom, and you know that our dear Mildred is not forthcoming. But I could see that the grandee ladies hated her. Not that she patronised them, but they could feel that she was of a different type, and they weren't prepared for it. That young person is going to raise antagonisms which her husband won't find it easy to settle."

The Utlaws' house was the ordinary suburban bungalow, but its mistress had made the interior delightful. It was furnished with economy and taste, the little drawing-room was full of flowers and books, and Adam was given tea out of very pretty china. Jacqueline was right. Florrie Utlaw had begun to take pains with her appearance. Her hair was better waved, her face was less thin, and a new air of well-being revealed its charming contours, while her deep eyes, though hungry as ever, were also happy.

She greeted Adam with a quiet friendliness. He was on her man's side, and therefore she was on his. She had given up her job at Eaton's she told him—Joe had insisted—and now she reigned in a little enclave of their own, which was going to enlarge itself some day into a great domain.

There was none of the uneasy inverted snobbery in her manner which he had formerly noted. She talked briskly of affairs and personages in the world in which Utlaw was making his mark, but with a cool, businesslike air. She condescended a little to Adam, for he was not of that world; he was not a person to be cultivated for any use he might be—only to be welcomed for his loyalty. . . . Of Judson, him of the smashing repartees, once to her a demigod, she was frankly critical. "He's so rough that people believe him to be a diamond," she said. "That's not mine, it's Joe's. I think the men are growing a little tired of him—the perpetual steam-hammer business is getting to be a bore." Gray was still a hero, for he had magnetism and poetry. About Trant, the party leader, she was enthusiastic. Joe had been seeing a lot of him lately, and was being brought into private consultation. "He is a great gentleman," she said, "for he has no vanity. Joe always says that the man without vanity can do anything he pleases." Friendliness to Joe was, of course, a sufficient passport to her favour, but Adam remembered also that Sir Derrick Trant belonged to a family that had fought at Crécy.

He asked how the new Mayor was doing. Her eyes sparkled.

"You remember what I said when we first met, Mr. Milford? I was utterly wrong. Lord Armine is a real man. He is on the wrong side, of course, but he has courage and big ideas, many of them quite sound. It's great luck that Joe and he were in the same battalion, for they met on a proper basis. They are like two schoolboys when they get together—it's 'Mr. Utlaw' and 'Lord Armine' at the start, and at the end it's 'Joe' and 'Sniffy'. I love Lady Armine, too, and think her perfectly beautiful. You know her a little, don't you? She told me she remembered meeting you."

There was no mention of the Utlaws' visit to the Court. If there was any snobbishness in Florrie, she was too clever to show it.

Chiefly she talked of Joe's career. There was a chance of an early seat in Parliament, for Robson was dying, and the East division of Flackington was in the pocket of the Union. She was anxious for him to get at once into the House. "He needs a proper sounding-board," she said, "to make his voice carry. Meetings up and down the country are all very well, but the papers only report the big men. In the House Joe would be a national figure within six months. He is a deadly debater, not a tub-thumper like Judson. Trant says he would give anything to have him at his back when the Factory Bill comes on."

But the urgent matter was the national secretaryship of the Union when Deverick resigned next month. Mrs. Utlaw's new matronly calm slipped from her and she became the eternal female fighting for her mate's rights.

"It's a test case," she declared. "Joe is far the biggest man in the show, and if it goes by merit nobody else can have a look in. If they pass him over, then there's no gratitude in the movement, and no decency."

She let herself go, and Adam was introduced to a long roll of grievances. It was a thankless job serving the people—plenty of kicks, no ha'pence, and only once in a blue moon a thank you. Florrie twined her fingers, her eyes glowed, and her words were like a torrent long dammed. Adam understood that this was her way of seeking relief; she could do it with him, for he was obscure and safe. He was very certain that to most of the complaints Utlaw himself would never have given a second thought; he had mentioned them in her presence in his expansive way, and she had docketed them and stored them up in her heart. He realised two other things. Florrie—perhaps Utlaw too— was getting a little out of sympathy with the whole Trade Union machine and the political party of which it was the centre. And there was a reasonable chance that Utlaw would not succeed Deverick.

Lord Lamancha, a member of the Cabinet, gave a dinner with a small party to follow, and, since a royal personage was to be present, Adam had to wear his miniature medals. They made a formidable string, for a number of foreign orders had been thrown upon him unsought, dispensed from the pool which his superiors had had at their discretion. He hated displaying them, but it was less conspicuous to fall in with the conventional etiquette than to disregard it. He had accepted the invitation, because a German statesman was to be there whom he wanted to meet.

It was a man's dinner, and his seat was on the right hand of the German guest, whose name was Hermann Loeffler, with on his other side Christopher Stannix. Loeffler was a small spare man who carried himself so well that he seemed to be of the ordinary height. He looked fifty, but was probably younger, for his thick black hair was prematurely grizzled. It grew low on a broad forehead, beneath which the face narrowed till it terminated in a short beard. This beard obscured the lower part, but Adam had a notion that, if the man were clean-shaved, his mouth and jaw would be seen to be firmly and delicately modelled.

Loeffler was in the uneasy German Cabinet—Minister of Commerce, Adam thought—and like most of his colleagues, his career had been variegated. He had begun life as a scholar, and long ago had published a learned work on St. Augustine. Then for a short period he had been a journalist on a famous Rhineland paper, where he had become a friend of Walter Rathenau, who had detected in him a special financial talent and had brought him into the banking business. He had served during the four years of war in a Westphalian regiment, and after the Armistice, again under the aegis of Rathenau, had entered politics. He was sprung from the lower bourgeoisie, and was the kind of man who would never have risen under the old regime, but who might have a career in a middle-class republic. Stannix had praised him—said he was honest and courageous and reasonable, the sort of fellow one could work with.

But it was not Loeffler's political prospects that interested Adam. Once early in 1918 a certain middle-aged Danish businessman called Randers, who had a neat blond moustache and wore big horn-rimmed spectacles like an American, had found himself in a difficult position in a Rhineland town. Circumstances had arisen which caused the military authorities to have their suspicions about this well-credentialled Dane. In particular there had been a Major Loeffler, who had been badly wounded at Cambrai and had been given a base job for six months. Of all his war experiences Adam looked back upon his examination

169

by Loeffler as his severest trial. He had liked him, he remembered, liked his honest eyes and his good manners, and he had profoundly respected his acumen. This was one of the men whom he had hoped to meet again, and the first mention of him in the press had set him following his career.

Loeffler spoke English slowly and badly, though he understood it fairly well, so after he had been engaged in an embarrassed conversation with Lamancha for a quarter of an hour he was relieved when his other neighbour addressed him in German. Excellent German, too, spoken with the idiom, and almost with the accent, of his own district. Adam pushed his name card towards him, and Loeffler read it with eyeglasses poised on the tip of his blunt nose.

"You speak our language to admiration," he said. "Ah, you learned it as a staff officer long ago? You English are better linguists than us Germans—your tongues are more adaptable. Maybe your minds also." He smiled in his friendly, peering way.

They slipped into an intimate conversation, for Loeffler found it easy to be frank with one to whom understanding seemed to come readily and who had an air of good-will. He spoke of the sufferings of his country—the middle-classes for the most part ruined, with all their careful standards of life crumbling about them—world-famous scholars earning their bread by typing and copying—little businesses that had been so secure and comfortable gone in a night. "They are bearing it well," he said. "My people have much stoicism in their bones, and they can endure without crying out." He spoke of evil elements, the financiers who flourished in any *débâcle*, the hordes of the restless and disinherited, the poison of Communism filtering through from Russia. "Yet there is hope. We have a stalwart youth growing up which, if it is well guided, may build our land again. The peril is that even honest men may be tempted to seek short cuts, and the good God does not permit of short cuts in this life of ours. If they are shown a little light, even though it is at the end of a long tunnel, they will endure. But if not—if they have no hope—they may break loose, and that will mean a world-confusion.

"There must be no more war," he said. "Now is the time,

when all men have seen its folly, to purge mankind of that ancient auto-intoxication. But you will not do this only by erecting a supra-national machine for peace. I am a supporter of the League of Nations—beyond doubt, but it is not enough. You cannot have a League without the nations, and these nations must first of all be re-made. Only then can you have a new world-mind. Chiefly Germany and Britain, for these are the key-points. France is a great people unlike all others, but France will never stand out. She will fall in—after protestations—with the general sense of humanity, and presently make herself its high priest and interpreter. That is her *métier*—she gives form to what others originate. America! She is a world to herself, and will walk alone and listen to no-one's advice till she learns the folly of it by harsh experience. Like our practical people she will practise the mistakes of her predecessors till she finds them out. But Germany must set her house in order without delay, for delay means disaster. Britain, too, for you are still the pivot of the world, and if you fall no-one can stand. I am not very happy about your Britain. You will pardon a stranger for his arrogance, but I do not think you are yet awake. We Germans are awake—to a far more difficult task than yours, and wakefulness, however unpleasant, is better than sleep."

He broke off to answer a question of Lamancha's, which had to be repeated twice before he grasped its purport. Adam turned to Stannix.

"Lord, I wish I had your gift of tongues, Adam," the latter said. "I am not much of a judge, but you seem to speak rather better German than Loeffler. . . . You asked me about Utlaw before dinner, and I hadn't the chance to reply. I heard this afternoon that he had missed the Union secretaryship. They have taken Potter. A bad mistake, I think, in their own interest, but that's not any concern of mine. What worries me is its effect on Utlaw. He is bound to be pretty sick about it. I only hope it won't make him run out."

"How do you mean?"

"Forswear his class. Utlaw's strength is that he is class-conscious in the only reasonable way. He knows his people through and through, and, while he is just a little above them so as to give him the vantage for leadership, he is bone of their bone and flesh of their flesh. He is loyal to them and they know it, but he's too loyal to them to tell them lies and mislead them, and they know that too. But he's devouringly ambitious, and a man of his brains won't stand being elbowed aside by nonentities. We mustn't forget the cut-throat competition among the Labour people. There are too many running for the same stakes, and if a man stumbles he's trampled down. It's a far crueller business than in our own jog-trot party. Besides, they are eaten up with vanity."

"Utlaw has no vanity."

Stannix pursed his lips.

"Perhaps not. But all his competitors have it abundantly, and that means that merit isn't given a chance. How can it be if everybody thinks himself God Almighty. . . . I am not so sure that Utlaw has none, either. He wouldn't be human if he hadn't. He has been up here at the Economy Commission, as you know, and has done amazingly well. I've rarely seen a better performance. Made his points clearly and neatly—always ready to meet a sound argument and genially contemptuous of a bad one—prepared to give way with a good grace when necessary—accepted gratefully half a loaf, and adroitly swapped it for a whole one—he has a real genius for affairs. Compliments were flying about, Trant made a pet of him, and Geraldine laid himself out to be gracious. The man couldn't help being flattered. Now what I ask is, with all this reputation behind him, how he is going to take being turned down by his own people."

"I don't think he'll play the fool," said Adam firmly.

"I hope not, but the temptation will be great, and I think too well of him to want him on our side. His strength is to stay where Providence has put him. . . . Happily I don't suppose he could afford to cut the painter. He hasn't a bob, I'm told."

After dinner Adam saw no more of Loeffler, who had a short talk with the royal personage, and then seemed to be engaged in conference with various members of the Cabinet. The Lamanchas' house was well adapted for entertaining, and the big rooms were not inconveniently crowded. Adam found a corner

172

by the balustrade at the head of the main staircase, where he could see the guests arriving in the hall below and the procession upwards to where they were received by the host and hostess. It amused him to watch this particular ritual on the few occasions when he went to parties—the free-and-easy ascent, the sudden moment of self-consciousness as they made their bow, the drifting off into absorbed little coteries. Most people had a party guise, something different in their faces as well as in their clothes, a relapse to the common denominator of the herd. But some retained a rugged individuality and so were out of the picture. Thirlstone, for instance, who looked a backwoodsman however he was dressed, and Manton, the steeplechase rider, whose trousers always suggested breeches.

One man he noted on the staircase who was different from the others. He was taking nothing for granted, for his eager, curious eyes darted about with evident enjoyment, as if he were a child out for a treat. Adam saw that it was Utlaw, rather smart, with a flower in his buttonhole, and a new dress-suit, which had certainly not been made in Birkpool. He saw too that the uplifted face had recognised him, recognised him with surprise. So he did not move from his place, for the time had come to drop the bagman.

Utlaw made his way to him.

"Good Lord, Milford," he said, "what are you doing here?"

"I dined here," said Adam. "The Lamanchas are old friends of mine."

Utlaw's eyes were on his medal ribbons.

"The D.S.O. and a bar. I thought you told me you weren't in the war. You didn't get that for staying at home."

"I didn't say I wasn't in the war. I said I wasn't fighting."

"Your service must have been pretty active, anyway, or you wouldn't have got that. Look here, Milford, what sort of a game have you been playing with me? What about the bagman in Mrs. Gallop's upstairs room?"

Adam laughed.

"You invented that for yourself, you know. I only didn't undeceive you. I went to Birkpool to make friends with you and I hope I have succeeded?"

173

Utlaw's face, which for a moment had clouded, broke into a grin.

"You jolly well have, old chap. And I can tell you I want all the friends I've got. Have you heard that they've turned me down for the Union secretaryship? Dirty work at the crossroads! My lads in Birkpool will have something to say about that. . . ."

He broke off and advanced to greet a lady who had just arrived, and who seemed to welcome the meeting. Adam saw that it was Mrs. Pomfrey.

III

For some months Adam was little absent from Birkpool.

His relations with Utlaw were on a new basis. He was still to most people the commercial gentleman who lodged with Mrs. Gallop, but Utlaw was aware that he played other parts, into which he forbore to inquire, though he showed his awareness by often asking his opinion about this man and that and his views on popular feeling. But he treated him now not only as a friend but as a counsellor, the repository of much knowledge which he did not himself possess.

Clearly Utlaw was going through a difficult time. Robson, though given up by the doctors, obstinately refused to die, and the East Flackington seat, which might have been a consolation for the loss of the Union secretaryship, had not yet come his way. He had lost something of his easy mastery of his job—was no longer "on the top of it", to use his own phrase; he was self-conscious and inclined to be irritable, and Florrie in the background was no peacemaker. He must have told her something of Adam's real position, for she showed a new desire for his society, and would pour out her grievances to him. Her politics now were her husband's career, nothing else. She was inclined to be impatient with any who raised difficulties for him in his daily work, and she was beginning to be contemptuous about the leaders of his party. "There's only one relic of feudalism left in Britain," she used to declare, "the super-fatted, hermetically-sealed, feudal aristocracy of the trade unions. People like Judson and Potter are the real oligarchs. Compared to them Lord Armine is a Jacobin." Adam recognised the sentence from a recent anonymous article in the press, of whose authorship he was now made aware. Florrie was trying to supplement their income by journalism, and succeeding.

It was his business to keep Utlaw to his job in spite of his wife, and he found it increasingly difficult. Utlaw had lost some of his old mastery over his people; he was still a leader, but a leader without any clear purpose. He had lost his single-heartedness, and appeared not to regret it. He invited Creevey to Birkpool to talk to a big debating society which he had founded, and though Creevey's brilliant opportunism may have been unintelligible to most of his audience, it seemed to be acceptable to Utlaw, and it helped to confuse the minds of some of his chief lieutenants. The man's opinions were in a flux. More serious, he seemed to be slipping away from his class. He was less a worker in a wide movement than the chief of a private army of condottieri which he might swing over to any side.

Frank Alban was also difficult. His first months at St. Mark's had been the biggest sensation Birkpool had ever known. The church was crowded, and Frank's sermons, to his disgust, were reported in the popular London press. That soon passed, but he remained a potent influence, and the Albanites became a force in the city. So long as he dealt with faith there was no opposition, but when he turned to works he encountered ugly obstacles. He had a remarkable way of handling boys, and his first big enterprise was a chain of boys' clubs in which he enlisted as fellow-workers an assortment of Birkpool youth. But presently he came hard up against social evils in the employment of boy labour and the eternal housing tangle, and he broke his shins against many educational and industrial stone walls. Birkpool did not know what to make of this turbulent priest who was not content to stick to his own calling, and Frank had moments of bitter hopelessness.

Adam was his chief consultant, and in his case, as in Utlaw's, the difficulty was to keep him to his job. He had much of Newman's gallant intransigence, but that inability to compromise, which gave him his power as a preacher, made his path thorny in practical affairs. The temptation was to retire inside his own soul, the old temptation of the saint. His high-strung spirituality was in perpetual danger of being introverted, and the crusader of retiring to his cell.

In dealing with him Adam had an ally in Kenneth Armine. The Mayor was not a saint, but he was notably a crusader. His father died about this time, and the new Marquis of Warmestre had now the House of Lords as a platform. On several occasions he uplifted his voice there to the amazement of his friends and the embarrassment of his party, and he could draw large audiences in most parts of the land. His creed was a hotchpotch, much of it crude and boyish, but it was preached with amazing gusto, and one or two dogmas stood out like rocks in a yeasty ocean. One was the gravity of the times, since Britain and the world stood at the crossroads. Another was the need for a great effort of intelligence, sacrifice, and discipline if the people were to pull through. When his critics pointed out that much of his stuff was not remarkable for its intelligence, he joyfully agreed. That was not his business, he said; he was no thinker, his job was to stir up the thinkers; but he knew the one thing needful, which might be hid from the wise but was revealed to plain fellows like himself.

"Send brother Frank to me," he would say; "I'll cure him of his megrims. Hang it all, does the man expect to find his job easy? Mine is as stiff as Hades, and it's by a long chalk simpler than his. I'll keep him up to the mark. . . . No, I'm enjoying myself. Jackie hates it, and I'm sorry about that, but I'm bound to go through with it. We've got a chance here, what with Frank and Utlaw to help me, and I'm going to see that we don't miss it. It's the only way, you know. You can't fire the country as a whole—too big and too damp. You must take it bit by bit. If we kindle Birkpool the blaze will spread, and presently we'll have a glorious bonfire of rubbish."

One day Adam visited Scrope at the same house in the Northamptonshire village where he had first met him. He had had a letter from Freddy Shaston telling him that the old man was failing rapidly and could not last long. "He wants to see you, and you must go. Take the chance, for a lot of wisdom will leave the world with him." Adam had come to know Shaston well. A partner in a firm of stockbrokers, his real business in life was to be Scrope's *chela*, to be his eyes and ears for a world in which he could no longer mingle. He had no desire to do anything, only to find out about things; as he said, his job was Intelligence not Operations, but it was a task in which he had few equals.

It was a bleak day in December, and there was no sitting out, as on the first visit, in a garden heavy with autumn blossom. The garden was now sprinkled with snow. Adam found Scrope propped up with pillows in an armchair beside a blazing fire, and the first glance showed him that he had not many weeks to live. The vigour which he had recovered in the war had ebbed, the face had fallen in and the cheekbones stood out white and shining, the voice had lost its crispness and came out slow and flat and languid. But there was still humour and interest in the old eyes.

"I have gone back to sanctuary," he said, "my last sanctuary. I am very near that happy island of which you told me. What, by the way, was its name? Eilean Bàn?"

He looked for a little into the fire and smiled.

"You still frequent it? Not in the body, of course. You cannot go back to it yet awhile. But it is more to you than a pleasant fancy, I think. It is a Paradise to which you will some day return. But you must earn the right to it. Is it not so? . . . You see I understand you, for all my life I too have lived with dreams."

For some time he seemed to be sunk in a feebleness from which he could not rouse himself. He asked questions and did not wait for their answer. Then some wave of life flowed back into his body, and he sat more upright among his pillows. "Give me a cigarette, please," he said, "one of the little black ones in the Chinese box. I allow myself six in the day. Now I think we can talk. . . . Have you found your Messiah?"

"No," said Adam. "I do not think there will be any one Messiah."

Scrope nodded.

"I think likewise. The day has gone when one man could

177

swing the world into a new orbit. It is too large, this world, and people speak with too many tongues. But you have found something? Shall I guess? You have found one who may be a John the Baptist, and you have found an apostle or two? Am I right? You see, I have been trying to follow your doings a little. I have learned much of Birkpool."

"I can have no secrets from you," Adam said. "I have found a man who preaches the fear of God. I have found a man who can lead. And I have found a man who has a fire in his belly and fears nothing."

Scrope mused.

"And your hope is that these may be the grain of mustard seed which will grow into a great tree—an Yggdrasil with its roots in the sea and its shadow over all the land? Something that will bind together the loose soil of the country? Well, I agree with you in one thing. Our malady today is disintegration. We are in danger of splitting into nebulae of whirling atoms. There is no cohesion in any of our beliefs and institutions, and what is worse, we have lost the desire for cohesion. It is a pleasant world for some people. Mr. Warren Creevey, for instance. He loves dilapidation, for it gives scope to his swift flashing mind. Also he makes much money by it. He would keep the world disintegrated if he could, for he has no interest in things that endure. He is a good Heraclitean, and worships the flux. . . . A pleasant world for such as he, but a dangerous world. Do you see much of Mr. Creevey?"

Adam replied that he met him occasionally, but did not know him well.

"No! Then my prophecy is not yet fulfilled that your lines of life would cross. But I stick to it. Somewhen, somewhere, somehow you will do battle with him. . . . And now for the apostles you have discovered."

"Do you know them?" Adam asked.

Scrope smiled.

"I can guess them. Yes, I know a good deal about them. I do not think your discernment has been at fault. But—but!! I would prepare you for disappointments. No one of them is quite of your own totem, and they may fail you. Your John the Baptist

178

may grow weary of the Scribes and Pharisees and flee to his hermitage—or, worse still, to a papal throne. Your leader may lead his people into the desert and lose them there. Your fearless man may become muscle-bound and the fire die out of him. One and all may get soft and sour. That is the trouble of working through other people. Are you prepared for that? You are? Well, what then?"

"I shall find others."

"Doubtless. But they also may fail you. And meanwhile time is passing, and any day crisis may be upon us. . . . You wish to be a kingmaker, but what if there are no kings? The king-maker may be forced in spite of himself to be royal."

Adam shook his head.

"Not this one. He knows his limitations. I have no power except in the shadows."

"I think you may be deceiving yourself. Power is one and indivisible. It is only an accident whether it works behind the scenes or on the stage. . . . Listen to me, my friend. You have a divine patience and have been content to work at that for which you are least fitted—imponderable, monotonous things—a touch here and an adjustment there. You have suc-ceeded—perhaps. But what of those other gifts—your real gifts? You say you have found the man who is fearless. But you yourself fear nothing but God. You have found a leader. But leadership is only courage and wisdom, and a great carelessness of self. Do you lack these things? Will you not be forced some day into the light?"

Once again, as at Birkpool after the Marrish business, doubt descended upon Adam's mind. Scrope's confidence in him seemed to be a searchlight which revealed his own incapacity. He was not a leader, and yet he was essaying the task of a leader—to shape men's souls. Was he succeeding? Could he succeed? Were they not slipping away from him? He had trained himself for one purpose, and that was sacrifice, but in this work the utmost sacrifice of himself would avail nothing. He was attempting a creative task, but had God destined him for any such high purpose? Was not the clay exalting itself above the potter?

A nurse entered to give Scrope his medicine, and to warn

179

Adam that the time permitted by the doctor was up. When she had gone, and Adam was on his feet to depart, the old man held his hand.

"This is goodbye. The troublesome accident we call death will come between us for a little. Presently I return to the *anima mundi* for a new birth. Let us put it in that way, for one metaphor is as good as another when we speak of mysteries. But I believe that I shall still be aware of this little world of time, and from somewhere in the stars I shall watch the antics of mankind. I think I shall see one thing. You will ride beside Raymond into Jerusalem . . . or if you cannot find your Raymond you will enter alone. . . ."

"I shall find my Raymond," said Adam, "but I shall not ride beside him. . . ."

Scrope was not listening.

"Or," he continued, his voice ebbing away into feebleness, "you will leave your body outside the gate."

Falconet had been a regular if not very voluminous correspondent, but he had stuck to his own country. Early in the spring, however, he visited England and occupied his old flat in St. James's Street. He had changed little; he was still lean and dark and hawklike and impetuous, but his full lower lip projected more than ever, as if he had encountered a good deal of opposition and had had some trouble with his temper.

"I'm mighty glad to see you," he told Adam. "I've a whale of a lot to tell you and to hear from you. Which will begin? Me? Right. Well, I've got my layout pretty satisfactory, and it's starting to work. Dandiest bit of organisation you ever saw. Cross-bearings come in a flood whenever I press the button. Any fellow we fancy is passed on by those that don't make mistakes. Result is, we've gotten some high-grade ore, and pretty soon we shall have the precious metal."

"Then you are satisfied?"

Falconet twisted his face.

"I'm satisfied that I'm going to add twenty per cent, or maybe twenty-five per cent, to the net competence of the American people. I'm on the way to grading up its quality. I'm saving for it a lot of fine stuff that would otherwise be stifled in its native mud. . . . That's something, anyway."

"But you don't think it enough?"

Falconet laughed.

"Say, Adam, do you take me for a man that's easy contented? I don't think it enough—not by the length and breadth of hell. I've got some lads that will make good—one of them is going to be the biggest chemist on earth, they tell me—another will make big business sit up in a year or two. Fine work, you say. Yes, but it doesn't come within a million miles of touching the spot. They're going to make their names and their piles, but they're not going to help America one little bit in the thing she needs. They're not considering the real things, and if they were they wouldn't be any manner of good. They're not the type that can swing opinion.

"We're in a mighty bad way," he continued, getting to his feet and, after his fashion, picking up the sofa cushions, pummelling them, and flinging them down again. "Oh, I know we're richer than Croesus—fat as Jeshurun, and consequently kicking. We have drawn in our skirts from poor old Europe in case we are defiled, and we are looking to go on prospering in God's country and letting the world go hang. It won't be God's country long at that rate. Our pikers don't see that in the end they can't keep out of the world any more than they kept out of the war. We're as smug as a mayor of a one-horse township that imagines his burg the centre of creation. How in hell can you get quality into a nation that don't believe in quality—that just sits back and counts its dollars and thanks God that it isn't as other men? What we need is a change of view—not heart, for our heart's sound enough—the trouble is with our eyes. But as I say, there's nobody that can swing opinion. I've done my best, and I've been giving a good deal of attention to my newspapers. You know I bought the *Beacon*. I've got a crackerjack of an editor, and day in and day out we keep on preaching common sense. But we're only read by the converted, and don't cut any ice with the masses. That's the cursed thing about a democracy. In the old days, when you had converted the King and the Prime Minister you had done your job, but now you have got to convert about a hundred million folks that don't know the first thing about the question. Cut out a strip of the East, and we're the most ignorant nation on earth about fundamentals. We have built up a wonderful, high-powered machine that don't allow us to think."

"There's the same trouble everywhere," said Adam. "We're too clever to be wise."

"And that's God's truth. I'm weary to death of clever men. That's what's muddying the waters. And I've gotten to be very weary of your man Creevey. At first I thought him the brightest thing I had ever struck. Well, he is too infernally bright. He has crossed to our side of the water pretty often—three months ago he was over about the French loan, and I can tell you that your Mr. Creevey hasn't been doing any good. He has a great reputation in Wall Street, and our newspapers have fallen for him, for he takes some pains to cultivate them and knows just the sort of dope to hand out. He can make a thing more clear than the Almighty ever meant it to be, and the ordinary citizen, finding its prejudices made to look scientific, cheers loudly and thinks himself a finer guy than ever. He has been doing his best to confirm us in our self-sufficiency. If money was his object, I would say that he was a bear of American securities, and was out to engineer a smash. That's partly why I came over here— to get a close-up of the doings of Mr. Warren Creevey."

Adam asked about Falconet's visit to the Continent.

"I had three weeks in Paris. There Creevey is their own white-haired boy. They told me there that he was the only Englishman with an international mind. . . . Then I went to Germany. That's a difficult proposition, and I haven't rightly got the hang of it. I'm going back next week. But I've got the hang of one German. A little dusty fellow. One of their leading politicians. Loeffler they call him. Heard of him?"

Adam nodded.

"Write his name down in your pocket-book and remember my words. Loeffler is going to matter a lot. He hasn't any cleverness, but he has a whole heap of horse sense, and all the sand on earth. That little man goes in as much danger of his life as a Chicago gangster, and he don't scare worth a damn. I'm going back to Loeffler. . . . And now let's hear what you've been doing."

When Adam had reported, Falconet scratched his head.

"You've got to put me wise about this island," he said. "It's a big disappointment that old man Scrope has died on me. I was sort of counting on a talk with him. . . . Maybe you've been wiser than me. I've been looking too much for brains, and you've gone for magnetism. You must let me in on your game, for I'd like to see your notion of quality. . . . I've heard of your man Utlaw. Say, do you know Mrs. Pomfrey?"

"A little. Have you been meeting her?"

"Yes. I got a note from her when I landed—with a line of introduction from Creevey, no less. I took luncheon with her yesterday. That's a fine lady. I'd like to check up with you on what she told me about England—I reckon she's likely to be right, though, for they tell me she's close to your Government. She has never been in America, but she seemed to have a pretty cute notion of how things were with us. She didn't mention you, but she had quite a lot to say about Mr. Utlaw. Said that in a year or two he would be the only one of the Labour men that counted. Do you pass that? On our side they don't signify—not yet. Our workfolk are too busy buying automobiles and radio sets to trouble about politics. Here I know it is different. But tell me, Adam. Is it healthy for a Labour man to be made a pet of by society dames?"

"I'm not afraid of Mrs. Pomfrey for Utlaw," said Adam. "I'm more afraid of Creevey."

Falconet looked thoughtful.

"Yep. I can see Creevey making mischief there. . . . Well, it's a darned interesting world, though mighty confusing. As my old father used to say when he was running a merger and had all the yellow dogs howling at his heels, it's a great game if you don't weaken."

183

CHAPTER III

I

IN the late summer things began to go ill in Birkpool. The big works had few contracts, and the extension which the war had brought about, and which had rarely been accompanied by any serious reorganisation or replacement of antiquated machinery, was beginning to prove so much adipose tissue. Men were turned away daily, and the programme of forward orders was so lean that the city anticipated a grim winter. One or two small expert businesses were still flourishing, but Birkpool had its eggs in few baskets, and the weight of taxation and the competition of foreign countries were playing havoc with its heavy industries. The minds of those who live by the work of their hands are not elastic or easily adjusted to a new outlook. The ordinary wage-earner was puzzled, angry, apprehensive, and deeply suspicious.

The weather did not improve matters. August is the Birkpool holiday month, and all August a wet wind had blown from Wales. September was little better, and in October gales from the North Sea and the fenlands brought scurries of cold rain. Lowering skies and swimming streets added to the depression which was settling upon Birkpool as thick as its customary coronal of smoke.

On one such day Adam was passing down a side street, where dingy tramcars screamed on the metals, and foul torrents roared in the gutters, and the lash of the rain washed the grease from the cobbles. There was a shabby post office, for in that quarter of Birkpool even the banks and post offices looked shabby, from the swing-doors of which men and women were emerging. They had been drawing their old-age pensions, the women were clutching their purses in their lean, blue-veined hands, and all had that look of desperate anxiety which the poor wear when they carry with them the money that alone stands between them and want. A miserable tramp on the kerb was singing "Annie Laurie" in a cracked voice, and from a neighbouring alley, which led to a factory, there poured a crowd of grimy workmen released at the dinner hour, turning up the collars of their thin jackets against the sleet. The place smelt of straw, filth, stale food and damp—damp above everything.

Outside the post office Adam found Frank Alban. He carried an umbrella which he had not opened, and the rain had soaked his ancient flannel suit. He was watching the old-age pensioners, some of whom recognised him; an old woman bobbed a curtsy, and a man or two touched his cap. But Frank did not return the greetings. He seemed wrapped up in some painful dream.

He gripped Adam's arm fiercely.

"I wanted to see you," he said. "Where are you going? I'll walk with you. Never mind the rain—I like it—a wetting's neither here nor there. I can't talk holding up an umbrella."

"I'm going to my rooms," Adam said. "I can give you luncheon—bread and cheese and beer. And a dry coat. . . . You're a fool to allow yourself to get wet," he added, as Frank coughed.

"I'm a fool—yes. But a risk of pneumonia is not the worst kind of folly."

He said nothing more, but held Adam's arm in a vice till they reached Charity Row, and Adam had insisted on his changing his socks and had sent his coat to be dried in Mrs. Gallop's kitchen.

"Now, what's your trouble?" Adam asked.

"The old one. I'm a misfit. A humbug. I have no business to be here. I'm not tough enough. You won't understand me, Adam, for you're tough in the right way. Most people are only tough because they are callous, but that's not your case. You're tough because there's very few hells you haven't been through yourself and come out on the other side. I'm not like that. I have to tell people to keep a high head and endure what I've never endured myself—what I couldn't stick out for a week. That's why I say that I'm a humbug."

"What has happened? You have done a power of good here."

"Have I?" Frank asked bitterly. "Well, I haven't it in me to do any more. Man, don't you see what is happening? The shadow of misery is closing down upon this place. It's so thick that you can almost touch it. I see the eyes of men and women getting fear into them—fear like a captured bird's. They see all the little comforts they have created beginning to slip away and themselves drifting back to the kennels. They are the finest stock on earth—there's nothing soft or rotten in them, and that's the tragedy. What in God's name can I do for them?"

He checked Adam's interruption with a lifted hand.

"Oh, I know what you are going to say. That my job is to give them a celestial hope to make up for their terrestrial beastliness. I believe in that hope—I believe in it as passionately as ever—but I can't hand it on to them. Why? Because I'm not worthy. I feel the most abject inferiority in my bones. I blush and get cold shivers in my spine when I try it. I ought to be one of them, sharing in all their miseries. I ought to be doing a day's work beside them in the shops, and then preaching to them as to brothers in misfortune. They would respect me then, and I should respect myself. . . . The day of the fatted parson is past. He should be a preaching friar as in the Middle Ages, or a fakir with nothing to him but a begging-bowl and the message of God."

"You wouldn't last long at that job," said Adam.

"I wouldn't. I wouldn't last a month—I'm not man enough. But it's the honest way. Only I can't do it, I've come out of the wrong kind of stable. That's why I say I'm a wretched misfit. It's killing me. That wouldn't matter if I were to go down in a good cause, but as it is I should only be perishing for my folly. I can't think with my head now—only with my heart."

"Or your nerves," said Adam.

"Call it anything you like. I'm beneath my job instead of being above it. I've been trying to puzzle the thing out, and unless I'm going to crash I must get back to thinking with my mind."

"We have often had this out before, haven't we?"

"Yes, and you've always cheered me up. A stalwart fellow like you heartens a waif like me. But not for ever. Things have come

186

to a pass when even you can do nothing for me. I'm in the wrong crowd and must get out of it!"

"What do you propose?"

Frank lifted a miserable face.

"I must get back to my cell—to some kind of cell. I must get my balance again. Perhaps there is still work for me to do. . . . Someone said that the great battles of the world were all won first in the mind."

"Who said that?" Adam asked sharply.

"I'm not sure. I think it was that man Creevey. You met him at Lady Flambard's, you remember."

"You've been meeting him?"

"Yes. He's a friend of Mrs. Pomfrey's. . . ."

There was a knock at the door, and Mrs. Gallop appeared, a breathless and flushed Mrs. Gallop. She saw Frank, recognised him, for she was a great church-goer, and bobbed a curtsy, a reminiscence of her village schooldays.

"Beg pardon, sir, but her ladyship is 'ere. The Marchioness—"

She ushered in Jacqueline, a picturesque figure in a white hunting waterproof, the collar of which framed a face all aglow with the sting of the rain.

"Hurrah, Adam!" she cried, "what fun to find you at home! This is the first time I've raided your lair. . . . And brother Frank no less! You oughtn't to be out in this weather, you know. I'm glad to see that Adam's looking after you. And food! May I have some luncheon, please? I love bread and cheese above all things— and beer—have you any more beer? I'm in Birkpool on my usual errand—the vet. Gabriel, my Irish setter, has got what looks like canker in the ear. I've just deposited him with Branker, and I thought I'd look you up. My car will be round in half an hour. I'm at the Court, a grass widow. Ken is off on one of his Provincial ramps."

Frank looked at his watch, got up, and announced that he must keep an appointment. He nodded to his sister, who had flung off her waterproof and laid a small dripping green hat on the fender.

"You're an unfeeling brute, Frank," she said. "You never ask after my health, though you see I'm as lame as a duck. Cubbing

187

the day before yesterday. I'm going to ride straddle, and have no more to do with those infernal side-saddles. They're all right when you fall clear in a big toss, but in a little one they hurt you horribly. No bones broken, thank you—only a strained muscle. Goodbye, Frank dear. Go and buy yourself a mackintosh. An umbrella in Birkpool is no more use than a sick headache."

When he had gone Jacqueline looked quizzically at Adam.

"Frank is a little shy with me at present," she said. "He knows I don't approve of the company he keeps."

As she munched her bread and cheese, her small delicate face took on a sudden shrewdness. The airy Artemis became for a moment the reflecting Athene.

"This is telling tales out of school, but he sees too much of Lilah Pomfrey. I don't mean that there's any philandering, and I've nothing against Lilah, but she's not the best company for Frank in his present frame of mind. She rather worships him and that brings out his weak points. He takes after my mother's side of the house—Highland sensitiveness and self-consciousness—and instead of laughing at his moods she encourages them. She is making a sentimentalist out of an idealist. And the next step, you know, is a cynic."

Jacqueline poured herself out a glass of beer with a most professional head on it.

"Didn't somebody say that the world was divided into the hard-hearted kind and the soft-hearted cruel? Ken is always quoting that. . . . More by token I want to talk to you about Ken. I can't stay now, but some day soon we must have it out. You've made him a perfectly impossible husband, Adam dear."

"I?"

"Yes, you," she went on. "You know very well that you're behind all Ken's daftness. He takes everything you say for gospel. But for you he would have been a most respectable Mayor of Birkpool, and at the end of his term of office would have been presented with a service of plate subscribed for by all good citizens. As it is, good citizens spit when his name is mentioned. He has made everybody uncomfortable, and has got nothing out of it except the affection of the ragtag and bobtail. . . . And look at his processing up and down the country. He is never off the stump, and he talks the wildest stuff. Oh, I know some people admire it. Charles Lamancha says that if you know Ken you understand the kind of fellows the Cavaliers were who rode with Rupert. But that is not much of a certificate, for as far as I can understand history Rupert muddled all his battles. He is getting a black name with his party, too. Mr. Stannix told me that he would have been safe for the vacant Under-Secretaryship last spring if he hadn't blotted his copy-book. As it was, they were compelled to give it to Jimmy Raven, who is a congenital idiot."

Jacqueline glanced through the rain-dimmed window and saw that her car had arrived. She rescued her partially dried hat from the fender, and with Adam's help struggled into her waterproof.

"I'm going to have all this out with you some day soon," she said. "I'm not thinking of Ken's career—I'm thinking of his happiness—and mine and young Jeremy's. And the country's good, too. Ken's digging up dangerous things out of people's minds—and dangerous things out of his own. The Armines are a queer race, you know, and I don't want any return to prehistoric freaks. Atavism is a kittle thing to play with. He says that he is getting back to Old England, but Old England had its unpleasant side. We learned that last June with our Women's Institute. Did I tell you about it? Well, we have an enlightened vicar who is keen on teaching the people history by ocular demonstration, and so he got them to act the founding of Arcote priory, and the flight after Naseby, and Lady Armine sheltering Charles—all with the proper clothes and correct detail. Then this summer he thought he would go a bit farther back and have the dancing on Midsummer Eve round the standing stones on Armine Hill. It was a fine moonlight night, but everybody was rather shy at first, and I thought it was going to be a fiasco. And then it began to go well—a little too well. You will scarcely believe it, but our village started to revert to type. You never saw such a pandemonium. The Sunday-school teachers became maenads, and those that weren't shingled let their hair down, and Pobjoy the earth-stopper behaved like a dancing

189

dervish, and Gosling the verger thought he was a high-priest and tried to brain the vicar. It seems that the chief feature of those revels had been the sacrifice of a virgin, and they dashed nearly succeeded—Jenny Dart it was—one of our laundrymaids. I can tell you we had the deuce's own job whipping them off."

II

A fortnight later Adam dined with Christopher Stannix in a private room at the House of Commons. The only other guest was Falconet, who was on the eve of returning to America.

Stannix held a curious position in the Government. He was reported to be a most competent administrator, and his actual department was little criticised. In the House he confined himself in his speeches to sober and incontrovertible arguments on facts. But he was also credited with a singularly receptive mind, and had become the acknowledged unofficial intelligence officer of the Cabinet. What his views on policy were the world was left to guess. He was believed to be often at variance with some of his colleagues, notably with Geraldine the Prime Minister, and his friendship with members of the opposition, particularly with Trant, was a scandal to the more precise. Yet no-one questioned his party loyalty, and the many who at the time professed themselves sick of politics and politicians were accustomed to except Stannix, and to wish him a cleaner job.

Adam and Falconet had been waiting for ten minutes before he joined them and dinner could begin.

"Well, we're in for it," he announced, when the waiter had left the room after serving the soup. "I ran across Judson in the Lobby just now, and he was positively menacing. You know how he slings the 'bloodys' in his talk. Tonight he was so excited that his conversation was mostly expletives and not very easy to follow. The big strike apparently is pretty well certain. The employers want a cut in wages in the new agreement and an extension of hours—they are on their uppers they say, and a lot of shops will have to close down if they don't get what they ask. They've been at the Ministry of Labour today presenting

190

their case, and I gather from Leveson that he is so convinced by it that he won't have the Government intervene."

"Have you seen their case?" Adam asked.

"Not yet. But I can imagine what it is like. A perfectly conclusive argument on facts and figures on the present basis of the industry. The only answer to it would be to question the basis. That is probably pretty rotten—all top-heavy from ill-considered war development and financial hokey-pokey."

"What do the men say?"

"Adamant, so far. Stuck their toes in. Won't budge and won't argue. The usual thing. They're certain they are getting a dirty deal, but they can't put it into reasonable English. Our people won't stand out for logic, but they'll fight like devils for an instinct. It's going to be an ugly business if it comes off, for God knows we can't afford a big stoppage. Our finances are running briskly downhill. I saw Creevey today—I don't much care for him as you know, but whenever he talks on finance I'm impressed. He was pointing out that we had established a standard of living for our people which was not warranted by the saleable value of our products—which means that we are not paying our way. He is not prepared to go back on our social services—says it can't be done. Perhaps he is right, for all parties go on sluicing out, or promising to sluice out, new benefits from the public funds—our own people are just as bad as any other. Creevey doesn't seem to mind that—he has no politics, he says, but I often think that he is the biggest Socialist of them all— he has the kind of quick autocratic mind that always wants to boss and regiment people. But he is clear that sooner or later we must face a scaling down of wages—money wages. As a matter of fact, it is quite true that we have enormously raised the standard of real wages in most trades as compared with before the war."

"That's because you have taught people to want a better kind of life."

"No doubt. And that is a good thing if we could afford it. But it looks as if we couldn't. A strike won't help matters. The poor devils will be beaten in the end, and the national income will have dropped by thirty or forty millions, and nobody, master or man, will be a penny the better off. . . . Leveson says there is only one hope. If the metalworkers stand out, the strike will probably never begin."

"Is there any chance of that?"

"I gather there is a fair chance. Potter, their new leader, is the ordinary thick-headed bellicose type, but there is Utlaw to be reckoned with. That means Birkpool. If Birkpool is against a strike it won't come off—at least so they tell me. You know more about that than I do, Adam. Could Utlaw swing his men the way he wanted?"

"Probably—any way he wanted. But what is to be his way?"

"Creevey seems to think that he is sound."

"What do you call sound?"

"On the side of common sense. He knows that it is folly to quarrel about the share from the pool, when the pool is shrinking."

"But aren't you all behaving as if the pool were bottomless with your policy of increased social services? Creevey and the rest of you?"

Stannix laughed. "That's a fair riposte. But it's easier to be provident in the finance of one industry, where you can get the facts into a reasonable compass, than in the finances of a nation, when you can get few of the facts agreed. . . . But tell us about Utlaw, for you know him better than I. By the way, I see that Robson is dead at last. That means a vacancy in East Flackington, and Utlaw will have a by-election to add to his other cares. We shall oppose him, of course—bound to—but not very whole-heartedly, and I fancy he'll get a lot of our people's votes. But about the strike—which way will he go?"

"I don't know," Adam replied. "But I know which way he ought to go."

"And that is?"

"Bring every man out, and keep them out till they win."

"But—hang it, man, what do you mean?"

"Look at it this way. Utlaw is nothing of your ordinary Socialist. He's an English brand that looks at facts rather than Marxian whimsies. He knows his people, and loves them—yes, loves them—that's half the secret of his power. He sees that they have painfully and slowly climbed a little way up the hill, and he wants to keep them there. He doesn't believe in a society where wage-earners are only a set of figures in a state register; he thinks of them as individuals, each of whom is entitled to some kind of free individual life. He won't have the moral fibre of his people weakened. Therefore he stands ·for high wages. Wages, he says, are the key to everything. It's the old question of property. A reasonable amount of property is necessary for liberty. Therefore any attack on wages is to be fought tooth and nail. If the masters produce figures to show that they can't pay, he says he is entitled to ask whether the masters are not muddling their businesses. That's what the ordinary workman is asking. You don't find much belief in the plenary inspiration of employers today. Utlaw would go farther. If the extravagance of the State is crippling the employers, he would have that checked in the interests of the worker. He has no notion of expensive pauperisation. Wages are his Ark of the Covenant, for he regards them as the price of individuality. . . . One thing more. He admits that matters may get worse with us, and that if we are to go on we may have to ask for a great effort of sacrifice and discipline from everybody. But that must be equal all round. He won't have the chance of that appeal spoiled by compulsory, one-sided, premature sacrifice."

"Good God, Adam," said Stannix, "that's the longest speech you ever made in your life. Is that your confession of faith?"

Adam laughed.

"I'm sorry to be so verbose. No, it isn't my creed. I should put it quite differently, and nobody would agree with me. But I know that it is what Utlaw believes."

"Then it looks as if Creevey and Leveson were backing the wrong horse. Will he stick to that?"

"I don't know. If he doesn't, he ceases to be a leader. I should be sorry, for we want all the leaders we can get against the evil days that are coming."

"Hallo!" said Stannix as the door opened. "Here's another rebel. Come in, Ken, and join us. Here, waiter, lay another place for Lord Warmestre. You'll soon catch us up. Do you know Mr. Falconet? Adam has been talking the wildest heresies, and they came out so pat that he must have been bottling them up for months. Where have you been? Putting spokes in their Lordships' wheels?"

"I've been listening to the dullest debate you ever heard in your days. I think I went to sleep. I heard that Adam was dining here, so I tracked you to this underground den. I never know whether I'm still on speaking terms with you fellows."

"I don't mind you," said Stannix. "I rather like your way of behaving. But Geraldine is looking for you with a tomahawk. To crown all your other offences, you've stolen his thunder. It appears that he has been incubating an emigration scheme on the same lines as yours, and now the thing has gone off at half-cock. He can't touch it now that you've given it the flavour of heterodoxy."

"He can't—and he never would," said Kenneth grimly. "None of your crowd wants to get things done. They're content if they get a nice little formula for their perorations. I don't mean you, Kit. You're not so bad, but you're a lone wolf in the pack."

Kenneth in his new mood was contemptuous of social customs. He was so full of his cause that he overflowed with it on all occasions. Now, long before coffee was served and cigars were lit, he was expounding his emigration ideas.

"Ken is the new Rhodes," said Stannix. "Can't you see him leading out a colony in the ancient Greek fashion? What will you call it? Warmestria? No, Arminia would be better. Did you see Creevey in the *Times* on your figures?"

"I can answer that blighter. You'll see me in the paper to-morrow. And Linaker says his talk about inflation is all moonshine. He is going to write a letter to the Press on the subject. No, my trouble is not Creevey or any of his kind. It's the black, blank apathy of your Government crowd, Kit. I can't get a move on with them. They'll neither bless nor ban, only shilly and shally. . . . I've sweated hard for a year, and what's the result? I've stirred up Birkpool, but whether or not it settles down again into a mud-hole depends upon one man."

"You mean Utlaw, and the strike," Stannix put in.

"What strike? I haven't heard of it. I mean Utlaw." And he looked across the table at Adam.

194

"Then there's this emigration racket. That depends upon the dozen fatted calves who call themselves a Cabinet. Well, I've had my try. If they won't play then I chuck the game. Back to the land I go and breed 'chasers.'"

"Not you," said Adam.

"Why not me?" But his truculent voice and the firm set of his jaw did not suggest an easy surrender.

Falconet accompanied Adam a little way on his homeward walk along the Embankment.

"I like your Marquis," he said. "He's a fighting man all right. He's got the eye of an old-time marshal in the Bad Lands. But I wouldn't put it past him to fling in his hand. Seems as if he were up against too many pikers."

III

Andrew Amos one morning found Adam at breakfast in Charity Row. It was dark February weather, with a swirling east wind that stirred up the dust of Birkpool and made the streets a torment. Andrew had a cold, and a red-spotted handkerchief was constantly at his snuffy nose.

"I've come to report," he said. "I was at the meeting last night. Joe Utlaw is in bigger danger the day from himsel' than he ever was from Davie Marrish. He has come out against the strike."

Amos fixed Adam with a fierce and rheumy eye.

"Aye, and he'll get awa' wi' it. That's my judgment. Seventy per cent of the men will vote his way. Joe will be the biggest strike-breaker in history. For, mind you, if Birkpool stands out the metalworkers will stand out, and the strike is broke afore it's begun.

"It was a most remarkable occasion," he went on. "Ye might ca' it a triumph o' personality. Joe was arguin' against a' the instincts o' his folk, and what's more, he was goin' back on a' he had been preachin' for five years. And yet, ma God! he kept the upper hand. He had four mortal hours o' it, and the

195

questions cam' like machine-gun fire, some o' them gey nesty yins. Man, he never turned a hair. He had a grand grip on his temper, too, for the mair impident a question was the mair ceevil his answer."

Adam asked what line he had taken.

"The cleverest. He wasna arguin' the employers' case. If he had, he wad hae been doomed from the start. He put it to them that they were up against the granite o' economic facts. If they chose to kick against the pricks, says he, the pricks wad be ower muckle for them. They couldna win, says he, and at the end o' three months or six months they wad be where they were—only their belts wad be drawn tighter and their wives and weans wad be thinner, and the country wad hae gotten anither shog doun the brae. . . . Man, it was an extraordinary performance, and though ye kent that every man in his audience was girnin' in his soul, he got the majority on his side. In my judgment he has done the job. There'll be nae strike."

"What about himself?" Adam asked.

"Oh, he's done. Joe is done. He has won this ae time, but he'll never win again. A' the purchase he has gotten will be exhausted by this effort. Besides, he has defied his Union, and there will be nae mercy for sic a blackleg. I's inclined to think—"

Amos stopped abruptly, for Utlaw himself had entered the room. He crossed and stood by the fire behind Adam's chair.

"I heard your last words, Amos," he said. "You think I have done wrong?"

Andrew was on his feet.

"I think ye've done black wrong, though maybe your conscience is clear and ye think it is right. I'm no here to judge ye—I leave that to whatever Power sums up in the hinder end. Ye're a Union man, and ye've gone back on the ae thing on which the Unions have never weakened. Ye've betrayed the men's wages. No doubt ye have put up a great argument—I heard ye last nicht—but you havena convinced me, for to my mind there's a thing ayont logic, and that's a man's freedom, and if ye take that from him ye'd better far wind up the concern. Ye've relapsed on the fosy Socialism that a' parties dabble in the day, Tory and Labour alike. Ye'll be for makin' it up to a warker

196

wi' mair education and widows' pensions and a bigger dole, as if onything on God's earth could make up to a man for the loss of the right to guide his life in his ain way! . . . But I'm no gaun to argue wi' ye. I've ower bad a cauld. I just cam' here to report to Mr. Milford. Guid-day to ye." Amos departed in a tornado of sneezing.

Utlaw sat himself in a vacant chair.

"Do you agree with Amos?" he asked Adam.

"I haven't heard your case. I gather you can carry the men with you."

"I think so. The big majority. . . . My case? It's simply common sense. When we have wasting assets, it's folly to waste them further. In a crisis we must sink legitimate interests and—and revise principles." He looked at Adam a little shyly.

"I've been going pretty deep into the facts," he went on. "Creevey—you know him?—Warren Creevey—has been helping me. Half our troubles are due to ignorance. Well, I've been sweating at the facts of the case. Our whole industrial fabric needs remaking—on that I agree—but meantime the storm is coming, and we can't start rebuilding in the thick of it. Also we have to take precautions against the storm, and one of them may be shoring up the walls which we intend later to pull down. That's how I have come to look at it. It is pretty nearly the case of all the intelligence of the country arrayed against the obstinacy of the Unions."

"Your power has been in the Unions?"

"I know. And all my loyalty has been with them. That's what has made this step a bitter one for me. It would have been far easier to go on thumping the tub with Potter and Judson. It takes some nerve to break with old associations."

"Did I ever deny your courage?"

Utlaw, who had been speaking to the tablecloth, looked up sharply.

"But you think I am wrong? You agree with old Amos?"

"It doesn't matter what I think. The question is, what at the bottom of your heart do you believe yourself?"

"I don't know what I believe. My creed is a collection of layers, and I don't know which is deepest. You think I may find that I have been mistaken. I don't know. God, life is an awful muddle! But if I disregard one truth for the moment it is only because there are other and more urgent truths which have to be attended to. I haven't forgotten what I stand for, and I'll return to it."

"But can you? You have lost your hold on the men's instincts, and that is not compensated for by a temporary grip on their minds."

Into Utlaw's eyes came an expression of sheer misery.

"That's maybe true. I've given up a good deal. The Union will spew me out. You think I have wrecked my career?"

"I think you are going to be a very successful man. You'll be in the Cabinet in a year or two, if you want that. Only the poor devils who believed in you will have to find another leader. . . . I'm sorry. . . . They won't find it too easy, and a man to lead them is the most important thing in life."

The Birkpool metalworkers broke the strike, and Utlaw became a figure of public importance. What was said about him in Labour circles did not reach print except in a bowdlerised form, but to nine out of ten newspapers he was a national hero. He had had the grit to defy his class, his Union and his party, and he had won; a hundred leading articles descanted on the scarcity and the potency of such courage. Speculations about his future were, for a time, the favourite pursuit of the gossip-writers. The East Flackington election was treated as a chance of testifying to a rare virtue. He was not yet disowned by his party, but at the last moment an Independent Labour candidate had appeared, so the fight was triangular.

Presently the rumour spread that things were not going smoothly there. One afternoon at Euston Adam met Florrie Utlaw, just returned from the North, and looking rather weary and battered. She would not admit the possibility of defeat, but her confident words seemed to lack conviction. It was a horrible election, she said, of personalities and mudslinging. The Tory candidate was behaving like a gentleman, and seemed to wish Joe to win, but Latta, the Independent, was a scurrilous savage. Joe was marvellous, but he had to fight against organised interruptions, and Judson and Potter, and even Gray, were up there doing mischief. "He will have his revenge on them," she said, with a tightening of her determined little mouth. "He will show up Judson for the noisy fool he is."

Three days later Kenneth Warmestre found Adam in the vestibule of the club, and drew him towards the tape. "East Flackington is coming out," he said, and edged his way to the front of the little crowd. He returned with a grin on his face.

"Utlaw is bottom of the poll," he said. "Serve him dam' well right. He should have stuck to his crowd, even if they had the wrong end of this particular stick, if he believed them right on the main point. I don't like fellows that run out. I see he has resigned his Union job. He'll have to get his friend Creevey to find him something else."

IV

On an afternoon in May, when the London streets were bright with the baskets of flower-girls, and the smell of petrol and wood-paving could not altogether drown the vagrant scents of summer, Adam went to see Mrs. Pomfrey at her great house in Curzon Street. He went by appointment. He had been summoned that morning by an urgent telephone message from Mrs. Pomfrey herself. "I want to see you so badly," she had said, "and we have much to talk over. Things have become extraordinarily interesting, haven't they?"

Adam had a conviction as to whom he should meet in the big sunny drawing-room. Mrs. Pomfrey was making tea, seated in a straight-backed chair with something of the look of a wise Buddha, and beside her was Frank Alban. Frank had abandoned his shapeless grey flannels and wore the ordinary garb of his profession. The clothes accentuated his leanness, but somehow they also gave him an air of greater solidity. He was no longer the lone wolf, but a member of a pack—perhaps of a hierarchy.

His eyes met Adam's with some embarrassment, for that morning he had had a curious talk about him with his brother-in-law. He had found himself slipping into criticism, and that

199

had roused Kenneth to a vigorous defence. He had called Adam self-centred, and had been roughly contradicted.

"You don't understand what I mean, Ken," he had said. "Not selfish. There isn't a scrap of selfishness in him. But he has this mission of his, and it narrows him. He is like a wind forced through a funnel, terrific in its force, but limited in its area of impact, and that funnel is himself, remember. He couldn't, if he tried, get outside himself."

"Rot," said Kenneth. "Adam's power is just that he wants to be only a funnel. How can you call a man self-centred if he looks on himself as a tool to be used and then scrapped. He has the self-forgetfulness of a saint."

"I don't agree," Frank had argued. "A saint is not only a servant of God, but a son. Adam is a bondman. He obeys, but without fellowship. He lacks what I call religion."

"Your kind, anyhow," Kenneth had answered rudely.

"We wanted you to be the first to hear our news," said Mrs. Pomfrey. "Dr. Colledge has got his deanery at last—it will be in the papers in the morning, and Frank is coming back to St. Chad's to take his place. Isn't it wonderful? Now he will have a platform from which his voice can really carry. Mr. Geraldine says he will very soon be the most important figure in the Church.

"Of course it is a terrible wrench for him," she went on. "He hates leaving Birkpool and all the poor people who have come to love him. But it was his duty, don't you think? He has to do the work he can do best. It would not have been right for him to bury his talent in a napkin, and Birkpool was a napkin. One oughtn't to use a razor to peel potatoes."

Frank spoke.

"No, Lilah, that's not what I feel. My trouble is that I have only the one talent, and it is no use for peeling potatoes. If it were I'd be happy to peel them for the rest of my days, for I should be doing honest work. . . . But all I have got is a brittle thing and I must use it for the only job it is fit for."

"Nonsense, my dear," said Mrs. Pomfrey. "You have ten talents and you must use them all for the good of the world. It would be sinful waste if you didn't. Do you call vision a small thing? Or the gift of awakening people. Or poetry? Or the power of thought? What we need is a new revelation and you can give it us. All the battles of the world, you know, are first won in the mind."

Frank looked a little shyly at Adam.

"Don't believe her. She rates me far higher than I rate myself. I want something very humble. I'm the preaching friar going back to his cell. I told you, you know, that I was coming to feel that it was my only course—to find a cell."

"Or a papal throne." Adam remembered Scrope's words.

A flicker which may have been pain shot across Frank's eyes. "What do you mean?" he asked.

"Only that your kind of cell may easily become a papal throne." Mrs. Pomfrey clapped her hands.

"He is right. That is the way to put it. A papal throne. A new and better Vatican. The Power of the Keys to unlock men's hearts. . . ."

At that moment Lord Warmestre was announced. At the sight of Adam he seemed for a moment put out. "Hallo! I didn't expect to find you. . . . I'm looking for Jackie, and thought I might run her to earth here. She must have gone back to the flat. Yes, please, I'd like some tea. I'm going to Warmestre tonight. You heard that we are going to live there and let the Court if we can. We are pretty well pinched by the death duties."

"Surely you are not crying poverty," said Mrs. Pomfrey.

"No. We'll be right enough presently. But Warmestre wants a deal of looking after. My father was old, and the agent was old, and things were allowed to slide. It's wonderful farming land, and I'm going to try out some notions of mine."

"And your 'chasers?"

Kenneth glanced at Adam.

"Perhaps. It's the right place for a training stable. Perfect downland without a stone in it. But that's for the future. Meantime Jackie and I will have our work cut out getting the house habitable. It's an immense barrack, and we shall have to begin by camping in a corner."

The conversation passed to other topics. Mrs. Pomfrey discoursed of Utlaw.

"He has come over to us. Oh yes, complete allegiance. Ours is the only party for him, for with us a man is given liberty to use his brains. He has behaved magnificently and has been abominably treated. Mr. Creevey has found him a post in Addison's—he is to look after the labour side of the business, and he is on the board of the new evening paper. He ought to be quite well off soon. A seat in the House? Yes, of course we want him there as soon as possible. There may be a vacancy in Birmingham, if Mr. Platt gets a peerage in the Birthday Honours. Why do you smile like that, Kenneth?"

"I don't like it. I wish Utlaw had gone the other way, for I fancied the chap. A man should stick to a half-truth, if it is his own, rather than swallow the truths of other people. . . . Not that I have any right to judge him." And again he looked at Adam.

The two walked away from the house together. There seemed to be some constraint in Kenneth's mind, for his manner lacked its customary exuberance.

"The mayfly will be on in another week," he said. "You'll be coming down to the Court. What about Friday week? I won't be there, for I must stay on at Warmestre, but you'll find Jackie when you go in for tea. Oh, by the way, I had a message to you from her. She specially wants to see you. Told me to tell you if I saw you that she had to have it out with you. Have you been getting into her black books?"

In Berkeley Square they met Florrie Utlaw, a very different being from the drab little woman whom Adam had first known. She had a new gown, a new hat, and what seemed to be a new complexion. Also she had acquired a new manner, vivacious, confident, pleasantly and audaciously youthful.

"I can't stop," she said, "for I'm late already. Yes, we've got a flat in Westminster. You must come and have tea with us. I saw Lady Warmestre last night at Jean Rimington's dance. Were you there? Jos is very well, thank you." (She had dropped "Joe" as too painfully reminiscent.) "He is desperately busy, but very happy. You see, he is working with white men now. But he has so much to do that I don't know how he will manage the House. You've heard about that? Yes, it is practically certain."

She cried them a gay goodbye, and tripped off in the direction of Mount Street.

The meeting unloosed Kenneth's tongue.

"Ye gods, it's a crazy world!" he said. "Utlaw in Creevey's pocket and destined to be a Tory silver-tongue! . . . His wife Jean Rimington's latest find! . . . Brother Frank returned from the styes to the fatted calf and soon to be a fashionable Pope! . . . It is a nice thing, Adam, to see virtue rewarded. All the same, they have left a lot of poor disappointed devils behind them."

They stopped at the corner of Berkeley Street and Piccadilly. Kenneth looked round him at the motley throng on the pavement and the congested stream of traffic, and up to the blue May sky.

"It's a crazy world," he said, "but it's a busy one. An amusing one, too. I'm going back to my corner of it. Yes, I'm chucking my work, for it wasn't mine. I'm not man enough to knock the heads of a thousand idiots together and teach them sense, and for all I'm concerned they can go on with their jabbering. What's the thing in the Bible? 'Ephraim is joined to his idols—let him alone.' I've had my run and I've failed, and I'm going back to my paddock."

He put his hand on Adam's shoulder.

"I'm sorry for you, old man. Sorry—and rather ashamed. You have backed three bad 'uns, and two have gone soft and one has gone sour."

CHAPTER IV

ADAM had in his bag the three brace of trout which were the recognised limit of the water, the rise was over, and now he was amusing himself with idle casting, dropping his fly by the edge of a waterlily or a snag at the far side of the stream. It had been a day of gentle sunshine and light western breezes, the day of an angler's dream. The hay in the meadows was already high, and the wind tossed it into eddies of grey and green, but by the riverside the turf was short and starry with flowers.

His fishing had had many interludes. He stopped to watch a kingfisher dart from a bole, and a young brood of moorhens scuttling under the shadow of the bank, and a diving dabchick. He sniffed the rich rooty scents of the water's edge, moist and sweet, the fragrance of the summer midlands—and wondered why it seemed to change to something salt and fresh, as the terrestrial scene faded from his eyes and he looked inward at a very different landscape.

Disappointment had not troubled him. He had no sense of failure. These things were ordained and it was not for him to question the ordering. The long monotonous grind behind him, the struggle with imponderables, the effort to keep his grip on what in his hands became slippery and evasive, the anxious thoughts and the baffled plans—the memory of these did not oppress him. That had been his task and it was finished; he was waiting for fresh marching orders. He was only a subaltern obeying a command: the setting of the battle was with the general-in-chief. He was in a mood of passivity which was almost peace. He had aimed too high; now he waited for a humbler task.

As always in such moods his fancy ranged, and he was back

in his secret world. As the vigour of midday declined to the mellowness of afternoon, his rod fell idle. He was not looking at the deep midland pastures or the green waters fringed with white ranunculus. He was on the western side of Sgurr Bàn, on the thymy downlands with their hollows full of wild-wood, their shallow glens and their singing streams. Nigel was with him, babbling happily, his small firm hand clutching one of his fingers, except when it was loosed to permit him to dart aside after a nest or a flower. This was their favourite afternoon ramble, when they could watch the sun moving down to the horizon and bask in its magic. The horizon should have been the sea, but Adam knew that it was not yet permitted to come within sight of it. He was aware of it—somewhere just a little ahead beyond the ridges of down and the hazel coverts—they could even hear the beat of the green waves on the white sands. Nigel was full of it, always asking questions about the wonderful pink and pearl-grey shells, and the strange nuts carried by the tides from remote lands, and the skerries where the grey seals lived, and far out the little isle called the Island of Sheep where had dwelt the last saint of the Great Ages. But Nigel was not impatient. They were going there of a surety, but perhaps not that afternoon. Meantime there were the blue rock-doves and the merlins, and the furry rabbits in their burrows, and an occasional loping hare—and his father's hand which he sometimes pressed against his cool cheek. . . .

About five o'clock Adam woke from his absorption, and remembered his engagement at the Court. He crossed the stream by a plank bridge and turned up through a fir-wood over the intervening ridge of hill. He had regard and loyalty for his friends, but he was aware that it was not the fierce rapturous thing which it had been in the old days. For him the world had now sharper and harder lines and dimmer colours. But Jacqueline was a little different. She reminded him somehow of Nigel, and he felt for her just a little of the same wondering affection. Besides, she understood him best. When he was with her he had the comfortable feeling of being with one who comprehended him without the need of explanation—comprehended him, sympathised with him, humoured him a little, perhaps, as she humoured her small Jeremy. Those bright eyes of hers saw very far.

He reached the Court on the garden side and entered the house by the open window of the library. There was no-one in the room, so he passed through the big drawing-room out on to the terrace. He found a tea-table set where a great magnolia made a forest in the angle of the east wing. Below was the Dutch garden, and the view was to the west through a glade in the park to far-away blue hills.

Jacqueline appeared on the terrace steps. She had been gardening among the lily ponds, and wore Newmarket boots a little splashed and stained. Her long limbs, her slimness, and her retinue of dogs gave her more than ever the air of the huntress.

The kettle was boiling, so she at once made tea. Then she flung herself into a chair, took off her gauntlets, and tossed them into another.

"Had a good day?" she asked. "You must have, for you're late. When Ken has no luck he is back clamouring for tea by four o'clock. I hope you're as hungry as I am." She was busy cutting slices from a wheaten loaf and buttering them.

To Adam she seemed a little nervous. She talked fast and busied herself about giving him tea, all with a certain air of preoccupation. She had much to say about Jeremy, and she was not in the habit of talking about her son. Also of Warmestre—regret at leaving the Court, complaints of the magnitude of the task that awaited them in Devonshire. Adam listened with half an ear. Jacqueline's presence always gave him a sense of well-being and ease, but now she was notably restless.

"Kenneth told me that you specially wanted to see me," he said.

"Yes, of course." She did not look at him, and was busy taking shots at a thrush on the terrace with bits of crust. "I always want to see you. I wanted to talk over our friends with you."

"Which ones?"

She laughed. "Well, let's begin with Mr. Creevey."

"Why Creevey?"

"Isn't he the rock on which you have shipwrecked, Adam dear?"

206

"You think I have shipwrecked?"

"Haven't you? I'm desperately sorry for you. But of course I don't pity you. I would as soon think of pitying God."

She sat upright and for the first time looked straight at him.

"You and I are too close friends to have secrets. What do you make of Mr. Creevey?"

"I don't know him well."

"You don't. No-one does. But you can feel him. . . . Shall I tell you what I think about him? First of all, I don't like him. His manners to women are atrocious. Not to Lilah Pomfrey, who is too old, or to Sally Flambard, who is too ethereal. But with anyone like myself whom he thinks good-looking he has a horrid streak of the common philanderer. But let that pass. We all know that he takes his pleasures rather in the farmyard way. . . . Apart from that there's nothing much against him. He has made heaps of money, but no-one ever suggested that he was a crook. I took the trouble to ask a lot of questions about that. He is not supposed to go back on his friends. Lastly, he is amazingly, superhumanly clever. Everyone admits that. It's the chief thing about him, and his chief passion. He lives for the exercise of his splendid brain and cares for nothing much else. Kit Stannix says that he is the perfect sophist, and I think I know what he means. Life is for him a very difficult and absorbing game of chess.

"Well, you have come hard up against him," she continued. "The apostle against the sophist! And the sophist has won the first round. If you had any human failings, Adam, you ought to hate him. For he hates you."

"He scarcely knows me."

"But he *feels* you and you feel him. And he hates you like sin. Trust a woman's instinct. Perhaps he fears you a little too. You don't fear him? No, you wouldn't, because you're scarcely human. . . . Don't you realise what he has done?"

"He has taken Utlaw away from me."

"Yes. Utlaw was clay in his hands, and Mr. Creevey succeeded just because he was mostly clay, not gold. I like the shaggy Jos— Jos, remember, for the future, not Joe. I prophesy that he will

207

be a prodigious success—the one honest working man, the darling of the gentlemen of England. I like little Florrie too. In a year she will be so smart she will scarcely be able to see out of her eyes. She will drop me as too dowdy. Jean Rimington is a fool, but she always backs the right mare for those particular stakes. But the Utlaws were easy fruit. Mr. Creevey made a bigger *coup* than that."

"Your brother?"

She nodded.

"Brother Frank. Make no mistake about it—Frank is a saint. You're not. You're an apostle, which is something very different. Frank has a wonderful soul, which he is going to cosset and polish and perfect. You don't care a rush about your soul. You'd sacrifice it tomorrow if you thought the cause was big enough. . . . How was it done? Through Lilah Pomfrey of course. Lilah was born to be a nursing mother to saints. She is full of all kinds of wonderful emotions and ideals, and she has the supreme worldliness which can make them all fit in nicely with each other. No, no. She won't marry him. Frank is incapable of marrying, and she knows very well that Frank's wife would never be more than a morganatic one. She'll be his mother, and his confidante, and his good genius, and—his impresario. I adore my Frank and want him to have a pleasant life. He'll get it, I think. He will be a tremendous figure before he is done. He will be the greatest preacher in England, and there will be scores of little birthday-books with his comforting sayings, and little manuals about his teaching. He'll do a lot of good too. All kinds of dingy beings will warm themselves at the fires he lights. And he'll die in the odour of sanctity, and people will say that a prophet has fallen in Israel, and it will be quite true. Only—you see Frank is not a fool, and at the end I think that he may have some rather bad thoughts about it all."

Jacqueline got up.

"Let's walk," she said. "A cigarette? Not for me, thank you. I give up smoking in summer because it spoils my nose for the flowers."

They crossed the terrace, and descended into the Dutch garden which, with lupins and the first delphiniums, was all a mist of blue. Jacqueline linked her arm in Adam's, for she had the habits of a friendly boy.

"What are you going to do now?" she asked. "I'm anxious about you, Adam dear. You've been slaving—oh, I've watched you—slaving at what was no job for a man like you. You have been a bottle-holder to champions that won't fight. What next?"

"I shall find champions who will."

She withdrew her arm.

"Why will you be so absurdly modest? You say you are trying to find leaders. But you have more grit than anybody. Why won't you do the leading yourself?"

Adam shook his head.

"You don't understand. I could never make you understand. I am only a servant—a bottle-holder if you like. I can never lead. It isn't the task I have been given."

"Stuff and nonsense!" she said. "I have prophesied about Mr. Utlaw and brother Frank, and now I'll prophesy about you. You'll be forced to come into the open and take charge. If you don't, you'll go on being beaten. By people like Mr. Creevey and Lilah Pomfrey. . . . And by me."

Jacqueline moved away from him and stood with one foot on a low parapet—a defiant huntress.

"I have a confession to make, Adam," she said. "It was I that took Ken away from you. He is far the best of them—far more grit and fire. He has the makings of an apostle. He would have followed you in sandals and a hair shirt. It was I that stopped him."

She stood up, very slim and golden in the light of the westering sun, and if there was defiance in her pose there was also a sudden shyness.

"You couldn't compete with me, you know. I often felt rather a cad about it, but I had a right to fight for my own. . . . How shall I explain? Four years ago I married Ken. I wasn't madly in love with him—perhaps I wasn't in love with him at all. But I greatly admired and liked him. There was no glamour about him, but he was the best man I knew, the most really good and reliable. A woman, you know, generally marries for safety. She may fall in love for all kinds of reasons, but when she marries

209

she takes the long view. Ken stood for something in England which I wanted to see continue, and as his wife I could help to keep it going. Marrying him gave me a career. I knew that if I had a son he would have a career also—he would be born to all kinds of fine sturdy obligations—with a niche ready from the start. So I married Ken partly for himself—quite a lot for himself—and partly for the great system behind him. Do you understand me?"

Adam nodded. He remembered his feelings the first night when he descended the broad oaken staircase at the Court.

"Well, since our marriage I have come to like him enormously—the solid affection into which people grow when they live together. And there's Jeremy, too. Jeremy is Ken and Ken is Jeremy. . . . And I have found out things I never guessed before. When I married I thought that if Ken had a fault it was that he was commonplace, the ordinary banal Christian gentleman. I was a blind little fool. There are queer things in the Armine blood. I'm half Highland and therefore half daft, but my daftness is like summer wildfire, and Ken's might be a steady, devouring flame. He has it in him to fling everything to the winds and tramp the world. . . . And I did not marry to be a beggar-wife."

Jacqueline's singing voice sunk to a whisper.

"I hadn't the courage. I wasn't good enough. Besides, it was all against reason. I saw his restlessness, and at first I encouraged him, for I didn't want him to sink into a rustic clod. That's another side of the Armines. If they don't happen to go crusading, they will relapse into the perfect chaw-bacon. I encouraged him to become Mayor of Birkpool, because that was a family job. But his doings there opened my eyes—and frightened me. And then I saw the power you had over him, and that frightened me more. I realised that I had to fight for my rights. Not my rights only—it wasn't altogether selfish. I was fighting for Jeremy and for all the old things—for the Court here and for Warmestre, and for the people who lie carved in stone in the chapel, and for all the kind, peaceful life that depended on him. I was fighting for Ken, too—for his peace of mind, for if he had gone crusading there would have been no more peace for

210

him. He's not a saint, you see, and he is only part of an apostle—the other strain in him would have been pulling hard and a good deal of his life would have been hell. . . . Do you blame me?"

"I don't blame you."

She sighed.

"'It was a stiff fight, and I only won on the post. I had all the chances, of course. I had Jeremy, and I had Ken's affection for us both to help me. I knew him much better than he knew himself, and I could play on all kinds of secret strings. His love of country life and horses. His laziness—he has plenty of it. His sentiment—he is a mass of it. His feeling for the past and for his family—he is no respecter of persons, but he has a big bump of veneration. But I could not have won, I think, if Mr. Utlaw had not run out—and brother Frank. That gave Ken a kind of nausea about the whole concern, and I worked on that. . . . So I have got him back to me and to Jeremy, and to all the Armines that ever were. But sometimes I feel as if I had sinned against the Holy Ghost, the sin my old nurse used to frighten me with. I'm not sure that I mind that—I'll face up to the Holy Ghost when my time comes—but I mind horribly having fought against *you*. I have beaten you, and I hate myself for it."

She looked at him timidly, as if much hung on his words. He did not speak, and she continued, her voice low and rapid, as of one making a difficult confession.

"You see—you see I could have been madly in love with someone—you, perhaps—someone like you. I think you are the only one in the world who could have made me feel like that, and then I would have flung everything behind me. My grandmother used to say that the women of her family would either sell their shift for a man, or make a packman's bargain with him. Nobody wanted my shift, so I have made my bargain. Do you blame me for fighting for my share in it? . . . I would like you to say that you forgive me."

Jacqueline's eyes had become solemn, like a wise child's.

"There is nothing to forgive," Adam said. "I think you did right—entirely right."

211

She came towards him and put her hands on his shoulders. Her lips were trembling.

"I believe you mean that," she said. "God bless you for it. . . . If I were a man I should wring your hand and wish you well. But I am going to kiss you. . . ."

Adam was scarcely conscious of her kiss. But there was something novel in his heart, which he recognised as tenderness. As he walked across the park the light touch of her lips seemed in the recollection like the clutch of Nigel's hand.

A week later he had a letter from Jacqueline, who was in London.

"Last night," she wrote, "I went to a wonderful little party at Lilah Pomfrey's. Ken was asked, but wouldn't go—said he was sick of monkey-tricks. The Utlaws were there, and Mr. Creevey was in great form, and Frank of course, and one or two young men and several yearning women. Lilah has a regular group now, and this was their second meeting. The invitation card may amuse you."

The card she enclosed had Mrs. Pomfrey's name in the centre, and neatly printed in the left-hand top corner *The Seekers*.

BOOK III

CHAPTER I

THE little low-roofed café in the Rue des Célestins in which Falconet sat on a certain October afternoon was flooded with the hazy golden light which is the glory of Paris in a fine autumn. The patron was busy in a corner with his own avocations; a party of four stout citizens were drinking bocks and disputing vivaciously; but otherwise the place was empty, for it was the slack period when *déjeuner* is over and the hour of *apéritifs* has not arrived. Falconet was waiting for Adam, and as he smoked a delayed after-luncheon cigar he let his mind run over the events of the past week, since he had landed in England.

In the retrospect the chief was a talk with Christopher Stannix, for whom he had acquired a puzzled respect. Falconet loved politics and their practitioners no more than the rest of his countrymen, but Stannix was unlike any politician he had ever met. He seemed to stand aside, intervening now and then to put his weight into the scales to adjust the balance. He was a noted pricker of bladders, and had deflated some of Falconet's pet ones, but he was as much in earnest as Falconet himself. He called himself a "trimmer", and had justified the name from a period of English history with which Falconet was not familiar. But above all he was Adam's friend.

For Adam, Falconet had come to entertain one of the passionate friendships which were as much a feature in his character as his passionate dislikes. At first Adam's ways had seemed to him inertia, and his fastidiousness mere pedantry. But his disillusionment with his own bustling methods across the Atlantic had made him revise his views. The breakdown of Adam's plans the summer before had been to him less of a disappointment than a relief. His friend was free to start again, and to start again with him as an ally. For Falconet was at heart an artist, and

215

could never be content with the second-rate. His own complex organisation in America he regarded without pride, as a useful nursery of talent. But it would not produce genius, the rare quality which was needed to heal the world's ills. Now, as ever, he was a pioneer in quest of the major secrets.

Adam was a hard man to know, and Falconet, in spite of their months of close companionship in the Arctic ice, felt that he had only penetrated the outer fringe. His explorer's instinct was aroused, and he sought enlightenment from Stannix; and Stannix, detecting an honest affection, opened his heart to him.

"Melfort," he had told Falconet, "is a religious genius. I don't know how to define that, for it is a thing which you can feel better than you can explain. I don't know what his religion is—never talked to him about it—it's sure to be very different from any orthodox brand. But whatever it is, it is a living fire in him. . . . Yes, I have known him since he was a boy. As a young man he was, I think, the most remarkable fellow I knew—'remarkable' is the word—you couldn't help noticing him, for he was unlike anybody else. We used to put him in a class by himself, not for what he had done, but for what he was. He had an odd spiritual distinction, and an extraordinary fineness—fine as a slim, tempered sword. Then the crash came, and he went under. After that I can only guess, but some time eight or nine years ago—yes, in prison—he had a great visionary experience. Like Dante's, and much about the same age as Dante. He has never breathed a word to me about it, but the results are there for anyone to see. Everything about him is devoted—dedicated—consecrated—whatever you choose to call it."

Falconet had nodded. That much he had long been aware of. He asked further questions.

Stannix puckered his brow.

"Oh yes, there are flaws in him. One is that he is—just a little—inhuman, and he used to be the jolliest of mortals. I wonder if I can make you understand me, for it is not ordinary inhumanity. My old tutor, I remember, used to define Platonism as the love of the unseen and the eternal cherished by those who rejoice in the seen and the temporal. Adam rather lacks the

216

second part. He thinks about God a great deal more than he thinks about the things and the creatures He has made. He is a little too much aloof from the world, and that weakens his power. If he could only be in love with a woman again!—but of course that's all past and done with. I wonder how much he really cares about his friends. Not a great deal for them in themselves, only as instruments for his purpose. He might have made a better job of Utlaw and Frank Alban if he had got really close to them. There must have been something a little chilly about those friendships. Kenneth Warmestre was different perhaps—I believe there was a sort of affection there—but, then, Warmestre was hopeless from the start."

Falconet had dissented. "I know what you mean, but I don't think I agree. My grouch with Adam is that he is too infernally modest. He rates himself too low and the other fellows too high."

"You haven't got it quite right," Stannix had replied. "He doesn't rate other people too high. He rates them too low—he's bound to do that, considering the sort of standard he has—and they are bound subconsciously to recognise it, and perhaps resent it. That is one bar to the proper sort of friendship. But you are right on one thing—he is too modest about himself. He's always contrasting himself with perfection and feeling a worm. He has made up his mind that his business is only to serve—not to serve God only, but to serve other men who are the agents of God's purpose, and the trouble is that there is nobody big enough for him to serve. He wants to untie our shoe-latchets, and none of us is worthy of it. He has the opposite of *folie des grandeurs*—the folly of humility, I suppose you might call it. But he hasn't found the Moses whose hands he can hold up, and I don't think he ever will."

Falconet had agreed, but with a cheerful air. For he believed that he was on the track of a Moses.

An hour slipped away in the sunny café and Falconet still waited. The party of four finished their bocks and their argument and went out. A man in a blue blouse came in and talked to the patron. The patron himself came over to Falconet's table and

217

spoke of the weather, politics, and the manners of travelling Americans, thereby showing that he took Falconet for an Englishman. Then a great peace fell on the empty place, and a white cat, who had been sunning herself outside on the pavement beyond the green awning, came in and slept on the top of the patron's little desk.

A man entered, a typical French bourgeois, wearing a bowler hat, a tightly buttoned grey coat, a stiff white collar, and a flamboyant tie. He ordered a vermouth, and after a glance at the empty table came towards Falconet. He took off his hat with a flourish, revealing a head of close-clipped fair hair—the familiar Normandy type.

"I await a friend, Monsieur," said Falconet. "But pray take the seat till my friend arrives."

The stranger sat down and sipped his vermouth. He summoned the patron, and commented on the quality of the beverage, a friendly comment with much advice as to how to secure the best brands.

"Monsieur is a connoisseur," said the patron. "He travels much?"

"I go up and down the land," was the answer, "and I find out things, and I share my knowledge with my friends." He spoke a rapid guttural French, with a curious flatness in his voice.

"You come from the East," said the patron. "Lille, I should say at a guess."

"But no. I am out of Lorraine. As are you, my friend."

He proved to be right, and for a few minutes there was a quick exchange of questions and recollections. Then the patron was called away and the stranger turned to Falconet.

"It delights me to detect the origins of those whom I meet by chance. You, Monsieur, I take to be American. Your eyes are quicker and hungrier than the English, and your mouth is shaped to the smoking of thin cigars. Is it not so?"

"You've got it in one," said Falconet. "Now, I'll guess about you. You're a Lorrainer, but you live in Paris. You're in some kind of trade—high-class *commis-voyageur*, I presume. What exactly do you sell?"

218

"I do not sell. I am looking for something to buy; but what I want is not easily bought."

"Meaning?"

"A man," was the surprising answer given in English. "But I think I have found one."

Falconet stared. Then he burst out laughing, and leaned forward with outstretched hand.

"You fooled me properly, Adam. I'm mighty glad to see you, but how in thunder did you get into the skin of a French bourgeois? You're the dead spit of one, and even now I've got to rub my eyes to recognise you. You've a face one doesn't forget in a hurry, but you've managed to camouflage it out of creation. I've been sitting opposite you for five minutes, and, though I was expecting you, I wasn't within a thousand miles of spotting you. How d'you do it?"

"I had four years' practice," was the answer. "Well, I have got alongside your great man. Tell me, what was there about him that first took your fancy?"

Falconet considered. "I think it was his old-fashioned face. That was a phrase of my grandmother's, and it means just what it says. Loeffler looks like the good old tough New England stock I remember as a boy. A plain face with nothing showy about it, but all the horse-sense and sand in the world. Like Abraham Lincoln—only not so darned ugly. Then I had some talk with him and I liked him better still. He wasn't like my friend Creevey, who between drinks will sketch out a dozen plans of salvation for everything and everybody. Loeffler don't talk much, but what he says counts a hell of a lot. He sees the next job and sits down to it—stays still and saws wood, as Lincoln said. I've gotten to be suspicious of all showy fellows, for what glitters isn't often gold. It's the plain people that are going to pull us out of the mess. That little Cosgrave man in Ireland is one, and I'll bet my last dollar that Hermann Loeffler is another. What do you say?"

Adam nodded.

"Well, let's hear what you make of him. You started from London twenty-seven days ago. How often have you seen him?"

"Only three times. But they were pretty useful occasions. First, I started in at the top. I got the right kind of introductions from the Foreign Office and the City, and I sat down at the Adlon as an inquiring cosmopolitan with a liking for Germany. I had my pedigree arranged—aunt married in Würtemberg, school-days in Heidelberg, a year in Munich under Luigi Brentano—all the proper credentials."

"Did my man Blakiston help you?" Falconet asked.

"Tremendously. I could have done nothing without him. He had your millions behind him, and I shared in their reflected glory. . . . It's a long story and it falls into three parts. First, there was the week in Berlin. Then the scene changes to the Black Forest. Last, I spent three days in the Rhineland, and had a little trouble in getting away. Yesterday I wasn't sure that I would be able to meet you here. It looked as if I mightn't be alive many hours longer."

Falconet lit a fresh cigar. "Go on. I'm listening. You start off at the Adlon all nicely dressed up."

Adam told his story slowly and dryly. He seemed more in-terested in his evidence than in the way he had collected it.

His introductions had given him ready access to Loeffler, now for two months the German Chancellor. The meeting at Lamancha's dinner-table had been recalled, and Loeffler, who forgot nothing, was intrigued at the transformation of the former British staff-officer into the amateur publicist, with Blakiston and the American millions in the background. Adam played his part carefully, his role being that of the honest inquirer, and some-thing in his face or his manner must have attracted Loeffler, for he talked freely. The little man was drabber and leaner than ever, for he was engaged in the thankless job of demonetising the old mark, and getting his country's finances straight by a colossal act of sacrifice. He talked finance to Adam, but, when the latter disclaimed expert knowledge, he turned to the things behind finance—the national temper, the attitude of other Powers, the forces in the world which made for stability or chaos.

"He doesn't deceive himself," said Adam. "He knows what he is up against down to the last decimal. When he has stated the odds against himself, he has a trick of smiling ruefully, just

220

like a plucky child who has to face up to something he hates. I wanted to pat him on the back—like a good dog."

That was the first meeting in Loeffler's flat, late one night, over several tankards of beer. The second was a grander occasion. It was at a private dinner given by a great banker, a dinner at which the guests sat on into the small hours and at which momentous things were spoken of. Loeffler was there and two of his colleagues in the Government; several bankers and financiers, one of them a noted figure in Paris; a general who had had to face the supply question of the armies in the last year of war, and who was now grappling with difficult questions of public order; a Swedish economist, Blakiston, and Creevey.

"That yellow dog!" Falconet exclaimed at the mention of the last.

"He behaved well enough," said Adam. "You see, his intellectual interest was aroused and he tackled the thing like a problem in mathematics. He's honest in one thing, you know—he'll never be false to his mind."

The atmosphere had been tense, since destiny hung on that talk. It had been tense in another way, for the guests were shepherded in and out of the house as if they had been visitors to a gun factory. Everywhere there were solid, quiet-faced watchers.

At this point Adam became more expansive. Loeffler, he said, had dominated the talk, a solemn, pale little man in a badly-cut dinner jacket among people starched, trim, and resplendent. They had talked of the London Conference fixed for the beginning of November, and of the burden of war debts and reparations which was to be the staple of the discussion there. The General was inclined to be explosive and melodramatic; and the German bankers to make a poor mouth about it, but Loeffler was as steadfast as a rock. He was a loyal nationalist, but he was also a citizen of the world, and to him Germany's interests and world interests could not be separated. Again and again he brought the debate down to the test of the practicable, but his conception of the practicable was generous. Clearly he was speaking against the prepossessions of his colleagues, but they could not gainsay his stubborn good sense. It was, said Adam, like a masterful chairman at a company meeting comforting and soothing recalcitrant shareholders, and sometimes like a wise old sheep-farmer pricking the bubbles of agricultural theorists.

But it was on the question of Germany's internal finance that he rose to the heights.

"He put the grim facts before them and what seemed to him the only road out. Here he had the others with him—all but the General, who hadn't much to say. You could see that Loeffler hated the job—hated those glossy people who did not need to look beyond the figures. There was one of them, a fellow with a big fat face and small eyes—I needn't tell you his name—who talked as if he controlled the flow of money in the world. I daresay he did. He was almost insolent with his air of cold dictation. They were all insolent, even Creevey, though he was better than some. It was the dictation of masters who were thinking only of their bank balances to a poor devil who was responsible for millions of suffering human beings. Yet Loeffler was on their side. He took their view, because he thought it was right, though his instinct was to beat them about the head. That wanted grit, you know, and he never betrayed his feelings except that he half-closed his eyes, and sank his voice to a flatter level. There was another side to it, too. He knew that in the interests of his country he was sacrificing his own class—the professional people with their small savings, the tradesman with his scanty reserves—all the decent humble folk who are the best stuff in Germany. They had trusted him, they had put him in power, and now he was sacrificing them. He was in hell, but he went through with it and never winced. I don't think I have often respected a man so much."

Falconet nodded. "I see you've gotten my notion of Loeffler. I'm glad about that. What next?"

"Next I took a holiday because he took one. He was pretty nearly all out, as anyone could see, and I discovered that he was going off for a few days to the country. I had a hint about what he meant to do. He was determined to give his bodyguard the slip, and be alone for a bit. I decided to follow him, for you can get a good line on a man when he is on holiday."

"Did you find him?"

"It took some doing. Blakiston was useful, for he has a graft with the police, and the police of course had to keep an eye more or less on his whereabouts, though I fancy he must have gone several times clean out of their ken. Anyhow, I was lucky. I got into tramping kit and I came up with him at a little inn in the Black Forest at a place called Andersbach. He had come north from Freiburg way, following the course of a stream that makes a long glen in the pine-woods. He was tired and dusty, wearing an old suit of *loden* and carrying an ancient rucksack, and he was alone.

"The inn as it happened was packed—it was a small place with cellars on the ground floor and a dining-hall up wooden steps which was pure Middle Ages. The place was like a bee-hive with trampers—the *Wandervögel*, you know—boys and girls holidaying on twopence a day. A queer crowd, but a merry one—shorts and open shirts—determined to enjoy life though the ground was cracking under them. They overflowed into the meadows round the stream and into the clearings among the pines, and slept anywhere, and ate sausage and rye bread and made coffee round little bivouacs. Innocent jolly folk, ready to talk the hind-leg off a donkey. I was swallowed up in them at once, for my rig was much the same as theirs, and they were not inquisitive. Loeffler, too. That was what he wanted. None of them had a guess who he was—probably took him for a small provincial professor. But he and I were the elders of the party, so we naturally came together. That was when I had my real talk with him."

"Didn't he spot you?" Falconet asked. "He had been seeing you a few days before."

"No. You see I was a different man—a chemist from Freiburg talking with a Breisgau accent. I learned long ago that disguise doesn't consist in changing your face and sticking on a beard, but in having a different personality. There was nothing about me to link me up with the Englishman who had been Blakiston's protégé and had been greeted as an acquaintance by Creevey. We were in a different world of mind and body."

"What did he pretend to be?"

"Nobody in particular. I think that he meant to let me imagine he was of the professor class. He is a bit of a scholar, you know, and we talked a lot about books. It was that that made him take to me, when he found that I had read Augustine and could recognise a tag from Plato. Loeffler's an extraordinary being to have the job he has. He has to work twelve hours a day at stony facts and figures, and yet all the time he is thinking of a little house in the Jura where he can look across at the Alps and botanise and read his books. He is uncommonly well read— even in English, though he talks it badly. You won't guess who his favourite authors are—Landor and Sir Thomas Browne! He was meant for the contemplative life, but he won't get it in this world. An exile from the cloister."

Falconet grinned. "Same as you, maybe. Did he talk politics?"

"Yes—the abstract kind—as if he were looking down at Germany from a great height. He seemed to enjoy that, for I fancy he doesn't get many chances of letting his mind run free. He was very illuminating. I suppose you would call him a common-sense Nationalist. One thing he said that struck me, that Communism and Capitalism were growths from the same root, both involving a servile state. He hates both as the spawn of hell, and he thinks that Germany is near the edge of the first and can only be saved by curbing the second. He would go a long way in that direction, by limiting rates of interest and striking at the sanctity of free contract. You see, he doesn't mind going back a step or two to get a run for his leap. But it's freedom that he cares about—he has the sound bourgeois clutch on the individual. One felt all the time that this fellow might have dreams but had no liking for theories. Always the practical man stuck out, but the kind of practical man who is ready for anything that will take him one step forward. That's how he struck me, since I knew who he was, and could read between the lines. To a stranger he might have seemed a windy provincial who talked boldly about things he was never likely to have much to do with."

"What did the *Wandervögel* make of him?"

"Only a friendly elderly chap who wasn't accustomed to being in the sun and had got all the skin peeled off his nose. He had a lot of trouble with that nose of his, and was always doctoring it with lanoline. . . . He talked to the hobbledehoys and joined

224

in their games—he's a useful man still on a hill walk—and we all shouted songs after supper. They chaffed him and romped with him and called him uncle."

"Did they call you uncle?"

Adam laughed. "No. I don't know why, but they didn't. I'm not as good a mixer as Loeffler. We were there three days, for it was a kind of base-camp for the trampers, and it did Loeffler a world of good. He got hill air into his lungs, and the sun comforted him, and the sight of youth cheered him. I had a walk with him one night after a blistering day, up on a ridge of the forest, where we could look down upon the meadows with their twinkling fires, and the noise of speech and singing came up to us in a queer disembodied way as if it were a sound of wild nature. There was a moon, and I could see his face clearly, and for the first time he looked happy. I remember he linked his arm in mine, and his voice had a thrill in it, as if he were repeating poetry. 'See, *mein Herr*,' he said, 'yonder is the hope of the world. These children have fallen heir to a heritage of troubles, but they have the spirit that makes light of them. They are very poor, and sweat all the year in dismal places for a pittance, but their youth will not be denied. Comfort is the foe of enthusiasm—and enthusiasm is everything, if only we can keep it from becoming madness. That is our good German folk. They have the patience of God, but their slow blood can kindle to noble things.' Then he gripped my shoulder and almost cried, 'What does it matter about the old men—you and me and our like? We have the stain of blood and folly, but these young ones are innocent. Can we ask for anything better than to be the manure for the fields from which will spring a better grain?' He went off next morning before I was awake, without saying goodbye. Four days later I read in the papers that he was in Berlin."

"Where did you go next?"

"I thought I had better look into the question of Loeffler's becoming manure too soon. That can't be allowed to happen. I knew that he was in constant danger. Blakiston told me as much, and that frozen-faced bodyguard of his was proof of it. So I went back to Berlin, and after certain preparations

225

descended into the shadows. I knew the road, you see, for I had spent three years among those particular shadows. I had confirmation of my fears. Loeffler's life is not a thing an insurance company would look at if it knew a quarter of the facts."

The café was filling up as the hour of *apéritifs* approached. "This isn't quite the place for the rest of my story," Adam said. "We'll adjourn till after dinner."

That night, in the hotel, Adam resumed.

"The danger lay in two directions—the Iron Hands and the Communists, the two groups that hanker after short cuts. The second was the easier job, for in the war I had laid down my lines there. But the first promised to be difficult, and I had to get the help of a queer fellow. His name was La Cecilia, an Italian by descent, but through his mother the owner of a little estate in Pomerania. He had English relations, and his parents died young, so he was sent to school in England. One of the smaller schools—I can't remember which. He was an undersized, dirty, ill-conditioned boy, but the most daring young devil I ever knew. I met him several times in the holidays, when he was staying in the same neighbourhood, and we rather made friends. You see, I was the elder, and he took it into his head to believe in me.

"I lost sight of him till after I joined the regiment. Then we met at a deer-forest in Scotland. He had been asked there because he was a wonderful shot with a rifle, but he didn't mix well with the other guests. He was in the German Army by that time, and had more than the average conceit of the old-fashioned Prussian officer. His manners were good enough, but they had lapses. He and I got on fairly well, for he hadn't quite forgotten his boyish respect for me. . . . There was a regrettable incident during the visit. He lost his temper with one of the stalkers and struck him, and the stalker knocked him down, and, since he looked nasty, confiscated his rifle. Cecilia went raving mad about it, and made a scene at the lodge, and—well, public opinion was pretty hot against him. I helped to smooth things over, and got him quietly off the place. He handed me a good deal of abuse, but I suppose, when he came to think it over, he was grateful.

"Anyhow, the next time I ran across him he was friendly. It

was at a little mountain inn in the Vosges, where I had turned up on a push-bike in one of my private explorations. I was then at the Staff College. Cecilia was on the same errand, I think— for the other side. He was using a different name, and was got up like a clerk on holiday. We both knew what the other was doing, and we didn't refer to it. But we had a great evening's talk about things in general. At first he was cold to me—you see, I had been a witness of his humiliation at Glenfargie, and the man was as proud as Lucifer. But he thawed in the end, and gave me about a quarter of his confidence. He had grown into a tough, lean, sallow little fellow, with a quiet manner hiding the embanked fires. A real volcano, for he was the complete dare-devil, with a passion for all that was desperate and spectacular and incalculable, and at the same time as cunning as a monkey, and with shrewdness behind his grandiose imagination. A sort of D'Annunzio. I remember thinking that, if war came, he would be killed in the first month.

"But he wasn't. I had a letter from him in 1920. He did not know what I had been after in the war, but somehow or other he had heard that I had done something, so he assumed that I must be a fire-eater like himself. It was a long, crazy epistle. He complained that the world was no longer fit for a gentleman, but that there was still hope if the gentlemen would only get together. National hatreds, he said, were over, the battle was now between the gentlemen and the rabble, and it was for all men of breeding and courage to work together. I gathered that he was in the inner circle of the Iron Hands, and he wanted to connect up with those who were fighting the same battle elsewhere, for, as he saw it, it was a world conflict. . . . I took some pains in replying to his nonsense. I didn't choke him off, but told him that just at present I was out of action and lying low. I was interested in the Iron Hand business, and wanted to keep in touch with Cecilia.

"Well, I succeeded in doing that, and I found out a good deal. The Iron Hand movement was on the face of it just an organisation of ex-soldiers, like the American Legion, partly benevolent and partly nationalist. There were thousands of members who only joined to keep up the fellowship of the trenches. But there was an inner circle to it which was playing a big part in politics, and an innermost circle which meant real mischief. This last cherished the old idea of iron discipline and class supremacy, and meant to win or perish. Peace in the world was the last thing they sought, for their only hope lay in a new and bigger ferment. They were violent German Nationalists, but they were cosmopolitan too, in their outlook—they wanted to brigade all the elements in every land that would help to restore the old world. They were true storm-troops, ready for any forlorn hope, and prepared to use any means, however devilish, and Cecilia was one of their brains.

"As soon as I left the Black Forest I went to Cecilia—I had been keeping track of him, you see. I didn't say much, but he believed that I was ready for the field again. Anyhow, he welcomed me. He sat and stared at me for a minute or two, and seemed to be satisfied."

Falconet laughed.

"I judge he was," he said. "If I was looking for a confederate in a desperate job, your face would be enough for me. Go on, Adam."

"He told me that if he took me among his friends there would be no going back, and he fixed me with his solemn, mad eyes. I said that I perfectly understood that. Then my doings became like a crude detective yarn, and I needn't trouble you with the details. He gave me passports to the inner circle, but I had to find my way there alone—that was part of the ritual. I had to pass through layers and layers of vedettes—all kinds of people you wouldn't suspect—bagmen, and small officials, and tradesmen, and peasants, each doing his appointed job in the dark. In the end I landed in the upper room of a squalid little eating-house in—never mind where. And there I became an honorary member of a fairly mischievous brotherhood.

"Cecilia was there, but he wasn't the most important member. There was a small, plump man with the thick rings on his hands that people wear for rheumatism, and a face all puckered into grey bags. He only spoke in grunts, but he seemed to be the final court of appeal. They called him Gratias—Dr. Gratias. And there was one wonderful fellow, with a neck like the busts of

228

Julius Caesar, and atop of it a small round head. He looked the pure human animal, one-idea'd, with the force and fury of a bull. He was a noble of sorts—the Baron von Hilderling. There were others too. . . . No, there was no melodrama. No signature in blood, no swearing of oaths—those gentry are beyond the inhibitions of oaths. They treated me with immense civility, but rather as if I was a criminal whose *dossier* was wanted by the police. They most politely took down every detail about my appearance, every measurement—even my fingerprints. You see, they were determined never to lose sight of me again, and if I turned traitor to make certain of a reckoning."

Falconet looked grave. "That's bad. They've gotten a tight cinch on you."

"It was the only way. I had to put myself in their hands. It adds to the odds in the game, but only a little. . . . After that was done they were perfectly frank with me, and Cecilia was almost affectionate. They took it for granted that I was heart and soul on their side, but they didn't ask me to do anything—not yet. I was only a friendly foreign associate. But I learned a good deal about their plans."

"Loeffler?" Falconet asked sharply.

"Yes, he is the enemy. Partly because he is Chancellor, and therefore the prop of a system which they detest. Partly because he is Loeffler. They are black afraid of him, for they are clever men, and recognise that he is the greatest force today making for peace. They have the wits to see that he is utterly honest and utterly courageous, and therefore they fear him more than anyone else. . . . But they are not yet quite sure, and that is the hope. He has always been a Nationalist, remember—he had a first-class war record—he's not a Jew—and he's not a Socialist. They are waiting, and watching him. As soon as he declares himself, the thumbs go up."

"How do you mean?"

"They may let him attend the London Conference if his policy is still in doubt. But if, in order to prepare the ground, he thinks it necessary to make some preliminary declaration— some gesture to France or to America—then they will do their best to see that he doesn't cross the Channel."

229

Falconet whistled.

"But he means to say something. I heard that from Blakiston."

"Yes, he means to. I gathered that in Berlin. . . . Well, so much for the Iron Hands. The Communists were an easier proposition. I dropped back into the underworld in which I moved in '17 and '18, and I had no trouble in picking up the threads. With the Iron Hands I was Melfort, formerly a lieutenant-colonel in the British Army, but among the anarchs I was somebody very different—a shabby Munich journalist called Brasser—Hannus Brasser. Some of them remembered me—one of them had actually hidden me for twelve hours in his woodcellar.

"I met the Iron Hands in a room in a slum public house, but the other lot were gathered in a castle! It was a great, empty, shuttered *Schloss* in a park of a thousand acres, and it belonged to one of them who bore a name more famous in history than Hohenzollern. What a mad turn-up the world is—gutter-blood out to restore aristocracy, and blue blood eager to blast it! . . . It was a funny party, but not as impressive as the Iron Hands. You see, the Iron Hands are a new thing, idiomatically national, with a single definite purpose, while the others are only cogs in an international machine. Active cogs, of course. The last word in cold, deadly fanaticism. They accepted me in my old role of fellow-worker, and didn't trouble to ask what I had been doing since we met in cellars in '17. I noticed changes in them—they were wilder, less confident, a little more desperate. There was a woman among them called Probus—Netta Probus—who struck me as nearly the evillest thing I had ever set eyes on."

"How do they look on Loeffler?" Falconet asked.

"With respect—and utter hatred. He is the triumphant bourgeois who may just pull Germany out of the mire, which is the last thing they want. They don't underrate his abilities—if anything, they overrate them. They are as afraid as the Iron Hands of the London Conference, and they will do their best to keep him away from it. Oh yes, murder is their usual card, and no doubt they will have a try at it—they are an unimaginative lot, with a monotonous preference for the crude. But they are less to be feared than the Iron Hands, for they have been trying that game for years, and the police have a line on most of them. I

230

had some difficulty in getting away from that cheerful party, for it broke up in confusion. Yes, a police raid. It was piquant to be hunted by Loeffler's own watchdogs, when I was trying my hand at the same game."

Falconet demanded the full story, but he got little of it, for Adam seemed to regard it as a thing of minor importance.

"Two, I think, were caught. The woman Probus got away, unfortunately. I had a bit of a cross-country run, with several automatics behind me to improve my speed. A good thing that I was in pretty hard condition! Lucky for me, too, that I had kept my communications open. I had rather a difficult twelve hours till I reached one of my hidy-holes. After that it was easy, and I emerged the spruce Parisian *commis-voyageur* you saw this afternoon. Flew into France with a watertight passport and a valise full of samples."

Adam yawned. "I'm for bed. Tonight I am a Christian gentleman, but Heaven knows what I shall be tomorrow. You and I must part for a week or two, for I'm going to be rather busy. My job is to see Loeffler safe in England. There we can leave him to the best police in the world."

"And after that?" Falconet asked.

"One stage at a time. The London Conference is the thing that matters most to the world at this moment. After it I stand back. I leave Loeffler to have it out with Creevey and his friends. By the way, Creevey has a bigger international reputation than I thought. The Iron Hands know all about him, and don't approve of him. Same with the Communist lot. He's their pet mystery man, and they have built a wonderful bogy out of him, something which they can fear and hate to their heart's content. He may find some day that his life isn't as healthy as he would like."

Adam stretched his arms like a tired boy. For one of his years his movements were curiously young. Falconet dragged his long limbs from his armchair and complained of stiffness.

"I'm growing old," he said. "I get rheumatism if I sit long in the same position. How in thunder do you manage to keep so spry, Adam? You look happy, too."

The other laughed.

"I have an active job to look forward to. And I haven't had much of that since you and I left the Polar ice. . . . Also, I now know where I am. I have been flying too high, and my pinions won't carry me. I have been trying to work on the stage, when my proper job is in the wings. Loeffler has the right word for it. I'm content to be the manure to make the corn spring."

CHAPTER II

I

ON the 23rd of October the Chancellor spent a busy day
in the important city of Rottenburg. He arrived in the
morning by special train from Berlin, and drove to the apart-
ments taken for him at the Kaiserhof, which stands near the
middle of the Koenigplatz, the famous street which divides the
new industrial and residential city from the older quarter of
Altdorf. In the forenoon, attended by the burgomaster and
councillors, he opened the new Handelshochschule, one of the
extravagant public buildings which Germany has indulged in
since the war, and made a speech on his country's industrial
future. After luncheon he fulfilled many engagements, including
visits to the new technical museum and to several schools, at
each of which he had something pleasant to say, for the Chancellor had a gift for apposite occasional speeches. Thereafter he
had long interviews with certain steel magnates, and then retired
to deal with his papers. It was understood that he proposed to
himself dinner in his rooms with his secretaries and a quiet
evening, leaving early next morning for Cologne.

But this programme was only for the public. The Chancellor
did not dine at the Kaiserhof, and the dinner ordered for him
was eaten by his secretaries alone. As the October dusk fell he
descended, wrapped up in a heavy ulster with a white muffler
round his neck, and, emerging from a side door in a narrow
street which ran at right angles from the Koenigplatz, entered
a waiting motor-car. Outside the town he stopped the car, and
took his seat beside the driver, for the evening was fine and he
was a glutton for fresh air.

Twenty miles from Rottenburg is the important railway junction of Neumarkt, on the main line between Paris and eastern

Europe. It is the junction from which travellers branch off to Switzerland and the south. The main day express from Paris arrives there at seven o'clock, but the night express which crosses the Alps does not leave till nine-thirty, having to wait for the connection with the Rhineland and the north. Passengers for the south have consequently two hours and a half at their disposal, which they usually spend in dining at the excellent table of the Hôtel Splendide, adjacent to the railway station.

A certain French Minister of State left Paris that morning, his destination, as the Press announced, being a well-known holiday resort on the Italian lakes, where he proposed to take a week's rest before the toil of the London Conference. But the Minister did not dine at the Hôtel Splendide. He left his secretary to see to his baggage, and hurried into the street, where a car awaited him by arrangement. After that he was driven rapidly through the pleasant woodland country to the north of Neumarkt to a village called Neustadt, where a little inn stood apart in a rose garden. There he found a modest dinner awaiting him, and he ate it in the company of a small man with a peaked beard to whom he had much to say. At a quarter to nine he left the inn, rejoined his car, which was waiting in a retired place, duly caught the south-bound express, and next morning was among the pines and vineyards of the Italian foothills.

A quarter of an hour later his companion paid the bill and ordered his car. Night had fallen, but it was the luminous dark of a fine autumn. As on the outward journey he sat beside the driver, partly for fresh air, and partly for another reason. He wore a white scarf round his neck, a dark ulster, and a soft black hat.

A mile from Neustadt the road was under repair for several hundred yards, and there was passage only for a single car at a time. Traffic had to wait at each end at the dictation of a man with a red lamp, who blocked ingress till the other end was clear. At the Rottenburg end several men with motor-bicycles might have been seen, lounging and smoking. They were men with unsmiling faces and broad shoulders that had once been drilled, and, though in ordinary civilian dress, they had the air of being on duty. They had inconspicuously accompanied the Chancellor from the Kaiserhof as his bodyguard, and now awaited his return, for their orders had been to stop short of Neustadt.

A car came out of the alleyway which they recognised. It was a big Mercedes, and beside the driver sat a small man in a dark coat with a white muffler. That white muffler was their cue. They mounted their bicycles, and two preceded the car, and two followed it. They attended it till it stopped in the side street running up from the Koenigplatz, and they saw the passenger descend and enter the hotel, after which they dispersed for supper. But one of them had stopped for a moment and rubbed his eyes. "His Excellency has dined well," he said. "He trips like a young 'un."

Five minutes or so after the cyclists had started, another car passed the road-mending operations. It was exactly the same as its predecessor—a Mercedes limousine, and beside the driver sat a small man in a dark greatcoat and a white scarf. There were no cyclists to accompany this car, which made its best speed along the fine broad highway towards Rottenburg.

Presently the speed slackened, and the driver stopped to examine his engine.

"She pulls badly, *mein Herr*," he said. "I do not know why, for she was overhauled but yesterday."

The journey continued, but it was a limping business, scarcely ten miles an hour. Loeffler looked at his watch, and compared it with the far-off chiming of the half-hour from the Rottenburg clocks. He was in no hurry, for he had nothing more to do that night, and he was enjoying the mild autumn weather.

But when the Rottenburg lights were near and lamp-posts had begun to dot the country road, the car came to a dead stop. The chauffeur descended, and, after examination, shook his head.

"As I thought. It is the big end which has had some mischief done to it. Somehow it has not been getting its oil. We cannot continue. I must wait here in the hope of a tow, and you, I fear, must go on on foot. We are almost in Rottenburg. That is Altdorf before you, and in half an hour you will be in the Koenigplatz."

Loeffler was not unwilling. He had had too little exercise of late, and he was glad to stretch his legs. He took off his ulster and bade the driver leave it at his hotel when he reached the city. But he retained his white neckerchief, for his throat was weak, and he had a good deal of public speaking before him in the near future.

"You will continue till you meet the tram-lines," said the driver. "See, there is their terminus just ahead. But stop, there is a better road, I think." He removed his cap and scratched his head. "I am a newcomer to this place, but it sticks in my mind that the tram-lines fetch a circuit. Here, friend," he cried to a man who stood on the side path. "What's the nearest way to the Kaiserhof hotel?"

The man, who looked like a workman, took his pipe from his mouth and came forward.

"The Kaiserhof?" he said. "Through Altdorf undoubtedly. It will save the gentleman a mile at least. By the Ganzstrasse which enters the Koenigplatz almost at the hotel door. See, *mein Herr*. After the tramway terminus you take the second street on your left and continue. That is the Ganzstrasse. You cannot miss it."

Loeffler thanked him, gave some final orders to his driver, and stepped out briskly. He had many things to think about and was glad of this chance, for he thought best when he was alone and using his legs. He looked back once and saw his driver sitting on the kerb, lighting his pipe. He did not notice the workman, who had crossed the road and was following him.

The Chancellor had had for many months to submit to the perpetual surveillance of a bodyguard from the secret police. He submitted, for he knew that it was wise, since his life was not his own, but he did not like it, and he welcomed a chance to escape from tutelage. He felt happier mixing freely with his own people than set on a guarded pinnacle. He liked, too, the spectacle of the evening life of the streets—it was not yet ten o'clock and they would be thronged—and he enjoyed the soft dry air into which was creeping the first chill of the coming winter. He strode vigorously along, and had soon reached the entrance to the Ganzstrasse.

This was a narrower street with no tram-lines. At the beginning it ran through a new workman's quarter of small houses

236

interspersed with timber yards. Here it was open and well-lit, and there were few people about. But presently it entered the old quarter of Altdorf, for it had been the principal street when Altdorf was a fortified town, whose inhabitants kept geese on the wide adjoining pasturelands. A good many new tenements had been erected, but between these rookeries were the bowed fronts of old buildings, and there were many narrow lanes running into mazes of slums. Loeffler remembered that Altdorf did not bear the best of reputations. There had been bread riots and other disorders in recent years, and he had a vague recollection of reports in which certain notorious suspects were said to have harboured here. The street certainly did not look too respectable. The broken pavement was crowded with people, sauntering youths and shopgirls, workmen, seedy-looking flotsam and jetsam, and the cafés seemed of a low type. He glanced in at a window now and then, and saw ugly heads bent over beer mugs. But the crowd was orderly enough, and he noticed a policeman here and there. Somewhere, too, must be the watchful figures of his bodyguard. He had to abate his pace and keep close to the wall to avoid being uncomfortably jostled. Several loutish-looking fellows had pushed against him, and one or two had peered suspiciously into his face. The height of the houses made the lighting bad. Between the lamps there were patches which were almost dark.

In one of these dark patches he found himself suddenly addressed. It was by a man in rough clothes, who had a cap with a broken peak and a knitted scarf knotted about his throat. The fellow rubbed shoulders with him and spoke low in his ear, and the voice and speech were not those of a workman.

"Excellency," he said, "do not look at me, but listen. You are in danger—grave danger. You must do as I tell you if you would save your life."

Loeffler in the war, and ever since, had lived in crises and had been forced to take swift decisions. Now he did not look at the speaker. In a level voice he asked: "What are your credentials? Why should I trust you?"

The man sidled away from him as they passed a lamp-post, and drew near again as the street darkened.

237

"I am the man Buerger who walked with you in the woods at Andersbach a month ago. We talked of St. Augustine."

"Good," said Loeffler. "I remember. Tell me, what must I do?"

"Your bodyguard have been decoyed away," was the answer. "There are men close to you who seek your life. In three and a half minutes, when you have passed the third lamp-post from here, shooting will begin farther up the street, and the police whistles will be blown, and the few people here will hurry to the sound. But the shooting will be a blind, for it is you—here—that matters. Your enemies will seize you. They may kill you now, if they are hustled, but anyhow they will kill you soon."

"So!" Loeffler's voice was unchanged. The news only made him slow down his pace a little. "And you propose?"

"When the shots are fired we shall be abreast a little slit of a passage. It is called the Ganzallee, and is very ancient. It turns south from this street and then runs parallel to it and debouches just where it meets the Koenigplatz. It is narrow, so that two men can scarcely walk abreast. You must turn down it and run—run for your life. If you reach the Koenigplatz you are safe, and within fifty yards of your hotel."

"But they may catch me. I am not a young man."

"Your Excellency is not slow with your legs, for I have seen you. But I will lead the pursuit—and shepherd it. The others will not be allowed to pass me, and the place is so dark and narrow that they cannot shoot ahead. . . . Are you ready, Excellency? We are almost there."

"I am ready," said Loeffler. Under the last lamp-post he had glanced at the dirty, white face of his companion, and seen there that which he had recognised—something he believed he could trust.

The man slowed down a little, and Loeffler fell into step. It seemed to him that figures were crowding in on him on the pavement, all keeping pace with him. But he did not turn his head, though his eyes shifted to the left to look out for the crack in the masonry which was the Ganzallee.

Then suddenly a hundred yards up the street shots rang out,

238

and at the same moment his companion hustled him. "There!" he whispered. "Run for your life and do not look back. Straight on. There is no turning."

Loeffler cannoned against an iron post in the entrance of the alley, bruising his thigh. Then he charged into a slit of darkness, while behind him he heard a sudden babble like a baying of hounds.

Things moved fast in that minute. The shots up the street were followed by a tumult of shouting, out of which rang shrilly the whistles of the police. The crowd at the mouth of the Ganzallee thinned, for some fled back down the street, and others ran towards the tumult. One or two policemen with drawn batons passed at the double. But half a dozen figures remained and drew quickly towards the man who had warned Loeffler.

This man behaved oddly. He whistled on his fingers, and waved his hand. Then he shouted something which may have been a password. Then he turned down the Ganzallee with the half-dozen at his heels. Each man of them had a pistol drawn.

The place was as dark as a tunnel, but now and then it was pricked with light from some window far up in the ravine of old masonry. The men behind saw nothing of the fugitive, but it was quiet in there, away from the noise of the street, and they could hear him slipping and stumbling ahead. The ground was cobbled and uneven, but the soft-soled shoes of the pursuit did not slip, while those of the quarry were clearly giving him trouble. The contest looked to be unequal in another way, for the seven men ran confidently in the dark as if the ground was familiar to them, while the man they sought could not put forth his best speed, in case of colliding with the wall at the many windings.

The chase was mute, except for laboured breathing. The man who led the pack may not have been the slowest, but he was far the clumsiest. Unlike the rest he wore nailed boots, which scrawled on the cobbles and made him often stumble. Yet none of the others succeeded in passing him, for he had the trick— learned long ago on an English football field—of edging off a competitor.

239

Once they were nearly up to the fugitive—he could not have been more than five yards ahead—but at that moment the leader tripped and staggered, causing the next two men to cannon into him and thereby delaying the chase for at least ten seconds. A second time success seemed to be within their grasp, at a point where the alley turned to the right and sloped steeply towards the Koenigplatz. They could see the glow of an arc lamp dimly reflected, and in it the figure of the man they sought, twisting like a hare, as his nails slipped on the greasy stones.

Undoubtedly the pursuit would have caught him, for he was making bad time, had it not been for the mishap to its leader. For his feet seemed suddenly to go from under him, and he came down with a crash, blocking the narrow road. The next three men cascaded over him on to their heads, and the last three sat down violently in their attempt to pull up. For a minute there was a struggling heap of humanity in the alley, and when it had sorted itself out the fugitive was in the bright light of the alley's debouchment.

"Our bird has escaped us," said one of them after a mouthful of oaths. "God's curse on you, Hannus, for a clumsy fool."

The leader, whom they called Hannus, sat on the ground nursing a bruised shoulder.

"God's curse on the cobbler that nailed my boots," he groaned. "Who was to guess that he would turn in to this rabbit-run! Had I known I would have come barefoot!"

Loeffler had some anxious moments when he almost felt the breath of his pursuers on his neck. Even at the sound of the final cataclysm he dared not turn his head, and he did not slacken pace till he emerged, breathless and very warm, in the Koenigplatz, with the lights of the Kaiserhof just across the street. He had a glimpse of the upper end of the Ganzstrasse, where the row seemed to be over. He went straight to his rooms, and informed his secretaries that he was ready for bed.

"And by the way, Karl," he said, "you might have up the police escort that Goertz insists on, and give them a wigging. They lost me tonight for the better part of an hour. Bad staff-work somewhere."

The packet boat had scarcely passed the end of the breakwater which outlined the river channel when it encountered the heavy swell of the Channel, tormented by a north-easter. The tourist season was over, and it no longer ferried backwards and forwards crowds of cheerful trippers. Very few passengers had come on board, and those few were composing themselves in the cabins or in corners of the lower deck for several hours of misery.

But the steamer carried a good deal of cargo, and in the loading of it had fallen behind her scheduled time of starting. There were several touring cars, the owners of which had crossed by the quicker route, and left their cars to follow by the cheaper. There was also a certain amount of perishable fruit from the Normandy orchards. So the French harbour had witnessed a busy scene before the boat's departure. On the quay there had been none of the usual sellers of picture postcards and chocolates and cherries, but there had been more than the usual complement of stevedores and dock labourers to assist with the cargo.

There had indeed been a bustle opposite the after-part of the steamer, which contrasted with the meagre traffic at the passengers' entry. The gangways to the hold had been crowded, and when the whistle blew for departure there was a scurrying ashore of blue-breeched dockers. One man, who had been fussing about the position of a motor-car and giving instructions in excellent French, did not leave with the rest, though he did not seem to be a passenger. He remained inconspicuously on the side farthest from the quay, where a ladder led to the middle deck, and, when the ship was leaving the river and the bustle in the hold had subsided, he ascended the ladder and found a seat in a place which the spindrift did not reach. He was dressed in a worn trench waterproof, and he wore a soft green hat well pulled down over his brows.

Loeffler had come aboard early, and had sat himself in a corner of the smoking-room with a novel. After much thought he had chosen this route across the Channel. It was of extreme importance that he should be in England before the other delegates to the London Conference, for he had many preliminary matters to discuss. Had he crossed from Calais or Ostend his journey would have been conspicuous, and would have been broadcast throughout the world, thereby raising suspicion when suspicion must, at all costs, be avoided.

There was another reason. In a speech at Bonn, three days earlier, he had said things which had been nicely calculated to prepare the atmosphere for the Conference, but which, as he well knew, meant a declaration of war against certain potent forces in his own country. He had repeated them in a statement to an international news agency. He was perfectly aware of the danger he ran, and understood that these words of his would make certain people determined that he should not sit at the London council board. He was dealing, he knew, with enemies to whom human life meant little. His colleagues would have had him travel by some way where he could be securely guarded. An aeroplane had been suggested, but by air he could not preserve his incognito, since it was the most public of all methods of conveyance, and his arrival would immediately be known. The same argument applied against the ordinary routes. There, indeed, he could have been well guarded, but it meant publicity, and that must be shunned.

So he had chosen the long sea-route from a western French port at a season when few people were travelling. It fitted in with his plans, for he had to have certain conversations in Paris, which could not be missed. Instead of an escort he had decided to trust in the protection of obscurity. He had reached Paris inconspicuously, and there had been no official greetings at the station. He had met the man to whom he wished to talk in an obscure café on the Rive Gauche. His hotel had been humble, and he had driven to the coast in an ordinary hired car. His passport did not bear his own name. On the English side all had been arranged. There he would be met by his host and driven to a country house. Once in England, he believed that any risk would be past, for he would have the guardianship of the famous English police till the Conference was over. Beyond that he did not look, for it was his habit, so far as he himself was concerned, to live for the day. If the Conference succeeded, much of his task was done, and the rest was in the lap of the gods.

Loeffler was a good sailor, and did not mind the violent pitching of the vessel. His novel did not interest him, and he relapsed into those complex reflections from which he was never for long free. Much of his power lay in the fact that he really thought. He gave less time to official papers than do most men, for he had the gift of plucking the heart swiftly from them, but he gave many hours to thought.

There was only one other man in the smoking room, a plump gentleman in knickerbockers, who was trying to write at a table and finding it difficult. He was smoking a rank cigar, and was bespattering himself with ash and ink. Loeffler lit his pipe to counteract the cigar, and half-shut his eyes. But he found the place ill-suited for his meditations. It was stuffy and smelly; each minute it seemed to hurl itself into the air and settle back with a disquieting wriggle, while spray lashed at the closed windows. He took off his short overcoat and laid it beside his big white waterproof. Then he changed his mind, put on his waterproof and went out.

He sought the upper deck, from which a bridge led across the hold to the after-part of the ship. All morning he had sped along the French roads amid scurries of rain, but now the skies had cleared and a cold, blue heaven looked down upon the tormented seas. But from stem to stern the vessel was swept with salt water—stinging spray, and on the starboard side great grey-green surges. Loeffler had always loved wild weather, and his spirits rose as he inhaled the keen air and felt the drive of spindrift on his cheek. He put his thoughts back under lock and key, and prepared to enjoy an hour or two of sanctuary.

Sanctuary—yes, that was the right word. He was enclosed between sea and sky in a little cosmos of his own. There was no sign of human life about, sailor or passenger; the vessel seemed to be impelled by no human power, like the ship in the strange English poem which he admired. Loeffler had been a mountaineer from his youth, because of his love of deep solitude. He was far from that nowadays, in a life which was all

243

heat, and sound, and movement, but the gods had sent him a taste of it this afternoon. He strode the deck, his mackintosh collar buttoned round his throat. The seas were breaking heavily over the after-deck. He would like to go there and get wet, as he had often done when a boy.

There was another figure on the deck, and he saw that it was the knickerbockered gentleman of the smoking-room. He had finished his cigar and had put on oilskins. A hat with the brim turned down almost met the oilskin collar, so that only a nose and eyes were visible. Loeffler realised that he had been wrong in thinking the man plump, for as he moved he gave the impression of immense strength. Those shoulders were overlaid not with fat but with muscle.

The man seemed to be in the same mood as Loeffler. He cried out in French about the weather, not in malediction but in praise.

"Here is the wind to blow away megrims! Like me, I see, you are fond of a buffeting."

He fell into step, and paced the deck beside him, laughing loudly when a wave more insolent than the rest topped the bulwarks and sent its wash swirling round their feet.

They covered the length of the deck twice, and then came to a halt above the hold, where there was some little shelter from the wind. The capstan and anchors in the stern were almost continually awash, and waves seemed to strike the place obliquely and half-submerge the staff from which the red ensign fluttered.

"We are well defended, both of us," the man cried in a jolly voice. "Let us adventure there. We can dodge the bigger waves. My God, that is the spectacle!"

Loeffler followed him across the bridge, bending to the buffets of the gale. A man in a trench waterproof, ensconced in a corner of the deck below, watched the two and smiled. He had been getting uneasy about Loeffler's sojourn in the cabin. He knew that if he did not leave it he would die there, since those who sought his life were determined to have it at all costs, but that they preferred another plan, with which Loeffler had now obligingly fallen in.

244

The starboard side of the after-deck was running like a river, but on the port side there was a thin strip which the waves did not reach. There were no bulwarks here, only a low rail; in quiet summer passages travellers would sun themselves here in deck-chairs and watch the track behind them outlined in white foam amid the green. There had been some carelessness, for several of the stanchions of the starboard railing had been removed and not replaced. For a yard or two there was no defence between the planking and the sea.

"What a spectacle!" repeated the large man in knickerbockers. "It is a parable of life, Monsieur. A line, a hair, a sheet of glass alone separates man at all times from death." He was looking at the sea, but now and then he glanced forward over the empty ship ploughing steadily through the waste. Not a soul was visible. He did not see the man in the trench waterproof, who had scrambled halfway up the iron ladder from the hold, and was now flattening himself under the edge of the after-deck. Nor could the man see him, though he could hear his voice.

Loeffler, awed by the majesty of the scene, and thinking his own thoughts, found his arm taken by the other.

"See, that big surge is past. Now we may look over the other side, and be back before the next one."

Obediently he took three steps amid the backwash of the last wave, and looked into a trough of green darkness over which the little vessel was slightly heeling.

Then suddenly he found himself grasped in arms like a bear's, grasped so firmly that the breath went from him. The big man was bracing himself for some effort against which he was powerless to struggle. He felt his feet leave the deck. . . .

The grip slackened. A sharp voice had cried out behind them. It cried a single word, but that word was enough to check Loeffler's assailant.

Then it spoke in fierce German.

"You fool, Kurbin. You have got the wrong man."

The giant let his arms relax, and Loeffler found himself switched from his grasp by a man in a trench waterproof. The ship was heeling again to port, and a shove sent him reeling against the port rails.

"Back," a voice shouted. "Run, man, run for your life."

Loeffler had heard that voice before. When the next surge broke over the stern he was already halfway across the bridge over the hold. He glanced back once and saw the after-part of the ship blotted out in a shroud of spray.

Loeffler's going seemed to rouse the knickerbockered man to berserk fury. He flung himself upon the other, and the two swung against the port rails. But the man in the trench water-proof was equal to the occasion. The giant was wearing rubber-soled shoes which had a poor purchase on the swimming deck. He slipped, and the other wriggled out of his clutch and managed to clasp him round the middle from behind. Then, while his balance had gone, he swung him in his arms against the low rail which defended the place from the hold. The rail gave under the weight, and the big man pitched down among the motor-cars. His head hit the bonnet of one, and he rolled over and lay quiet.

The man in the trench waterproof glanced forward and saw that no-one was in sight. He slipped down into the hold and had a look at his adversary. The man was bleeding from a gash on the head, and was doubtless concussed, but his neck was unbroken.

Then he went forward and found a sailor. "There has been an accident," he said. "A gentleman has fallen into the hold from the after-deck. He is unconscious, but not, I think, badly hurt. Get him moved to a cabin. Meantime I will see the captain."

He showed the captain certain papers, and told him a story which caused that honest seaman to rub his eyes.

"There need be no fuss," he said. "There must be no fuss, since no harm has been done. You know Lord Lamancha by sight? He will meet the small gentleman in the white mackintosh and take charge of him. Never mind who the gentleman is. He travels incognito, but he is a person of some importance. As for the other, the doctor had better attend to him. He has no baggage, but he has plenty of money—he will probably wish to return to France with you tomorrow. Only, till we reach England, his cabin door must be kept locked."

246

III

As Lamancha drove Loeffler through the dusk from the coast, by way of a broad river valley into wooded uplands, he did not talk politics.

"You'll have five days of peace here," he told him, "peace very slightly interrupted by discussion. Geraldine is coming down, and Stannix, and that is the party. It is a jolly place, and the weather looks to be mending. Don't you call this time the 'Old Wives' Summer' in Germany? You don't shoot, I know, but I will take you for some long rides on the Moor. One doesn't often get the chance of entertaining a man like you in our simple country way. The last European celebrity who came here had three secretaries with him, and Scotland Yard sent down a couple of men."

Loeffler observed that it was a pleasure to get away from the surveillance of detectives, and Lamancha laughed.

"Well, as it happens, you won't quite escape that. The fact is, we had a burglary two nights ago. Oh no, nothing serious. It was very much the usual business—my wife's room, while we were at dinner, open windows, a ladder from the garden. The burglars were scared away by the return of her maid, and had no time to pinch anything. But the police have chosen to take it seriously, and there are London men in the village making inquiries. It has nothing to do with you, of course, for nobody knows that you are here. But I thought I'd let you know about it, in case you are surprised by the sight of sharp-faced fellows looking on at our doings."

The weather mellowed, as Lamancha had hoped, into a St. Luke's summer, and for five days Loeffler enjoyed a leisure the existence of which he had almost forgotten. The old house, set among meadows of hill turf and flanked by russet woods, seemed a sanctuary remote from a fevered world. The hostess was the only woman in the party, and Mildred Lamancha's low, sweet, drawling voice gave the appropriate key of peace. Geraldine, the Prime Minister, shot all day with Stannix, while Lamancha and his guest, mounted on hill ponies, quartered the uplands, and Loeffler's face took on a wholesome colour from wind and sun.

At night they talked, and their talk ranged far. In such company Loeffler felt at his ease, and threw off much of his habit of caution. Through his dogged matter-of-factness there came glimpses of enthusiasms and dreams. Geraldine, who of the three ministers knew him least well, was moved to confide to his host that he had got a new notion of the little man.

On the evening before they were due to leave for London there was a small party. "Old Jocelyn is coming to dine," Lamancha told Loeffler; "asked himself and I didn't like to refuse. He used to be our Ambassador at Vienna, and he speaks good German—not the limping affair of the rest of us. You'll like the old fellow. He's uncommonly knowledgeable, and he'll be thrilled to meet you. There's no more need for secrecy, for tomorrow evening the papers will announce your arrival. I hope you have had a pleasant time here. It has been a very educative time for all of us, especially for the P.M. I don't mind telling you that I have been rather anxious about him. He sees a little too much of Creevey and his lot."

"I have learned much," Loeffler replied with his slow smile, "and I have seen many beautiful things. Also my English has improved, is it not so?"

To his wife later in the day Lamancha brought a message.

"Jocelyn wants to know if he can bring a friend to dinner tonight. He has a man staying with him, an American doctor. Upcott's the name. Trust Jocelyn to have an assortment of odd friends. He collects them up and down the world like rare postage stamps. I suppose it's all right, for Jocelyn thinks it's only a country dinner-party. Anyhow, it's too late to matter. Things have gone well so far, I think."

"I have loved it," said Lady Lamancha. "I have completely lost my heart to the Chancellor. He is like one of the old wise collie dogs at Leriot. I don't suppose he realised he was being so closely looked after. He has been, you know. Kit spoke to me about it. He asked what dark secret we were hiding. The police have been simply squatting round the place. You didn't notice it perhaps, for you were out most of the day, but there's always been somebody hanging about each of the gates. And then there's the absurd old Scotsman that Adam Melfort insisted on our having in the house. I believe he is the life and soul of the housekeeper's room, but he is an odd figure for a servant. I am sure that he is wearing his best Sunday blacks."

Lamancha laughed.

"Amos is a wonderful graven image, but you couldn't get a better watchdog. There's a new ghost haunting the west corridor, the wraith of an elder of the kirk. . . . By the way, you remember that Adam himself is coming tonight. He'll arrive late, and will have dined already."

Sir Francis Jocelyn was a stately old gentleman, verging upon eighty, whose gout made him lean heavily upon two sticks. He was a little surprised at finding himself in what looked like a committee of the Cabinet, and his eyes opened wide when he was presented to Loeffler. Retirement from the world had not dimmed his interest in the world's affairs. Mr. Upcott, the American doctor, proved to be a youngish man with a cheerful, clean-shaven face and a mop of fair hair brushed back from his forehead. He spoke almost with an English intonation, for it seemed that he was a Bostonian, though now a professor at Baltimore. Jocelyn introduced him with a short sketch of his attainments, and he gravely informed each member of the party that he was pleased to meet them.

On a side table in the hall stood the materials for making cocktails.

"I told Upcott that he would find here what he was accustomed to," said Jocelyn. "Better let him mix the drinks. He has already turned my butler into an artist."

Mr. Upcott announced his willingness, and set to work at the side table with a professional air. Lamancha, who detested cocktails, drank sherry, but the others accepted an agreeable mixture which appeared to be known as a "Maryland sidecar." Loeffler raised his glass to the health of the compounder.

It was a pleasant meal. Jocelyn was too skilled a talker to steer near the shoals of current politics. His memory dallied with old days in pre-war Vienna, and Geraldine, who had many continental friendships, kept up the ball of reminiscence. It was a world which Loeffler knew only by hearsay, but he was eager in his questions, and the Maryland sidecar seemed to have thawed his gentle taciturnity. But the success of the dinner was Mr. Upcott, who showed that medical science had not monopolised his interests. He seemed to know everybody and to have been everywhere in the civilised world. He was enlightening in his comments on his own land, and he had the lovable solemnity on public questions which characterises one type of young American. But he had also a wealth of idiomatic slang and curious metaphors which introduced an agreeable spice of comedy. He had often to be explained to Loeffler, generally by Jocelyn, who professed to specialise in American idioms, and the explanations produced that rare thing in the Chancellor, hearty laughter.

After dinner Jocelyn, Lamancha, Stannix, and Geraldine made a four at bridge. Loeffler and Mr. Upcott did not play, and sat with Lady Lamancha round the library hearth, for the autumn frosts had begun. Their talk was desultory, for the Chancellor had relapsed into his customary silence, and sat with his eyes on the fire, as if he were seeing pictures in the flames. Mr. Upcott was as sparkling as before, and entertained his hostess with an account of the last St. Cecilia's ball at Charleston which he had attended, and which he said was the ultimate outpost of the well-born South against a vulgar world. He was very amusing, and the third in the group was forgotten.

Suddenly Loeffler raised himself from his chair.

"I think if you will permit me, gracious lady," he said, "I will go to bed. I am feeling weary, and I have much to do tomorrow."

He spoke in a small, strained voice, and his face was very white. Lady Lamancha was full of kindly anxiety.

"No. I am quite well," he said. "Only tired. Pray do not disturb yourself. I will have a long sleep."

He swayed a little as he passed the bridge table.

"What! Off already!" Lamancha cried. "Well, perhaps it's wise."

Loeffler shook hands ceremoniously with Jocelyn and left the room. Lamancha rose and came over to the fire.

"Anything wrong, Mildred? Can his food have upset him? He had the complexion of a deerstalker when he came down to dinner. Perhaps it was your cocktail, Mr. Upcott!"

The young American looked grave.

"He certainly doesn't look good. Say, Lord Lamancha, hadn't I better go up to him? It's my job, after all. We oughtn't to take chances with so big a man."

"That's a good idea. It would ease my mind. I'll show you his room."

He said something to the bridge players, and led the young doctor up the main staircase to where the west corridor turned off from the upper hall. In the dim light at the end of it stood the rock-like figure of Andrew Amos. Lamancha knocked at the door of Loeffler's bedroom, and opened it for Mr. Upcott to enter. "You'll find your way down again all right," he said. As he turned away he noticed that Amos was no longer in the corridor.

Loeffler had taken off his coat and waistcoat and was lying on his bed. He opened his eyes languidly as the young doctor entered, and made an effort to sit up.

"You stay still, Excellency," said Mr. Upcott. "Lord Lamancha thought I might as well have a look at you, for I'm a doctor by profession. Just keep as you are."

He felt his patient's pulse, looked at his tongue, and listened to the beating of his heart.

"Nothing much the matter, Excellency," he said. "But I'm going to fix you so that you'll have a good night and wake in the morning as jolly as a bird. We doctors don't work with coarse medicines now. Just a prick of a needle and a spot of the right kind of dope. Give me your arm."

Mr. Upcott took from the pocket of his dinner jacket a small flat leather case, from which he selected a tiny syringe. He did not fill it, so it appeared that it had been already prepared. He was about to take Loeffler's arm, when suddenly his right hand was seized from behind and the syringe was forced from his grasp.

Mr. Upcott turned to find that two men had entered from the adjacent sitting-room. One was the grotesque figure in black that he had noticed in the corridor. The other was a tallish man in tweeds.

"No," said the latter. "You do nothing more, Mr. Upcott."

He balanced the syringe in his palm, and then picked up the leather case from the bed.

"You have made your preparations well," he said. "One touch of this and your job would have been done. It's the new stuff, hamaline, isn't it? Doesn't kill, but atrophies the mind and drugs the body for a week or two. I congratulate you on your ingenuity."

Mr. Upcott had been transformed from the bland doctor into something alert and formidable. He looked as if he were going to strike, but there was that in the air of the two men that made him think better of it.

The man who had spoken handed him back his case.

"I take it there's nothing much wrong with Herr Loeffler," he said. "Something in your cocktail, perhaps. They tell me you are very adroit at that game. . . . You will go quietly downstairs and tell Lord Lamancha that everything is well. Then you will go home with Sir Francis Jocelyn. You had better leave England tomorrow or there may be trouble. Do you understand me?"

Mr. Upcott lifted the bedside lamp and looked at the other's face. Then he put it down and shrugged his shoulders. He laughed, and his laugh was not pleasant.

"I've got you now," he said. "Colonel Melfort, isn't it? One of us too, by God! Well, we shan't forget this evening."

Adam appeared in the library about eleven o'clock after Jocelyn and his friend had departed.

"Just arrived," he explained. He glanced at the array of glasses around the siphons and decanters.

"Hallo, have you had a party?" he said. "Where is the great man?"

"Gone to bed," said Lamancha. "He wasn't feeling his best, but a man that old Jocelyn brought to dinner, a young American doctor, had a look at him and reported him all right. Amusing chap, that doctor. Mildred went upstairs whooping at some jape of his on the doorstep. I must get her to tell it me in the morning."

IV

After breakfast next day Adam sat in Loeffler's sitting-room. The Chancellor had breakfasted in bed, but had sent word to his host that he was wholly recovered. Lamancha had interviewed him, and then Adam had been sent for.

"I have to thank you, Colonel Melfort, for a great service," Loeffler said in his shy, deprecating voice. "How great a service I do not know, but I can guess. That man last night—he would have drugged me? Would the drug have killed?"

Adam shook his head.

"I do not think so—from what I know of hamaline. But it would have made you useless in the Conference. The Iron Hands are artists, and do not take stronger measures than the case requires."

"What do you know of the Iron Hands?"

"A good deal. I am by way of being one of their inner brotherhood—the extremists who stick at nothing. You cannot defeat such people unless you are of them. For three weeks, Excellency, you have been leading a dangerous life, but now, for a little, you are safe. Since you are now officially in England you are in the keeping of the English police. As a matter of fact you have been in their charge for the last five days, but your anonymity made it difficult to take full precautions."

Loeffler had been staring at him, and suddenly recognition awoke in his eyes.

"You were the man on the boat," he said, "the man who saved me from being flung into the sea? Am I right?"

"I was the man. Do not blame the Iron Hands for that. That was the work of another branch of your enemies who are clumsier and more desperate."

Loeffler's puzzled face broke into a smile.

"It is a world of marvels," he said. "I did not think when we sat at dinner in August in Berlin that at our next meeting you would save my life. You have been my good angel."

"We met in between," said Adam. "Consider, Excellency; search your memory. What of the Freiburg chemist at Andersbach and the *Wandervögel*?"

Loeffler sprang to his feet.

"Then you were the man at Rottenburg that plucked me out of the Ganzstrasse business? Him I recognised. God in Heaven, who and what are you? Can you change your person like a wizard? You are miraculous—beyond belief. I can observe and my memory is good, but you have vanquished me utterly."

"I served a long apprenticeship to the job," said Adam. "You think we first met at dinner with Lord Lamancha in London eighteen months ago. But you are wrong. We met before that."

"It cannot be."

"It is true. Do you remember a day in February '18 at Bodenheim? You were then Major Loeffler, a convalescent recovering from wounds. You had before you for examination a neutral commercial agent, a Dane called Randers, with whose doings you were not altogether satisfied. You and your colleagues—you especially—gave Randers a pretty hot time. More than once you nearly broke through his defences. Had you succeeded Randers would have died, and I think that you yourself would not be alive this morning."

Loeffler passed his hand over his eyes.

"It comes back to me. A middle-aged man with a high colour and a blond moustache. Rather a vulgar fellow? I suspected him, but I had not enough to act upon. But I was right, you say?"

"You were right. I was a British officer, and for three years of the war I was behind your front. Thank God I was able to do your country a fair amount of harm."

"And now you would atone for it by doing my country much good. No, not atone. There was no need of atonement, for you were doing your rightful duty. But you are chivalrous, and now you would do an old enemy a kindness."

"May I put it differently? I want to help to build up the world. You are at the moment the chief builder, so my services are at your disposal. I cannot direct—I cannot even carry a hod—but I may be able to keep wreckers away."

"I thank you." Loeffler spoke gravely and held out his hand. He seemed to be under the influence either of some emotion or some sudden thought, for he walked to the window and stood there in silence looking out at the morning landscape.

254

"Come here," he said, and Adam took his place beside him.

The view was over the terraced garden to the park, which rose to a low wooded ridge. The early hours had been clear and sparkling with frost, but now banks of vapour were drifting athwart the landscape. The garden was plain in every detail, with its urns and parapets and statues, its rose beds and grass plots drenched in dew. But the park was dim, and the trees were wreathed in mist, and the ridge was only a shadow. But, far beyond, some trick of light revealed a distant swell of moorland, dark as a sapphire against the pale sky.

"Look!" said Loeffler. "That is how I see the world. The foreground is plain—and the horizon—but the middle distance is veiled. So it is with me. I see the next stage very clear, but all beyond that is hidden from me. But I see also the horizon to which I would move. . . . Let us sit down, Colonel Melfort, and talk a little. I can lay open my heart to my preserver. You are a friend of Germany, but still more you are a friend of the world. I, likewise—for Germany cannot be safe until the world is safe. Nor, I would add, can the world be safe until Germany is at peace. These things are a circle, which the pessimist will call vicious and the optimist virtuous."

He held his head low, and dropped his clasped hands between his knees, looking, thought Adam, much as Ulysses Grant might have looked at some difficult hour of the Wilderness Campaign.

"This Conference," he said, "I now think that it will succeed. But its success will only carry us a little way. We shall have a breathing space, no more—not yet a place to rest. After it there will come for Germany the slow business of waiting and toiling and suffering. She will face it, I think, and she will go through with it, but she must have some streak of light on her horizon. If that light is denied, she will despair and sink into the slough of anarchy, from which it will be hard to raise her. Then she will suffer most, but all the world will suffer much, and all our dreams of peace will have gone. We shall be back in the old cruel world—crueller than before, because there will be deeper poverty and no hope. Do you understand me, Colonel Melfort?"

255

Adam nodded. "You look to the Conference to give you the streak of light?"

"Assuredly. Your country will not deny it us. Nor will America, I think. Nor France, if she is wisely handled. Such a promise of an ultimate dawn will be much. After that my task, if God permits me, is to keep my people steady. That will not be easy, for there are many who are impatient and would cut the knot. Some of them—your friends of the past week—think that my life is the barrier to prosperity, and that with me out of the way the road will be clear. They are foolish, for I matter little. I am only the housemaid sweeping the floor and opening the windows. If I were gone the dust would be thicker, for I do not make dust. But most of my opponents are not violent or criminal, but they are obstinate and short-sighted. They cannot endure to wait. Therefore they will try other ways, and unless they are held there will be disaster."

Adam looked at Loeffler as he sat with his head poked forward, his voice grave and level, and his eyes abstracted as if in an inward vision.

"I think you can hold your people," he said.

"I think I can," was the answer. "But on one condition only—that the streak of light is not allowed to die out of their sky."

He got to his feet and stood in front of the fire.

"I will be wholly candid with you, Colonel Melfort. It is your right, since you have made yourself my friend. . . . That streak of light does not depend upon Germany, but upon the world outside. It does not altogether depend upon the Governments. They may be difficult at times, but I think they will be reasonable, for, after all, they understand their own interest. As for the Press, it does not greatly matter, since the Press is not an independent power. But there is a great and potent world which the Governments do not control. That is the world of finance, the men who guide the ebb and flow of money. With them rests the decision whether they will make that river a beneficent flood to quicken life, or a dead glacier which freezes wherever it moves, or a torrent of burning lava to submerge and destroy. The men who control that river have the ultimate word. Now most of them mean well, but they do not see far, and they are

256

not very clever; therefore they are at the bidding of any man who is long-sighted and a master of strategy. Such a man has the future of the world—the immediate future—in his hands."

"Is there such a man?" Adam asked.

"I am coming to believe that there is. And I think you know him. He can command money, and he can dictate its use, for he is clever—no, not clever—he has genius, a persuasive genius. If he wished, he could move—what? Not the State treasuries, which are difficult things. Those responsible for them have to give strict account and carry with them in their policy millions of uninstructed voters. No, he could move the private hoards of which the world is full, and apply them wisely to sowing here and irrigating there in the certainty of a rich harvest. The Rothschilds, you remember, made their great fortunes by helping a bankrupt Europe through the Napoleonic wars, by moving money to the point where it was needed. Such a man as I speak of could do more today, for he could move money not to pay bills for war material and war damages but to nurse throughout the globe the new life which is waiting to break forth. The world is richer today than it has ever been, but the communications are choked, so that one half of it is waterlogged and the other half a parched desert."

"The man you speak of is not doing what you want?"

Loeffler shook his head.

"He is moving money but capriciously, without any wise purpose. I do not think that he cares greatly for wealth, but he is scornfully amassing it—nothing more. He has persuaded finance to trust him—in America, in France, to some extent in Britain—and the trust is not misplaced, for he will earn for it big dividends. He provides loans for many lands, but at too high a price, for he exacts in return a control over certain things which in no land should be under foreign control. He has his pound of flesh, and the flesh is taken from vital parts of the body. Therefore his loans do not benefit. They tide over a momentary difficulty, but in the end they cripple recovery—and they may kill it.

"That is not all," he went on. "They foster a bitter nationalism which I would fain see die. A people is not grateful when

257

it sees its choicest possessions go in payment for this foreign help. Such a man may create violent antagonisms—dangerous for himself, more dangerous for the world."

"Let's get down to names," said Adam. "There would be more hope for things if Creevey were out of the way?"

"Yes," said Loeffler. "And also No. You open your eyes, but I will tell you what I mean. Mr. Creevey has genius beyond question, but it is a misdirected genius. Misdirected, not in its essence malevolent. As I read him he is still immature. You may laugh, but I am very serious. He has immense abilities, but he uses them like a clever child. His fault is an arrogance of intellect. He is so wrapped up in the use of a superb intelligence that he does not permit himself to look to ultimate things. He is, if you please, not awakened. Now there is so little genius in the world that I cannot wish for its disappearance, even if it stands in my way. Mr. Creevey is no common man; he is no mere money-spinner. He is no doubt very rich, but I do not think that he pays much heed to his private bank account. He seeks nobler game—the satisfaction to be won from the use of a great mind. But it is not the noblest, and in its results it may be disastrous. He is at present a dark angel in the world, but could his power be orientated otherwise he might be an angel of light."

"Why do you tell me this?" Adam asked. "I cannot help you." Loeffler smiled.

"I tell it you because you are my friend, and I want my friend to understand me."

There was a knock at the door and Lamancha entered.

"The cars will be ready in half an hour," he said. "You're coming with us, Adam, aren't you?"

"If I may. I'm by way of dining with Falconet tonight."

V

Adam and Falconet dined in the latter's rooms in St. James's Street. Another man joined them after dinner, whose name was Blakiston, an Englishman who had been for thirty years in New York and was Falconet's partner in many enterprises. He was small, grizzled, and clean-shaven, and when he spoke he had the habit of dangling tortoise-shell eyeglasses at the end of a black ribbon. He looked the conventional banker, and he had a note-book, which was seldom out of his hand.

He gave a list of businesses which sounded like an extract from the speech of the chairman of an investment company.

"Which of them are going to raise questions in the next few months?" Falconet asked.

Blakiston considered. There was a group of wood-pulp propositions in East Prussia which might be difficult—an attempt to combine several had been blocked by the local boards. An Italian artificial silk concern was at loggerheads with the Government over certain labour questions. Then there were the michelite mines in Rhodesia—something had to be done there in the way of a working agreement with the Swedish and American interests. The financial arrangements, too, with Leigh and O'Malley of New York were due for revision, for some of that group were kicking about the German municipalities loan. Blakiston had a list of other activities—a coffee combine in Brazil, the vast estates of a Westphalian syndicate in the Argentine, the proposed match monopoly in Turkey, and a new harbour on the Adriatic.

"All of them boiling up to be nasty, you think?" Falconet asked. "And with a little trouble you reckon you could make them boil faster?"

Blakiston did not consult his notebook.

"Sure," he said, smiling. "Up to a point, that is. Our interests are so widely scattered that we can bring some kind of pressure to bear in most parts of the globe."

"Enough to make it necessary for Mr. Creevey to give the business his personal attention? I mean, go out and look at things for himself?"

Blakiston considered.

"Yes, I think so. He won't go to Rhodesia—couldn't be spared that long from England. But we could so fix it that he would have to visit New York."

"Mr. Melfort wants the chance of a long private talk with him, and that can't be got in London. What do you recommend?"

"Why not an Atlantic Crossing? We could arrange that they had adjacent cabins."

Adam shook his head. "I'm afraid that wouldn't do. I want rather more than Mr. Creevey's company. We must set the stage a little."

Presently Blakiston had to leave for an appointment, and the two others sat on till Big Ben tolled midnight.

"I don't quite get you," said Falconet. "You want Creevey to yourself for a bit. What do you hope to do with him? Convert him?"

"No," said Adam. "I couldn't live with him in argument for ten minutes. I don't talk his language. If Kit Stannix can do nothing with him it's not likely that I should succeed."

"Agreed. Then, what do you mean to do?"

"Put myself alongside him—and keep there."

"In the hope that fate will shuffle the cards for you?"

"In the certainty," said Adam simply. "My job is sharpened to a point now, and that point is Creevey. He is the grit in the machine, and the grit has to be removed."

Falconet whistled.

"Pity we don't live in simpler times. Or that you were something of a ruffian. It would be so easy to knock him on the head. . . . I don't say you're not right. There are other kinds of appeals than argument, and you're an impressive fellow when you get alongside a man. You say you want to set the stage? How d'you mean?"

"I want to isolate him—get him out of his padded life into a rougher one. I want to put him outside all the fortifications he has built and make him feel naked. The Arctic ice would be the place—or the desert—but, since these are impossible, I must find a substitute."

Falconet grunted.

"I see. You want to reason with him as man to man—not as the amateur and the big professional."

"I want to make facts reason with him."

"And you believe that they will? It's a great thing to have your grip on predestination. Well, I daresay something could be managed. Blakiston will have to get busy. Our job is to shepherd

Mister Creevey out of boardrooms and special trains and big hotels into the wilderness. It might be done, for, though we are darned civilised, the wilderness is still only across the road. Count me in. I'm going to get a lot of quiet amusement out of this stunt. But it's a large-size job. You're right to look solemn."

As Adam walked home along the Embankment, he stopped to lean over the parapet and watch the river bubbling with the up-running tide. He had shown a grave face to Falconet, and gravity was the key of his mood, a grave expectancy. His mind ran back to the first sight of Creevey, when he had dined with Scrope at the restaurant, and Scrope had spoken significant words about the man with the big forward-thrusting head and the ardent eyes. He remembered his first meeting with him in Falconet's room, and his own puzzled antagonism. Later meetings were telescoped into one clear impression—of something formidable, infinitely formidable, perverse, and dangerous. He had no personal feeling in the matter; he neither liked nor disliked him, but regarded him as he would have regarded a thunderstorm or a cyclone, a perilous natural force against which the world must be protected.

And yet—was this man only an angel of destruction? In the talk in Berlin in August he had detected in him a fiery honesty; to one thing he would never be false, the power of reason with which he had been so nobly endowed. Loeffler, too, believed that if fortune were kind this capricious disintegrating force might be harnessed for the world's salvation. . . . Adam had one of those moments of revelation in which he saw life narrowed to a single road moving resolutely to a goal. His mission had been to find quality, and he had found it. His task was now to release that quality for the service of mankind—or to clip its wings and render it impotent for ever.

He had a passing moment of nervousness. His opponent was now not the perversity of the world, but a single man, and that man a genius. He mistrusted his powers, till he remembered that he was only a servant of great allies. A servant—the humblest of servants. He was not architect or builder, not even a labourer with a hod, but something lowlier still, and in his lowliness was strength. As he let himself into his rooms on the quiet Temple

261

staircase, he was in the same mood which had sent him to his knees years before in his prison cell. The sign he had asked for had been given him.

BOOK IV

CHAPTER I

M R. WARREN CREEVEY took his seat in the reserved compartment of the boat-train, and, as the whistle sounded, unfolded his *Times* and settled down to a slightly cynical study of the foreign page. It was his custom to travel in a modest state, with the best reservations; his private secretary was in an adjoining carriage, and somewhere in the train his assiduous valet; he travelled so much that he was respectfully greeted by the railway company's servants, and could count on the way being made smooth for him. The weather was sharp, so he wore a heavy fur coat, which he removed in the warm compartment. As he regarded the luxurious garment he smiled, for it reminded him of a thought which had crossed his mind as the train was starting.

A secretary and two clerks had seen him off, bringing him papers to sign, and receiving his final instructions. This hasty visit to Italy was a nuisance. What had caused the Brieg-Suffati people to get suddenly at loggerheads with the authorities, when hitherto they had pulled so well together? He had a great deal of work on his hands in London, and resented this interruption, even if it were only for a few days. . . . Yet, as he waved a farewell to his secretary and tipped the guard, he realised that he was not altogether displeased. Mr. Creevey was not a vain man—the lack of vanity was part of his strength—but he could not but be conscious that he mattered a good deal in the world. The sable-lined coat on the seat beside him was an emblem of the place he had won.

Old General Ansell, who sat on one of his boards, had a metaphor which he was never tired of using. It was drawn from the Western Front in the war. He said it had been like a great pyramid with its point directed to the enemy. Behind the lines was a vast activity—factories like Birmingham, a network of railway lines like Crewe, camps, aviation grounds, square miles of dumps, hospitals, research laboratories, headquarters full of anxious staff officers. But as one went forward, the busy area narrowed, and the resources of civilisation grew more slender. And then at the apex of the pyramid you were back in barbarism, a few weary human beings struggling in mire and blood to assert the physical superiority which had been the pride of the cave-dweller.

The General had usually applied his parable in a far-fetched way, for he was a little sceptical of the plenary power of science and harped on human quality. But Mr. Creevey gave it a different application. He, so to speak, inverted the pyramid. All great human activities expanded from a single point. Their ultimate front might be as wide as the globe, but it drew its power from the brain at the apex. His was such a brain, and it amused him to reflect how much depended on him. He was not the soldier in the trenches, but the directing mind in the impressive hinterland, from which both hinterland and trenches drew their life. . . . While the train flashed past deserted hop-fields and pastures dim under a November sky, Mr. Creevey smiled as he lit a cigar. How far was old Ansell's world of mud and blood from the guarded ritual of his life!

In Paris he drove to the Meurice, dined in a private room, and then, having no work on hand, decided to pay his respects to an old friend, the Duchesse de Rochambeau, in her flat near the Champs Elysées. The day was Tuesday, and it was her custom to receive on Tuesday. Mr. Creevey had a vast acquaintance, which he carefully tended, for he was a student of humanity. He had a weakness for a certain type of aristocratic relic-worshipper, especially in France; their sentimentality did not appeal to him, but they cherished wit, a rarity in these days, and he liked the free play of their minds. Their illusions were kept apart in a modish shrine, and did not, like the illusions of democracy, taint and muddy the springs of thought. It pleased him to share in the delicate swordplay of a world without seriousness or passion. . . . But the Duchesse had a cold in her head, and her *salon* that evening was dull. There was a contentious old gentleman who buttonholed him and discoursed of Loeffler with the dismal platitudes of the Nationalist press. Mr. Creevey left early and retired to bed.

The long journey next day bored him. He was fond of a day journey, for it enabled him to make up arrears of reading, and this one he had marked out for the study of a new Swedish work on currency. But he found the arguments of Professor Broester so ill-coordinated, that he turned to a couple of sensational romances which he had brought from England. These did not please him more—indeed, they exasperated him with their pictures of a world where strange things happened at every street-corner. Heavy-footed nonsense, he reflected; strange things happened, but not in this mode of childish melodrama. Life was conducted nowadays by great standardised machines, as exact and ruthless as the processes of nature, and no casual accident could deflect them. Adventure lay in designing, altering, regulating this cosmic mechanism, and not in inserting a foolish spoke in the wheels. The spoke would be as futile as a child's beating of the dome of St. Paul's to annoy the Dean.

The train was very empty. In the restaurant car that night at dinner he sat opposite a lachrymose German who harped on the sins of France, much as the old gentleman at the Duchesse de Rochambeau's had harped on the misdeeds of Loeffler. He was a youngish man with fair hair who chose to talk English. Mr. Creevey, always impatient of amateur politics, did not linger over his meal. He felt irritated, almost—a rare thing for him—depressed, so he summoned his private secretary and bent his mind to business. His spirits did not recover till next morning when they ran into sunlight in the Lombard plain.

In Rome he had two days of warm blue weather which was almost oppressive in his over-heated hotel. He had never greatly cared for the Italian capital, and, for a man of his multitudinous acquaintance, knew comparatively few of its citizens. He had luncheon with a few business associates, at which the affairs of the Brieg-Suffati company were discussed, and a long afternoon with various departments of State. He was received with the civility to which he was accustomed, and realised that the difficulties which had arisen would not be hard to settle. But he found that his necessary interview with the head of the Government must be postponed till the morrow, and he had the prospect of some hours of idleness, unpleasing to a man who chessboarded his life between strenuous work and strenuous play. He called at the British Embassy, and was promptly bidden that evening to dinner.

Before dressing he sat for a little in the hall of his hotel, watching the guests. Many were foreigners on their way home, but there was a considerable sprinkling of Roman residents, for the hotel had a reputation for its *apéritifs*. It was rare for Mr. Creevey to be in a place where he did not know by sight many of the people. Here he saw only two faces that he recognised. One was the lachrymose German whom he had met in the train; he sat by himself in a corner, and seemed to be waiting for someone, for his pale eyes scanned with expectation every newcomer. Mr. Creevey was thankful that he escaped his eye, for he had no wish for more international politics. The other was Falconet, who entered, cast about for a seat, thought better of it, and went out. Falconet, of course, was to be looked for anywhere and at any time; he was the most notorious globetrotter of the day.

But if Mr. Creevey saw few acquaintances, he was conscious that several people looked at him, as if they recognised him. He was not vain, and did not set this down to his celebrity, for he was not the kind of man whose portraits filled the press. Nor was there anything sensational in his appearance; he dressed quietly, and looked the ordinary travelling Englishman. But he was aware that he was being covertly studied by several men and one woman, who hastened to avert their eyes when he looked in their direction. He was a little puzzled, for this habit seemed to have been growing in the last few months. Wherever he went he was aware that somebody in his neighbourhood was acutely interested in him. He considered the matter for a minute or two and then dismissed it from his mind. He had no time to spare for the minor inexplicables of life.

The dinner at the Embassy passed the evening pleasantly. Falconet was the only other guest at the meal, and Falconet was in an urbane mood and on his best behaviour. Mr. Creevey

268

rarely asked himself whether or not he liked a man; his criterion was whether he respected him, and he was not disposed to underrate the American. At their first meeting he had thought that he had discovered one with whom he could work, and, detecting Falconet's imaginative side, had set himself to cultivate it. But presently he had found him intractable, the type of American whose mind had two compartments, realistic business and *schwärmerisch* dreams, and who let the one spill into the other. But Falconet was formidable, for he had immense wealth, and, when roused, could return to the predatory brilliance of the grandfather who had made the fortune. So he had tried to avoid antagonising him, and, though they had differed often, they had never quarrelled.

Tonight he found him polite and unassertive. Falconet gave no information about his own doings, and was incurious about Creevey's. He was full of Rome, of which he talked with the enthusiasm of a schoolmarm on her first visit. He asked the ordinary questions about Mussolini, and showed himself grossly ignorant of the machinery of the Catholic Church. Indeed, there was a pleasant touch of the schoolboy about him.

Mr. Creevey, whose father and the Ambassador had been at school together, did most of the talking, and did it very well. For example, he gave an amusing account of his talk with the lachrymose German in the train, to point an argument about the confusion in the popular mind of Europe. He quoted several of his phrases, and one of them seemed to impress Falconet—an odd and rather forcible metaphor. Falconet asked to have the speaker described, and Mr. Creevey did his best. "I saw him in my hotel this evening," he said, and Falconet for some reason knitted his heavy dark brows. Mr. Creevey observed this, as he observed most things.

Falconet was anxious to know his plans for the return journey. "I'd like to join you," he said. "Leaving tomorrow night? Not stopping off anywhere?"

Mr. Creevey answered that he was going straight through to London, having wasted enough time already.

He was just about to take his leave when, to his surprise, Jacqueline Warmestre appeared. He had a great admiration for

Lady Warmestre, the greater because she was one of the few women with whom he made no progress. She had never made any secret of her dislike of him, and in his eyes her frankness increased her charm. Her beauty was of the kind which fascinated him most, and tonight she seemed especially lovely, for she had been dining with some Roman friends, and her long, white-furred cloak contrasted exquisitely with her delicate colouring and her brilliant hair. Mr. Creevey felt a patriotic thrill; after all, English women had a poise and a freshness which no other nation could match. She had been in Italy for the vintage, staying at the country house of some Italian connections, and was spending a night at the Embassy on her way home. She seemed to have something to say to Falconet, and carried him off downstairs to the Ambassador's library.

Next day Mr. Creevey duly had his interview with the head of the State, and found it satisfactory. What he did not find so satisfactory was a telegram which awaited him at his hotel on his return. It was from the general manager of the Brieg-Suffati, announcing that the local board desired a meeting with Mr. Creevey, and suggesting an hour the following day. Mr. Creevey almost wired consigning the local board to the devil. But he reflected that he could not afford to antagonise them, for they had it in their power to make infinite mischief. He remembered the trouble he was having over his wood-pulp concern in East Prussia because the local people had got out of hand. So he replied consenting. It would mean leaving the main line at Arsignano, and motoring to the works, which were situated in a little town which bore the odd name of Grandezza. That would involve a couple of days' delay. Why could the fools not have fixed the meeting in Milan or Turin? It was too late to arrange that now, so he must make the best of the stupid business.

Mr. Creevey left Rome that night in a bad temper, and, since he was of an equable humour, this departure from his normal condition lessened his self-respect. He felt himself needlessly irritable, and the sport of petty annoyances. He saw the lachrymose German in the train, and, for some reason, the sight displeased him—he had come to dislike the man. Also the

270

Italian railway people were less careful of his comforts than usual. His secretary was many coaches off, and his valet had difficulties with his baggage. Twice he found strangers entering his reserved compartment—withdrawing, to be sure, with apologies, but looking at him with inquisitive eyes. Was he being subjected to some ridiculous espionage? The notion was so ludicrous that it amused him, and almost restored his good humour. It reminded him of his power. That very morning a great man had quite humbly asked him to do certain things as a kindness to Italy.

Falconet was on the train. He came out on the platform at Arsignano, and wanted to hear the reason of the change in Mr. Creevey's plans. "Too bad!" he exclaimed. "I was looking forward to having a talk with you on the road. I've got some notions I'd like to put up to you, but I'll be in London for a week, and I'll call you up when you get back."

The board meeting at Grandezza proved, as Mr. Creevey half-expected, a farce. There was nothing before the directors which could not have been settled by correspondence. The whole affair was fussiness. But there must be some reason for his colleagues' disquiet, and he ascertained that, besides the labour troubles, there had been a certain pressure from unexpected quarters, and rumours of more coming. He allayed their fears, for he was an adept at conciliation, but he was not quite easy in his own mind. Some hostile influence was at work which he must seek out and crush, for he was not accustomed to sit down under threats— at any rate not till he had uncovered them and assessed their importance.

Then a telegram was handed to him. He had kept London informed of his movements, and this was from his London office, from his most confidential manager. It urged his return at once without an hour's delay, for certain difficulties with New York had come to a head, and O'Malley himself had arrived on his way to Berlin, and must be seen at once.

This was a matter of real urgency, and he cursed the fate which had brought him on a false errand to Grandezza. Mr. Creevey was instant in an emergency. He liked his comfort, but he was aware that the game must be played according to its

271

rigour. The board meeting was summarily wound up, and he had some private talk with the general manager, in whose competence he believed. His secretary and his servant could travel to England by train, but he himself must fly part of the way home, and that at once. He ought to be in Paris that evening, and in London by ten o'clock the following morning. Could it be done?

The manager thought that it could. An aeroplane could be obtained from Arsignano—he himself had flown several times to Paris, and the service was to be trusted. Mr. Creevey disliked travel by air, for he was generally sick, and especially he disliked long-distance travel. He remembered with disgust a flight from London to Vienna the year before. But he bowed to the inevitable, and bade his servant put a few necessaries in a small suitcase, while the manager telephoned to the Air Company at Arsignano. The reply was that a good machine was available and an experienced pilot. Two hours later Mr. Creevey was clambering into the aeroplane, which had landed in the sports ground of the factory.

He settled himself down to some hours of boredom or discomfort. Chiefly the latter, he thought, for he did not like the look of the weather. It had become colder, and a wind from the north-east was moving up masses of cloud over the Grandezza foothills. The wind would be behind him at the start, for they would make a wide circuit towards the coast so as to turn the butt-end of the Alps and follow the Rhône valley. The first stage would probably be the worst, he reflected, as he buttoned the collar of his fur coat round his ears. He was not interested in the champaign spread far beneath him, and by a conscious effort of will he switched his thoughts to certain startling theories of Professor Broester's, expounded in the book which had bored him in the train.

The movement was so smooth that he must have dozed, for he woke to find that they were among clouds and that it had become much colder. He looked at his watch. By this time the sea should have been crawling beneath them, but, when there came a gap in the brume, he saw what seemed to be wooded hills. Then came a spell of bumping which stirred his nausea, and then a swift flurry of snow. This was getting very unpleasant, but things might improve when they turned into the Rhône valley. He drank a little sherry from his flask and ate two biscuits. He spoke to the pilot, who could not be made to hear. Then he scribbled him a note in his indifferent Italian, and the man glanced at it, nodded, and grinned.

After that they came into more snow, with a wind behind it which made the machine tilt and rock. Mr. Creevey became very sick, so sick that he was no longer interested in his whereabouts, or the journey, or anything but his miserable qualms. In a stupor of discomfort the time dragged on. The pilot was no doubt steering a compass-course, for nothing was visible beneath them but a surging plain of cloud.

Then it seemed that they were dropping. Mr. Creevey felt the wind abate as if it were cut off by some cover on his right hand. No doubt the flank of the mountains above Nice. Lower still they went, till they were out of the clouds and saw the ground. The pilot exclaimed, and examined the big compass. He said something which Mr. Creevey could not understand. Had the fellow missed the road? He seemed to be uncertain, for he cast his eyes round him as if looking for a landmark. What Mr. Creevey saw was a valley bottom in which a stream tumbled among rocks and trees, and on each side what looked like the rise of steep hills.

At the same moment the machine began to behave oddly, as if it were not answering to the helm. Mr. Creevey found himself pitched from side to side, and there were strange noises coming from the engine. Then the bumping ceased and they began to glide down at a long angle. The pilot was about to make a landing. There was a grassy meadow making a kind of mantelpiece in the valley and this was his objective. Mr. Creevey held his breath, for he had no experience of forced landings, and he was relieved when the aeroplane made gentle contact with the earth, taxied for fifty yards, and came to a standstill.

The pilot climbed out of his machine, and, turning a deaf ear to his passenger's excited questions, began an elaborate inspection of his engine. Mr. Creevey also got out and stretched his cramped legs, on which his nausea had made him a little shaky.

The pilot finished his researches, straightened himself and saluted. He spoke excellent English.

"I am very sorry, sir. We have come out of our course, for something has gone wrong with the compass."

"Where the devil are we?" Mr. Creevey shouted.

"I cannot tell. We have come too far north, and are in a valley of the mountains. We were in luck to strike this valley, for it was very thick. We must retrace our course. But meantime my engine must be seen to." And he added some technical details which Mr. Creevey did not understand.

Mr. Creevey was very angry.

"What an infernal muddle!" he cried. "How long will you take to get it right? I should be in London tomorrow, and now I'll be lucky if I'm in Paris."

"An hour," said the man. "Not more, I think. Perhaps less. See, there is an hotel above us. Perhaps your Excellency would prefer to wait there. It will be warmer, and no doubt there will be food." He was a youngish man, and the removal of his cap revealed fair hair brushed back from his forehead. He had an impassive, rather sullen face.

"Then for God's sake hurry up," said Mr. Creevey. He was choking with irritation, but he put a check on his utterance, for the situation was beyond words. A little, pink, square hotel was perched on the hillside a few hundred yards above him, and he started out towards it. It had become very cold, and the powdery snow was beginning again.

In his thin shoes, and cumbered with his massive coat, he plodded up through the coarse grass and scrub till he reached a road. It was an indifferent road, but it was just possible for wheeled traffic. There he halted, for he heard a sound below him.

The aeroplane was rising. It left the ground, climbed steadily, and curved round till it headed the way it had come. Then it flew steadily down the valley.

Mr. Creevey's voice died in his throat from sheer amazement. He stood staring at the departing machine and saw the pilot turn his head and wave his hand. . . . The thing was beyond him, but his predominant feeling was anger, and anger with him

274

always meant action. He gathered up the skirts of his fur coat and ran towards the hotel door.

He pushed it open and entered. He shouted for the landlord, but there was no answer. The place was fairly warm, and ashes were still red in the stove. But the hotel was empty.

In the library of the Embassy, Jacqueline Warmestre had much to say to Falconet. He knew this imperious lady as one of Adam Melfort's friends—a closer friend, he thought, than any other; but he had met her only a few times, and had never had more than a few words with her. He was a little surprised therefore at her cross-examination, but it fell in with his own mood. She was anxious about Adam, and so was he—acutely.

"I want the latest news," she said. "You can give it me, I think. Where is Adam? In the summer we had—well, a difference of opinion—but we did not quarrel. We are good friends and we write to each other. I will tell you all I know. He has been acting as a kind of bodyguard for the German Chancellor. I got that from Mildred Lamancha. But now? . . . I am afraid for him. You see, he failed in what he was working at—other people let him down—but he will never give up. He is trying some other way, and it is sure to be very difficult and desperate. Can you help me, Mr. Falconet? We both love him?"

Falconet was shy with beautiful women, but as he looked at Jacqueline's face he saw something behind the beauty. There was a fierce loyalty in her eyes, and gallantry in the tilt of her small chin. This was an ally about whom he need have no fear.

"I will tell you all I know," he said. "Adam is stalking Creevey."

"What do you mean?"

"Just that. He was shadowing Loeffler in the early fall, and by all accounts had a tough job of it. He put it through and got the Chancellor safe to the London Conference. But, of course, that couldn't be the end. Loeffler put him wise about the real trouble. To pull out he has got to have certain forces on his side that just at present are fighting against him. The biggest of them is Creevey. Well, you know Adam. When he sees where the mischief is he makes straight for it, though it's as big as a mountain and as tough as hell. He is out to immobilise Creevey."

"But how?" Jacqueline's eyes were wide and perplexed.

"God knows. The old way, and maybe the right way, would have been to knock him on the head. But that isn't allowed today, and Adam's a gentle fellow, so he is trying another line. He wants to get alongside him, and have him to himself, and he thinks that the Almighty will do the rest. That's his philosophy, I reckon. The Almighty is on his side, and all he has got to do is to give the Almighty a fair chance."

"But it's lunacy. He can't argue Mr. Creevey round—no-one can, they say—he is the cleverest man alive."

"Adam has allowed for that. He's not trusting to his own power of argument. He is looking to what he calls facts, by which he means the Almighty. He wants to get Mr. Creevey and himself away out of his familiar world, and he believes that something may happen then. It isn't sense, I know, Lady Warmestre. But it's Adam's way, and I'm not going to say it isn't the right way. He's like an old-time prophet and has inspirations."

"But how can he get him to himself? Mr. Creevey is the busiest man going, and he is surrounded by hordes of secretaries."

Falconet grinned.

"There are ways—and means, and that's where I can help a bit. We're shepherding Creevey out of the flock into our own little fold. We brought him to Rome when he didn't want to come, and, please God, before he gets back to England we're going to shepherd him to other places where he doesn't want to go. I would have you know that I'm not in big business for nothing, and I've got a considerable graft up and down Europe."

Jacqueline put a hand on his arm.

"I want to know everything, Mr. Falconet. Please tell me."

"I don't mind giving you the layout. First of all, way up in the north there is a valley in the mountains called the Val d'Arras."

Jacqueline nodded. "I know. My father was a great mountaineer, and preferred the Italian side of the Alps, and he used to take me with him when I was a girl. The Val d'Arras runs up from Colavella. At the top is the Saluzzana pass leading to the Staubthal. An easy pass, except in bad weather."

"Right. Way up the Val d'Arras is a little summer hotel where there's nobody at this time of year. Well, Adam's notion is to get Creevey there. That has all been arranged, and it ought to work to plan."

"But after that?"

"After that I don't know. Adam may have his own notion, or he may be leaving it to the Almighty. I guess he means to get him over the Saluzzana, for my orders are to be waiting at Grunewald in the Staubthal. If Adam has gotten Creevey into the right frame of mind I might be able to put in my word."

Jacqueline wrinkled her brows. "It sounds the wildest non-sense. That sort of thing isn't done nowadays. Mr. Creevey will either have the law on Adam for kidnapping, or he will get pneumonia and die. Perhaps you want the second."

"No. Adam doesn't and Loeffler doesn't. They think Creevey is too valuable to the world to lose, if only his head could be turned in another direction. Still, that may be the solution the Almighty fancies."

"Then Adam is in Italy?"

"Yep. And that is where my own private worry comes in. You see, Lady Warmestre, Adam has just lately been wading in deepish waters. To look after Loeffler he had to go way down into the underworld, and as a consequence I've an idea that some of those gentry are out gunning for him. I've seen one of them today, and I've heard of another. It don't look good to me that they should be in Italy when Adam is here, and, besides, it shows that they have a pretty correct line on his movements. Now, if Adam is stalking Creevey, it will cramp his style if other fellows are stalking him. I'm going right back to my hotel to call up my man Blakiston in Milan and put him wise to it."

Jacqueline leaned forward with her chin in her hand and looked her companion in the face.

"I'm coming into this show, Mr. Falconet," she said. "I did Adam a great disservice, and yet all the time I was on his side, and now I'm going to atone for it. I think his scheme is raving madness, but he is the only great man I have ever known, and I want to help. I believe I could be of some use with Mr. Creevey. When do you plant him in the Val d'Arras?"

277

"According to schedule about the evening of the day after tomorrow."

"Well, I'm going to the little pink hotel. I needn't hurry home. I have my car here and I meant to go back by easy stages. I'll start out tomorrow morning and with any luck I'll be in time. It's a Lancia and can face the mountain roads. I'll bring a friend with me—Andrew Amos."

Falconet exclaimed. "The old Scotsman with the chin whiskers! He's a crackerjack."

"He is Adam's watchdog. Ken—my husband—adores him. I found out that the dream of his life was to see Italy, so I brought him with me as my courier. He doesn't know a word of any language but his own, but you can't defeat him. He can drive a car too."

Falconet protested.

"It's no place for a lady."

"I'm not a lady. I'm a woman."

"But Adam wants to be alone with Creevey."

"We won't interfere with their privacy. . . . If Adam is in danger, as you think he is, I'm going to plant Amos beside him, and if the good God is going to work a miracle a woman and an old Scotsman won't be in the way."

Jacqueline spent the night regretting her rashness. As she lay awake in the small hours she seemed to herself only a foolish child who had forced itself into a game where it was not wanted. She half resolved to ring up Falconet in the morning and cry off. Falconet would be relieved, for he had not welcomed her intervention. In the end she fell asleep without having come to any decision, and when she woke she discovered that her mood had changed.

As she dressed she found it difficult to disentangle her thoughts, but one thing was clear. She was wholly resolved on this adventure. At the worst she could do no harm, and if Adam did not want her she could go back. A clear recollection of the Val d'Arras came back to her. The road was bad after Colavella, but it was possible for a car as far as the little pink inn which she remembered well; after that there was only the mule track across the Saluzzana. She would leave her maid and chauffeur at

Chiavagno, and Amos would drive the car; he was a first-rate mechanic, and a cautious, resourceful driver. No-one would know of the escapade but Amos and Falconet, and her hosts at the Embassy would believe that she was starting decorously on her journey home.

By and by her thoughts arranged themselves and she realised the subconscious purpose which was moving her. . . . She had made her choice with open eyes and did not regret it. She had done the right thing for Ken and her child and all the long-descended world built up around them. She had played for peace and had won it for them. Ken was settling down into the life where he would be useful and happy. But for herself? She had had a glimpse of greater things and had turned her back on them, but they had left a void in her heart. She had chosen the second-rate—for others and for herself, but she was paying for her choice in an aching wistfulness. . . . She was not in love with Adam, for love did not belong to that austere world of his, but he had come to represent for her all the dreams and longings which made up her religion. She felt like some fisherman of Galilee who had heard the divine call and turned instead to his boats and nets.

Yet the cause from which she had held back others she might embrace herself—for a little only—for one small moment of restitution. Jacqueline had fatalism in her blood, and Falconet's talk had given her an eery sense of some strange foreordering. She had come to Italy on a sudden impulse, for she had felt restless at Warmestre before the hunting began. In coming here she had thought that she was leaving behind the world which had perplexed her, and lo and behold! it had moved itself across the sea to meet her. This was destiny which could not be shirked. She had always guided her life with a high hand, for no man or woman or beast had so far made her afraid, and she had welcomed risks as the natural spice of living. But this was different. This was no light-hearted extravagance of youth and health, but an inexorable summons to some mysterious duty. Jacqueline felt strangely keyed-up, but also at peace.

The mood lasted during the day while the car sped up the Tuscan coast and through the Apennines into the Lombard plain. It was still, bright weather, and as mild as an English June. But when Jacqueline and Amos left Chiavagno the following morning the skies had clouded and a sharp wind was blowing from the mountains. They stopped for lunch at Colavella, at the mouth of the Val d'Arras, and the little town set amid its steep woody hills bore the aspect of winter. The hotels were mostly shuttered, the vine trellises leafless, and the Arcio, foaming under the Roman bridge, looked like molten snow. Snow-covered peaks showed through gaps in the hills; these were not the high mountains, so there must have been a recent snowfall.

Their troubles began when they left Colavella. The first part of the road, which wound among pines, had been vilely rutted by woodcutters' wagons. When they climbed to the higher and barer stages of the valley, the going became worse. It was a lonely place, where few came except mountaineers seeking an easy road to the west face of the Pomagognon, or occasional botanists and walkers bound for the Staubthal. Now it seemed utterly deserted, for there were no farms on its shaly slopes. Moreover, the road was far worse than Jacqueline remembered it. There were places where landslips had almost obliterated it, and Amos had much ado to pass. Jacqueline was puzzled. This might have been expected in the spring after a bad winter; but it must have been set right in the summer, and since then there had been no weather to account for the damage. It almost looked as if it had been wrecked by the hand of man.

They made slow progress, and presently ran into snow-showers which blotted out the environs. In one of these Amos violently put on his brakes. Ahead of them was what had once been a wooden bridge over the deep-cut gorge of a winter torrent. It had been destroyed, and the road came to an end at a brink of raw red earth and a forty-foot drop.

Amos hove himself out of the car and examined the broken timbers of the bridge.

"Queer!" he observed. "This brig has been cut down wi' an aixe, and that no mony hours back."

The sense of fatality had been weighing all day upon Jacqueline, intensified by the lowering sky, the cold, and the frowning hills. She had been like a child feeling its way into a dark corridor where fearsome things might lurk. But the sight of the broken bridge comforted her. Adam had staged the business well.

"Back the car into the trees," she told Amos. "We can't be far off. We must walk the rest of the road."

Amos, laden with baggage, including some provisions which Jacqueline in a moment of forethought had added to the equipment, led the way down the side of the ravine, across a trickle of water, and up the farther bank to where the road began again. As they reached it, the snow ceased, and there came a long rift in the mist. It revealed a small square hotel about a mile ahead. In half an hour the dark would have fallen.

Shortly after noon on that same day Adam Melfort sat in a little restaurant near the aerodrome at Arsignano. He must snatch a meal, for he had much to do that afternoon. So far all had gone according to plan. The aeroplane which Creevey had ordered by telephone had just started for Grandezza. It had been a delicate business, depending on many minute arrangements, but, with the help of Blakiston's organisation and his own network of queer contacts, it seemed to have so far succeeded. There was only one 'plane at the moment in the aerodrome suitable for a long-distance journey, and one pilot who could be selected—it had taken some doing to arrange that. This pilot, a veteran of the Alpini, had had dealings with Adam before, and had been brought into the conspiracy. His fidelity was beyond question, and his part was simple. He was to have a breakdown in the Val d'Arras and leave Creevey at the inn, while he flew back for certain repairs; he would lie low for such time as was necessary to complete the journey to England and back, and then present himself at the aerodrome in the usual course of business. Creevey had paid the fare before leaving. That afternoon Adam proposed to go by car to the Val Saluzzana, and cross the intervening ridge to the Val d'Arras by a col which he knew of. Creevey would be at the little inn in the care of a friendly innkeeper, an old acquaintance of his, and some time in the late evening Adam would join him, arriving casually as if on a walking tour. There would be a moon that night, though it might be obscured by the weather, but he knew the col well and had no fears for his journey. Then he would have Creevey to himself. The man would be in a fever to get home, and, when no aeroplane appeared, and the alternative was to tramp the long road back down the valley, Adam would persuade him to cross the Saluzzana with him to the Staubthal, from which return to England would be simple. Somewhere and at some time, at the inn or during the crossing of the pass, he hoped to bring him to another mind. He did not attempt to forecast the method of conversion—in that task he felt himself like a boy with a sling before a fortress—but he believed that behind him destiny might range great artillery.

The restaurant was a dim little place and at that hour almost deserted. Two waiters and an elderly man of the shopkeeper type were the only occupants when Adam sat down. His meal had been brought him, and he ate it greedily, for he had had no food that day save a cup of coffee. . . .

Suddenly, as he lifted his eyes from his plate, he saw that two men had taken their seats at the other end of the room. They still wore their ulsters, and seemed to have entered merely for a glass of wine. The one with his back to him had thick dark hair, and something in the shape of his head seemed familiar. About the one who faced him there could be no mistake. He saw a big man with a small bullet head on a strong neck, and a flat face as hard as hammered steel. He knew him for that von Hilderling whom he had last seen in the upper room of a shabby eating-house in a Rhineland slum.

The two men were talking low to each other and did not look his way. Then the one with his back to him rose and came towards him. He recognised the trim figure, the fine oval face, and the deep mad eyes of La Cecilia.

Cecilia smiled and took a chair beside him, and his smile was not pleasant.

"Well met, Colonel Melfort," he said. "May I have the honour of a word with you?" The Baron von Hilderling had poured himself out a glass of wine, and seemed to be absorbed in the contents of a small notebook.

"It would appear that we are on the same errand," Cecilia said. "You have something to say to Mr. Warren Creevey, I

282

understand. So also have we. My instructions are to order you to drop out. We will deal with the rest of the business ourselves."

"I wonder what you are talking about," said Adam.

"Oh no, you don't. You know very well. You have a grudge against Mr. Creevey, for which we commend you, for we share it. You have been stalking him for some days and are very ingeniously manoeuvring him into a position where you can have him to yourself. I won't ask what you propose to do with him, but I can guess. We know what we propose. We have been following his trail—and yours—for it is easy to stalk a stalker, and we have taken over your arrangements, of which we approve. This evening Mr. Creevey will find himself in an empty inn in a remote Alpine valley. There will be no-one in the inn—that we have seen to. The innkeeper has gone to see a sick father in Turin, and will not return for a while, and the two servants have been dismissed on holiday. The 'plane which takes Mr. Creevey there will proceed by the ordinary route to Paris, but will have an unfortunate accident on the coast, in which the world will regret to learn that Mr. Creevey has perished. Meantime, up in the Val d'Arras we shall deal with him at our discretion. The pilot is not the man you selected, but one of ourselves—that is the only serious change we have made in your otherwise admirable arrangements."

Adam had learned to wear an impassive face in any crisis, but his brain was working busily. "I see," he said. "Will you have a drink? I would like to hear more of your plans."

"I'm afraid I have no time," said Cecilia. "I came only to bring you the thanks of our brotherhood for what you have done. . . . Also to say one little thing. In this matter you have unconsciously been working with us, and we approve. But there was a certain incident some weeks ago in an English country house when you opposed us, and frustrated an important policy. That we do not forget—or forgive. You may have had reasons to justify you—that we do not yet know. But I bring you this message from Gratias. According to our laws you will be judged for that act—and if necessary you will be punished. You are one of us, and cannot escape us, though you took the wings of a bird and flew into the uttermost parts of the earth."

Adam smiled. "I don't quite follow you, but you have the same old rhetorical tricks, my dear Cecilia. Well, you know where to find me."

The full mad eyes regarded him unwinkingly.

"We shall always know where to find you. Meantime you will please to go home—at once. There is a train this evening. You understand. *Auf wiedersehen*, my friend."

Cecilia went back to his companion, and a minute later the two left the restaurant.

Adam finished his meal and drank a cup of coffee, while he made certain calculations on the back of an envelope. His plans still held, but now there had entered into them an element of desperate haste. He felt curiously at ease. The game was out of his hands, for destiny had taken hold of it.

CHAPTER II

M R. CREEVEY looked at the dying ashes in the stove, and, though he was warm with walking and the weight of his fur coat, he shivered. He opened the door of the *salle-à-manger*, and saw that the table was bare and the chairs stacked in a corner. Several times he shouted, and his voice echoed eerily in an empty house.

The thing was utterly beyond his comprehension. The breakdown of an aeroplane he could understand, but how in Heaven's name could the pilot have blundered so far out of his course? And why, without a word, had he righted his machine and flown away? He was accustomed to an orderly world where all things were explicable, but this folly was beyond explanation. Unreason always exasperated him, and for a little his anger blanketed all other thoughts. Some fool would be made to pay heavily for this. It was a blunder—it could only be a blunder—he refused to admit that there could be any purpose behind it. To whose interest could it be to play so infantile a trick on him?

But the chill of the place and the silence cooled his temper. He began to sum up his situation. He was marooned in an empty inn in a remote valley, and he had not the dimmest notion of his whereabouts. He had no food except the remains of a little packet of biscuits and half a flask of sherry. There was no fire, and probably no bed—the place was empty as a shell. But it was less the immediate prospect that perplexed him than the next step. How was he to get out of this hole? The aeroplane might return for him; or he might make his way down the valley to some place where he could hire a conveyance; he remembered a little town many miles back of which he had had a glimpse through the fog. But he was not dressed for walking, with his modish clothes and his thin shoes, and, anyhow, he had never been much of a pedestrian. With a feeling which was almost panic he realised that he had been pitchforked out of civilisation into a barbaric world, and that he was ill-adapted to cope with barbarism. With all his power and brains the commonest day-labourer was better fitted for this situation than he.

He forced himself to be calm, for he had a great gift of self-command. But he was desperately uneasy, for the mystery tormented him. . . . Clearly he must spend the night here, for nothing could be done till the morning. The aeroplane might return—must return—that was his best hope. He liked the comforts of life, but he was man enough to forgo them if needs be; the prospect of a miserable night dismayed him less than the intolerable inexplicableness of the whole situation. . . . And something more weighed on him. He was not a nervous or a hypersensitive man, but there was that in this accursed place which sent a chill to his heart. Its loneliness weighed on him like a pall, for it was not the solitude of wild nature, but of a deserted human habitation. Deserted, and why? Could there be some malignant purpose somewhere?

He had left the door open, and he noticed that the twilight had begun. He went out and looked at the dismal scene. The valley was perhaps a mile wide, filled with coarse grass and big boulders, and with the narrow gorge of a stream in the centre. He could hear the water churning among its pot-holes, but for the rest there was deep silence. There was a sprinkling of snow on the ground, but the snow-scurries had ceased, as had the wind. Across the valley he saw the steep rise of the mountains—raw scars of winter torrents, cliffs of shale with stunted pines perched insecurely on their face. There was a little square mantelpiece of gravel before the door, and a number of green wooden seats from which summer visitors no doubt admired the prospect, and little iron tables where they had their meals. This sight seemed to put the last edge on his sense of desolation. He looked down the valley where the road, rough as a river channel, was presently lost in mist.

Then suddenly out of the mist came two figures. In a moment his mood changed. This infernal desert had, after all, its inhabitants. He hastened towards them, and saw that one was a short, square man heavily laden with baggage, and the other a woman. Peasants no doubt; perhaps the people of the inn returning.

He halted and stared. The man was an odd figure in a heavy chauffeur's coat. But the woman he had seen before. She was wearing a tweed ulster with a collar of fur, and her light walk was not that of a peasant.

A minute later he had recognised her as Jacqueline Warmestre. He forgot all his dismal vaticinations, for he had now made contact with his old world.

She was the first to speak.

"Mr. Creevey! I didn't expect to meet you again so soon. Where have you come from, and what are you doing here?"

He felt at ease, indeed, he was pleasurably excited. The appearance of Jacqueline had taken all the unpleasantness out of the situation. It was less of a mischance now than an adventure.

"A ridiculous accident," he explained, and briskly and humorously he described his recent doings. "The half-wit of a pilot left me—God knows whether he means to return—and here am I stuck like Robinson Crusoe." He felt obliged to speak lightly, for he knew that Jacqueline was not apt to make much of the rubs of life.

"What atrocious bad luck!" she cried. "Well, we are companions in misfortune. I was motoring home and took a fancy to spend a night in this place. I used to come here with my father ten years ago. But my Lancia broke down some way back, and we've had to hump our swag and foot it. My ankles are aching from this terrible road."

"A car!" He remembered his urgent business in London. "Can't we get it going? I was flying back because of cables from home."

"Tomorrow morning we'll have a look at it and see what can be done. Meantime I want food and fire. I'm rather cold, and perfectly ravenous."

"But the hotel is empty—deserted."

Jacqueline stopped short. "Is there nobody staying there?" she asked. She had expected to hear of Adam.

"No guests, no innkeeper, no servants. Silent as the grave!"

She was puzzled. This was not quite the scene she had gathered from Falconet that Adam meant to stage.

"That's odd. It used to be the snuggest little place. Antonio Menardi the landlord was a great friend of mine, and his wife made the most wonderful omelets. Do you mean to say that there's not a soul there? Is it shut up? It used to be open all winter, for people came for the bouquetin shooting?"

"It isn't shut up, for the door is open. But it is empty, though it can't have been empty long. Here we are, so you can see for yourself."

Amos dropped his packs on the floor of the little hall, while Jacqueline sat herself on a stool and proceeded to remove gravel from her shoes. "Go and forage, Andrew," she said. "You must find a lamp. It will be dark in half an hour."

Amos's heavy step could be heard pounding through the rooms and penetrating to the back regions. Presently he returned to report, carrying a lit paraffin lamp.

"There's lamps," he said, "and plenty o' wud, so we can hae a fire. There's bedding in some of the rooms, but no muckle. Otherwise it's like the bit in the auld sang, 'Neither man's meat, nor dowgs' meat, nor a place to sit doun.' "

Jacqueline laughed merrily. Her spirits were beginning to rise. No doubt Adam had a plan of his own, and he must soon arrive.

"Then thank Heaven we brought some food," she said. "Andrew, get the stove going, please, and prepare some kind of supper. We are orphans of the storm, Mr. Creevey, and must camp here and make the best of it. I hope you are grateful, for if I hadn't turned up you would have starved."

Soon a roaring stove and three lamps gave an air of comfort to the bleak little hall. Amos fetched a table from the *salle-à-manger*, and set out on it a variety of cold food.

"Wait on," he said, "and I'll boil ye eggs. I've fund some in a press in the back kitchen. I'm nae hand at coffee, but I'll get ye a cup o' tea."

Mr. Creevey made his toilet in icy water, and borrowed a comb from Amos's pack. At supper he was a brisk companion, for he was beginning to see merit in this adventure. Somehow, by 'plane or by car, he would get off next morning, and, though the delay was a nuisance, it was not disastrous. His position was too solidly established for petty setbacks. Meantime he had the luck to have as companion one of the most beautiful women in England, one who had always piqued him by her undisguised aversion. He was not accustomed to such treatment from women, and it did his reputation no good, for Lady Warmestre, though she concerned herself little with the ordinary social game, had a supreme distinction of her own, and a host of admirers. Tonight she had been very gracious to him and had treated him like a playfellow and an ally. Mr. Creevey felt a slight quickening of the blood. This was a real adventure.

So at supper he exerted himself to be both discreet and agreeable. He spoke of common friends, of the humours of certain negotiations in which he had been recently engaged, of politics high and low. He spoke of Lord Warmestre. "Cincinnatus, they tell me, has gone back to the plough," he said. "I am rather glad of it. Publicists and politicians are as common as black-berries, but we have too few capable landowners. You approved, I think?"

"Yes, I approved," Jacqueline answered. She had lost her vivacity and her attention wandered. She had an odd air of expectancy, too, and seemed to be listening for something.

After supper Mr. Creevey lit a cigar. The meal had been satisfying, and Amos's strong tea had not poisoned but fortified him. Jacqueline was rather silent, but he was exhilarated by her presence. He had never seen her look lovelier, for Mr. Creevey, while paying due homage to the voluptuous charms of Aphrodite, had a secret respect for Artemis. Her figure, now—there was no woman or girl in London who could compete with her there— every movement was a thing of precision and grace. She was wearing just the right shade of blue to go with her hair. Then her voice. That of course was famous for its caressing beauty. He wished that she would talk more, and he laboured to draw her out. But she remained rather silent and *distraite*.

Twice she sent Amos out to look at the weather. The first time he reported that it was "black dark, gey cauld, but nae wund." The second time he announced that the moon was up,

289

a moon nearly full. "It'll freeze the nicht, but there's cluds bankin' up north and there'll be mair snaw or morn."

"Is there no-one about?" she asked. "On the road?"

"Not a mortal soul."

"I thought that the inn people might be coming back," she explained. "I simply can't imagine why this place is empty."

Mr. Creevey had a sudden idea. It was not the weather or the return of the inn people that she had sent out Amos to investigate. She must be expecting someone. Had she chosen this lonely place for an assignation? He searched his memory for gossip about Lady Warmestre and could find none. She had always been a pillar of decorum, devoted to husband, child, and home; free-spoken of course, and sometimes startling in her frankness, but that was only proof of her innocence. No-one had ever credited her with a lover. The thing was unthinkable. And yet—

Mr. Creevey made it his business to chatter freely, and to bring in the names of her friends. He did not want his suspicion to be confirmed—Jacqueline was too rare a being to have the foibles of many women of his acquaintance—but something puck-like in him made him itch to discover secrets. He had no luck.

Her face did not change from its brooding expectancy.

Still he gossiped on. It was partly good manners, for long silences would be awkward, partly a desire to stand well in her eyes. He must appear to take misfortune airily, as she did. . . . Then he said something that roused her interest. He was describing his visit to Berlin in August, and giving, after his fashion, admirably clean-cut sketches of his associates. He mentioned Adam Melfort.

"You know Colonel Melfort?" she asked. "How well?"

"I know him as other people know him. The surface only, but I guess at what is behind. I believe him to be that uncomfortable thing which Lilah Pomfrey calls an apostle, and to understand an apostle you must be a disciple."

She awoke to attention. Her eyes had a sudden light in them.

"That is true," she said; "but even if you refuse his evangel you can recognise the apostle."

"I remember now. Of course you and Lord Warmestre are friends of his. You admire him?"

"I believe in him," she said.

There was a movement as if someone were coming from the back quarters, and he looked up, expecting to see Amos. Instead, he saw a tall man in soiled tweeds, whom he recognised. Jacqueline had sprung to her feet.

Mr. Creevey smiled, but a little ruefully. He was sorry that his guess about an assignation had proved right.

Adam finished his coffee in the restaurant and then walked leisurely to his hotel. It was important that he should be observed, for it was certain that Cecilia and his friends would be on the watch. At his hotel he gave instructions for his things to be packed in readiness for the evening train. Then he telephoned to the garage where his car had been ordered, and directed that it should meet him at a point on the east side of the town. He left the hotel by a back entrance, wearing an old waterproof coat and a tweed cap, and made his way by unfrequented streets to the place where the car awaited him. By ten minutes past one he was on the road, driving in a heavy drizzle of rain due east from Arsignano.

He was in no wise excited or perturbed. This was the way that fate had chosen to arrange the cards, and he must shape his game accordingly. His plan had always been to strike in on the Val d'Arras by the col from the Val Saluzzana, which would give him the appearance of arriving accidentally from a tramp in the hills. To have flown to the Val d'Arras, even had an aeroplane been obtainable, would have aroused Creevey's suspicions, and the way thither by road was rough and roundabout. . . . Now everything was changed. Creevey was at the pink hotel—or would be there before the evening—and his enemies were drawing in upon him. He would be left alone for a little—but how long? Some time that evening or during the early night Cecilia and his gang would be upon him. How would they travel? Not, he thought, by air. They had already used the air so far as it was needed, and soon the 'plane in which Creevey had started would crash in its appointed place, and the passenger would officially pass out of the world. They would probably travel by road. All the more reason why he should avoid the direct route to the Val d'Arras.

His immediate business was to be in time. As to what he should do when he arrived at the inn he had no plan, and did not attempt to make one. If the enemies were there, his task would be rescue; if they had not arrived, the task would be escape. For ways and means he had no care—these he knew would be provided when the moment came. Somehow or other he and Creevey would be enclosed in a lonely world of their own, and his mission would be accomplished. It might be that Creevey would die; that was one solution; but it must come only after he had done his utmost to keep him in life, for he felt himself in a strict sense this man's keeper. If Creevey lived he was assured that he would live to a different purpose. . . . One precaution only he had taken. Years ago he had made himself a fine marksman, but he had never in all his life fired a shot at a man in offence or defence. Now he had brought a pistol with him. It was in the right-hand pocket of his coat, pressing comfortably against his side as he drove.

He was forced to make a wide circuit, for he dare not risk meeting Cecilia on the road, so it was half-past three before he had threaded the foothills and climbed to the skirts of the great mountains and entered the Val Saluzzana. The road had been almost deserted, for the weather, as he ascended, had changed from rain to sleet and from sleet to a powder of snow. But the surface was magnificent, for it was one of the great through-roads of the Alps. As every traveller knows, it ascends the Val Saluzzana to the hamlet of Santa Chiara, and then turns up a subsidiary vale and crosses the Staub pass to the Staubthal and Switzerland. The main stream descends from a trackless glen, at the head of which is the famous Colle delle Rondini, a route attempted only by expert mountaineers. The Saluzzana pass, threaded by a mule track and not by a highway, is not in the vale of that name, but in the parallel Val d'Arras, and why the name should have been transferred no geographer has yet explained. A little north of Santa Chiara the containing ridge is indented by a saddle, which is reached from the Val Saluzzana by a long tortuous cleft, and offers, towards the Val d'Arras, a descent by a series of steep but practicable shelves. There is a track over the col once used by smugglers in winter-time, and long ago, when Adam had been on manoeuvres with the Alpini, he had played the war-game, and this col had been the key of his plan. By it he had led a force concealed in the Val d'Arras to attack in flank the invaders coming over the Staub. He remembered the details as if it had been yesterday. Twice he had himself made the crossing, and he had no doubt about his ability to do it again in any weather. He could do it in darkness, he thought, and, anyhow, there would be a moon. But time was the problem. He dared not delay one unnecessary minute, for fate was busy beyond the hills.

Never in his life had he driven a car at such breakneck speed. Twice he was held up by woodcutters' wagons, and once in a village he had to back out and make a round to avoid a wedding procession. But when he reached the great Saluzzana road there was good going, and he was at Santa Chiara by a little after four. The inn was shuttered, but he drove the car into a farm shed, and gave the farmer money to keep an eye on it till his return. In two miles he was at the mouth of the gorge which led to the col, and turned up the track by the stream side. Twilight had fallen, and he looked up the left into a pit of dark vapour, out of which loomed menacingly a black sentinel crag.

A great peace was on his spirit, peace which was more than the absence of care, and was almost happiness. He felt as if a burden had fallen from his shoulders. For one thing he was drawing again upon the strength of that body which for years he had so scrupulously tended. Not since the Arctic ice had he used his muscles to the full, and they responded like a young horse at the first feel of turf. Also he felt as if he were in some sense in sight of his goal. His duty had narrowed to a strait road which he could not miss, and the very fact that he could have no prospect but must wait for light increased his certainty. He was being led, and he rejoiced to follow. But indeed there was no room for self-examination, for his first purpose must be speed. He went up the steep track among the boulders and pine-boles like a hunter running to cut off a deer.

Above a waterfall the gorge flattened out into an upland glen strewn with the debris of old rock-falls. This made slow travelling, for the bigger rocks had to be circumvented, the track had disappeared, and sometimes there was scarcely room for passage between the cliffs and the gorge of the torrent. Beyond that the ravine bent to the right, and a long steep had to be scaled, down which the stream fell in a chain of cascades. It was dark now, though the white water was still plain, and bits of old snowdrifts. There was one point where the only passage was between the gorge of the stream and a rock which seemed perilously poised. He felt it shake as he passed, and he realised that at any minute it might fall and block the road, since there was no possibility of a circuit on either hand among the sheer crags. He passed in safety and then had the main slope to breast. The rocks were glazed by the recent snowstorms, and even his nailed boots bit on them with difficulty. This was the most arduous part of the road, but he did not slacken his pace. Often he slipped and fell, and there were parts where it took all his skill and strength to surmount some icy boiler-plates. When he reached the top his watch told him that it was nearly seven. He was not yet halfway across.

After that, for a little, it was easier going. The slope was less violent, and the road was mostly across shaly screes and patches of snow. He was far above the pines now, above even the coarsest herbage. The wind which had been drifting intermittent snow-showers had dropped, and the air seemed to be sharpening to frost. He still strode furiously, but the lack of the need for the severer kind of exertion left him leisure for his thoughts. . . .

He was back in Eilean Bàn, and the time was afternoon. Just of late it had always been afternoon; still, golden weather, when the ardours of day were beginning to melt into the peace of evening. He was on the west side of Sgurr Bàn, his favourite place, a long way to the west, for he was conscious that he was very near the sea. Hitherto the sea had always eluded him, however far he rambled, though he was never out of sound of its murmuring. But now two strange things had happened. One was that he knew—though how he knew it he could not tell— that never before in all his dreams had he been so close to the sea. Surely a very few steps more must take him to the white sands, where the tides were never silent. The other was that Nigel had escaped him. It was a long time since Nigel had gone off to play by himself; usually he stuck very close to his side, clutching his hand, and babbling like a brook. He could still hear him only a little distance away shouting among the hazels. But he wondered what fancy had taken Nigel off by himself. . . .

The pale bright skies of the isle disappeared, and he was looking at a narrow saddle between rocks. It was light now, for the moon was rising. He was at the col, and a freer air blew in his face.

Far below him the Val d'Arras lay in a deep olive gloom. The hotel was out of his sight, blocked by a shoulder of hill, but there was enough light to see the valley narrowing northward towards the pass. He felt quickened and braced and utterly tireless. He had made good time, and unless he were hung up on the descent he must reach the inn before the others. Eilean Bàn vanished from his thoughts, and he addressed himself to the precipitous screes that led to the first shelf.

It was a wild descent, now in the darkness of a cleft, now in open moonshine, when he was forced on to the face. He did not trouble to look for the track, for in his head he had a general picture of the route. Often he would slip for yards, and once on a patch of snow he had a furious glissade which ended miraculously at a rock above an ugly drop. A little stream began, and at one time he had to take to its channel and got soaked to the skin. The first flat shelf was a slower business, for the way had to be picked among ankle-twisting boulders. With the second shelf the trees began, gnarled old relics, with ugly pitfalls in the shape of rotting trunks. But the moist smell of vegetation cheered him, for it told him that he was nearing the valley. At one corner he caught a glimpse of the hotel. There was a light in a window. Who were assembled behind that light?

Almost before he knew it he had reached the valley floor. He straightened himself, and wrung out the wet from his sopping trousers. He looked at his watch, and had a moment of pride. In five hours he had finished a course to which most mountaineers would have allotted ten, and he was as fresh as when he had started. He forded the stream at a shallow, and ran towards the light which twinkled a mile down the valley.

He must move carefully, for he was now on enemy's ground. He left the track, and approached the hotel from behind, where the hill rose steeply. He vaulted the wall of the little garden and tiptoed stealthily towards the back door.

As he approached it it opened, and a man emerged and looked up, yawning, at the sky as if to prospect the weather. He was an oldish man, very square and stocky, and he had in his hand a frying-pan. He dropped it as the stranger came out of the earth and stood before him.

"Great God, Amos," Adam cried, "what are you doing here?"

The old man peered and blinked.

"Losh, it's the Colonel," he whispered. "I cam' here wi' her leddyship—the Marchioness, ye ken. We've been ryngin' about Italy."

"Who are here?"

"Just Mr. Creevey and her leddyship and masel'."

Adam pushed past him through the kitchen and into the little hall, where before a cheerful stove sat a man and a woman beside the remains of supper. He had not grasped Amos's information, for the sight of Jacqueline made him stand and gasp. He had no eye for Creevey's surprised face or his outstretched hand.

"Are you mad?" he asked her. "Do you know that you have come into a place of death?"

CHAPTER III

I

THE three made a strange group around the glowing ashes of the stove—Creevey and Jacqueline as neat as if they had been denizens of a common summer hotel, and Adam wet and dishevelled and about him the tang of wild weather.

Jacqueline, under the spell of his demanding eyes, felt her wits wandering. What had happened? What was his purpose? Why did he talk fiercely of death? She had to make some kind of answer.

"I came by accident," she stammered. "I have been motoring in Italy. . . . I used to come to this inn long ago. . . . I wanted to see the place again."

"And I," said Creevey, "am here by misfortune. I have been left stranded by an infernal aeroplane which should have taken me to Paris." He spoke cheerfully, for indeed he was relieved in mind. There had been no assignation, for Melfort's surprise at the sight of the lady was too real to be assumed. At the meaning of his words he could make no guess, but apostles must be permitted a little melodrama.

Adam strode to the door. It was a heavy thing, which could be fastened by a thick bar let down from the adjacent wall. He dropped the bar and called for Amos.

"Go out," he said, "and look down the valley. There's a moon. See if anyone is coming up the road. By car or on foot."

"They'll hae to be on foot," said Amos, "for somebody has broke doun the brig a mile back."

"So much the better. If anyone appears in that last mile, come back and warn us at once. It is now half-past ten. If they don't come by midnight we may assume we are safe for the night."

He cut himself a wedge of cold pie.

"Forgive me," he said, "but I've had no food since midday. I have come over the col from the Val Saluzzana, and I didn't take it easy. Thank God I'm in time."

"Time for what?" Creevey asked a little sharply. He disliked mysteries, and Adam's peremptoriness offended him.

"Time to warn you. And, I hope, to save your life."

He seemed to be about to explain further when Amos appeared again from the back part of the house.

"There's no muckle prospect doun the road," he announced. "The mune's ahint the hill noo and the clouds are comin' up. It looks as if they were bankin' for mair snaw. There's naebody to be seen."

A light broke in on Adam.

"Of course. Fool that I am! They are not coming up the valley. That would leave too obvious traces. They are crossing the mountains by the Marjolana pass and are coming in here from the north. From the Staubthal. They can't arrive till morning. They have isolated this place on the south, and tomorrow they will complete the cordon. Well, that gives us some hours' grace."

He flung wood on the stove, and sat himself in a wicker chair. He took from his knapsack a pair of stout nailed boots and thick socks. "I brought these for you," he said to Creevey. "I think you may need them."

"For God's sake have done with mystifications, Melfort," Creevey cried. "What is all this fuss about? For the last ten hours I seem to have been in a lunatic world!"

Adam smiled.

"You have been in a lunatic world much longer than that, and perhaps you are a little responsible for its lunacy. That is what the fuss is about."

"You are in danger, Adam," Jacqueline put in. "Mr. Falconet told me."

"I? Oh, no doubt. But I am not the one that matters. I will tell you what I know, but half of it is guesswork."

He turned to Creevey.

"You remember Berlin in August? You saw how Loeffler was guarded and you thought it natural, for he was head of a nation and therefore the chief mark for the discontented. He was in greater danger than you thought, and he ran some heavy risks before he got to the London Conference. But have you never considered that others may be in the same position? Not such conspicuous public figures as Loeffler, but men who have aroused as deep antagonisms. Remember that the desperate today have good information and look below the surface of things. They have organised themselves like an army."

"Do you mean me?" Creevey asked.

"Why not you? Everyone who knows anything is aware that you have more power today than most Governments. You use it, shall we say, in a certain way. To you that way is natural and reasonable, but to other people it may seem an infamous way, the way of the wrecker. Madness, you think? Yes, but an effective kind of madness. A disintegrated world lets loose strange forces which do not bother about the conventions."

Creevey did not answer, for he recalled some curious things that had been happening lately, words casually dropped, cryptic warnings, inexplicable little hindrances. He had set them down to a perverse chance, but he remembered that the notion had flitted over his mind that there might be purpose behind them.

"Do you know a man called La Cecilia?" Adam asked.

Creevey shook his head.

"Or a Baron von Hilderling?"

The name seemed familiar to Creevey, but he could not place it.

"Or a Dr. Gratias?"

This stirred his memory. He had met Gratias, who had been the head of a big German industrial combine which crashed in the inflation period. The man had once had a great reputation, not without its sinister element, and he had marked him down as one to be watched. Lately he had disappeared from view, and he had sometimes wondered a little uneasily what had become of him. Not a month ago he had instructed his people to try to get news of Dr. Gratias.

Adam saw that he had moved him. He told in detail what he knew of the inner circle of the Iron Hands, of the meeting at the Rhineland eating-house, of what happened during Loeffler's visit to Lamancha. Then he told of his sight of Cecilia and von

Hilderling that very day in Arsignano, and his talk with the former. He said nothing of his own plan to get Creevey to himself; that had failed and might be forgotten.

At first Creevey did not speak. He sat with his big head sunk on his chest and his eyes half-closed. That which he had believed impossible had come to pass. The world of reason, on which he had so firm a hold, had dissolved into a chaos of crude passions. His alert intelligence told him that this hideous transformation had always been a possibility. As for Adam's tale he must credit every word, for he had too strong a respect for Adam's acumen to think that he could be mistaken. He was a brave man, but this sudden crumbling of foundations sent a chill to his heart.

"What do they want with me?" he asked hoarsely.

"I do not think that you will live long in their hands," was Adam's reply. "Some time tonight the aeroplane in which you are supposed to be travelling will be wrecked and your death will appear in the evening papers tomorrow. That report will not be contradicted if our friends can help it."

"You are in danger too? You risk your life in coming to warn me? Why do you do it? We have never been friends. I was under the impression that my doings were not so fortunate as to have your approval."

Again Adam smiled, and there was that in his smile, in his fine-drawn face, and the steady friendliness of his eyes, which stirred in Creevey a feeling which no human being had ever evoked before. So novel it was that he scarcely listened to Adam's words.

"I didn't approve of you. But I have always admired you, and thought that some day you would awake. I have a notion that this may be the awakening. For you are going to escape—make no mistake about that. You will escape, though we have to climb the Pomagognon."

"But how?" Jacqueline had been roused out of her first stupefaction, and was struggling to grasp a situation which she had never forecast. Her first thought had been that her mad escapade had added to Adam's burden. Then she remembered her car, the only means of transport at their disposal. If danger was coming from the north, might they not escape by the south?

"My car is all right," she said. "I lied about it to you, Mr. Creevey. It is in perfect order, backed in among the trees beyond the broken bridge. Let us go off by it at once. It's the only way."

Adam shook his head.

"Not a ghost of a chance. If our friends are coming up the valley they will meet us. If they are coming down the valley, as I am certain they are, the route to the south will be picketed. Those gentry leave nothing to luck. They have already made the road difficult and broken the bridge. Amos says it had been hewn down with axes and that the cuts were fresh. I am afraid there is no hope in that direction."

"Then we are caught. We cannot get into Switzerland."

"We must get into Switzerland. Once there we are safe. Falconet is at Grunewald—and more than Falconet. Once in the Staubthal we are out of their net."

"Can't we get away from the inn and hide in the mountains?"

"How long could we keep hidden? It is going to be wild weather, and we should starve. Besides, the men we have to deal with are old hands at the game. They won't be plump, sedentary folk like Gratias, but the real Iron Hands, like Cecilia, and Hilderling, men who will take any risk and can endure any fatigue. They have the best mountaineers in Europe at their command. It would be a lost game to play hide-and-seek among the hills with the people who will come over the pass tomorrow."

Jacqueline dropped her hands on her knees with a gesture of despair. But the sight of Adam's face gave her hope.

"Our chance," he said, "lies in our start. I know the Marjolana route and I know the Saluzzana, and I do not believe that they can be here before eight o'clock tomorrow. If the roads forward and backward are shut to us we must take to the flank. We must try the col by which I crossed tonight from the Val Saluzzana. At Santa Chiara you strike the main road over the Staub."

"Then let's start at once." Jacqueline's anxiety had made her eager for instant movement.

301

"Impossible. The moon is down, and the road is not easy. If I were alone I might do it in the darkness, but I could not take another with me. We must have daylight—and a little sleep first. Remember that we are dealing with athletes and trained mountaineers."

Creevey had gone white, but by an obvious effort he kept his composure.

"Won't they have men on the col?" he asked.

"They may—in which case we are done. But I don't think so. Few people know it and fewer use it. It was my own discovery, and was shared with about half a dozen Italian officers, most of whom are now dead. . . . But we may be followed, and must allow for that. They will have men with them who are experts at winter hunting and can follow spoor. That means that we shall be in rather a hurry."

Creevey got himself out of his chair, and stood up, an incongruous figure in his neat blue suit, his coloured linen, and his dark tie with its pearl pin. He stretched out his arms as if to assess his bodily strength, and he shivered as if he felt it to be small at the best. Certainly as compared with Adam's lean virility he looked heavy and feeble.

"Do you think I can do it?" he asked. "I never climbed a mountain in all my days. I am not in good training—I never am—I live too well and too much indoors."

"I think you can do it," said Adam gently. "You must do it. You see, the stake is your life. Much more than that, I think, but first and foremost your life."

"What about Lady Warmestre? Hadn't she and her servant better get off at once, if her car is in order? She, anyhow, won't be stopped by whoever is on the watch down the valley."

"Nonsense," said Jacqueline, "I'm coming with you. I'm as active as a cat—I've climbed the Pomagognon by the west ridge. My father said—"

She stopped, for Adam's eyes were on her, and she read in them a knowledge of all the things that she had left unsaid. He knew for what purpose she had come here—her mention of Falconet had enlightened him. He knew that she had come to make restitution, to settle an account between two souls

302

predestined to a strange community. He knew, and the knowledge had awakened in him something which she had not seen before in his face. He was looking at her in a passion of tenderness.

"I am going to ask more from Lady Warmestre than that," he said. "She is our chief hope. I am going to ask her to stay here and receive our guests from over the mountains. If she can delay them for an hour she may save your life."

Then Creevey did that which surprised at least one of the other two, and may have surprised himself. The pallor left his face, and his voice came out, clear and masterful.

"I won't have it," he cried. "Damn you, Melfort, do you think I'm so little of a man as to take shelter behind a woman? God knows what those devils might not do to her! It's the most infamous proposal I ever heard in my life."

"She will be in no danger," said Adam. "Our enemies are no doubt devils, but in their own eyes they are gentlemen, rather punctilious gentlemen. They won't harm her—"

"I refuse to allow it. Lady Warmestre must start off at once in her car and by tomorrow morning she will be out of danger. I'm in the hell of a fix, but if I can help it it won't be anybody's funeral but my own. Except yours, of course, and you asked for it—"

He said no more, for Jacqueline's face silenced him. It had a new, strange beauty, the like of which he had never seen before. He felt suddenly that here was a woman in relation to whom it was merely foolish to talk of danger or fear.

"Thank you, Mr. Creevey," she said. "You are very kind and I am very grateful. But I wouldn't miss doing what Adam wants for anything in the world. It will be the greatest thing in my life. I'm not in the least afraid—except of not succeeding. I'm . . . but I'm going to do more than delay the enemy. Have you thought of the next step, Adam?"

It was her turn to rise. She had put her travelling cloak about her shoulders and now dropped it and stood up to her full height, a head taller than Creevey, almost tall enough to look from the level into Adam's eyes.

"They are bound to let me go," she went on. "I think they will try to speed my going. Very well. Somehow or other I will get the car round to the Val Saluzzana—to Santa Chiara—and meet you there. It's a long road over the Staub . . . and you will be very tired . . . and you may be pursued. I will be there to pick you up and we will finish the run together. Do you understand, both of you? That is my final decision, and nothing will shake me."

Her face was flushed and gay, her voice had a ringing gallantry. To Creevey in his confused dejection it was like a sudden irradiation of the sun. But Adam did not lift his eyes.

"It's about time we found somewhere to sleep," she said, and she called to Amos.

That worthy presently brought candles. "I've been outbye again," he announced, "and it's snawin' hard. The auld wife is pluckin' her geese for Christmas."

Creevey slept little; for his will could not subdue his insurgent thoughts. He had moments almost of panic, which he struggled to repress, but his chief preoccupation was to adjust his mind to a world of new values. Oddly enough, in all his confusion the dominant feeling was surprise mingled with something that was almost pride. This man Melfort was ready to risk his life for him. He had been a leader of men, but what disciples had he ever made who would have been prepared for such a sacrifice? And Melfort was no follower, but a stark antagonist. He had hated him and been hated in turn. Something very novel crept into his mind—a boyish shame. He could not allow himself to be outdone in this contest of generosity.

Adam and Jacqueline slept like children, for the one was physically weary, and both had suffered a new and profound emotion.

Amos woke the party an hour before dawn. It was very cold, and the storm of the night had covered the ground with two inches of snow. He gave them hot chocolate in the little hall, where he had lit the stove. Creevey looked pinched and haggard in the candlelight. He had put on the nailed boots which Adam had given him, and tucked the bottoms of his trousers into the heavy socks. He drank his chocolate but could eat no food.

But Jacqueline was a radiant figure. From the baggage which

Amos had brought she had extricated a thick jumper and a short jacket of russet leather, and the lack of a maid had imparted a gracious disorder to her hair. Even so she had often appeared to Adam's eyes on winter mornings at Armine Court, a little late after a big day's hunting.

Adam gave his last instructions. He was still yawning like a sleepy child. They went out of doors, where the skies were beginning to lighten over the Val Saluzzana peaks, and a small wind, which would probably grow to a gale, was whimpering down the valley.

"Confound the snow," Adam said. "It won't melt before midday, and it shows footsteps. Amos, you follow us and blur our tracks. We'll get off the road a hundred yards down, for on that long spit of rock we'll be harder to trace. There's a shallow place in the gorge where we can cross. We must be inside the big ravine before daybreak."

He took Jacqueline's hand, as she stood in the snow at the doorstep. There was no word spoken, and the manner of each was cheerful, almost casual—*au revoir*, not goodbye. But in the candlelight which escaped from the hall Creevey saw her face, and it was a sight which he was never to forget. For her eyes were the lit eyes of the bride.

II

Amos was busy indoors removing all signs of occupation, other than that of himself and Jacqueline. The relics of breakfast for two remained in the hall, and only two beds upstairs showed signs of use. He repacked the hold-all, which had carried Jacqueline's baggage and the provisions. As he worked, he repeated to himself the instructions he had been given by Adam and his mistress, and his gnarled face wore a contented smile. "It's like auld times," he muttered. "Man, Andrew, this is the proper job for you. Ye're ower young to sit back on your hunkers. But it beats me how the Colonel is to get yon Creevey ower thae fearsome hills."

Jacqueline put on her hat and her fur-lined coat and stood

in front of the inn watching the shadows break up in the valley. The dawn wind blew sharper, but she did not feel cold, for her whole being was aglow. Adam had trusted her, and had asked of her a great thing—asked it as an equal. She fired with pride, and pride drove out all fear. She did not attempt to forecast what would happen at the inn in the next few hours, for her thoughts were with the two men now entering the long ravine which led by difficult shelves to the col. They would succeed—they must succeed—and in the evening she herself would carry them to sanctuary. It was the hour of miracles—she had witnessed them. She had seen a man emerge from Creevey's husk, a man who with white lips was prepared to forget his own interests and sacrifice himself for a whim of honour. She did not forget his stubbornness about her own safety. Could he ever return to his old world? Had not a new man been born, the leader of Adam's dream? And there was still before him a long day of trial and revelation. Of Adam she did not allow herself to think; she had fallen in with his code, and kept her thoughts firm on that purpose which was his life.

The eastern slopes of the valley were still dark, but the inn and its environs were flooded now with a cold, pure light. She looked up at the sky, and saw that the growing wind was drifting clouds from the north, clouds contoured and coloured like ice-floes in a Polar sea. Snow would fall again before midday. She occupied herself in recalling the road to the Val Saluzzana—down the Val d'Arras to Colavella, and then east in a detour among the foothills to the great Staub highway. She remembered it vividly; it would be open even in rough weather, and the Staub pass was low and rarely blocked by snowfalls. What about their stock of petrol? She turned to look for Amos, and saw him in the doorway. . . .

He was held by two men, and was spluttering in well-simulated wrath. She was aware of other men. . . . One was advancing to her from the north side of the inn. He was a slim, youngish man, rather below the middle height, dressed like a mountaineer, in breeches and puttees, with a waterproof cape about his shoulders. He had been in deep snow, for he seemed to be wet to the middle.

Jacqueline cried out to Amos.

"What is wrong, Andrew? What do these men want?"

"I dinna ken. They grippit me when I was tyin' up the poke. I don't understand what they're sayin'." Then to his warders: "I'll be obliged if ye'll let me get at my pipe. I haven't had my mornin's smoke." He spat philosophically.

The young man addressed her. He had a finely cut face, dark, level brows and sombre eyes.

"We want to know who you are, madam, and what you are doing here?" His tone was civil, but peremptory.

"What business have you with me? This is an inn."

"It was. But for a little it has been the private dwelling-house of myself and my friends. By what right have you entered it?"

Jacqueline laughed merrily. "Have I made a *gaffe*? It is like the story of the Three Bears. I'm so sorry. Have I been trespassing? You see, I had a fancy to come here again—I've been motoring in Italy—and I thought I would like to have a look at the place for auld lang syne. Antonio Menardi used to be a friend of mine, and I came here often with my father. He was a famous mountaineer. Hubert Alban. Perhaps you have heard of him?"

There were now four men on the snow by the inn door, besides the two who still held Amos in custody. One was tall, with massive bull shoulders and a curiously small head. All six looked preternaturally alert and vigorous, just such as she remembered among the Alpine heroes of her youth. But in their faces there was a sullen secrecy which she did not remember, and in their eyes a mad concentration.

One spoke, not to her, but to the others. "I have heard of Herr Alban. Yes, I have seen him. He did many famous courses in the mountains."

Her first inquisitor spoke again.

"Will you tell us your name, please?"

"I am married. My husband is Lord Warmestre."

Recognition stirred in the big man.

"I did not think I could be mistaken," he said. "She is the Marchioness of Warmestre, a very famous lady in England. I have seen her at the Court balls, and elsewhere."

"Will you tell us how you came here?" the young man asked.

He seemed to be bridling a deep impatience, though his voice was still polite.

"I motored here. The road was bad, and a little way down the valley a bridge was broken. But I was determined not to be beaten, so my servant and I left the car and walked the rest of the way."

"And you found here?"

"An empty house. No Antonio, no servants. No food, but, thank goodness, I had the sense to bring some of my own. . . . Oh, and I found something else. Another unfortunate guest. A man I have met occasionally in London. A Mr. Creevey."

They were masters at their game, for no flicker of interest moved their faces.

"Will you tell us about this other guest?"

"Oh, he was a dreadful little cross-patch. He was so angry that he could not explain properly, but I gathered that he had had a mishap in an aeroplane, though I can't for the life of me see how he got here. He was in a desperate hurry to be gone, and after my servant had given him a cup of tea he started off down the valley. He must have had a rotten night of it."

The faces were still impassive.

"You did not offer to take him away in your car?"

Jacqueline laughed. "No. I didn't tell him about the car—or rather, I said it had broken down hopelessly. You see, I am not very fond of Mr. Creevey. I didn't see why I should help him out of his troubles when he was as uncivil as a bear, and I certainly didn't want his company. I was very glad when he decided to go away."

"And now—you propose?"

"To go home. We camped the night here, but I can't say it was very comfortable. I was just about to start when you turned up. My maid and my luggage are in the hotel at Chiavagno."

The young man bowed. "Will you please to go indoors, Lady Warmestre? My friends and I must talk together."

Jacqueline sat down in the inn hall, where Amos's fire had almost burned itself out. Amos, a little way off, puffed stolidly at his pipe.

So far she had managed well, she decided. Her tone had been

right, the natural tone of a crazy Englishwoman, and by a great stroke of luck her father's name had been known to them and she herself had been recognised. Now they were trying to verify her story. She could hear the tramping of heavy boots upstairs, and twice a weather-beaten face looked in from the back parts. The others would be outside ranging the environs.

Presently the young man entered.

"When did Mr. Creevey depart last night?" he asked.

Jacqueline considered. "Just when it was growing dark and I got my servant to light a lamp. I think it would be about five o'clock."

"There are footprints in the new snow."

"Aye," said Amos, "They're mine. I gaed out for a daunder afore it was licht to prospect the weather."

When he had gone Jacqueline had a sudden disquieting reflection. She had thought it very clever to bring in Creevey, but had it not been the wildest folly? Could they let her go? Had she not fatally compromised their plans? Creevey was supposed to have perished in an aeroplane accident the night before somewhere on the coast, and here was she, a witness to his presence in a remote Alpine valley no earlier than five o'clock. For the first time she knew acute fear. If she was permitted to go away, permitted even to live, their story was exploded and their schemes brought to naught. They had failed to manoeuvre their victim out of the ken of the world. Even if they found his trail and caught him on the col, she and Amos would share his fate. Those mad eyes were capable of the last barbarity.

She told herself that it was impossible. They could not cumber themselves with her as a prisoner. They would not dare to silence her in the old crude way. An English great lady—it would be too dangerous. They were cunning people and would somehow adapt their policy to the changed circumstances. She must carry off things with a high air. . . . And meantime, thank God, she was holding them up. Every minute that she sat shivering in that wretched inn was bringing Adam and Creevey nearer to their goal.

At last the door opened and the young man appeared.

"You can take up your baggage," he told Amos. Then to

309

Jacqueline: "Are you ready, Lady Warmestre? We have inspected your car, and it is in good order. We wish you to leave—now."

Outside she found four men waiting like terriers about an earth.

"You will take one of us with you as a guide," said the young man.

"To Chiavagno?" Jacqueline asked, with a new fear in her heart.

"To Chiavagno—perhaps. At any rate he will guide you. I will accompany you to your car."

The others bowed ceremoniously as the three set off down the road. The clouds were no longer floes, but pack-ice almost covering the sky, and a dull leaden light filtered through them, while the wind volleyed in bitter gusts. Jacqueline did not turn her head towards the eastern wall, lest it might wake suspicion, but she wondered if from any vantage-ground on the lip of the ravine Adam could see the party. He had, she knew, his field-glasses. . . . One thing she did not like. Two of the men were busy looking for prints beside the road, and they were danger-ously near the long rib of rock down which Adam had gone. Would the enemy after all hit the trail?

They scrambled across the gully of the broken bridge, and Amos with a good deal of trouble started the engine and ran the car into the road.

"I will drive, please," said Jacqueline. "I am more used to difficult roads than my servant. Will your friend sit beside me?" The rudiments of a wild plan were forming in her brain.

"My friend will sit behind you. Get in, Franz." The young man said something in German to the other which Jacqueline did not catch, but his face interpreted his words. The sullen figure behind was there as a guard—she saw the bulge made by the pistol in his coat pocket. What were his orders, she won-dered dismally. Was it Chiavagno, or some darker goal?

"*Bon voyage*," said the young man. "Remember my instruc-tions, Franz," and he turned to re-cross the ravine.

On a rough piece of road a mile farther on the car gave so much trouble that no-one heard a whistle blown behind them. Had he heard it, Franz might have insisted on turning back.

310

That whistle meant portentous things. For the trackers by the roadside had found the spoor on the rib of rock, spoor leading down to the stream, and, five minutes later, the pack were following it.

Jacqueline was surprised at her own coolness. She was certain in her mind what orders had been given to Franz—that their goal was not Chiavagno. And even if they went to Chiavagno her plan would fail, for then she could not pick up Adam and Creevey at Santa Chiara, and she had a premonition that if she failed them they were doomed. But not a shadow of personal fear lurked in her heart. Her whole being was keyed up to the highest pitch of active purpose.

Sometimes she turned round and nodded friendlily to the man behind. He sat rigid and expectant, his sullen eyes watchful, and one hand in his coat pocket.

It was a great thing to have Amos beside her. She talked to him in a loud voice about the road and the weather, so that Franz might hear, but interpolated in her remarks some words in a lower tone. Amos responded. He modulated his great voice to a whisper and that whisper was in the broadest Scots.

"We maun find the richt kind o' place," he crooned, "and then I'll pretend to be no weel. I'll gie ye the word when I see a likely bit. You leave the rest to me, mem. . . . Dinna you stop the engine. . . . This cawr is a fine starter, and it accelerates brawly. . . . Watch me and play up till me, and God be kind to His ain." When Amos, a bigoted unbeliever, dropped into the speech of piety, there was trouble awaiting somebody.

Before they were out of the Val d'Arras the wind dropped and the snow began, a steady, resolute fall. There were people on the vile road—one or two men who might have been woodcutters, and Jacqueline observed that they stared not at her but at Franz, and that some signal seemed to be exchanged. Once a fellow who looked like a gamekeeper dropped from the hillside, and the car was halted while he whispered to Franz over the back of it. Jacqueline preserved an air of aloof inattention, as if such a meeting were the most natural thing in the world.

After Colavella Franz proposed to drive. "Please let me go on," Jacqueline protested. "I'm not in the least tired, and we shall be on better roads now. It is only driving that keeps me warm." Franz consented with an ill grace, but he shifted his station so that he sat directly behind her.

Half an hour after leaving Colavella they came to a fork where the road to Chiavagno branched to the left.

"Straight on," Franz commanded.

"But we are going to Chiavagno."

"We are going where I direct. Do as I bid you, or I will take the wheel."

The snow was thickening, and already it lay an inch or two on the highway. "We'll have to do something soon," Jacqueline whispered to Amos.

"Aye," came grimly through closed teeth.

Soon after that he began to groan. He huddled himself into the left-hand corner and sat with shut eyes, so that Franz could see his profile. He had the appearance of a man in extreme distress.

Presently they turned down the side of a mountain torrent flowing in a deep-cut wooded ravine. Only a low wall protected the road from the gorge, and in parts the wall had crumbled into stone heaps.

Suddenly Amos cried out. He pawed feebly at Jacqueline's arm. "Stop," he groaned. "I've an awfu' pain. Let me oot—let me oot."

Jacqueline brought the car to a standstill. "What is it?" she asked anxiously.

Amos's voice came small and weak between his gasps.

"Colic," he answered. "It's the cauld. Let me straughten mysel' on the roadside. Oh, mem, for God's sake!"

Franz was standing up and demanding angrily the reason of the delay.

"My servant has been taken ill. He says he must be laid flat. Will you help him, please?"

Franz leaped from the car, and hauled out the groaning Amos, who staggered a step or two to the edge of the gorge and then fell flat among the snow. It was at a point where there was a gap in the protecting wall.

He bent over the prostrate figure and his face was wrathful.

"A nip o' brandy," Amos whined. "There's a flask at the bottom o' the big green poke."

Franz addressed Jacqueline fiercely. "There is no time for doctoring. The fellow must lie here till he recovers. People will pass . . . he will be seen to. . . . Give me the wheel, madam. I now will drive. . . ."

His back was to the stricken man, and he was about to re-enter the car, when a strange thing happened. Amos drew his legs up with astonishing agility, and in a second was crouching like a broody fowl. Then he flung his enormous arms round Franz's knees. To Jacqueline it seemed as if the body of the latter suddenly rose from the ground and described a curve backward in the air over Amos's shoulder. It disappeared into the ravine, and could be heard crashing among the snow-laden undergrowth.

In an instant Amos was beside her, and the car was in motion. Amos dusted the snow from his disreputable breeks.

"That's settled him," he said complacently. "A dodge I learnt lang syne at the fitba'."

After that there was no delay. Jacqueline swung to the left, cut across the road to Chiavagno, and after being at fault once or twice among the valleys of the foothills and consulting her map, struck the main road which led to the Val Saluzzana. There the snow lightened, but much had fallen, and the pine-woods were white like the mountain tops. But on the broad highway it was little hindrance to speed, and by four o'clock they had passed Santa Chiara. The temporary clearness of the air enabled her without difficulty to follow Adam's directions, and presently she had drawn up at the mouth of the gorge which led to the col and to the Val d'Arras. She could see the faint outline of the track which followed the stream.

Amos descended, stamped his feet, and swung his arms. "I'll gang a wee bit up the burn to meet them," he said. "Losh, it's a fearsome-lookin' glen! Yon puir Creevey will hae an ill journey."

Jacqueline watched his gnome-like figure stumping up the track till it disappeared among the draggled pines. . . . The place was hushed and solitary. She saw the highway bearing to the

313

right for the Staub pass, the road that was to carry them to safety. In front was the sword-cut of the upper Val Saluzzana, and she could make out dimly the gap which was the Colle delle Rondini and the famous ice-ridge of the Pomagognon. . . . But her eyes were chiefly on the cleft which led to the col. The twilight was falling, and above the pines and the fitful gleams of white water she saw nothing but a pit of shade across which blew thin streamers of mist. That was the way of salvation. Out of that darkness would presently come two men on whom the fate of the world depended. They must come—they could not fail—not if there was hope on earth or mercy in Heaven. But as she peered up into that savage wilderness she shivered.

Suddenly she caught sight of Amos. He was far up on a jut of crag and he was looking towards her. He was waving his hand. He had seen them.

Relief made her choke and filled her eyes with happy tears. She started the engine.

III

Scarcely a word was spoken between Adam and Creevey for the first half-hour. With difficulty they crossed the torrent at a place where the gorge flattened out and the water ran wide and shallow before plunging into a new abyss. After that the way lay along the east slope of the valley in a chaos of fallen rocks and straggling pines. Creevey, like all novices, forced the pace, but Adam made him fall back into a slow, steady stride. "We have a long road before us," he said. "You must keep your breath for the hills."

Under the lee of the slope it was still very dark, and Adam had to take the other's arm at many points to help him over clefts hidden by scrub. He was straining his ears for sounds from the other side of the stream, from the track that led to the pass, something that would tell him that their enemies had crossed the mountains. That route was easy even in the darkness for hardened mountaineers. But the noise of furious water and the soughing of the dawn wind blanketed all other sounds. The

314

light in the inn was soon hidden from them, and they moved in a shell of loneliness.

Adam was in such a mood as he had not known before. He was supremely confident. He felt that his task was nearing fulfilment, like a runner who has entered the straight with the tape clear before him. He had no fear of failure, so that he did not attempt to forecast the next difficult stages. These would be surmounted—somehow or other Creevey that night would be beyond the reach of danger. A new Creevey, too, for the gods would not leave their work half done. . . . But to this assurance happiness had been added, and in recent years he had known peace, but not happiness. Now something jubilant and ecstatic seemed to have been reborn in him, and he was aware of the reason. He had discovered tenderness, for Jacqueline had taught him. She had thawed his chilly, dutiful soul. He was no longer content to pity humanity, for he had come to love it. Creevey, stumbling along at his side, was not merely a pawn in the game to be guarded, but a friend and a fellow. The aching affection which had once been confined to Nigel was now given to Jacqueline, and through her to all mankind. "I am a full man and a free man again," he told himself. "I have come out of the shadows."

The slopes on which they moved bent inward, and down the cleft in the mountains there came the first grey light of dawn. "Thank God," said Adam, "we are now in cover. We must take it quietly, for we have four thousand feet to climb to the col."

Adam led at a slow even pace up a track which was only a deeper shadow among the shadowy fern. Here the wind was cut off, and the snow, warded off by the pines, lay thinly on the ground, but it was damply cold, as if the trees still held the chill of midnight. It was steep going, but not difficult, though Creevey's heavy breathing soon proved the poverty of his training. It was Adam's business to keep him cheerful, for he knew the potent effect of the mind on the body. "You are doing famously," he told him. "After the trees we have the first shelf where the slope eases off. Then there comes a bit of a scramble, and then a second shelf. After that we must hug the stream till it stops, and the last bit is slabs and screes. The snow should be lying there

315

fairly deep and that will help us. Then we are at the col and there's no more climbing. The descent into the Val Saluzzana is longer, but far less stiff. In two hours from the col we should be in the valley."

"You think that Lady Warmestre will be there?"

"I am certain of it."

"You're a queer fellow," said Creevey. "You go a good deal by instinct. . . . Perhaps you are right. . . . I'm not built that way."

They came out of the trees to the lip of the first shelf. There the track, to avoid an out-jutting crag, bent to the right, and reached a vantage-point from which the valley beneath could be seen. It was here that, the night before, Adam had first caught the lights of the inn. He made Creevey keep low in cover, and wriggled forward to where he could rake the trough of the Val d'Arras.

There was no-one on the road which led to the pass, nor on the road below the inn, as far as he could see it. Outside the inn itself stood a solitary figure. The glass told him that it was neither Jacqueline nor Amos. It was a tall man, and he had the air of being on guard. As Adam watched him he shaded his eyes and seemed to be watching something to the east in the valley bottom.

The enemy had come. More, some of them were now down by the stream. They might be only casting about for the fugitives; on the other hand, they might have found the spoor down the rib of rock which would show up in the snow. They were bound to have skilled trackers with them, men accustomed to the winter trails of bouquetin and chamois.

Adam snapped his glasses back into their case. "We must push on," he said. "Our friends are below at the inn. They may pick up our trail."

"Are they faster than us?"

"Than us two? Perhaps twice as fast. But we have a long start. Never fear, we shall beat them."

Creevey seemed to have exhausted his strength on the first steeps. He had not the mountaineer's gift of walking delicately in difficult places, and he slipped and stumbled among the

316

boulder-strewn herbage, and several times fell heavily. Adam took his arm and forced the pace, so that when they reached the place where the stream fell in great leaps down a broken rock-wall he was puffing hard and limping.

In summer there was a faint track up this wall, but there was no sign of it now in the waste of glazed rock, snowy cracks, and boggy ledges. Creevey was most of the time on his knees, for he retched with vertigo whenever he rose to his feet. Over most of the ground Adam simply dragged him, blaming himself bitterly for not having brought a rope. Sometimes they came to an *impasse* up which Creevey had to be lifted like baggage. His crawling soaked him to the skin, and it was a limp and sodden figure that dropped on the ground when the second shelf was reached.

"Get your breath," Adam told him. Creevey lay flat on his back looking up to the sky from which occasional flakes fell, while Adam made a short detour to the right, to a point where from a steep overhang he believed that a view could be got of the foot of the ravine where it debouched on the valley.

He got the view and something more, something which sent him racing back to Creevey. For on the spit of open sward below the trees, on the track by which they had come, he saw four figures, their heads bent like dogs following a trail.

He plucked Creevey to his feet. "On," he cried, "the hounds are out. At the speed they go they are less than an hour behind us."

The words woke the other's drugged mind to life. Never before had he known what it was to be in physical danger. He, the assured and authoritative, was being hunted like a fox, and the price of failure was death. He felt a cold clutch at his heart, but a new nervous power in his limbs. This shelf was more difficult than the first, but there was no drag on Adam's arm. Creevey covered the ground at a shamble which was almost running. "Don't strain yourself," said Adam's quiet voice in his ear. "We shall win all right," but the sense of the words hardly penetrated to a brain obsessed with the passion of flight.

They were now at the last tier of the ascent, where at points, to avoid knuckles of sheer cliff, it was necessary to take to the bed of the infant stream. A round of the clock before Adam had descended the place like a falling stone, leaping in the strong moonlight from boulder to boulder. But now the rocks were more glazed and treacherous, and the snow, which was falling thickly, made the route harder to prospect. There were points where Adam simply took Creevey in his arms and jumped with him; others where he forced him up the tiny couloirs on his shoulders. It was a toil which few men could have compassed, but he scarcely felt it—at long last he was finding use for that physical strength which he had so jealously conserved. As he clutched the dripping, inert body of his companion he felt a strange affection. This sodden thing, so feeble and yet so precious!

The stream ceased, a few hundred yards of snowy screes followed, and then they stood in the throat of the col. Adam let Creevey drop on the ground, and looked at his watch. It was a little after one o'clock.

The consciousness of having reached the summit seemed to rouse Creevey to a new vigour. He swallowed some brandy from Adam's flask and found his voice.

"Will the snow help us?" The words came from blue lips. "Will it hide us? What about leaving the road?"

"There is no route but the one, and these men could follow tracks in any weather."

"Then for God's sake let us get on." He started downhill at a stumbling run. So far the wind, which was from the north, had been shut off by a wall of mountain, but the ravine on the Val Saluzzana side took a northward turn, and they had now the drift in their faces. Adam caught the other's arm, for the way down the long broken moraine was not easy, but his help was scarcely needed. Creevey had got a new reserve of vigour with the downward slope, his foothold was surer, and his face, plastered with the drift, was human again. On the last stage it had been washed clean of life like a sick animal's.

"How much longer?" he gasped.

"Two hours—not more. If the snow lasts we shall be safe, for it will prevent them shooting."

Then the wind seemed to be shut off again, and they moved in a soft feathery blanket. Creevey spoke.

"I did not know the world was so savage," he muttered, and it sounded like an apology.

"It is very near the edge," said Adam.

"You think I have helped to bring it to the edge? . . . That is what Loeffler believes. . . . I thought it hysteria—he has a good many blind patches in his mind. . . . But he was right. . . . If we come through, you and I . . . I will go to Loeffler."

"Don't try to talk," Adam said. "You will want all your strength." The snow muffled sounds, and they moved in a world of deathly stillness, but he had the sense of proximity which wild things have, and it told him that the enemy had passed the col and were on the moraine. The hunters were faster by far than the hunted.

The snow was thinning. Presently they struck the torrent which came down from a tributary ravine, and the road now was in a narrow gully. The wind caught them again, and their immediate environs were blown clear—the beetling cliffs on their left, like chocolate dusted with sugar, the leaping white water, the icy ledge lipped by it where the track lay.

Adam looked back, and saw that the moraine by which they had come was visible almost as far as the col. There were figures on it, moving fast like plover in a spring plough. Half a mile behind—less. Within the next half-hour they must be overtaken.

A dozen plans flitted through his brain as he dragged Creevey down the gully. The latter had gone numb again, and was maintained only by the other's resolution. They were taking crazy chances, and again and again Adam's arm saved him from disaster. But no audacity could avail them, for the relentless trackers behind were their masters in pace, and the trail was for a child to read. Creevey's breath was labouring and he was stumbling drunkenly. Where was a hope, for hope there must be? They could not fail on the brink of success.

Suddenly they came to a point which Adam remembered. A huge boulder on the right was delicately poised above the track. He recollected it clearly, for here he had had to walk warily, since a very little would have sent it crashing down to block the route for ever. A man could dislodge it—a man on the upper side—and bar any further descent. But that man must remain on the near side of the chasm which he had created. He would be shut off himself from reaching the valley.

It was the sign which he had awaited, and a solemn gladness filled his heart. He had not been wrong in his hope, and his purpose was now certain of fulfilment. Creevey saw that his face was smiling, and wondered.

"You must go on alone for a bit." Adam's arm pulled him to a standstill. "We are almost over the bad patch. After this the road is easy. The snow has stopped, and you will see where the track runs. Soon you will be among the trees."

"What do you mean? . . . Are you going to stay and fight? . . . I'll be damned if I leave you." Creevey was nearly at the end of his tether, but the weakness of his body was not reflected in his angry eyes.

"There will be no fighting. But I see a chance of blocking the road. On with you, for it is our only hope—a certain hope."

There was that in Adam's voice which could not be gainsaid.

"You will follow me? Promise that, or I won't stir. I must have you with me—always. . . ."

"I will follow you. I will be with you always." Creevey heard the words, but he did not see the look on the other's face.

Adam circumvented the boulder and reached a point on the cliff above it, where its shallow roots clung to the mountain. His vantage-ground gave him a view of Creevey stumbling down-ward towards the easier slopes where the first pines began. Very small he looked as his figure grew dim in the brume.

Then Adam put forth his strength. He found a stance where, with his feet against living rock, he thought he could prise the boulder from its hold. . . . It quivered and moved, but at first it seemed as if it were too deep-rooted to fall. Desperation gave him the little extra force which was needed, and suddenly the foreground heaved, slipped, and with a sickening hollow sigh dropped into nothingness. Thunder awoke in the narrow glen, and the solid flank of the mountain seemed to shudder. The air was thick with dust and snow, and Adam, perched above the

320

abyss, was for a moment blinded. Presently it cleared, and he saw that the side of the ravine had been planed smooth, smooth as the glassy rock-wall of the torrent. Only a bird could reach the Val Saluzzana.

Creevey was safe. He would be alarmed at the earthquake, and might totter back to look for his friend, but, sooner or later, he would reach the valley. It did not matter how long he took, for he was now beyond the reach of his enemies. . . . Presently he would be restored to a world which had sore need of him. Loeffler would have a potent ally. The rock-fall was a curtain which cut him off from his foes and inaugurated a new epoch in his life. He would be the same man—hungry, masterful, audacious, infinitely resourceful, still striding with long quick steps, but his face would be turned to another goal. The gods did not stop halfway when they wrought miracles.

Adam looked into the chasm which was filled with a fine dust like spindrift. That way lay the long road he had travelled since boyhood. Did his eyes deceive him, or was there some brightening of the mist, as if somewhere behind it there were the fires of sunset? Pleasant things were there—all his youth with its hopes, and all the striving of the last years—the grim things forgotten and only the sunshine hours remaining. His friends, too, and Jacqueline above all. He felt a warm uprush of affection, but it was an affection without longing or regret. He had seen life and beauty and honour, and these things did not die; they would endure to warm the world he was leaving.

He turned his face up the ravine whence he had come, and there the air had the bitter clearness of an interval between snow-showers. His range of vision was small, but every detail stood out hard and bleak. It was like the world he had seen from the Greenland ice-cap, a world barren of life, the antechamber of death. It was motionless as the grave, for the wind had fallen. But there was movement in his ears. He could hear the rasp of nailed boots on stone, and what sounded like human speech. The pack was closing in on him.

Then suddenly he saw beyond it. His eyes were no longer looking at clammy rock and lowering cloud, or the icy shoulder of the Pomagognon lifting through a gap of cliff. . . . They were on blue water running out to where the afternoon sun made a great dazzle of gold. He knew that he had found the sea which had eluded him in all his dreams. He was in a bay of white sand, and, in front, crested with light foam, were the skerries where the grey seals lived. The scents of thyme and heather and salt were blent in a divine elemental freshness. Nigel had come back to him—he saw him skipping by the edge of the tide—he saw him running towards him—he felt his hand in his—he looked into eyes bright with trust and love. From those eyes he seemed to draw youth and peace and immortality.

A voice which was not Nigel's broke into his dream, but it did not mar his peace. There only remained the trivial business of dying.